THE LOST SHERIFF OF ORCHARD BEND

a novel by
Patrick Lemieux

Published by
Across The Board Books™
Toronto, Ontario, Canada

ISBN: 978-1-926462-14-1

First Trade Paperback Edition: December, 2019

Cover Illustration
© Patrick Lemieux, 2019

For Corrie and Lisa,

Two candles float on the water beneath the stars.

Also by Patrick Lemieux

Fiction:

The Orchard Bend Series:
 The Prisoner of Orchard Bend
 The Murder Ballad of Orchard Bend

Non-Fiction:

The Chronology Series:
 The Queen Chronology:
   The Recording & Release History of the Band
   (Co-written with Adam Unger)

 The Mike Oldfield Chronology:
   The Recording & Release History

 The Barenaked Ladies Chronology:
   The Recording & Release History of the Band

 The Rush Chronology:
   The Recording & Release History of the Band

 The David Bowie Chronology, Volume 1: 1947 – 1974
   The Recording & Release History

Art & Storytelling:

Revenge Of The Dark Witch Of Oz:
   The Illustrated Screenplay

Horizon Line, Vol. 1 (A Comic Book Collection)

Play Of Light: The Art of Patrick Lemieux

Acknowledgments

Writing this book took longer than anticipated, but I must thank the following people for their direct and indirect involvement and support:

Michael Wiley – Like the man says, "To edit is divine." I didn't follow every suggestion you made and that's on me.

Heidi Loney – Always there when I need some sanity. And some insanity.

Malinda Prud'homme – I think you'll agree that this book was worth the wait.

Elysia White – Superhero Ninja Warrior and inspiration.

Tim, Mel, Emmet, Jill, Dave, Jack, Josephine, Mark and Liv – My posse.

Mom and Dad – With me everyday.

1

December 22, 1861
Black Barrel

Under the glow of the half moon, Sergeant Kenna Decker stomped across the thin, icy snow. It crunched beneath her boots with each awkward step, and drops of blood accompanied every footprint she left behind. Her right hand ached through its numbness in the frigid night air. She'd have stopped to put on her gloves, but her hand was keeping her face from falling off. Or so it felt like. Blood oozed between her fingers from the very real gash in her right cheek, trailing down her arm, staining the snow at her feet. By some mercy, she hadn't lost her eye, though by all rights she knew she probably should have. And as much as her hands hurt, she welcomed the slow deadening of feeling in her face as the cold air numbed the pain from the wound.

"It pulled us in," Decker muttered, "the moment the captain blew it all to hell. That's how I survived."

The explosions had gone off around her and... now she was here in this cold, dark, snow-covered plain, a faded blue-white landscape dotted with the dark shapes of trees. Her own moonlit shadow stretched a few feet ahead of her. She looked at the small square watch on her wrist and saw only the message:

Geo-sync update
required.
Unable to acquire
signal.
Manual? Cancel?

The watch's operating system would continue to scan in the background for a satellite, a tower or a mobile signal, so Decker left that problem for another time and continued across the field.

At the sound of growling behind her, she spun around.

Several dozen feet away stood the grey shape of an animal. Decker thought it was a dog until more of them came into view, approaching slow and cautious, sniffing the air as the snow on their grey hides speckled in the moonlight.

Wolves.

She picked out more than twenty of them. Some darted back and forth, making an exact count difficult. The lead wolf put his nose to the snow where she had walked, taking in her scent and the smell of blood. That's when Decker knew this would not end well.

The pack started to spread out as it moved closer. Decker wasted no more time. She dropped to a knee. Wet with blood, her hand drew her sidearm in one smooth motion from the holster on her tactical harness, leaving the gash in her face to fall open. The wound stung and burned in the bitter air. Her sudden movement made some of the wolves stop, but only for a moment.

And then they charged.

Using both hands to take aim, Decker fired two rounds into the lead wolf and it squealed in pain and fell. She then pivoted left and right, capping off rounds, taking down whichever attacker seemed closest. Some fell, but some kept coming, closing the distance second after second. When the automatic's slide locked open, she thumbed the release and the clip slid out. Decker replaced the magazine with a fresh one as the spent clip bounced on the hard icy snow.

When she resumed firing, the remaining wolves were all but on top of her. She took down two with headshots at close range before one leapt on her chest. Its jaw snapped close to her ear, but she rolled and pinned it. As it clawed and growled, Decker fired at another charging wolf. It landed only inches to her left, but Decker paid it no mind as she drilled the pinned wolf twice in the head, never taking her eyes off the pack.

Another charged her and she swung about, aiming and squeezing the trigger twice. Somehow, one got behind her and leapt at her back, knocking the sergeant off balance. She and the wolf hit the ground hard. The last of the pack saw their opportunity with the downed prey and were on her. Decker, on her back, kicked and screamed with rage, firing into the masses of fur and teeth. A set of jaws clamped down on her thick army boot. Without hesitation, Decker fired on the animal. More jaws snapped at her dark, camouflaged fatigues, tearing the fabric, trying to rip her flesh. The wolves got in their bites as she flailed and fought.

Decker knew she couldn't last much longer.

A wolf pounced, but Decker impaled it with her army knife. Decker stabbed it again and again as it fell bloody and dead on top of her. Firing from her back, aiming almost upside down and entirely through instinct and training, Decker took out another wolf baring its fangs a few feet from her head.

As one of the predators climbed over the carcass on her chest, growling and dripping saliva, Decker fired at it, striking its shoulder. She squeezed the trigger again and again, but the pistol's slide locked back. The gun was empty. The wolf lunged and Decker jammed the gun into its mouth to stop its teeth from gouging her already injured face. The weight of the two animals on her chest made it hard to breath and she gasped for air as she drove her knife into the wolf's neck.

She dropped back onto the hard ground and saw the other wolves watching her, easily ten of them now, probably more. With a grunt, she leveraged the first wolf off of her and took a deep breath. Two wolves charged and Decker screamed at them, "FUCK OFF!"

They stopped, uncertain.

Decker pulled the other wolf off her chest enough to reach the last clip on her harness. It wasn't as easy to reload this time. Her muscles trembled and her fingers felt like mere ghosts, but she somehow got it done and didn't hesitate to open fire once more, killing one of her attackers. The other jumped back, but Decker continued to fire, getting in a headshot and killing the second. The pack spread out again and Decker struggled to her feet. She advanced to her left, where more of them were concentrated. If this was to be her last stand, she was going to take the fight to them. She didn't know if it was the right move and she didn't care. Another burst of adrenalin coursed through her and she squeezed the trigger three times at the closest wolves. The pack darted about, uncertain now of their dominance in the situation. Decker held her knife in her other hand. When she heard the crunch of paws running toward her from behind, she spun around. She caught the wolf with the blade, twisted her body and let its momentum help her throw the animal to the ground between her and the bulk of the pack.

"COME ON, YOU FUCKERS!" Decker screamed at them, standing as tall as her injured body would allow. "I'LL KILL EVERY LAST MOTHERFUCKING ONE OF YOU!"

She fired at the nearest wolf and it cried out as it retreated. Decker fired again at another wolf that seemed to find some courage as it growled. Its bravery didn't last long as the sergeant put two rounds into it. That was enough to break the pack and send them scurrying away. Some of the wolves stopped, seeming to regroup and consider their options, eying her from a safe distance. Decker stood her ground and in the end, the remaining wolves took off across the plain.

Decker watched them go, ready to collapse in exhaustion, but she holstered her automatic, sheathed her knife and limped away from the carnage. No longer worried about her face, she took her gloves from the cargo pocket of her torn and blood-soaked pant leg and slipped them on to her shaking hands.

When she looked up, she saw the light of a single lantern approaching about a hundred feet away. It swung back and forth as the owner ran in her direction, its light reflecting off the snowy ground. Decker looked back at the scattering of wolf corpses behind her, then turned to face the man with the lantern. The man also carried a lever action rifle, but that wasn't what caught Decker's eye. Bundled against the winter air, the man's attire was more rustic than she'd ever seen. His long, unkempt hair covered his ears, reaching just about to his shoulders.

"Can I borrow your phone, sir?" Decker called out, her speech slurred from the cold and the gash in her face.

The man slowed a few yards from her, holding his lantern up.

"Good Heavens, you're a woman!" he said, his voice deep and dry. By the lantern light, Kenna Decker guessed him to be in his forties. As he drew near, he looked her up and down.

"Look, just let me use your phone, sir. I need to make a call," Decker said, her body shaking as her worn out muscles struggled for oxygen. The adrenalin wore away and pain seeped in from every wound, but her heart rate wouldn't slow down, nor would her breathing. Decker couldn't seem to catch her breath.

The man stared at her, his expression one of confusion. He looked away, to the bodies of the wolves left in her wake.

"You... you did this?" he asked, his tone one of awe.

"They didn't leave me much choice," Decker said, starting to feel nauseous and dizzy. "Do you live nearby?"

"My farm is back beyond the trees, over yonder," the man said. "I heard the gun shots and the yelling. I couldn't figure where it was coming from or I'd have gotten here sooner, but... Mercy, I can't believe my eyes. *You* killed all these wolves?"

Decker nodded, her eyes closed.

"Whoa there, little lady," the man said, rushing back to her side. She swooned and wanted very much to lie down.

The man took her arm and kept her from falling right over.

"Lord above, your face!" Decker heard him say. "Those animals are a vicious lot. We best get indoors. Can you walk?"

Decker tried to nod but wasn't too sure if she succeeded. The man put her arm over his shoulder and they started walking. Decker opened her eyes as they stumbled across the field and looked at him.

"Thank you, sir," she said, and closed her eyes again.

"Miss, I can't begin to fathom what on earth you were doing out here," the man said, breathing hard as he half-carried her along, "but you're in a right bad way and very lucky to be alive. When they get it in their heads to attack a person, wolves aren't known to leave many survivors, that's for darn sure.

This winter, though, it hasn't left them much of a choice, people reckon. Biting cold and no small game? They've gotten bolder."

That was the last thing Kenna Decker heard before she passed out.

* * *

When she came back around, Decker was lying on a bed. She felt hands jostling her and pressing into her ribs. She opened her eyes in the soft lantern light and saw a cramped bedroom with plain wood slats for walls, with little in the way of decoration. The man from the field knelt next to her, his attention fixed on his task, his hands working at something out of her view. Past him, through the door beyond, Decker made out a lit stone fireplace and a table with several chairs. He jostled her again, pulling on her combat harness. She tried to speak, but it came out thick and unintelligible.

"What are you doing?" Decker asked, her mouth dry. Disorientation and the cold bandage on her facial gash made coherent speech almost impossible.

The man looked up at her and smiled, his expression kind and full of concern.

"You're awake then, good," he said. "I got worried once or twice there when your breathing got too shallow for my liking. Your colour is coming back, too."

"I need a doctor," Decker said struggling with articulation.

"Too right, you do," the man said, nodding and looking her over, "Somewhat fortuitous then that I was one."

"Just my luck," Decker muttered.

"What's your name?" the doctor asked.

"Decker," she answered, "Kenna Decker."

"Miss Decker, I'm Charles Winstone," the man said, "I've cleaned and dressed your wounds, and they were considerable, but I have a very good feeling you are going to live."

"Hospital," Decker said, her speech slurred and her head pounding.

"We're pretty far from the city," Winstone said, "I wouldn't want to make that trip, not in your condition. You lost a good deal of blood."

"They'll airlift me," Decker said. "Call my people. I have the contact number."

The doctor gave her a quizzical look.

Decker scanned the candlelit room.

No electric light fixtures, she noted.

"No phone?" Decker asked. "No net connection out here?"

Winstone's brow furrowed.

"Can't say I follow you, young lady," he replied, shaking his head. "Best you not talk, what with the bandage and that cut on your face."

He started to pull against her harness once more. Decker leaned forward, wanting to ask what the hell he was doing down there, but then she saw the answer. The man grunted as he fidgeted and worked at releasing the buckle. Decker reached down and swatted his hands away.

"This is on you tight and probably isn't doing you any good in your condition," he protested.

Decker pressed the release between her thumb and forefinger and the latch let go. Winstone shook his head in wonder, then reached over her and did the same to the other buckle. He lifted her up a little to pull the harness away and let it drop to the floor, regarding it with some curiosity. He didn't dwell on it, but instead undid the first few buttons of her camouflage top.

"That should be more comfortable, Miss Decker," Winstone said. He took a wet rag and washed the sticky, drying blood that had gushed down her cheek to her upper chest. He rinsed the rag in a basin on the floor and dried her off with a towel.

With that done, Winstone looked at her, more serious than before.

"Now comes the hard part, Miss Decker," he said. "Your face is pretty badly cut. The gash is deep enough that I'm worried you may lose some feeling in it, even after it heals. I'm worried about infection, too. I cleaned it with alcohol, but to give you the best chance of it healing properly, I'd like to stitch up the wound right now. You were out in the cold and that helped keep the flesh around the cut from going bad, but time is important here. There's going to be a scar, but if I stitch you up right now, it may not be so bad. Do you understand?"

Decker felt her head clearing and knew that the man was right, it had to be now.

"I have morphine here, to dull the pain while I work," Winstone said.

"No," Decker said, grabbing him by the wrist.

"It's going to hurt and I don't have any ether," Winstone sighed, "It's morphine or nothing. And I really don't advise nothing."

"No drugs," Decker said. "I mean it."

"It's your choice," Winstone said, "It's going to hurt and because it's mostly your cheek I'll be working on, I can't even give you the belt to bite down on. Last chance before I get started."

"No drugs," Decker repeated. "I can handle the pain."

She could see he didn't believe her, but he nodded and said, "As you wish. Just try to hold still so I don't do too ragged a job."

Winstone eased the bandage from her cheek. The shot of agony as he did so made Decker wonder if he was tearing half her face off with it. She gripped the edge of the bed until the pain settled to a tolerable burning sensation. He looked up from the wound to fix her with a hard look.

"I mean it this time," he said. "Last chance for—"

Her hand, the one that had held the white-knuckle grip on the edge of the bed, now seized his wrist. She held it firm and steady, not trying to hurt him, but demonstrating that she had not changed her mind in the least. The move startled him and she let it sink in before she spoke.

"Get to work, please, doctor," Kenna Decker told him.

* * *

The first light of morning began to creep through the kitchen window when Winstone set about washing the bloody rags and

8

tools with soap and hot water. He let it all soak in the steaming pot as he went to check on his patient. The woman named Decker slept, finally succumbing to exhaustion. He'd replaced the bandage on her cheek and used an ice-filled cloth to keep the swelling down. Winstone knew he should get some sleep, too, but the grey fatigue that came from pushing well past one's tiredness told him proper rest was a long ways off right then.

He stepped outside into the frosty dawn and squinted against the sun's rays. They streamed through the line of trees that flanked his farmhouse to the east. Winstone double-checked that his rifle was loaded and then set out. He crossed through the line of trees and walked east across the flat icy snow.

The bodies of the wolves the woman had killed still lay where they had fallen. The blood from their wounds stained the white ground shades of red, pink and brown. Having seen to and mended Decker's wounds, Winstone knew some of this blood belonged to her, but most of it came from the wolves. Standing in the cold, still air, he counted the bodies.

"... Fifteen... sixteen... seventeen... eighteen," he tallied. Drops of blood streaked away from the scene and Winstone guessed they belonged to the wounded, those that had managed to escape with their lives.

Winstone saw that no snow had fallen overnight, so he easily picked out Decker's footprints. He followed her back trail across the plain, picking out the small drops of red that accompanied her trek.

At a large, disturbed patch of snow, he stopped. The shape in the snow almost resembled an angel children would make with their arms and legs. This form was nothing so elegant. Winstone knelt, examining the single frozen pool of blood at the head of the depression, about the size of his hand. He turned and looked west, back the way he came, unable to see his farmhouse past the tree line in the distance, but able to spot the rising smoke from the stovepipe's chimney. He stared in that direction for a long time, then rose and looked around. The plain spread to every horizon, with trees and hedgerows in the distance. He looked back at the ground.

The woman's trail ended at this spot.

Standing in the quiet winter landscape, Winstone shook his head. His eyes scanned the ground for man-made tracks. The small, distinctive marks of wolf prints dotted the snow, but Winstone found nothing else around the impression left by Decker.

He started to circle the depression. As he arced around it, a wave of dizziness overwhelmed him. Winstone staggered and almost doubled over. All around him, the air went out of focus. Winstone pressed his gloved fingers to his eyes to rub them, but it did no good. He spun around and stumbled, wanting to be ill. He closed his eyes and tried to steady himself.

"I'm tired, that's all," he whispered. "Just tired and cold."

The nausea faded and he opened his eyes, looking up at the blue morning sky. Except, the clear sky wasn't blue anymore, but shades of grey such that he had never seen before. On the horizon, the evergreens had been drained of their colour, too. Winstone looked to the bloody spot in the snow left by the wound on Decker's face and saw that the red stain had become a warm tinted grey, as well. He knelt and reached out to touch the now-colourless patch, but the sight his glove chilled him more than the cool air. To his horror and disbelief, Winstone found he could see the shape of his hand through the fur-lined leather. On closer inspection, turning his hand over, he could trace the lines on the palm and knuckles.

If I take off my glove, will I see through my skin to the very bones and ligaments? Winstone speculated.

With little warning, Winstone sensed someone behind him. He spun around to his left, raising his rifle and forgetting all about the bizarre sight of his hand—

It's not just my hand, he realized as the gun barrel came up, *I can almost see right through the metal and wood of my gun.*

—but he saw no one. Still, he couldn't shake the eerie feeling of being watched. The air around him seemed to flutter. He glanced about and caught movement to his right. He jerked in that direction, finding no one there. Then something else moved just out of view to his right.

Someone *was* there, he was sure of it.

He waited, staring straight ahead. The shape came again on his right, subtle, but murky. Winstone didn't look right at it, but instead let the shape move about his peripheral vision. The wispy form stood about his height, and even though he saw no discernable human shape in it, Winstone had the undeniable sense that this was a person. Somehow, in some startling way, he was seeing a living being. Another such form came into view to his left, moving this way and that. The first spectre stood still a moment and didn't seem to react to the second. A third appeared on Winstone's left, but did not seem aware of the other two. None of these beings seemed aware of the others, or of him, and Winstone was fine with that, as the uneasy feeling held tight to his gut.

The beings milled about and he started to wonder if they were lost. He wondered if he was lost, trapped in this unreal place where no God-fearing man should be. He wanted to turn and run back to his cabin, but a stronger instinct told him to stay right where he was, that running would not save him. There existed a danger here, one far beyond his comprehension, but he sensed it all the same.

To his right, out of the corner of his eye, he saw the first spectre move closer to him, one step at a time. Winstone gripped the rifle tighter, not knowing if the weapon would have any affect on this person that seemed both there and not there. The being stopped, but Winstone did not relax. When it started toward him once more, its pace was slow and tentative.

Panic seized him. When the being seemed a mere foot away, Winstone could stand the tension no longer. In a single motion he pivoted to his right, bringing the rifle to bear on the approaching shape and fired. The kickback brought the rifle up and Winstone staggered on his heels. Snow under foot and unbalanced, he slipped and fell, landing hard on his side. He cocked the Winchester rifle and reloaded in a flash, eyes darting about for the being that had approached him.

Whatever it had been, it was now gone.

The sky shone bright blue overhead and the dizzy sickness eased away. Blood still pounding in his ears, Winstone looked around. The scarce winter colours had returned to the world.

11

The blood on the ground stood out red against the snow once more, the firs in the distance rose tall and green in the yellow rays of the morning sun. Winstone got to his feet, relieved, but unable to shake the dread in his gut..

His voice shook as he said, "Something is very wrong here."

* * *

Kenna Decker awoke blurry-eyed to see the business end of Winstone's rifle pointed at her from the doorway of the bedroom.

"Miss, you have some explaining to get on to," Winstone said, his aim sure and steady, but with an ever-so-slight tremble to his voice.

"You saved my life," Decker said, her own eyes stern and fixed on him, "and now you're pointing a weapon at me."

"Where did you come from?" Winstone asked, his dry voice hard with a dangerous combination of seriousness and fear.

Decker didn't answer at first. She didn't know where she was, but she had formed an idea of *when*. And why.

The Breach.

It hadn't just transported her God-knows-how-far across the country, but also across time.

Winstone's resolve had not faltered in the few seconds that passed as she weighed her options.

"Put down the rifle and we'll talk," Decker said, her own voice even, but not giving the man an inch, not offering a hint of submission, even with a gun pointed at her head.

"No," Winstone said. "You tell me where you came from. Right. Now."

"Or you'll murder me?" Decker asked.

"There's something not right about you," Winstone said. "I found the spot out across the plain, the spot where your tracks start cold. There's something out there. Something bad. A broken place right where your trail starts. I think you came from there, because nothing about you makes a lot of sense."

Decker held her interrogator's stare a few seconds longer, then let it go with a heavy sigh, looking first past him, then around the narrow bedroom. The wound on her face seared and pulsed, and protested every movement of her mouth, even through the adrenalin rush of the moment.

"That broken place is the Breach," Decker said, her gaze drawing back to Winstone, "It sounds like you found a portal into it, probably the same one I came out of."

"You better start making a lot more sense than you are right now," Winstone said, adjusting the rifle's stock against his shoulder.

"I'm not from this place," Decker said, "or from this time. The Breach is a tear of some kind in reality. The people I work with studied it. Scientists, some of the best in the country. My job was to help guard it, but we were taken over by the new government. Don't ask me to go into specifics, just know that we couldn't give the Breach to them. My commanding officer blew up the facility, but before we were killed, the Breach pulled us in, one by one. And I arrived here, out in that field, last night. I traveled *through* the Breach, through *time*. I don't even know what year it is or where I am exactly. The United States, I supposed. Maybe Canada."

"You're in the United States, alright," Winstone said. Some of the fear had left his voice; some, but not all of it. "And the year is 1861."

Decker nodded, because it was just as she'd suspected.

"Does that answer your question?" she asked, knowing he probably had a whole host more now. That is, if he didn't think she was either lying or insane.

Winstone lowered his rifle and hung his head. His long hair blocked her view of his eyes and most of his face, so she could not read his expression. He stood there for several seconds before speaking.

"Get some rest," he said. "I'm going to make some coffee."

Winstone left the bedroom doorway and Kenna Decker watched him go.

13

2

The Ledger of Owen McCabe

May 3, 1895
Orchard Bend

I don't want to forget, that's why I'm writing all this down.
I don't want to forget any of it.
I have articles clipped from the Orchard Herald *and after I*
write this, I'm going to put them in this ledger too, so the story
is complete.
So that I never forget.
Of course it's all still fresh in my memory now, but come ten
years, twenty even, it could fade. Maybe not all of it, but losing
any of it would be unacceptable. If I ever waver or stray from
my path, I want to be able to look back on this record I'm
building and remind myself why vengeance is all I have left.
I'm doing this for my brother. His name was Henry.
My last real memory of Henry is of him reading a story to me
on New Year's Eve of 1886. I can't say I remember the story
itself, seeing as Henry read a lot of stories to me growing up,
but I think it might have been Little Lord Fauntleroy, *the one*
about a poor boy who inherits a fortune and moves to England
or some such nonsense. Let's just say it was *that book because*
I also remember dressing up like the little lord for the dinner
party that New Year's Eve and later for Henry's funeral. By
God, I hated that suit, lace collar and all.
I must have fallen asleep as my brother read the story and so
that's how I remember him, sitting on the side of my bed, book
open on his lap while I hugged the thick, warm blankets to my
chin. The next time I saw Henry was in his coffin in our
parlour. I kept thinking he'd open his eyes, sit up and everyone

would stop crying. *Things could get back to normal. But no, that didn't happen.* Mr. Allman the undertaker closed the coffin and took Henry away. My father and mother and I followed in our expensive coach, driven by Mr. Burke. It was cold that day. I remember that, too. I remember wondering if Henry was cold in his coffin. It had a lining, but surely that wouldn't be enough. I thought maybe the ground would keep him warm and in my seven-year-old mind that was all right. I asked Mr. Burke if he thought that was right and he patted me on the head.

"No, Owen," he said with a hint of a smile, "It's far too cold to bury Henry. The ground is too hard in the winter. A shovel can't break through. What will happen is that we'll put Henry in the receiving vault behind the church. I'll bet you didn't know what that building back there was, did you?"

I told him I did not know that. The vault of dark grey stone sat unassuming behind the small church. Its walls a stark contrast to the church's bright white paint. A thick oak door with heavy metal bracing and a great padlock barred entry most days, but when we arrived, Reverend Thomas stood by the open door, shivering against the cold air, waiting to receive the family and give a few words of comfort.

But all of that came after.

I woke from my last peaceful slumber—after Henry read me to sleep—to the sound of raised voices, shouts of surprise and anger. I admit that I felt fear, there in the dark under the heavy, warm blankets. However, the curiosity of a child is sometimes not to be denied, so I crawled from my bed, left my bedroom and arrived on the landing in time to see the dozen or more New Year's Eve guests being hurried out the front door by Mr. Burke. I watched from the shadows as they departed. They spoke in murmurs and whispers, the voices we use to pass secrets and rumours. Gone was the jovial air of the party—and with good reason—replaced by the sound of harsh sobs from the parlour. Some of the guests looked back over their shoulders at the sound, but they tucked their heads down in awkward shame and continued out into the frigid night. When the last guest left, Mr. Burke hurried to the parlour.

I started down the steps, heart pounding. I took each tread carefully, knowing this was serious. I had to know what was going on, but it was late and I didn't want to get in trouble for being up past my bedtime.

I'd made it only a few steps before the door opened and in stepped Sheriff Dale. She didn't see me and I stopped. She closed the door with great care behind her, as if she were sneaking in, which I thought was odd since she used to work for my father for years and used to come and go at her leisure beforet. I didn't then know, however, that she had good reason to be hesitant. I didn't yet know what she had done to our family.

Dale stood in the foyer almost unmoving, the snow from her boots melting into pools on the hardwood. In her hand she held her sword, her curious trademark if ever there was one, and I remember she held it backwards, almost hiding it behind her. The pummel, once smooth and round, looked bent and deformed, the metal damaged. The hood of the cloak she wore—yet another odd affectation of hers—hid most of her face. All I could see were her lips and her chin.

She seemed to me to be listening to the voices coming from the parlour, the voices of my father and Mr. Burke. As she did, her head titled, she spotted something hanging by the door, the scabbard of her sword. She took it from the peg on the wall and sheathed her weapon, then slung it over her shoulder. She must have known she could put it off no longer and so crossed the foyer to the parlour.

I was going to proceed down the stairs but didn't get a single step before I heard my mother's anguished cries of "What did you do?! WHAT DID YOU DO?!"

I heard the sheriff try to answer, calling my mother by name. I heard the schoolteacher, Miss Adelaide, call out to my mother to let the sheriff explain, and I heard my father demand that Mr. Burke rid them all of Emery Dale's presence. The voices grew louder until the sheriff herself spoke in a sharp, commanding tone.

"Gertrude, Mr. McCabe, I had no choice!" Dale said. "Henry attacked me with my own sword!"

16

"Why would he do such a thing?" my mother pleaded.

"I suspect he found out I'd discovered his secret," Dale said. "He murdered Laura O'Malley."

"LIES!" my mother screamed. The conversation degenerated into shouts and accusations, but all I took from it was that something happened to Henry. That was when the fear grew stronger than the curiosity and I scampered back upstairs to my bed. I didn't even close the door. That negligent act allowed me to hear with awful clarity my mother yell at the sheriff, "YOU DIDN'T HAVE TO KILL MY SON! You didn't! You didn't!"

"Gertrude, I'm so sorry," Dale answered. Even to my young ears it sounded pathetic and trite and wholly useless.

"GET OUT!" my mother said. "NEVER ENTER THIS HOUSE AGAIN!"

Soon after, I heard the door open and close as the sheriff left.

I was crying by then, soaking the thick blanket that had become my hiding place. I cried for my mother and I cried for Henry. That woman took my brother from me and never again would he read a bedtime story or pick me up and carry me around or help me with my schoolwork.

I cried and I cried until there was nothing left and I lay in my bed under the blankets. The wind slammed our house, but it couldn't mask the outbursts from my mother and father, the sobbing and harsh words and agonized laments.

And when the night was at its darkest, HE *appeared from the gloom, a dark apparition both there and not there, like a shadow, a thing without substance, but in the shape of a man. At once, I thought it was the ghost of my brother and whispered his name.*

"Henry?" I asked.

I am not your brother, *the man of shadows answered.* Nor will I hurt you. I was Henry's friend once upon a time, when he was near your age.

The man spoke, yet it was much more than that. The voice filled my mind and with it came a flood of pictures and moments, like I was seeing into his head and glimpsing the different thoughts there. I saw Dale before she was sheriff, standing in a strange room of lights and metal things. I saw a young Henry and our home. I then saw the Sheriff Dale I knew, standing over Henry's dead body in our barn.

"She killed him," I said.

Yes, she did, *the shadow answered.*

"I hate her," I said. I did. I truly did.

And I still do.

"Who are you?" I asked.

A prisoner, *the man of shadows replied.* I am trapped in a place between places and I can't get out.

Again, more pictures came, first that of a man running through a dark place of white trees, being shot at. I realized that I was seeing what the Prisoner saw, seeing through his eyes, things he'd done or witnessed. After that I didn't understand what I was seeing. The world changed around him, colour replaced by grey, and everything became like smoke that has been trapped inside glass. I saw things that made no sense, something like a window in that grey world. The Prisoner punched and punched at it, but could not break through.

It made me sad and angry for him, but not as much as I was sad and angry for Henry. Tears poured down my cheeks and my face quivered and shook as I cried again.

You should sleep now, Owen, *the Prisoner said.*

I found comfort in his presence and it was enough for me to close my eyes and do just that.

Over the next few days, the whole town would find out what Dale had done.

3

The Ledger of Owen McCabe

The Orchard Herald, January 4, 1887
KILLER UNMASKED? TOWN IN SHOCK!
by Thomas Buchanan, Editor

As Orchard Bend braces itself against a most harsh and terrible winter, the coldest in recent memory, it begins the New Year not with the annual sense of hope and optimism for what lay in store, but instead with a palpable sense of dismay. For a chill descended on the town the morning of January 1ˢᵗ, delivered not by bitter Mother Nature, but by mercurial, cruel irony.

Since last August, Orchard Bend has felt the dread brought on by the unsolved murder of Miss Laura O'Malley. For months, her unidentified killer eluded detection, evading the best efforts of our previous sheriff Clement Wilson, May God Rest His Soul. Wilson's successor, Ms Emery Dale, has previously been written about in these pages, for her heroic deeds in defence of Orchard Bend. Before taking up the mantle of sheriff, Ms. Dale was in the employ of Mr. Maxwell McCabe.

Laura O'Malley's murder remained yet-to-be-solved when Sheriff Dale took her post last November, but where Sheriff Wilson came up short, Sheriff Dale broke the case in dramatic fashion. The details of just what transpired during the festivities at the McCabe house on the evening of December 31ˢᵗ, 1886, are still being sorted through. However, Sheriff Dale claims to have discovered the identity of Laura O'Malley's killer. She had been a guest there by personal invitation of the McCabes. She further claims that said killer confronted her with *murderous intent in the McCabe barn, offering her no choice but to end his life with her Colt revolvers.*

The person she accuses of the heinous deed, the person she claims to have shot dead in the line of duty, is Master Henry McCabe, son of Mr. & Mrs. Maxwell McCabe, her former employer.

The truth of the events will be determined by due process of public hearing, where Sheriff Dale will stand before the Council of Aldermen in one week's time to present facts and testimony. The hearing is scheduled to begin at 9 AM on Monday the 10th of January at the Town Hall.

4

The Ledger of Owen McCabe

The Orchard Herald, January 11, 1887
"HE WAS TRYING TO KILL ME!" DECLARES DALE
by Thomas Buchanan, Editor
with notes from A.C. Clapton, Contributor

Barely two months old, the Town Hall in Orchard Bend has played host thus far to only one other gathering of nearly all its citizens, that being the grand opening fair held late last October, to mark the official opening of the building. Where that night gaiety flowed through the great assembly hall, on the brisk morning yester-day, questions and morbid curiosity dominated the gathered souls. With seating yet to be furnished to accommodate all and sundry, most were left to stand. Cordoning the townsfolk was a line of sawhorses, beyond which sat Sheriff Emery Dale, positioned before the stage at a long table. Upon the table was a collection of papers and items, amongst which were a hatchet, a locket and Sheriff Dale's own sword. Next to the long table was a smaller table and chair, unoccupied except for a pitcher of water and a cup.

What follows is offered as a transcript of the relevant points brought up at the hearing. Presiding over the event was the attorney and committee Chair Mr. Martin Griesbach. Other members present of the Council of Aldermen were Mr. Earl McManus, Mr. Edgar Allman, Mr. Wayne Statler and Mr. Geoffrey Holland. Positioned on the assembly hall's stage, the committee cast an imposing presence over those gathered.

Mr. Griesbach called the hearing to order and thanked everyone to remain respectful. The committee was introduced and the purpose of the hearing announced:

"To inquire as to the circumstances of the shooting of Henry Maxwell McCabe by Sheriff Emery Ann Dale, and to rate her competency to remain in that appointed position."

Mr. Griesbach called upon Dr. Alfred Shaw, who took the witness post at the small desk. Mr. Griesbach questioned him about the cause of Henry McCabe's death.

"Young Mr. McCabe was killed by five gunshots, apparently from a .45 calibre Colt Single Action Army revolver," Dr. Shaw informed the committee. "The two most mortal of those wounds were the ones closest to his heart."

"When did you examine the body?" asked Mr. Allman, the undertaker.

"Soon after death," Dr. Shaw replied, "Within 20 minutes. I was attending the soiree at the McCabe home and Sheriff Dale found me at the piano. She quietly asked me to join her outside. She first asked that I retrieve the lantern from my buggy. After I did, I followed her to the barn where, before allowing me inside, she told me she had shot Henry McCabe in self defence."

"How did you react?" asked Mr. Griesbach.

"I was surprised and disturbed by the news," Shaw answered.

"When you examined the body, did you find cause to doubt Sheriff Dale's claim of self defence?" Mr. Allman asked.

"Henry lay dead on the dirt floor of the barn," Dr. Shaw explained. "There was evidence of a confrontation all about. The dirt, hay and frost on the ground suggested a fight of some sort. And he was holding Sheriff Dale's sword."

"What was the sheriff's demeanour during all this?" Mr. Statler asked.

"Collected, if a touch shaken," Dr. Shaw answered.

"Neither angry nor upset?" Mr. Statler asked.

"No," Dr. Shaw answered.

With no additional questions, the committee thanked Dr. Shaw for his time and dismissed him. Mr. Griesbach called Sheriff Dale to answer the committee's questions, which she did from her table.

"Sheriff Dale, you admit to shooting Henry McCabe?" Mr. Griesbach asked.

"In self defence, yes," the sheriff replied.

"Please describe in your own words how this came about," Mr. Griesbach said.

"I was attending the party at the McCabe's house and Henry asked to speak to me in private. We agreed to meet in the stables across from the barn. On my way to the stables, I had reason to go to the barn," Sheriff Dale explained. "There, I discovered evidence that pointed to Henry McCabe as the killer of Laura O'Malley."

"What was this evidence?" Mr. Griesbach asked.

"A hatchet was visibly absent from their tools stored in the barn," Dale said. "You see, there was space designated for four hatchets and only three were present. I suspected the missing fourth to be what the killer used to decapitate Laura O'Malley..."

And then Sheriff Dale held up the hatchet she had before her.

"...Deputy Green found this hatchet in the East River below the trestle bridge during our investigation into Laura's death and I believe it to be that weapon."

"Allow me to go back a little in your narrative, Sheriff," said Mr. McManus. "What prompted you to visit the barn before going to the stables?"

Dale let forth a long sigh at this question and collected her thoughts.

"A sudden moment of insight," she said. "Laura O'Malley left a secret note in her locket that I felt was a clue to her killer's identity."

As she spoke, the sheriff worked open Laura O'Malley's locket and drew from it a bit of paper.

"I verified with her teacher, Miss Adelaide, that this was Laura's handwriting," Dale said. "On it she claims mutual affection for a 'Mr. H.' I previously had not considered Henry McCabe as a person of interest because it did not occur to me that they knew each other. Laura attended school in town and Henry was home-taught by his mother. At the New Year's Eve party, the idea came to me and I went to the barn to investigate."

"How did you come to confront Henry McCabe?" Mr. Griesbach asked.

"I didn't," Dale answered. "He confronted me, brandishing my sword."

"How did he get your sword from you?" Mr. Statler asked.

"He didn't take it from me," Dale said, her tone becoming apologetic. "In my haste to check the barn, I left my sword in the house."

"Unattended," Mr. Griesbach said.

"Yes, unattended," the sheriff replied. "It's not an oversight I plan to ever allow again."

"And there were no witnesses you know of to your confrontation with Henry McCabe?" Mr. Griesbach asked.

"We were in the barn, just him and myself," Dale answered. "Several men on the front porch saw me leave the house, Mr. Trask and Mr. Porter among them. They were smoking cigars. But no one besides Henry and me was in the barn to see him attack me. So no, there were no witnesses to the shooting."

"Sheriff, do you feel it was necessary to shoot and kill Henry McCabe?" Mr McManus asked.

"Unfortunately, I do. He was trying to kill me! I only had a moment to react. He said, 'Now you have to die like the others.' Those were his exact words," the sheriff told the committee.

At this, the townsfolk let out a collective gasp. Mr. Griesbach tapped his gavel and brought the room to order.

Sheriff Dale continued, "I drew both my guns and moved to avoid his attack. He swung at me repeatedly and at one point I dropped one of my guns on the ground and drew a knife to deflect his sword strike. It gave me the opening to fire my remaining gun, killing him."

"Five bullets?" Mr. Holland asked. "You saw fit to use that many?"

At this question, Sheriff Dale let out a weighty breath.

"I aimed for center mass and used all the bullets in my gun to stop the person intent on murdering me," Sheriff Dale said. "I shot to kill. I had no other agenda in that moment."

"What happened to the sixth bullet fired from your gun?" Mr. Holland asked.

"After Henry attacked me, my first shot hit the pommel of the sword," Dale said and held up her sword to show the damage. The pommel, the piece below the grip, was misshapen apparently from being struck by the bullet in question.

"Sheriff, if what you say is true, then it begs the question: what 'others' was he referring to?" Mr. Griesbach asked.

"I believe he was referring to Laura O'Malley," Sheriff Dale responded, "and to Sheriff Wilson."

The fervour of surprise swept through the crowd again and Mr. Griesbach threatened to have the hall cleared.

"Sheriff Wilson's death was determined to be a suicide," Mr. Griesbach said.

"Based on the sole account of Henry McCabe as the witness," Dale replied. Muttering and whispers filled the hall, but the sheriff went on, "Dr. Shaw tells me he found gunpowder burns on Wilson's face, yet the common story from Henry McCabe is that Sheriff Wilson had the barrel of the gun in his mouth. Burns like that should only be left if Sheriff Wilson had held the gun out from his mouth, not inside it."

"Doctor, do you agree with this?" Mr. McManus asked.

Dr. Shaw came forward once more to reply.

"I'll tell you what I told Sheriff Dale: that's one way of looking at it," the doctor answered. "I've seen my share of bullet wounds. The powder and heat leave marks sometimes, depending on where a person gets hit and how they were shot. I saw the burns, but concluded at the time that they came from the cylinder, which would have been outside Wilson's mouth. I had no reason to think Henry McCabe was lying that night. Sheriff Wilson was distressed, having had to deal with Laura O'Malley's mother and the unsolved case."

"Doctor, do you think it's possible Henry shot Wilson?" Sheriff Dale asked him.

Dr. Shaw gave a nod so slight it would be easy to miss, but he replied, "Yes. It's possible."

More chattering arose from those assembled, followed by more rapping of Mr. Griesbach's gavel on the table to settle them down. Dr. Shaw stepped back from the committee.

25

"After you shot Henry McCabe, what did you do?" Mr. Griesbach asked.

"I holstered my empty gun, retrieved the one I dropped and kept it pointed at him as he died," Dale said.

"You didn't think it advisable to fetch Dr. Shaw?" asked Mr. Holland, "To make an attempt to save the man's life?"

"I was still focused on my own survival, Mr. Holland," Dale replied. "His well being was not my greatest concern right then."

"I see," Mr. Holland said.

"Did he say anything else during your confrontation?" Mr. McManus asked.

"No," Dale answered, "But as he lay on the ground, I asked him 'why?' He replied that he was the master of life and death."

The next few minutes were near pandemonium in the assembly hall. Clearly, none present expected such revelations. A heated Mr. Griesbach demanded order and eventually got it.

"Have you anything further to add, Sheriff Dale?" Mr. Griesbach asked.

"I wish Henry McCabe had surrendered peacefully, but he chose not to," Sheriff Dale said. "I can't say I entirely understand his motive for killing Laura O'Malley, but I hold little doubt he was her murderer and that the likelihood is great that he also killed Sheriff Wilson, presumably to cover his tracks."

"You presume much," came a voice from the crowd. Mr. Maxwell McCabe, father to Henry, stepped forth in dramatic fashion. When Mr. Griesbach brought the attendees back to a state of order, he addressed this unexpected interruption. Mr. McCabe asked to speak on behalf of his family and in particular his son. Mr. Griesbach yielded him the floor.

"I have listened to the proceedings and held my tongue," Mr. McCabe said with great oratory. "Much has been presumed about my son during this hearing and I will stand for it no longer. The thought that he could murder a girl in cold blood is beyond absurd. The idea that he could kill Sheriff Wilson, an experienced lawman, is equally ridiculous. Dr. Shaw declared poor Wilson's death a suicide hardly two months ago. Sheriff Dale is seeking to sully my son's good name to save her own!'"

In the growing din of comments from those gathered, Dale rose to her feet at the accusation and spoke loudly so all could hear.

"Mr. McCabe, I regret what happened," Dale said, "but there is enough evidence here to support my claim."

"Evidence coloured unfairly towards my son," Mr. McCabe replied.

"Maxwell, that's enough," Mr. Griesbach said, slamming his gavel. "You've said your piece for the record."

"I want this woman stripped of her badge and arrested for Henry's murder!" Mr. McCabe demanded. "I want her tried and hanged!"

At Mr. Griesbach's urging, Mr. Edward Burke—an employee of Mr. McCabe's—escorted Mr. McCabe from the Town Hall. When all had settled once more, Mr. Griesbach spoke.

"While this committee reviews the facts and evidence, Sheriff Dale will relinquish her title and authority," Mr. Griesbach announced. "Should the committee find her capable of resuming her duties, both will be restored. Deputy Turnbull will assume the title and duties of Sheriff until this committee reaches its decision. That is all for today and this hearing is adjourned. Good day to you all."

5

A Letter from Rose Adelaide

January 13, 1887
Orchard Bend.

Elizabeth, My Dearest Cousin,

Our correspondence has become less frequent of late and I bear responsibility for that. The winter school term has occupied much of my time, and other events, which I'll relate in due course, have kept me from putting pen to paper.

Thank you for sending along the R. L. Stevenson book and arranging its delivery. I gave it to my dear friend, Emery, for Christmas. I look forward to reading it myself when she finishes it, though that may take longer than excepted now. Speaking plainly, an impossible, terrible situation has developed.

In my last letter, I told you how Emery was made sheriff of Orchard Bend. She has been my friend for many years and now faces a trial of the spirit against which I fear I can do little more than offer my undying support. In pursuing the truth behind a murder, Emery had to take the life of the young man she suspected had committed the heinous deed. Evidence supports his guilt and Emery shot him in self-defence, but there is much more. The young man, Henry, was the son of our close friend, Gertrude. As Gertrude mourns, I cannot help but feel the knit of friendship unraveling between the three of us. While Emery and I remain close, I fear Gertrude will be lost to us.

Being winter and with the ground too firm to dig, Henry was placed in waiting in the receiving vault behind the church until the spring thaw. A service was held and I attended, hoping to find a moment to speak to Gertrude. You see, her son was shot on New Year's Eve at their home and I was there at the house both when it took place and when Gertrude found out. The magnitude of her sorrow I cannot put into words. Myself, I was overcome with a sense of awful detachment, like I was watching a tragic play unfold upon a stage. When Emery tried to explain—an impossible task—Gertrude sent her from the family's home with the edict never to return. I departed a short time later with our Dr. Shaw after he tended to Gertrude. She had become withdrawn and silent soon after Emery left. Her husband Maxwell assured the doctor Gertrude would be seen to. Dr. Shaw being my means of travel that evening, he and I made for town.

At the service days later, I had hoped to learn Gertrude's disposition. She remained silent as Rev. Thomas read from the Good Book and did not look about the room, her gaze remaining fixed straight ahead, in the direction of the vault where Henry lay. When the service concluded, I approached, but was intercepted by Mr. Burke, Maxwell's employee. He deftly placed himself between Gertrude and me, and his expression was grim, though soft in its way. He said nothing, but shook his head. I called out to Gertrude, but she did not respond, nor did she acknowledge me in any way. The family drove off and I was left at the church door with Rev. Thomas. I thanked him for the lovely service, then in the sunny cold, I walked home, my heart heavy.

Emery came to visit and I consoled her, as I have several times in the days since the shooting. Her burden is unfathomable. Then came the hearing wherein her actions were scrutinized and dissected. She has been relieved of her duties, which we hope is merely a temporary state of affairs. Henry attacked her and she defended herself, however Henry's family holds sway in town. There is a good chance they will rule against her.

That evening, after the hearing, Emery presented me with her sword.

"It no longer feels like its mine," she said with great melancholy. "I don't want to wear it and I don't want to draw it *ever again. Henry used it against me. The price I'm now paying for that act makes me sick to look at it. I'll decide later what to do with it, but for now, please keep it safe. I don't even want it at my cabin, not after what happened."*

I promised her I would do as she asked.

A cold spell tightens its grasp on the region, much as it does on the rest of the country according to the reports in the Orchard Herald. Fewer of my young scholars make the journey from their farms to attend school in this inclement weather. On the coldest days, only those who live in town venture forth. There is talk of heavy snow in the forecast and it's difficult to imagine even more descending on us than we've already been dealt. I long for the milder California winters of my youth

I fear I have rambled a good deal too long, so will bid you goodbye and await your response.

Be well, Fairest Cousin

Rose

6

The Ledger of Owen McCabe

Minutes of the Orchard Bend Council of Aldermen
McCabe house (study), January 14ᵗʰ, 1887, P.M.

Mr. Maxwell McCabe presided.
Mr. Edgar Allman recorded minutes.
Mr. Wayne Statler led opening devotional exercises.
First considered was the recognizing of the minutes of the
January 13ᵗʰ committee hearing on the matter of Sheriff Dale.
Vote to approve given by Mr. Griesbach, head of the committee.
Vote seconded by Mr. McManus, committee member.
Mr. McCabe was given the floor. Transcribed is a letter to the
committee read by himself (original appended):

> *"Committee and fellow aldermen,*
> *In humble fashion, I apologize for my outburst*
> *at the hearing Monday last. Such an act was*
> *unbecoming a man, grieving father or no. I beg*
> *your forgiveness and hope this evening you will*
> *hear my words and give them due consideration*
> *without bias or malice.*
> *I believe the woman Emery Dale to be unfit for*
> *the position of Sheriff and the tragic incident*
> *with my son only reinforces my belief. Her*
> *handling of the matter wherein, by her claim, she*
> *suspected my son Henry of foul play led directly*
> *to his avoidable death. Yes, I say avoidable. If*
> *she thought him suspect, she ought to have made*
> *arrangements to control the situation, to keep*
> *the worst of outcomes from playing out as they*

did. Had she come to me before speaking to Henry, I would have done everything in my power to see my son answer whatever questions she had in the peace and comfort of our home. In reflecting on the matter, I cannot deny that Henry may have felt threatened by the prospect of being interrogated by Sheriff Dale about young Laura O'Malley's equally tragic death. It had been two months since he witnessed Sheriff Wilson's suicide and any young man would be affected. Lashing out, as Sheriff Dale claims he did, was the act of a scared boy. However, as sheriff, Ms. Dale had other options available to her. If she was unable to subdue Henry, she ought to have sought assistance, from myself, my employee Mr. Burke, or Dr. Shaw, or even his mother, my wife Gertrude. Together, any or all of us could have calmed the child and prevented a tragedy.

And Dale's assumption of Henry's guilt based on evidence quite circumstantial shows a deep character flaw, a lack of reason, understanding and logic. The hatchet is one of many owned by farmers in Orchard Bend, and Laura O'Malley's secret 'Mr. H.' could be any one of a dozen or more people with that initial. And the absurd notion that Henry murdered Sheriff Wilson, a man in his prime and experienced in the enforcement of the law, well, I can only shake my head in disbelief. Dr. Shaw, himself an expert, questioned the validity of her claim to all present at the hearing.

I don't believe it was in my son's nature to murder Laura O'Malley, and lest the real killer strikes again, God forbid, we may well now live with the knowledge that her real killer still roams free. Such is the magnitude of Emery Dale's mishandling of this case.

32

Therefore, I urge the committee to recommend the dismissal of Emery Dale as Sheriff and if it sees fit, to have her arrested and tried for Henry's wrongful death.

A father and husband in mourning,

Maxwell McCabe"

Mr. Griesbach voted to recognize and include Mr. McCabe's letter in the minutes. Mr. Holland seconded.

Mr. Griesbach re-iterated the facts of the committee's findings, reviewed in brief the statements and evidence presented to the committee in hearing, and opened the matter to discussion.

Mr. McManus began by highlighting that Sheriff Dale had only a second or two to react to Henry's alleged attack, respectfully dismissing the claims that other options for subduing Henry were available.

Mr. Holland argued that Sheriff Dale ought to have fled and sought assistance.

Mr. Statler reminded the committee that Sheriff Dale left her sword unattended, itself an act of negligence.

Mr. Allman reminded the committee that Sheriff Dale says Henry asked to speak to her in private, before Dale suspected him of the crime and offered the suggestion that Henry meant to ambush her, because why else would he bring her sword?

Mr. Holland contended that Henry would have had no reason to ambush Sheriff Dale if Sheriff Dale didn't suspect him.

Mr. Allman asked again, "Why then did he bring the sword to their meeting?"

Mr. Griesbach brought the committee to order and reminded them that Henry's guilt or innocent was not the purpose of the committee's formation, that its mandate was determining Emery Dale's fitness to remain Sheriff. He called for a vote on the matter of removing Emery Dale from the Office of Sheriff. The results came thus:

Mr. Griesbach: In favour
Mr. Holland: In favour
Mr. McManus: opposed
Mr. Allman: opposed
Mr. Statler: In favour

Mr. Griesbach asked for a vote on the matter of arresting Emery Dale and bringing her to trial before a judge to answer for the death of Henry McCabe. The results came thus:

Mr. Griesbach: In favour
Mr. Holland: In favour
Mr. McManus: opposed
Mr. Allman: opposed
Mr. Statler: abstained from voting at this time

Mr. Statler gave his reason for abstention as wanting more time to consider the matter, which was only put forth to the committee at this very meeting and was beyond the purview of the committee's intended purpose. He suggested the matter be revisited in two days' time. Mr. Griesbach voted to reconvene on January 16ʰ and Mr. Holland seconded the vote.

Mr. Statler led closing devotional exercises and the meeting was adjourned by Mr. Griesbach.

7

The Journal of Rose Adelaide

January 16, 1887
Orchard Bend

The air grows colder each day. Sometimes, it seems, even hour by hour. In my church classroom, the stove does little to ward off the imposing frigidity. My students and I keep layers on and doing so makes lessons difficult. Mittened hands struggle to write. Shivering makes concentration almost impossible. If this keeps up, I may cancel the winter term until this cold wave breaks. To-day was a rare day of sunshine, free from snowfall and the ominous clouds that deliver it, and for fleeting moments as the winds settled the winter-scape truly was beautiful. One could not stray far in one's thoughts about the scenery for too long before the next gust all but struck their face with an icy hand, stinging their cheeks and nose.

Few souls are to be found on the streets amid this bleak assault, only those with business that cannot be avoided. Having put off too long delivering a letter to my cousin Elizabeth, I did so after school let out. The post office has moved from Anderson St. to the Town Hall. After the ordeal of Emery's hearing, I find myself reluctant to set foot there. Yet, I set my resolve upon the task and hurried through the snow-covered streets both to get the chore completed and to spare myself the chill.

The post occupies an office to the rear of the building, so I was spared entering the hall proper where Emery had faced her interrogation. This being my first visit to the new post office, I took in the craftsmanship of the space, which was larger than the post's previous location. The widow Bentley sat at the fine cherrywood counter, a book open before her. We exchanged pleasantries and she told me I was the first visitor she'd received all day. I told her the cold and the snow would keep most folks indoors.

"Too right you are, Miss Adelaide," Mrs. Bentley said, speaking in her rapid, conspiratorial way. "Mrs. McManus stopped by two days ago and told me it was practically the first time she'd left the house this year. Not including that business with the sheriff, mind you. Everyone suffered the elements to see that. All except for one person. I'm sure you know who I mean."

For the life of me I did not.

"Poor Mrs. O'Malley," Mrs. Bentley whispered, perhaps fearful that to say the woman's name aloud would conjure her before us. It's unchristian of me to think ill of Laura O'Malley's grief-stricken mother, but the loss of her daughter has caused her to grow a vicious, cruel tongue towards anyone who crosses her.

"I had not noticed, but you are correct," I agreed.

"I heard from Mrs. McManus that Herman Statler rode past the O'Malley farm the other day. Herman was heading to the Clarke farm, you see, with a late order of nails. You know how Ben Clarke's been trying to get that addition built on his barn? He's had the lumber since November, but those nails have been on back order, see. <u>Well</u>, Herman is riding out that way out of the goodness of his fool heart and happens by the O'Malleys'. I guess it belongs to only the one O'Malley now, what with Laura gone and her husband making off for parts unknown."

I wanted to interject, but Mrs. Bentley hardly paused for breath. Her gurgitation of details was not to be slowed by a mere schoolteacher, regardless.

"So, according to Mrs. McManus, Herman sees no smoke coming from the O'Malley chimney, no disturbance of the snow around the property," Mrs. Bentley continued as I stood patiently with my letter in hand, nearly forgetting why I had visited the post office in the first place. "Herman knocks on the door. No answer. He calls out to Mrs. O'Malley—not something you could pay me to do, poke that sleeping dragon—!"

"Mrs. Bentley!" I said, appalled.

"Oh, I only mean that figuratively, Miss Adelaide," Mrs. Bentley replied, "you know how she could get, the sharpness of her tongue. No need to invite a lashing from it if you can help it, that's all I meant.

"Now, Herman knocks and calls out and gets no response. He peeks in the window, hoping he doesn't see the poor woman has passed on," Mrs. Bentley crossed herself at this, "but no, from what he can see, the home is in order. Only there's no Mrs. O'Malley."

I waited for more. So used to her monologue had I become that I had to rouse myself and ask, "Where was she?"

"No one seems to know," Mrs. Bentley said, a satisfied grin on her face. "I thought maybe she was staying with someone, but the subtle inquiries to that end have proven fruitless."

"I hope she's not in distress," I said.

"I have half a mind to wonder if she's left town, now that this business with her daughter is concluded, the killer unmasked, they say," Mrs. Bentley said with breezy opine as the door opened behind me. A shock of winter air made us both shiver.

Sheriff Turnbull stomped the snow from his boots, looked up and saw me. He had a difficult time looking me in the eye as he tipped his hat. While I understand that the decision to remove Emery as sheriff was not his, he now occupies her rightful post.

"Sheriff Turnbull!" Mrs. Bentley said, full of delight. "I believe I have a letter for you. From Blue Creek, if I recall. I didn't know you have family there."

"I do, yes," the sheriff said, "but I believe Miss Adelaide is next in line."

"Yes, yes! How silly of me," Mrs. Bentley laughed. "I was so caught up on our little chat, Miss Adelaide, I completely forgot. You have a letter, yes?"

"I do," I said, handing her the envelope. "To California, to my cousin. Same as the other times."

I paid the fare and she stamped the letter, then placed it with the other outgoing mail.

I thanked her, said goodbye to the sheriff and hurried from the office, eager to get home as the sun was now below the horizon and the temperature was dropping with it. I shuffled away from the Town Hall, making slow progress through the snow. I was almost at Church Street when Sheriff Turnbull caught up with me.

"Miss Adelaide," he said, "I wanted to tell you I'm sorry Sheriff Dale is in this predicament. Please let her know that. You're her friend. Would you do that for me?"

"Sheriff, I haven't seen Ms. Dale since the hearing," I told him and it was the truth. The sheriff frowned. I confess to letting my gaze linger on the deep, rough scarring that covers his right cheek. It's impolite to stare, so I let my attention turn to the direction of my cottage. "If that's everything, Sheriff, I'll bid you good afternoon."

"Bet you miss California in this cold, huh?" he smiled. It was a warm smile and the scar did not diminish it.

"Good afternoon, Sheriff," I said politely and turned away, thinking only of getting home, making cocoa and preparing dinner. My fingers were beginning to hurt and my face tingled like so many needle pricks from the evening frost. I think now I may have been too abrupt in my departure. I'll apologize to the sheriff when I next see him.

I do worry for Emery, though, and hope she is safe from the cold. Her cabin in the ravine must be hard pressed as winter deepens. I would go to her, but the roads west are treacherous with snow right now and my buggy would not fair well. So I must wait for her to come to me, if she so desires. I hope she knows she is not alone

8

The Ledger of Owen McCabe

The Orchard Herald, January 18, 1887
DALE ARRESTED! CHARGED WITH KILLING McCABE!
by Thomas Buchanan, Editor

The charge is manslaughter and the accused, Emery Ann Dale, former Sheriff of Orchard Bend, will answer before a judge in the days to come.

Dale awaits trial in a jailhouse cell.

She was arrested yester-day outside Reed's General Store & Feed and surrendered peacefully to Acting Sheriff Turnbull, who is expected to be appointed to the post permanently following these developments.

Dale stands accused of wilful negligence in dispatching her duties as sheriff in the matter of questioning Henry McCabe, leading to his death, according to the lawyer Mr. Martin Griesbach, who will try the case as prosecutor at the judge's discretion. Ms. Dale may retain council or chose to defend herself.

The incident with young Henry McCabe occurred on New Year's Eve, when, as Dale claimed in testimony previously given during a hearing on the matter, Henry attacked her rather than be questioned about Laura O'Malley's murder. The charge of negligence against her, brought by Mr. Griesbach on behalf of the Town of Orchard Bend and it citizens, argues that then-Sheriff Dale had other recourse in handling the situation, recourse she wilfully ignored in favour of killing Henry McCabe, whom she suspected of the murder of Miss O'Malley.

Judge Archibald Grenville is expected within the week to preside over the case and to dispense justice.

* * *

The Orchard Herald, January 18, 1887
ORCHARD BEND CELEBRATES 25 YEARS!
by Thomas Buchanan, Editor

As the hardness of winter sets in, Orchard Bend may take warmth from the knowledge that the Year of Our Lord 1887 marks the 25th Anniversary of the town's official incorporation.

Settlers first arrived in the area that would become Orchard Bend in the summer of 1811. The families McCabe, Statler, Sullivan, Pine and O'Toole traveled from the east seeking to build a community. They put down roots around the land between the banks of the winding east, west and south rivers.

Over the next fifty-one years, the combination of hard work, perseverance and commitment allowed the township to grow. Community leaders such as Mr. Liam McCabe and Mr. "Doc" Reed guided and helped shape the town through times both hard and prosperous. The McCabe Orchards and the McCabe Mill were and still are stalwart fixtures of the landscape. Doc Reed, a natural philosopher with acumen in matters of commerce, wed the eldest of the two Sullivan daughters. With her family's money, Reed successfully managed a mercantile business, and the development of property. Both McCabe and Reed also created opportunities for new shops and businesses to establish themselves.

The first public building erected, in 1813, was a church. Then as now, it served many roles, first as a house of worship, but also as a school and community meeting place. Dorothy Sullivan, the younger daughter of the family, was the schoolmarm there until 1865. The original church burned to the ground in 1825, replaced on the same land with the church that still stands to this day. Ms Sullivan taught out of a corner of the Statler livery for a time during construction of the new church.

The war years from 1861 to 1865 saw the formation of companies and cavalry throughout the state, with brave young

40

men volunteering to serve. Following the end of hostilities, many displaced families and individuals ventured to our humble county, ever increasing the population.

Incorporation came in 1862, granted by the State and presided over by the elected Council of Aldermen.

The now-annual town picnic began that year, held to celebrate the incorporation, repeated every year since without fail. Recently unearthed by the Sutter Grove Gazette is a photograph taken at that first town picnic. An engraving of the photograph is shared here for the first time in the pages of the Orchard Herald. This rarest of finds is an historical treasure, as it is one of the few known images of Mr. Doc Reed, capturing a candid moment where, even at his advanced age of ninety years, he partakes with the merry revelers that day.

Plans are underway by the town aldermen to celebrate in grand fashion the silver anniversary at this summer's annual picnic, to be held on the lawn of the newly erected Town Hall, with more details forthcoming.

9

The Journal of Rose Adelaide

January 20, 1887
Orchard Bend

I've made a terrible mistake.

Before I delve into that assertion, I must explain the preceding events.

As school let out on the afternoon of the 17ᵗʰ, I learned of Emery's arrest. I was standing at the door as my students departed and the street was abuzz with the news. I was aghast. My dear friend Emery in jail! I spared no time in going to the jailhouse. There I found a crowd gathered outside, excited and curious. Deputy Green stood on the boardwalk in front of the jailhouse, trying his best to manage the barrage of questions.

"What's the charge?"

"She murdered the McCabe boy, didn't she?"

"Never trust a woman to do a man's job! Lady Sheriff, my foot!"

"She gonna hang, Green?"

Mr. Buchanan of the Herald stood off to the deputy's right, scribbling notes. When the jailhouse door opened and Sheriff Turnbull stepped out, Mr. Buchanan went to him. The two spoke in hushed voices as I pushed through to Deputy Green.

"Miss Adelaide," he said as I approached, "This is no place for you, I reckon."

"May I see Sheriff Dale?" I asked, fixing him with my sternest schoolteacher gaze, one I knew he'd recall, having been among my first pupils in Orchard Bend.

Allen hesitated under my stare, stammering and looking over his shoulder at Sheriff Turnbull, then back to me.

42

"Um, just a moment," Allen said, and he waved the sheriff over.

"Miss Adelaide wants to see Sheriff Dale," the deputy told him.

"She's not the sheriff anymore and never should have been!" came a shout from a man behind me. I knew his voice, but won't dignify his sentiment by naming him in my journal.

Sheriff Turnbull addressed the onlookers.

"Go on about your business!" he told them, "You all have better things to get up to right now!"

More questions and snide remarks came about Emery's arrest and only a few people went on their way. The sheriff turned to me and said, "Miss Adelaide, I understand why you're here, but it's not the best time. Come back to-morrow and perhaps then you can visit your friend."

He was correct, of course, but I turned away with reluctance. Making my way through the small crowd, I caught the cold stares of some of the men and women, and I made haste departing the unpleasant scene.

Under the late afternoon sky, as the clouds sat golden high above, I stopped a dozen yards from my cottage. My body shook, but not only from the cold. I imagined myself going inside, lighting the stove and making myself hot cocoa. And I saw myself there alone as Emery sat in jail. I could not even ride out to Gertrude for company. I quite literally cast about, looking around me in the deepening winter dusk, as if a friend might emerge, but there came no one. So go inside I did and prepared my cocoa and later my dinner. I thought about writing in my journal, but couldn't set my thoughts still enough to try, so I sat listening to the wood burn in the stove.

Then a knock came at my door.

I opened it to find Irene Sullivan there.

The night was cold now and I ushered my former pupil inside.

"Miss Adelaide, of course you heard about Sheriff Dale!" she exclaimed, talking quickly, as was her excited habit. "I came as soon as I could. At the tavern, there's talk of nothing else! And some of the things being said are dreadful!"

"Yes, I can well imagine," I said as I took her coat and hung it by the door.

"Some said she will stand trial for Henry McCabe's murder," Irene said, "but Sheriff Turnbull now says the charge is negligence, that Sheriff Dale did wrong by shooting McCabe. It defies belief! He killed Laura O'Malley... and he..."

Irene spoke so fast as she paced the room, her words seemed to catch in her throat, and she threw her hands up in frustration, letting out a long growl before finding her voice again, "...He quite possibly murdered Clem! She said so! Sheriff Dale said as much at the hearing. Clem would never take his own life! He loved me and I loved him!"

She stopped suddenly then, looking at the door, her voice now almost a whisper.

"I blamed Mrs. O'Malley, because of the vile things she said," Irene looked at me, guilt and shame in her eyes. "I was wrong. I see that now. She said terrible things, but she didn't drive Clem to..."

I took her hand and brought her to the sofa by the wood stove. Lord forgive my anger at the troubled boy, but even from the grave Henry McCabe finds a way to bring sorrow and pain to this town.

"It was a time of great fear and confusion for everyone," I told her. "She was suffering and so were you. She spoke awful, hurtful things, there's no denying that."

Irene nodded, looking down at her clasped hands, saying nothing.

"The charge is negligence, you say?" I asked.

"It seems so," Irene said, not looking up. "It's cruel to put her through that after she saved this town from a murderer."

"She did nothing wrong," I said, "and we can pray a judge and jury will see that."

Irene nodded again.

"And as I told you once before, Irene," I continued, forcing a smile, "you may call me Rose."

Irene offered a grin at the reminder and after some small talk, the time came for her to leave.

The next afternoon, the 18ᵗʰ, Sheriff Turnbull allowed me to see Emery. In her cell, I found her collected and dispassionate about the situation.

"I will have my day in court," Emery said. "I did nothing wrong. I had no choice, as I told everyone at the hearing."

"This isn't right," I told her. "I'll try to speak to Gertrude. Maybe she can speak to her husband about reconsidering all of this."

Emery shook her head.

"You are persuasive," Emery said, "but the McCabes see this as justice. I'm not at all surprised it came to this."

"Well, I am surprised," I said, "Gertrude has known you a very long time. This is not the way of good friends."

"That ship has sailed, I'm afraid," Emery said, taking a step toward the cell bars and speaking low. "But Rose, I need you to do something for me."

"Anything, Emery," I said.

"At my cabin, in the chest at the end of my bed, you'll find a locked box. Keep it safe for me until this passes," Emery said.

"I will," I said, "and I trust you won't be in here for very long. A few days at most, then you can settle this foolish matter."

Resolve and bravery lined Emery's face as Sheriff Turnbull put down the newspaper he'd been reading and insisted we draw our visit to an end.

Checking my pocket watch, I felt I had enough daylight left to make the journey Emery had asked of me, so long as I set out promptly. I prepared my buggy and packed a small meal, famished as I was after a day's teaching. In the cool winter air, I set out to the west river and the ravine where Emery makes her home. Even with the roads well-travelled, my progress was slow, all the while the sun descending ahead of me.

At the ravine, memories arose of the day I first met Emery Dale in that very place, memories that made my heart race and my shoulder ache where a bullet struck it. So vivid was the memory and so quickly did it come that I almost seemed to relive the encounter with the Underwood Gang as I descended the hill and crossed the bridge.

Evidence that I should hurry came with the deepening blue sky. I left my buggy on the road by the bridge and walked through the mud and snow down the path along the river to Emery's cabin. The forlorn quiet there almost made me want to weep, the enormity of Emery's plight felt as a great weight on my heart. I did not delay letting myself in with the spare key Emery leaves at my cottage. The ravine grew darker with each passing moment. Inside, the one-room cabin was darker still. I set alight a lantern and went to the chest at the end of her bed, leaving my muddy boot prints on the floor. I made a silent promise to return to clean up another day when I had more time.

Inside the chest I found Emery's hat and duster, which she now wore less often—if at all—in favour of her hooded cloak. Next to these was the box she asked me to retrieve, plain wood with a dark varnish, slightly smaller than my own jewellery box. As expected, I found it locked, and as I moved it, the contents shifted inside.

With no time to ponder what might lie within, I closed the chest and looked about the cabin, considering what else might be important to collect for her. I took a change of clothes from her dresser, her toothbrush and a jar of toothpaste. After tucking all the items into her satchel, I closed the lantern light and opened the door.

The dark blue sky above dazzled the eye, with its endless stars reaching from horizon to horizon, but it also showed me it was too late now to return to town. I decided the best thing to do would be to stay the night and leave at sunrise, giving myself ample time to return to my cottage before school started. So, I left the satchel at the cabin, took the lantern back to the road and unbridled my horse. I led him to Emery's small stable, watered and fed him, covered him with the horse blanket and went back inside.

Even with the lantern and the wood stove lit, the bitter cold of the air seeped into the corners of the cabin, never quite warming the space. I thought of Emery and the many nights she slept here. My sadness turned to anger at the injustice of her being charged and jailed. I prayed to Our Lord to set her free, that she be rightly exonerated of any wrongdoing. As I calmed myself, I set to work cleaning my muddy tracks on the floor, tidying the kitchen area and retrieving more wood from outside. I checked on my horse, who seemed much more content than I felt.

The blue had left the sky by this time and I gazed up at the beautiful, nearly moonless star-scape once more. I saw a shooting star and thought of Ptolemy and my lessons as a girl. He believed a person could wish on a shooting star, that it was a sign the gods were listening. The Almighty already knew my greatest wish, but another desire, almost as powerful, rose within my heart and I whispered, "Please let me mend our friendship with Gertrude."

My words seemed like little more than wisps of breath in the still, cold air, but I hoped this desire would come true.

I slept in Emery's bed, which proved a greater comfort than I would have imagined, and before dawn broke the next morning I was awake and making coffee. Alas, Emery had no cocoa on hand.

After a small breakfast, I made for town as the sun announced the new day.

The wet snow and mud had hardened overnight and driving the buggy proved easier on the road, though less forgiving as I felt every bump and frozen puddle each mile of the journey. I made good time and reached Orchard Bend as the town awoke. On the streets, a scattering of people went about their various enterprises. I detoured off Anderson and kept to the back street. I passed the shuttered windows of the jailhouse cells and my heart dropped as I thought of Emery inside. I wondered whether she was asleep. I couldn't imagine anyone but a hardened criminal sleeping well in such a place. Or sleeping at all.

As I passed the window, I turned my attention back to the snow-covered street ahead of me and saw a man on his wagon, waiting at the back door of the Orchard Herald. He saw me, but didn't say or gesture any acknowledgement. Drawing closer, I recognized him as Mr. Burke and the wagon that of the McCabes. No sooner had I identified him, drawing up to his position, than the backdoor of the Herald opened and out stepped Gertrude McCabe. She looked up at Mr. Burke and then to me.

Our eyes met and she smiled.

I smiled back, wholly out of reflex and it was a bright and wonderful moment.

She turned away and climbed aboard her wagon.

My thoughts in such pleasant tumult I didn't think to call out to her as I passed. Mr. Burke cracked the reins and their wagon lurched forward, heading off in the opposite direction. I watched it go, craning around quickly, and saw Gertrude look back just as briefly.

My heart remained light and full of hope that my wish could be fulfilled. I resolved to visit Gertrude immediately after I dismissed my young scholars from school.

Henry's crimes, I told myself, were not those of his parents. I would explain to her that Emery is wracked with her own guilt over what happened and wishes she could have changed the outcome.

Things might never be the same, I knew that, but some of this pain could be healed. Despite being a long day already, I set out again swiftly after school and rode east to the McCabes' house, with the sun starting low behind me.

I passed Dr. Shaw as he rode in the opposite direction, returning to town. I smiled, but he must have had a lot on his mind, for his smile in return was brief, gone just as quickly as he gave it.

The McCabes' house stood a thing of beauty on the hill in the setting January sunshine, and I tried not to think of that night almost four weeks ago. I'd been the last guest to leave, after trying to comfort Gertrude in the aftermath. When Dr. Shaw at last left her sleeping, he drove me home. We'd travelled there together as friends and had left in grief and awe.

I knocked on the door and after a time, Mr. Burke answered.

"Miss Adelaide?" he said with a stone expression.

"Mr. Burke, I wonder if I might speak to Mrs. McCabe?" I asked.

"Come in," he said. "I'll see if she's available."

I had hoped Gertrude would answer the door herself or come to see who it was. Earlier, I'd entertained a scene wherein she'd welcome me, overcome with relief that I had read her passing smile quite correctly. Once inside, that fantasy vanished. The grandfather clock in the front hall clicked and clacked, seeming to be the only sound in the house. Of course the Christmas decorations were gone, but so too were the familiar, appetizing smells from the kitchen. The house, which had once been fragrant with bread and cider, now sat devoid of aroma. My lips became dry and I found myself wishing for a glass of water.

Mr. Burke returned and took me through the parlour to the small sitting room beyond. There I waited, looking at the cold fireplace. After a few minutes, I poured myself some water from the elegant pitcher on the sideboard and pushed away the curious feeling of being a stranger in the house I'd so often visited as a cherished guest.

"Hello, Rose," came Gertrude's soft voice, and I turned with a start. Overcome with emotion, I put down the water and went to her. I only got a few steps when she brought her hand up in a gesture that made me stop. A slight shake of her head communicated so very much and I could not sort all of it at once.

"Gertrude, I want you to know I am your friend," I said, the certainty that brought me there now gone.

Rose looked away with a sigh, but not one of relief or elation, but the kind one gives when a difficult task lays before them.

"Rose," she said, her tone making me feel small in the room, "Our friendship is concluded."

"Why?" I asked in a cracked whisper.

Her gaze returned to me. Where I hoped for a glimmer of the light that once marked our friendship, there was none. There had been none since she entered the room. There had been none at the church when they laid Henry in the receiving vault weeks before.

"You know why," she said.

"No, I don't," I said. "You smiled at me to-day as I passed. I did not imagine that."

49

Gertrude looked at the floor and shook her head once more, then looked back at me.

"There was a moment," Gertrude said, "but it passed."

"How," I said, shaking with embarrassment and rejection. "Why?"

Gertrude held my gaze.

"Her," was all she said. There was no anger, no accusation in the word, only a truth so cold and unforgiving.

"Emery is..." I began, but could not go on. What could I possibly say?

Gertrude watched as I struggled to find something to try to save what we had, her face impassive and pale in the soft light of the room.

Then she coughed.

I blinked, thinking it was directed at me, a cue to not even try rebuilding the bridge that had collapsed between us, but another cough came, deeper. Then another. When she doubled over, covering her mouth, I went to her and took her hand, meaning to help her sit.

She pulled away from me and found support with the back of a chair.

"Gertrude, sit," I said.

She gave another unhealthy cough and there was blood on her hand and mouth.

"Go," she said, as though the blood wasn't there.

"Gertrude, what's wrong?" I asked.

"I wish you to leave now, Rose," she said, sitting in the chair. "There's nothing more to say."

"No," I said, anger and frustration now taking hold of me. "I will say my piece! You don't get to break what's between us. I cannot fathom your pain and loss right now, but I won't let you hurt me this way. Be angry at me, be angry at Emery, be angry at God, but know that she had no choice in what happened."

"He was my son," Gertrude said calmly. "She killed him."

I hesitated.

I could say nothing more. It had been a mistake to go there.

"Please leave, Rose," she said. "Don't come back here."

And so I left.

50

And so it has ended.

10

The Ledger of Owen McCabe

Sheriff's Report, January 18, 1887
Orchard Bend

Around 6 o'clock in the evening, Prisoner Dale experienced a bout of swooning in her cell, collapsing to the floor and muttering without coherence. The spell lasted some thirty seconds, during which time she clutched to-day's newspaper, which she had been reading prior to the incident.

When Dale regained consciousness, I asked after her health and well being, suggesting I call on Dr. Shaw, which she declined, instead asking to see Mr. Buchanan. I asked what business she had with him and she said she wanted to ask him some questions. I told her it would have to wait until after her trial. She said she understood and asked for some water. I obliged her.

As the paper contained news of her arrest, I suggested she refrain from reading anymore, but she insisted on keeping the copy of the Orchard Herald with her, saying it helped keep her mind occupied. She asked that she be allowed to read the next day's newspaper after I finished with it. In the interest of keeping the prisoner in a peaceful state of mind, I agreed.

This report is brief due to both the suddenness of Dale's illness and the shortness of the episode therein, a blessing in that no real harm came to the prisoner and that I was able to put down the details prior to the end of my shift, to deliver this document in a timely fashion to Alderman McCabe for his signature. Should further details be required for the record, I am at the Council's service.

Acting Sheriff Reginald Turnbull

11

The Ledger of Owen McCabe

May 10, 1895
Orchard Bend

*A few days after the arrest of Dale, the Prisoner emerged
again from the shadows of my room.*

Owen, *he said,* how are you?

*"I don't know," I answered, my young mind still not entirely
grasping this apparition's presence. Somehow, it seemed easier
at night to accept the existence of the Prisoner.*

This must be a strange time for you, *he said, standing at the
foot of my bed.* I am here to help you, to be your friend.

*"Okay," I said. "I miss Henry. They say he killed that girl,
that's why Sheriff Dale shot him."*

Your parents told you that? *the Prisoner asked.*

*"No, they said Henry died because the sheriff didn't do her
job right," I said, "but I listen to them talk, all the grown-ups
that visit. And I can tell when my parents are lying to me."*

I know you loved your brother, but he was dangerous, *the
Prisoner said both speaking and projecting images into my
head. I saw Henry struggling with a man I later identified as
Edmond Reed, whose family owns Reed's General Store. Then I
saw the Reed storehouse burn to the ground as Henry fled. I
saw Henry strangle Laura O'Malley from behind, dropping to
his knee and holding her off-balance as he wrung her life from
her body. The Prisoner had been there, reaching out to try to
stop Henry, but unable to do so as rage filled my brother.
Henry didn't see the Prisoner in his murderous state, but the
girl did, her eyes wide at the sight of him. The Prisoner heard
her final thoughts.*

I am dying! *Laura said.*

It wasn't meant to be this way, *the Prisoner replied.* I'm sorry.

I feel strange, *Laura said,* and I can see you more clearly now. Oh, how you have suffered.

The Prisoner found he could say nothing, so taken aback was he by her observation.

I'm afraid to die, *Laura said as her eyes closed for the last time. The Prisoner reached out again, even though he knew the gesture was futile. He could not stop Henry—and the Prisoner knew it was too late, regardless—but maybe he could comfort Laura's last moment in this world. His dark, spectral hand passed over her cheek and to his shock, Laura's eyes snapped open. In that instant, the Prisoner believed she was looking right at him, just as the life left her body.*

Henry dropped her onto her back and then drew a hatchet from the rear of his belt.

The Prisoner's thoughts went no further. Given what I found out later, how Henry had beheaded the dead girl, I'm now grateful the Prisoner spared my younger self that sight.

Henry promised to help me, but now he can't, *the Prisoner said.* You're not like him, though.

"I'm not?" I asked.

No, *the Prisoner said, cocking his head to the side.*

I saw a memory of Dale in our barn, swinging her sword at a man, taking off his head. I saw a younger Henry there, too, about the same age in this memory as I was as he showed it to me. Blood marked Henry's cheek as he stood watching, scared beyond his wits.

What I showed you happened just after you were born. Men attacked your family and Henry was taken by one of them. Dale killed them, but the events of that night changed your brother forever, *the Prisoner said,* It only got worse for him in the days and years that followed, the sickness of his mind. He was broken and couldn't help me anymore. That's why I need *you.* In time, you can help me be free of this prison.

"How?" I asked.

We will get to that later, *the Prisoner said,* For now, just know that I am your friend. I know things and see things, and I can help you. Henry is gone and that's sad, but I'm here now.

"I'm afraid to go to sleep," I whispered, *"I have nightmares."*

You are safe, *the Prisoner said,* I won't let anything hurt you.

I fell asleep soon after, with the Prisoner standing watch at the foot of my bed.

12

The Journal of Rose Adelaide

January 22, 1887
Orchard Bend

Yester-day after school, Rebecca Clarke extended her parents' invitation for to dine with them at their home to-day. I accepted, not only because I hold the Clarke family in high esteem, but because it would afford me a welcome distraction from Emery's plight. She remains in jail and I've visited her every day of her incarceration. She surprised me the other day by having scratched on the stone wall of her cell a simple drawing of a rose, done with a bit of crumbling mortar. She told me it keeps her good company. I wanted to believe her to be in high spirits, but I've known her too many years to not be able to see the weight upon her.

"I did nothing wrong," Emery says each time in an attempt to reassure me. "I will have my chance again to speak and I will make them understand."

This fine morning, before I drove out to the Clarke farm, I paid Emery another visit. I found her sullen and introverted to-day and it hurt to see her in such a state. She would not confide in me the root of this despair, whether she had doubts about her legal defence or if her black mood was born of something else. I offered her words of comfort before Sheriff Turnbull brought our conversation to a close. His manner was kind, yet I cannot help but remain aloof of his apologies.

With reluctance, I bade Emery goodbye with the promise to visit her to-morrow before mass.

My drive to the Clarke farm proved pleasant enough, milder than it had been all month, and it cheered me somewhat. My thoughts dwelled on Emery and I decided to make a detour, a longer route, one that brought me back to the west river, the ravine and to Emery's cabin.

There I made my way down the lonesome, muddy path along the river, careful to hitch up my dress to keep it clean. My boots would not fair so well.

When I came to Emery's cabin, I was again swept over with melancholy at the forlorn sound of wind in the trees. However, I had come to this place with specific purpose and set that feeling aside. I went to her door and took from my handbag my pencil and I drew a rose upon the wood. It took a few minutes, and when I was finished I hoped it expressed everything I felt about our friendship. I then departed

I had a pleasant visit with Rebecca and her family. Mrs. Clarke cooked a wonderful meal of venison, which Mr. Clarke beamed about having shot only two days before. He also talked at length about the addition he could at last build on their barn, with the nails having arrived the previous week. Come spring, he would begin that project.

After dinner, Mrs. Clarke insisted her husband play some violin for us. Needing only the slightest prompting, Mr. Clarke fetched his old instrument—handed down from his grandfather, Rebecca told me— and played a grand assortment of pieces, some lively and some of rich emotion. We clapped and sang and for brief passages I could put my trepidation about Emery aside.

When I looked at my pocket watch, I saw the time approached 4 o'clock. The sky outside had begun to darken.

"Oh," Rebecca said, looking at my watch, "You'll want to go before it gets much later."

She bore a troubled expression as she spoke.

"Why would you say that?" I asked.

Rebecca looked to her father, who now played a lovely yet mournful piece. She looked back at me and said, "I don't really like going out after dark. _She_ is out there."

"Who?" I asked.

"Mrs. O'Malley," Rebecca said. "I've seen her. Twice. She walks the road at night, dressed all in black. I see her shape against the snow when the moon is bright. Both times I found the tracks the next day, but they fade away, buried in the blowing drifts. It's unsettling."

I looked from her earnest countenance to the window, indeed a little unsettled.

"I'm sorry, Miss Adelaide," Rebecca said. "I didn't mean to frighten you."

"I'm merely concerned, Rebecca," I said, perhaps bending the truth somewhat. "Mrs. O'Malley is not well and I hope that she stays safe. These nights can be wretchedly cold."

I took my leave not long after. I travelled by way of the most direct route across the farmland as the sun set. When I came to the dark O'Malley farm, I hurried my buggy past. I gave the farmstead as good an inspection as I could from that distance and saw there where no lights or signs of life to be found. It reminded me of Emery's cabin in the ravine, itself also unoccupied through cruel circumstance. My imagination conjured the idea that Mrs. O'Malley might now even be lurking in the shadows, watching me from behind one of the windows. I was content to drive on and leave the sad property behind me.

What to make of Rebecca's claim that the grieving mother had passed near their farm, walking the road by night? I believe the sincerity with which she spoke, and Mrs. O'Malley's behaviour since the murder of her daughter lends credibility to Rebecca's tale. If she's not living at her farm, then where is she? Has madness so devoured her mind and soul that she ignores the elements to embark on a purgatorial march across the frozen countryside? If so, I hope our Lord is watching over her and someday will grant her peace.

13

January 25, 1887
Orchard Bend

Early in the afternoon, the storm which had threatened from high above at last descended on Orchard Bend, bringing with it a deceptive stillness of the air that felt almost warm compared to the usual winter chill.

Rebecca Clarke and her beau, Billy Howard, reached the crossroads hand in hand when the snow began to fall. The dismissal of all the students from school came early that day when Miss Adelaide watched the darkening of the clouds and heard the wind pick up during lunch. Soon after, as the students sat reading quietly, the church shook and its timbre groaned. The schoolteacher gave strict orders for everyone to go straight home.

At the crossroads, Billy and Rebecca stopped and faced each other. He leaned in for a kiss and she let him. She smiled up at him and brushed a snowflake from his nose. He laughed his quiet laugh and looked around.

"It's pretty like this, don't you think?" he asked.

Rebecca delighted at the winter fields, everything accentuated now by the falling snow.

"It's quite lovely," she answered, holding him close.

"Do you remember when we used to play down by the stream on Laura's property?" Billy asked. "That time we tried to walk all the way along it, to see how far it went, to see if it would connect to the west river?"

"Yes!" Rebecca said, the pleasant memories from that childhood summer day bringing a brief grin to her face. It faded just as quickly. "I'd forgotten all about that."

"I find myself remembering things about her, stuff I hadn't thought about in years," Billy said. "But then I forget stuff. Like she had this little scar on her hand, but I don't remember for the life of me how she got it. I know I used to know that."

"She got it when Sammy O'Toole threw a dead mouse at us girls during the town picnic, remember?" Rebecca explained. "She tripped backwards and hit the back of her hand on a rock. It bled something awful. Good thing Doctor Shaw was right there to tend to it."

Billy nodded, with a far off look in his eyes as the details came back to him. Then he looked at her.

"The snow is getting thicker, we really ought to get home," he said.

"Alright," Rebecca said. She pulled him close for a peck on the cheek. Then she said with a wink, "Now you can go."

"I'd stay here with you forever," Billy said, backing away, smiling, "You know that."

"I know," she answered.

Instead of starting down the road toward his farm, Billy began climbing the narrow logs of the fence at the roadside.

"What are you doing, Billy Howard?" Rebecca asked.

"Shortcut," Billy said, dropping down on the other side. "Since the Douglases left town, it's a faster way. The snow's not that deep yet.

"I don't like it, Billy," Rebecca said. "The road is safer."

"I'll be fine," he said, starting across the field. "It's half the distance. And you should get going, too."

Rebecca shook her head at the persistent foolhardy way boys had of trying to impress girls they liked, and then started down the road towards home, all the while watching Billy as he made his way through the snow. She had to admit that he was making good time. His dark form went first grey in the thick falling snowfall, then disappeared altogether behind the white veil.

Directing her attention to her own journey, Rebecca pulled her coat tight around her. The fresh wet snow clumped on her boots and within minutes, visibility grew worse across the landscape. Having walked this way all her life, Rebecca did not fret, even as her legs began to ache against the effort each step required. Familiar markers came into view through the snow-filled world around her. First was the knotty, twisted post in the fence of the former Douglas farm, then came the gap in the fence where the driveway met the road. Further on, she saw the cluster of trees at the edge of her family's property. She wondered if Billy was still making good time. He might even have made it home by now.

Rebecca adjusted her wool bonnet and wiped the snow from her eyes, her mittens rough on her face. She pressed on, knowing her own driveway wasn't much further. When she glimpsed a dark shape looming not far ahead in the snowy distance, she wondered which landmark it could be. A few steps later, Rebecca thought her eyes were playing tricks on her. She realized the dark shape was in the middle of the road.

And it appeared to be a person, a mere dozen yards before her, heading in the same direction.

Who else would be out here? She wondered.

"Hello!" Rebecca called out. In a moment's inspiration, She suspected who it might be and shouted, "Mrs O'Malley, is that you?"

The dark shape stopped and as Rebecca drew nearer, she saw it was indeed a woman in a black dress and a bonnet. Rebecca had known Mrs O'Malley for most of her life. She was almost a second mother to the teenage girl. Rebecca still remembered the woman Mrs O'Malley had once been—pious, strict, but also compassionate—before the devil of grief replaced those virtues with outbursts of condemnation, profanity and vitriol. Those happy memories stayed any apprehension Rebecca might have had in addressing the woman in black.

"Mrs O'Malley, it's me! Rebecca Clarke," she called out. Mrs O'Malley didn't react, keeping her back to the girl. Rebecca stopped a half dozen yards from the woman. Even through the dense, falling snow, she could see that Mrs O'Malley's dress was tattered and dirty, even torn in places. "You don't need to be out here. Laura was my best friend. I miss her terribly, but I believe she's at peace now. Her killer is dead."

The woman's head turned just a little in Rebecca's direction, her face remaining hidden behind her bonnet. Rebecca waited for her to answer, but when no response came, Rebecca spoke again.

"Mrs. O'Malley, come with me to my house," Rebecca said. "You're always welcome there. Be warm and amongst people who care about you. My mother would love to see you again..."

A sound cut through the quiet, one that came to Rebecca's ears in such a subtle fashion she didn't realize she'd been hearing it behind her until just that moment. The rhythmic jingle of tiny bells made Rebecca turn. A horse-drawn wagon approached, sliding along on its sleigh bed. Rebecca turned back to Mrs O'Malley to tell her to get out of the way. She saw the woman's figure enveloped by the falling snow.

"Mrs O'Malley, get off the road!" Rebecca called out to her.

But the woman was gone from view.

The wagon drew closer and Rebecca waved her arms to get the driver's attention. He saw her and slowed his team to a stop next to the girl.

"Rebecca Clarke, is that you there?" Mr Slayton asked atop his wagon, reins in hand, snow clinging to his well-kempt beard. "This is no kind of weather for a young'un like you to be out in."

"I was on my way home, Mr Slayton," Rebecca said, "but I saw Mrs O'Malley. Just now. She can't have gone far. She should be just up ahead. If you drive slowly we can find her."

"Are you sure?" he asked, peering into the storm.

"Positive!" Rebecca said as she climbed up and took a seat next to him.

Mr Slayton eased his wagon forward, the sleigh offering a smooth ride, but Rebecca was too intent on trying to spot Mrs O'Malley to take much notice. They cruised along, each calling out for her.

After a few minutes, Mr Slayton shook his head.

"I don't think she's out here, Rebecca," he said.

"I saw her!" she said. "I spoke to her. I know she heard me. Her dress was in tatters, but it was her."

"Well, we're coming up on your farm," Slayton said. "I can't see her having walked this far without us passing her, but this snow can fool a person."

Rebecca didn't answer, still casting about through the growing blizzard to find Mrs O'Malley.

"Tell you what, I'll drive you home and I promise to keep an eye out for her," Mr Slayton said. "Reckon she'll spew some fire and brimstone in my direction should I happen on her, but I'll keep my eyes peeled."

"Thank you, Mr Slayton," Rebecca said.

A few minutes later, they came to the Clarkes' driveway and Mr Slayton drove the sledded wagon almost up to Rebecca's front door. Her father came out of the farmhouse as they pulled up.

"Slayton," he said by way of greeting.

"Came across your girl here out on the road," Slayton said as Rebecca climbed down from her seat.

"Miss Adelaide let us out early because of the storm, Pa," Rebecca explained.

"Was fixing to ride into town to get you," Mr Clarke said, giving her a hug. "You saved me a trip, Slayton, and brought my girl home. How about you come in for a cup of coffee?"

"Mighty tempting, but I gotta get back to the missus," Mr Slayton said, jerking his thumb in the direction of his farm. He tipped his hat to Rebecca, "And good day to you, young lady."

"Thank you for the ride, Mr Slayton," Rebecca said as he pulled away to loop back toward the road.

"Well, *I* could certainly use some coffee," Mr Clarke said as he started for the door. Rebecca followed him, watching Mr Slayton vanish into the snowfall. Then she looked out in the direction of the road where she'd encountered Laura's mother.

"Lord, take care of Mrs O'Malley," Rebecca said. "And make sure Billy gets home safely."

With that, she turned and went inside.

14

The Ledger of Owen McCabe

Deputy's Report, January 26, 1887
Orchard Bend

Writing these reports is an ache in the backside.

The sheriff says to keep it simple, so that's what I'll do. He says no one blames me for what happened, which is not of any comfort at all.

He wants my version of events, so here it is.

The snow started coming down heavy yester-day afternoon, sweeping through town and covering everything in a matter of hours. I don't recall a winter storm ever being this bad, like a frozen cloud descending to earth to swallow up everything in the county, it seemed.

Sheriff Turnbull and I being the only law in town right now took shifts to watch Sheriff Dale—that is to say, former Sheriff Dale—as she awaited trial. While in custody, she developed a darkness of temperament I found somewhat disquieting, the way a caged dog gets when left penned up too long. Doc Shaw even dropped by to look in on her the morning of the storm and he saw what the Sheriff and I saw.

"Would you excuse us, Sheriff? Deputy?" the doctor asked us. "I want to talk to my patient in private."

With reluctance, we gave them their privacy. We crossed to the other side of the jailhouse and stood by the window, watching the snow pile up outside and keeping an eye on Shaw and Dale. The two of them spoke in low tones for maybe fifteen minutes. She sat on her bed, hardly moving, and Shaw stood a foot from the cell bars. He never went any closer. At the end of their palaver, Shaw came to us and asked when the judge would arrive to hear her case.

"He's held up," the sheriff said, "We got a wire yesterday. Big case in the city that's taking longer than expected. And with a heavy winter fall threatening, who can say when he'll arrive?"

Shaw looked back at Dale, who still sat on her cot, now turning a bit of mortar over and over in her hand, staring at it, her eyes locked onto it. I remember that, the way she didn't just stare at it, but focused on it. When Shaw turned back to us, he sighed.

"How difficult would it be to let her of the cell for a short period of time?" the doctor asked.

"We're not in the habit of letting prisoners out while they're awaiting trial, Doctor," Sheriff Turnbull answered.

"I understand, but this is an unusual case," Shaw said, "The woman suffers from clauster-phobia. Do you know what that is, Sheriff?"

"No."

"It's a fear of small spaces," Shaw said, "Being trapped in a closet or locked in a jail cell. It's taking all her effort to not lose control in there after so many days."

"And you suggest letting her out to alleviate her strain?" Sheriff Turnbull asked.

"I do," Shaw said, "An hour, that's all. Once a day until her trial."

"What if she tries to escape?" I asked.

The sheriff had the same worry, I reckon. He paced the floor with his head down, considering Shaw's words. The fear of small spaces, it made sense and it explained Dale's mood.

The sheriff stopped and looked at me.

"She's not a runner," he said. "She surrendered when we arrested her and she's given us no grief since. If nothing else, she's earned my respect and my trust."

"I agree," I said.

"Okay, one hour," the sheriff said. "Will you stay, Doc? See that your remedy works?"

"I can't," Doc Shaw said, "I have to check in on old Mac Philips at his farm. I do that from time to time and I'm a bit overdue. With him living alone and not nearly as spry as he once was, someone has to make sure he hasn't met with an unfortunate misadventure out there."

Shaw left and I followed him outside.

"This fear of small places," I said, "what do you call it?"

"Clauster-phobia," Shaw said. "Some people are born with it, some come by it after a particularly awful experience. For Ms Dale's sake, I hope that judge gets here soon."

"Or what?" I asked.

Doc Shaw did answer, at least not with words. He looked past me to the jail, his expression grim. Then he climbed aboard his buggy and offered me this advice, "Keep your eye on her."

Under the darkening sky, he rode off to the Philips place and I went back inside.

"One hour," the sheriff said to Dale. "You have to stay in the jailhouse, it's the best I can do. This is pretty irregular, I dare say, but we're going to try it."

All Dale said was, "Thank you."

"Green, you stay by the front door," Turnbull said, "Ms Dale, you stay on that cot until I've opened the cell and ordered you can get up. Understand?"

She nodded and the sheriff unlocked her cell. The hinges creaked as he opened it and I thought I'd better get some oil on them later. When the sheriff had stepped away from the door, hand on his six-shooter, he told Dale she could come out.

I thought she'd jump at the chance, but she did not. She regarded the open door with a look I thought might be fear, though I couldn't imagine why. After a moment, she did get up, taking her time as she did. She crossed to the open cell door with a single stride and stopped before going through, just for a second. When she stepped out into the jailhouse, Dale let out a deep sigh, all the while looking at the floor.

I won't lie, it bothered me to see the former sheriff so... I don't know what the right word is. Vulnerable, maybe. At the mercy of this clauster-phobia.

Sheriff Turnbull had his pocket watch out and started timing her hour. Dale took some steps away from the cell and raised her arms to stretch. Again, I was reminded of an animal let out of its pen. I suppose it's unnatural for any living thing to be cooped up for too long.

"Can we open a window?" Dale asked. "Mine is shuttered for the winter. I'd like to breathe some fresh air, even if we can't go outside."

Turnbull obliged and Dale took a few steps toward the open window and the cold air coming in. With her eyes closed, she drank it in.

"Feel better?" I asked.

"Yes, Allen," she said, "Thank you."

She opened her eyes and looked at the sheriff.

"And thank you again, Reg," Dale said to the sheriff.

"Don't mention it," Turnbull said. "And I mean that. It would look mighty improper if people knew about this, Shaw's say-so or no."

"I won't say anything," Dale told him.

Over the next hour, we watched her every move. She didn't try to escape or have any opportunity to exploit the situation. Dale stayed in the open-most area of the jailhouse, simply relishing her time outside her cell. When she looked at me, I saw her mood had lightened, her eyes no longer distant.

When the hour came to an end, the sheriff reluctantly snapped his watch closed and said, "I'm sorry, Ms. Dale, you have to go back in your cell. To-morrow, if the judge doesn't arrive, we'll see about doing this again."

Dale only nodded, stretching her arms out once more and turning toward her cell. She paused for a moment at the door. For a split second, I thought she might resist going back inside as her body tensed. Yet, she didn't. Dale sat on her cot in the cell as before and the sheriff locked the door.

As I closed the window, I looked out and saw the foul weather now well advanced as it piled snow upon the town. I could hardly see across Anderson Street, it was that thick a sheet and dark now as the day crept into the evening.

Turnbull sent me to Sully's to bring back food for Ms Dale. I brought back some for myself, too, anticipating a long night holed up in the jailhouse watching our prisoner. Around 7 o'clock, Sheriff Turnbull retired. The snow had not relented one bit and I wondered if we would all be buried alive that night. Ms Dale curled up on her cot with a week-old newspaper, reading by the lantern outside her cell.

I was preparing coffee when the front door crashed open and Herman Statler stumbled in.

"Allen," Herman said, "where's the sheriff?"

"Back at Sully's, I expect. Why?" I asked.

"The snow, it..." Herman said, stamping the snow from his boots, "...I mean, you have to see it for yourself!"

"See what?" I asked, "What's happened?"

"I'll show you," Herman said.

"I can't leave the prisoner," I said, looking from Ms Dale to Herman, who was shaking his head.

"Okay, okay," Herman said, hurrying back outside. I followed him to the door.

"What's going on?" I asked.

"The church, it's gone! There could be people inside," Herman said and he raced off. I watched him go, tramping across the covered boardwalk, where the snow wasn't as thick. I wanted to go after him, but didn't. I went back inside and saw Dale standing at the bars of her cell.

"The church?" she asked.

"That's what he said," I answered, "It doesn't make sense."

"Go investigate," Dale said, "I'm not going anywhere."

"I can't," I told her.

She nodded and sat back down on the edge of her cot, restless nerves making her fidget.

"Ms Dale..." I said, feeling helpless. I heard voices and trampling footsteps outside as men raced to the church. Sheriff Turnbull stuck his head into the jailhouse long enough to grab the shovel and to check that everything and everyone was secure there. I asked if he needed my help at the church and he said no, to stay and guard Dale.

Too anxious now for coffee, I started becoming restless myself. Blocks away, men were gathered at the church. I found out later what had happened there, but for the moment I was left ignorant, with Ms Dale quiet in her cell again and soon only the sound of the blizzard outside.

10 o'clock came around and Sheriff Turnbull did not arrive to relieve my shift, too busy was he at the church. By 11 o'clock, I had bundled myself in a blanket against the chill that seemed to want to freeze the very air. I even gave Ms Dale an extra blanket, as the potbelly stove in the jailhouse could only warm the place so much.

To my shame, after twelve hours on shift, I fell into a doze at the sheriff's desk, intending to only rest my eyes. That was only a little after midnight and I thought I'd only nodded off for a few minutes. I could hear the wind outside, the shuddering of the wood frame of the jailhouse. With a start, I woke up again and yawned. I stood up and intended to make that coffee I'd set aside earlier. The jailhouse was dark apart for the lantern on the desk. The wind still howled as I gathered up the coffee and the pot.

"Would you like some coffee Ms Dale?" I asked quietly. "Looks like it'll be a longer night than expected."

No answer came from her dark cell and when I looked over, it was empty.

I put down the coffee and went to the cell, not believing my eyes. There was no denying it, though. She was not in there.

I grabbed the door and found it locked. The ring of keys was still in my pocket, but before I opened it, I relit the lantern by her cell, hoping against hope she was in there, maybe hiding under the cot. Even with full illumination, the cell was empty.

Emery Dale had escaped.

I never did open the door to her cell. I merely stood there a long time, looking at the empty space where she had been. The barred window above her cot was still shuttered. The blanket and pillow lay in a heap on her bed. I tried the door once again and it was still locked. I touched the keys in my pocket again, just to be sure.

Sheriff Turnbull returned around one o'clock in the morning to find me still staring at the empty cell.

His report will better explain his arrival on the scene and his reaction. I assured him, most emphatically, that I had not let Dale out. I explained that, without meaning to, I'd fallen asleep for a time and awoke to find her gone. He tested the door, as well, and found it still locked.

Our consensus after opening the door and looking inside is that there's no way yet to explain how she vanished. Her possessions, consisting of her cloak, knives and guns, all remained locked in the jailhouse cabinet, likely because Sheriff Turnbull kept the key in his possession, rather than leaving it in his desk. However Ms. Dale got out, she was unable to take much with her but the clothes on her back and the extra blanket I had given her earlier.

Sheriff Turnbull doesn't blame me for her escape, saying she is both crafty and resourceful, more so than any of us imagined.

Deputy Allen Green

15

The Ledger of Owen McCabe

The Orchard Herald, January 26, 1887, Special Edition
DALE ESCAPES!
By Thomas Buchanan, Editor

In the small hours of morning this day, former sheriff Emery Ann Dale escaped custody at the Orchard Bend jailhouse. While awaiting trial for negligence in her duties, resulting in the death of Henry McCabe, Dale seized the opportunity to slip from her cell unnoticed. Sheriff Turnbull would not elaborate on the details of the escape, saying only that Ms Dale picked a moment when the town's focus was on the destruction of our beloved church. As the winter storm raged, townsfolk hurried to the scene to sift through the devastation, fearing the worst if anyone had been inside the church when the roof collapsed. After hours of digging through the timbre, with efforts directed by Sheriff Turnbull, it was to everyone's relief that no souls had been inside at that late hour.

As the town dealt with the sudden loss of its spiritual home, Emery Dale made good her escape, fleeing from the jail and into the relentless fury of the blizzard. A brave posse formed under the sheriff's authority and searched much of the area in town, before the lateness of the hour and the danger of the heavy snowfall forced the search to be called off.

"I wasn't prepared to risk good men to battle the elements in an effort to find her," Sheriff Turnbull said this morning, looking haggard and spent after a long night. A respite does not await the sheriff and his men, however. As the storm passed in the night and the first rays of sunlight woke the county, Sheriff

Turnbull gathered his men at Sully's tavern and laid out a strategy to continue their search for Ms Dale.

"With the weather clear," the sheriff told the Orchard Herald, "we will set out to find the woman and return her to custody. She is to be considered a dangerous fugitive. She is skilled with weapons and is very resourceful, but I don't believe she poses a threat to citizens unless threatened herself. Should anyone see her, do not approach and do not engage with her. Notify the law."

Mr. Martin Griesbach, attorney-at-law and intended prosecutor in Ms Dale's case, was also on hand at the sheriff's briefing and spoke candidly with the Orchard Herald.

"In my experience, an innocent person doesn't run," Mr. Griesbach said.

* * *

The Orchard Herald, January 26, 1887, Special Edition
Winter Storm Claims Life of Doctor
by Thomas Buchanan, Editor

As the town reels from the news of the escape of Emery Dale and the devastation of our church during yester-day's vicious weather, more terrible news comes to-day, that of the untimely death of Doctor Alfred Shaw.

Found partially encased in snow on the northwest road atop his buggy, Dr. Shaw appears to have either succumbed to the elements or suffered a failure of his heart at a most unfortunate time and place. Mr. Edward Ramsay discovered the doctor's lifeless earthly vessel as he travelled into town at daybreak. After notifying the undertaker, Mr. Edgar Allman, the two retrieved the body and Mr. Allman is now performing his necessary duties. It is expected that the good doctor will be interred in the receiving vault until the spring thaw allows for a proper burial.

Speaking on behalf of the Council of Aldermen, Mr. Earl McManus said an emergency meeting will be held to-day to discuss placing an ad in county newspapers—and possibly *beyond, if needs be—for a qualified physician to fill the vacancy.*

Of mysterious note, Dr. Shaw's horse was not found with his buggy, either alive or dead, and appears to have been unbridled and possibly stolen. The whereabouts of the animal remain unknown.

16

The Ledger of Owen McCabe

About Town column, *Orchard Herald, February 1, 1887*

Mr. & Mrs. Maxwell McCabe and their son Owen departed Orchard Bend by train yester-day for a planned extended retreat in Sutter Grove to visit with Mr. & Mrs. Thomas Wilson. The family is accompanied by Mr. Morris Burke.

* * *

A Letter from Rose Adelaide

February 1, 1887
Orchard Bend

My Lovely Cousin, Elizabeth,
While I await your reply to my most recent letter, life for me in Orchard Bend has taken on a troubled and disquieting air. My friend, the former sheriff Emery Dale was arrested on the charge of misconduct in the death of Henry McCabe. While awaiting trial, she escaped custody. Now, the opinion of many in the town has shifted against her. They see her flight as an admission of guilt. Sheriff Turnbull has questioned me as to her whereabouts twice in the seven days since her disappearance, hoping I could provide some insight, but I could offer nothing. I believe her innocent of the allegation and cannot fathom where she might be and what she might be doing. I ask myself often what she hopes to accomplish evading the law. It seems unconscionable that she has simply fled, never to return.

Unexpectedly, the day after Emery's escape, the judge who was to preside over her case arrived in Orchard Bend. He has issued a warrant for her arrest, which by now has spread across the county. It tears at my soul to think what might happen if Emery, now a fugitive, is confronted by a lawman. I pray often that her dilemma does not end with bloodshed.

Work provides little respite from my concern. The great and awful storm that befell Orchard Bend last week brought about the collapse of the roof of the church that doubled as my schoolhouse. The receiving vault to the rear of the church stands intact, with its heavy, thick stone. I thank The Lord that no-one was hurt, but classes, as well as church services, have been relocated to the new Town Hall. Alderman McManus tells me this arrangement will likely remain until spring at the earliest. I raised the point of the construction of a dedicated schoolhouse, one separate from the church, and Mr. McManus said the issue would be addressed at the next Council meeting.

I wonder now if this winter will forever be remembered as one of tragedy following tragedy, as the storm that claimed the church also claimed the life of a dear old friend, Dr. Albert Shaw. It's unclear exactly what happened, but he passed away on the road during an ill-advised journey through that dreadful storm. Now at rest in the receiving vault behind the ruined church, awaiting burial when the ground thaws, Dr. Shaw is missed terribly. His absence only makes this hard winter even colder.

I took an opportunity, Elizabeth, to mend things not long ago with my former good friend Gertrude McCabe only to be harshly rebuked. She declared our friendship ended. Yesterday, I had occasion to encounter her again in passing. After releasing my scholars from their school study at the Town Hall, I ventured home to my cottage as light snow began to fall. When I reached Anderson St., the clatter of the McCabes' pristine black coach announced its approached. I very nearly turned and ducked into the millinery, but I tempered my discomfort and held firm as the coach passed. Inside, Gertrude sat with her young son Owen on her lap, both peering out the window. Our eyes met and neither of us offered any amount of warmth to the other with our gaze. I wonder what she saw in my expression. Hurt? Grim acceptance? Did her grief yet allow her to see past her own pain? If not, will it ever? Am I selfish to place my anguish in any fashion approximate to hers?

These questions haunt me daily and I see no reconciliation between what was and what now is. Perhaps you have some insight, Elizabeth?

When she moved out of view, I continued on to my cottage, only learning to-day from the Herald that Gertrude and her family were on their way to the train station when they passed. They have left Orchard Bend indefinitely.

Give my best to your family and know I am thinking about our sunny childhood together in warmer climes than that which surrounds me now. I am weathering this trial of the spirit and will pray it all resolves favourably soon.

Rose

17

January 25th, 1887
Orchard Bend

It stopped snowing around 3 o'clock in the morning, but
Emery Dale didn't have her pocket watch, let alone the small
technological marvel that was the watch she'd brought with her
from the future. There and then as the last flakes of snow
settled, time really had no meaning for her. Wrapped in the
blanket she brought with her from the jailhouse, she trudged
through the woods. The wind had picked up and she hoped the
blowing drifts would conceal her back trail. She also hoped Doc
Shaw's horse would find shelter. She'd let it loose a few
minutes before. As an escaped criminal now, she didn't want
the added charge of horse theft if she were caught with the
animal.

Are they looking for me? she wondered. Surely Deputy Green
wasn't still asleep. By now he would have discovered that she
was gone. Dale didn't think they'd venture too far from town to
search for her tonight, what with the snowstorm and the
church's collapse. With the storm now breaking, though, all
bets were off for what Turnbull would do come sunrise. Dale
knew she had to find a place to hold up before then, somewhere
out of the way, somewhere they weren't bound to look, at least
not at first.

As she pushed her way through the woods, where a thinner
layer of snow coated the ground—though not by much—, Dale's
legs and back ached once more, as they had after she fled the
jail. Riding Shaw's horse had allowed her some time to rest, but
now her muscles protested again.

She pressed on.

The house wasn't far away.

The lantern she took from Doc Shaw's buggy also provided some heat as well as much needed illumination. In the thin woods, Dale didn't think anyone from the adjacent farms would see the tiny point of light, but it was a risk she had to chance. With almost no moon in the sky, even with the fresh snow, darkness shrouded the land. Through the trees, Dale saw the clouds parting and stars twinkling above. Despite everything, it felt good to be outside, to not be caged anymore.

All those days behind bars, let out only to do her business in the outhouse, it had been a real test of her will. It couldn't last, though, and that hour of supervised release earlier in the evening should have eased her claustrophobia. In a small way it had, but going back inside, facing another dark night behind bars? Well, it had simply been too much. That was the moment she knew she would be breaking out, even though it would make matters worse for her as far as her case went.

And she had business to take care of.

As she marched on through the woods, Dale reached into the pocket of her jacket and felt the folded newspaper there.

With the dirty yellow light cast from the old lantern highlighting the snow and trees around her, Dale reached the edge of the woods and saw her destination at last.

The one-storey farmhouse stood almost black against the dark blue of the pre-dawn snow. Beyond, the trees that encircled the house opened up and the snow-covered farms rolled away into the distance. The sliver of the crescent moon lit the clouds with only the faintest light, yet Dale paused, shivering and exhausted, to take it in. Summoning her final reserves of strength, she ran as best she could through the knee-high snow to the O'Malley house.

Dale pounded on the back door and wondered again if this was a mistake. Through the gentle howl of wind across the flat farmland around her, she listened for movement inside. She knocked again, harder, and waited. Still nothing. With the windows shuddered, Dale could not look inside. She could only hope the O'Malley house was deserted.

The chill in the air stung her already aching fingers as she felt along the top of the doorframe. Finding nothing there, Dale knelt and pulled up the snow-covered mat, revealing the key.

She unlocked the door and a gust of wind seemed to throw it open as she turned the handle, pulling it from her grasp.

Dale wasted no time hurrying inside. The lantern swung in her hand, lighting her way. She closed the door behind her and stood motionless in the house, listening. Wind moaned and whistled outside and Dale's own heavy breathing filling the dark space. She heard no one else in the house. Holding the lantern up, Dale saw she was in the kitchen-dining area. A table for four sat across from a large stone fireplace. The lantern light also picked out the familiar shapes of kitchenware and tidy shelves around the room. Dale put the lantern on the table and shed the blanket from her shoulders, leaving it in a snowy pile on the floor.

When her eyes adjusted, Dale saw more of the room, the cupboards of dishes and cups, two armchairs in the hearth of the fireplace, and the mantle above it. An unmoving clock sat there, not having been wound recently, and next to it sat several candles and a box of matches. Dale had a box of her own, found with Doc Shaw's lantern on his buggy, but she didn't want to root through her pocket to find them, the skin on her fingers already raw from the cold. Even sheltered in the house, Dale could still see her breath float from her lips in icy wisps. She grabbed the candles and the matches from the mantle and brought them to the table. As she lit each one, the room grew brighter. Her face and fingers tingled in the warm air radiating from the candles. Dale moved around the room, checking that both doors were locked, that all the windows were shuttered. Having secured the space, she sat down at the table, throwing the blanket back over her for warmth. Her back and legs still burned sore, but they welcomed the rest. Dale thought about starting a proper fire in the in the fireplace, but even at night and assuming the neighbours were bedded down amid the storm, she didn't want to chance someone spotting smoke rising from the chimney of what should have been a deserted house. True, they might think Mrs O'Malley was home, but the woman's recent bizarre behaviour might draw someone to investigate. And she herself was now a wanted woman, so any unusual sightings could bring an armed posse to the O'Malley farm.

No, Dale thought, *the candles and lantern will have to do for now.*

In the dry, dusty air of the house, Dale licked her lips and went to the kitchen's water pump.

The plumbing might well be frozen, she mused, *do you chance it?*

She did, working the hand lever and drawing several pulls before water poured in the basin on the counter. Retrieving one of the cups from a shelf, Dale drank the contents and scooped up another cupful, downing it. She took the second refill back to the table and tried to ignore the growling of her stomach. More tired than hungry, Dale eyed one of the two thread-worn but sturdy armchairs by the hearth. She slipped off her boots and kicked them towards the door, then took off the light jacket she wore and placed it on the other armchair, wishing not for the first time that she'd been able to retrieve her cloak before escaping custody.

"Along with my knives," Dale said to herself, "and my guns."

She frowned in the dim light, taking the lantern and setting it on the upturned apple crate that sat between the armchairs like an end table. With reluctance, she blew out the candles and sank into the cushioned chair. She put her feet up on the little padded footrest, wrapped in her jailhouse blanket. The lantern next to her lit half her face and she stared at the blackness of the fireplace.

"What have I done?" Dale asked.

She sat up, reached into the jacket draped across the other armchair and pulled the folded newspaper from the pocket. By lantern light, she examined the engraving printed above the article titled *ORCHARD BEND CELEBRATES 25 YEARS!*

The picnic in the image looked like a grand affair, with decorations on and around the church. Picnickers dotted the lawn, some seated on the grass while some stood talking. In the center of the image was a dignified elderly man, Doc Reed, supported by his cane.

However, it was not Doc Reed who caught Dale's eye. On his right, her arm tucked under Doc's—not in affection but to help his balance—was a dark-haired woman in a simple white blouse and rugged-looking skirt, something a farmer would wear. She looked to be in her late twenties or early thirties. She'd pulled her hair back into a tight, efficient, no-nonsense ponytail. If that had been the extent of her appearance, nothing about it would have caught Dale's eye. Except that wasn't the extent of it. The woman looking at the camera sported a long, straight vertical scar down her right cheek, almost to her jaw line.

It had been the scar that had triggered Dale's episode in the jail the week before. Sheriff Turnbull had been kind enough to give her the paper and Dale had braced herself to read about her own arrest the day before. Doing so hadn't been as embarrassing or awkward as she'd expected. Somewhat relieved, she'd moved onto the other articles. When Dale saw the picture of the picnic from twenty-five years before, she'd stood up from her cot and moved closer to the lantern hanging outside her cell for a better look.

That's when she saw the woman with the scar.

That's when the migraine hit, dropping her to the floor.

These episodes would come when she least expected them. As she collapsed from the sudden intensity of it, an image filled her mind, as sometimes happened. The newly recovered memory surfaced from somewhere in the great wasteland of her amnesia, the scorched land of her psyche where memories ought to be, where little remained but fragments, broken and incomplete. When she happened upon a piece of her old life, the experience came as both exciting and terrifying. This new memory had been no different...

The woman from the picture lay on the floor of a cold place filled with machines, clutching her bloody face as Dale looked at her. The woman's face had been sliced open and blood gushed forth, covering her dark camouflaged uniform.

"Stand down," Dale said.

...The brief, vivid memory ended there. Dale kept the newspaper after that and Turnbull didn't protest. Over the days which followed, each spent locked behind bars awaiting her trial, Dale examined the image again and again, hoping more of that memory would come back to her, but nothing more did.

Looking at the woman in the engraved photograph by lantern light in the O'Malley farmhouse, Dale asked, "Who are you?"

She intended to find out, because this person from her old life had been in Orchard Bend twenty·five years before, had come from the same where and when in an unremembered future, and she might have answers.

More important than that, if she was still alive, it was more proof that Dale had not arrived in the past alone. She looked at her arm, pulling the sleeve of her shirt up to reveal the tattoo there, the odd shape that looked like an "L" growing out of a "P." In the grove near her cabin, someone had long ago carved the same symbol into an aspen tree. The woman in the picture might even have answers about that grove of aspens, the place she'd always felt drawn to.

Dale hoped it was so.

Emery closed her eyes and her thoughts went to Rose. She fought back the tide of conflicting emotions that threatened to break free. The escape would be hardest on Rose, Dale knew. Most of the town knew she and the schoolteacher were friends, including Turnbull. Rose's cottage would be the first place he'd look, and Dale's cabin would be the second. He'd question her, but Rose could honestly tell him she knew nothing of Dale's escape. After that, well, Dale knew it was almost cruel to leave Rose in the dark, but Emery had work to do finding the woman with the scar. Maybe after, Dale would return to settle the charge of misconduct and they could get on with their lives.

Dale let her mind fantasize about returning to Rose's cottage, free of her charge, knocking on the schoolteacher's door and surprising her when she answered. It was a pleasant thought and Dale fell asleep to it.

* * *

82

A cramp in her right leg woke her. Dale sat up in the armchair, grimacing and shaking, covered in sweat. Her breath floated from her mouth in the cold air of the unheated farmhouse. Gasping at the pain in her calf, she tried to stretch it out by putting her foot on the floor to bear the weight. She eased into it, slow to apply pressure until the cramp let go. When it did, she leaned back in the armchair, meaning to let sleep take her again, but a bout of sneezing followed and would not relent for some time. It left her clutching the chair's arm, her face wet with more than just perspiration. Dale scrambled to her feet, a mistake she regretted almost at once as her balance wavered. She stumbled forward and dropped herself on one of the hard wooden chairs at the kitchen table. Another round of sneezing hit and when it let up, she realized just how hard the throbbing in her head had become. Her sinuses felt like they would explode from the pressure at any minute. Through tear-soaked eyes she cast about the kitchen for a handkerchief or a rag. Seeing none, she got to her feet, careful this time not to overdo it. In the cupboard below the basin, Dale found what looked like cleaning rags, so grabbed one and blew her nose. The relief it brought came with tremendous pain from her tender, swollen sinuses. When that pain subsided, she looked around, noticing for the first time the thin shafts of light cutting into the kitchen through the shudders on the window. The surge of adrenalin gave her focus as she rushed to a window by the front door and looked out.

Through the space between the shudders, the bright daylight on the untouched snow outside blinded her until her eyes adjusted. The farms beyond the gap in the tree line rolled away and she could almost make out the homesteads themselves, including the Clarke farm in the distance if she had her bearings right. It looked to be almost midday. Dale watched for movement from the road or from the farms, but saw none. Few people would be in a hurry to navigate the roads this far west after last night's snowfall.

Dale wondered again if Doc Shaw's horse had made it to a safe haven, possibly even back to town and the Statlers' livery.

At the thought of poor Doctor Shaw, Dale stepped away from the window. Shivering and shaking a little, she returned to the armchair and couldn't stop herself wondering if anyone had found his body by now. She pulled the blanket around herself, against the growing chill in her bones, and closed her eyes. A steady pulse thrummed behind them.

It wasn't long before she gave into sleep again, this time a sleep filled with fevered dreams and memories weaving together. The ever-present snowfall provided the only consistency throughout.

Dale stood next to the buggy on the northwest road, its wheels buried up to the axle in the drift. Sitting on the buggy was Doctor Shaw, unmoving, staring straight ahead as if waiting for something. Or someone.

His horse gave a neigh as Dale worked the latches and buckles that bound the animal to the vehicle.

"I'm going as fast as I can!" Dale told her, knowing full well the mare wouldn't last much longer stuck to the buggy and unable to escape the storm.

"Better hurry," Doc Shaw said from his seat, giving Dale a start. When she looked at him through the blue-grey blackness, lit only by the lantern sitting on the seat next to him, he remained unmoving. Dale shook her head and continued unbridling the horse. When the mare was free, Dale guided it away from the buggy, all the while thinking the animal would bolt off into the night. The mare didn't move, even when Dale retrieved the lantern and the box of matches sticking out of Shaw's coat pocket. The horse even allowed itself to be guided into a kneel so Dale could climb onto her saddle-less back, sitting in the blanket she'd taken from the jail.

"You can't let him," Shaw said behind her. "Remember, 'key'... 'list.'"

Dale turned and saw only Shaw's motionless body. She guided the horse away without a word, riding the mare through the blizzard. The world became a moving shadow as the snow billowed and danced around her. She looked up at the sky, but saw nothing different. In that moment her balance failed and she fell. She kept falling for what felt like an entire minute before landing in the snow. Shivering, Dale got to her feet and started for the mare.

"Major, it's me," came a voice behind her. Not Doc Shaw's, but someone else's. Dread filled her and she tried to move faster to reach the horse, but it bolted. She cried out after it, but it disappeared into the storm. Dale stopped, not wanting to turn around, not wanting to see who or what had spoken behind her. She could sense him, it, coming closer.

"Stop," she whispered. To her surprise she felt the shadow stop.

"You know me," it said.

"Do I?" Dale asked. But she knew the answer already. She did know this being, somehow. In another life, one she could barely remember.

"Yes," the shadow said, "not all of your memories are gone, Major, you figured that out years ago, except..."

"Except what?" Dale asked.

"Except part of you wants to forget," the shadow said.

"No," Dale said, "I want to remember! I want to know who I was. I can't go back to my old life, I know that, but I want to at least remember where I came from."

Fear giving way to anger, Dale turned, ready to face the faceless shadow that had haunted her since she arrived in Orchard Bend all those years before.

Who she found standing behind her was not the shadow, however, but someone else. The woman's blonde hair, so like Dale's own, swirled in the blowing snow. The woman's eyes shone a bright green, nearly white, pierced the raging storm around them.

"Who are you?!" Dale demanded.

The woman drew a sword from the scabbard on her back and dropped into a ready stance. Dale put her hands up.

"I'm unarmed," she told the woman with the white-green eyes.

"No, you're not," the woman said. "As long as you keep your wits, you're the fiercest person I know."

"But who are you?!" Dale asked again.

"You'll remember," the woman said, sheathing the sword, "when you put the clues together."

The woman turned and walked away through the snow. Dale followed. Up ahead the O'Malleys' farmhouse loomed in the blizzard, with warm and welcoming light pouring from the windows and onto the mounting snowdrifts outside. The woman moved faster than Dale, who struggled to keep up. When she reached the farmhouse, the woman opened the backdoor and went inside. Dale pushed on through the snow. When she reached the door, it wouldn't open for her. Dale knocked on the door, calling out. Somehow in the storm she heard footsteps on the other side approaching. The door unlocked with a click and creaked opened.

Rose stood in the doorway and Emery Dale began to cry at the sight of her.

"Let me in, Rose!" Emery said, "They're after me! I have to get away!"

"No," Rose said, her expression stern, "you can't come in, Miss Dale. You're not supposed to be here."

"I know, Rose," Emery said, "but I have nowhere else to go."

"Yes, you do," Rose said, "it's the real reason you escaped."

"Miss Adelaide, who is it?" asked a girl's voice from behind the teacher. Rose turned and Laura O'Malley approached the two women, looking happy. Emery smiled, delighted to see the teenage girl alive. Strands of dark hair framed her face and a familiar locket hung from her neck. When she saw Dale, Laura's expression became serious. "Oh, it's you, Sheriff Dale."

"I hope you've found peace now, Laura," Dale said.

The girl said nothing, her form quickly becoming transparent, spectral. She raised an icy thread of a finger and pointed at Dale.

Dale jerked awake in the armchair. Almost at once a fit of sneezing followed. Her head pounded, worse than before. She blew her nose and then coughed up an ugly mess.

"Dammit, not now," she said, "I can't get sick now. Not here."

Her throat burned and her dry lips cracked as she spoke. Dale tried to lick them as she went to the basin again for some water, but her mouth felt full of sticky cotton. The cool water felt good as she drank, then she refilled the basin, dampening a cloth and holding it to her forehead. She staggered back to the armchair and picked up the blanket, wanting only to collapse back into sleep, to feel better when she woke up. Unsurprising, the blanket was patchy with dampness. Dale guessed it was from either the snow the night before or her fevered sweat, or both. Shivering again, Dale draped the blanket over one of the wooden chairs at the kitchen table and shuffled to the narrow hall at the back of the house. With the bedroom doors closed, the shadowy hall was not inviting.

Dale went to one of the bedroom doors and knocked, even though she knew no one was home. As expected, no one answered, so she opened the door.

A large bedroom awaited her. The bed was made and Dale guessed, judging by the modest personal items and décor, that this was the master bedroom that had once belonged to Mr and Mrs O'Malley.

You assume they're not coming back, she thought to herself.

"I do," Dale said, her voice hoarse and loud in the lonesome room. "Mr O'Malley is gone. Mrs O'Malley hasn't been seen in weeks. Clearly no one has lived here in just as long."

Dale took the heavy, folded quilt from the end of the bed, as well as one of the pillows, and disturbed nothing else in the room. She meant to return to the chair by the hearth, but stopped outside the smaller door at the end of the hall. Once more, she knocked (it seemed wrong somehow not to) and went inside. Sunlight poured into Laura O'Malley's bedroom through the window, where one of the shutters hung ajar. The light brought with it a few degrees of warmth, making it almost cheery by comparison to the rest of the house.

"Laura?" Dale asked. "Are you here?"

It didn't seem so wild to think her spirit might be there. The vivid image of Laura's ghost in Dale's dream flashed through her mind. But only silence hung in the girl's bedroom. If Laura was there, she wasn't letting Dale know. Dale closed the door, heading back to the kitchen.

A wave of dizziness swept through her. Dale propped herself up against the wall until it passed. Her head felt thick again, the pressure behind her eyes becoming unbearable. In the hall closet, Dale found a small stack of towels and took two of them with her to the kitchen, trembling as her body felt both chilled and over-heated. Sweat poured from her brow and she wiped it with one of the towels. Dale began to undress, shedding the sweat-dampened clothes piece by piece. Shivering, Dale used a towel and the wash bucket from under the counter to wipe herself down. The cold water on her body gave her focus through the hazy throb in her head. Drying each body part as she went, Dale cleaned herself up. Feeling refreshed even as the sickness filled her head and chest, Dale lit some of the candles to warm the room, the heavy quilt now covering her body. She picked up her clothes one by one and draped them about the table and chairs.

On the corner of the kitchen table, Dale saw the backdoor key sitting where she'd left it the night before. She picked it up and a recent memory came to her as she felt the hard metal between her fingers.

"You can't let him!" he had said to Dale. "Key... list..."

Those were Henry McCabe's dying words.

Dale had told no one this, not the committee at the hearing, not even Rose. Telling anyone would mean she'd be forced to explain what actually led her to the barn on New Year's Eve.

What... or *who*.

The shadow from her dream. It had led her to the barn to expose Henry's murder of Laura O'Malley. Dale didn't think the shadow meant for Henry to ambush her. When the shadow spoke to her, it was with a flood of words and images, like their minds were touching. Dale never got the sense that the shadow man meant her any harm. No, he'd brought her there so that she could stop Henry.

Was the shadow man benevolent or did he have an agenda?

Again, Dale didn't know.

She curled herself in the armchair, the heavy quilt pulled tight around her, doing its job of warming her up. Her eye sockets ached and she closed her eyes, putting the key down on the crate next to her.

Dale had encountered the shadow man twice before. The first time had been years ago in the McCabes' study. Dale had glimpsed the shadow but had not engaged it, nor it her. The next, more significant encounter—prior to New Years Eve— came later, nine months ago. A wounded Emery Dale had looked up from another dying foe, Daniel Underwood, and saw the shadow man there. His dark, spectral form had been more substantial. And, for the first time, he spoke to her.

Major, it's me, he had said.

"But *who* are you?" Dale asked out loud, tired and sick. "Who are you people from my old life?"

Settling into the armchair, Dale closed her eyes. Not for the first time she asked, "Who was I?"

* * *

Time stole away after Dale fell asleep. Later she remembered waking up, her throat burning and the vice grip of swollen sinuses making it difficult to balance when she tried to get up. The singular thought that she needed to find water floated about her fevered brain as she stumbled naked across the room to the hand pump. No water would come forth from the nozzle, no matter how hard she pumped. Consciousness faded then and the next thing she remembered was crawling to the back door on her hands and knees in the failing light, pushing an empty bucket in front of her. Dale opened the door and saw the sky was a brilliant electric blue. The brisk air of the unheated farmhouse was replaced by a gust of cold wind on her bare skin. For a moment, it eased the fever, but the sweat soon chilled and she was shivering again, now from exposure more than sickness. Dale tried to ignore the discomfort. She scooped up a handful of snow and ate it. It numbed her lips and hurt her teeth, but it soothed the fire in her throat. She stopped herself after several more handfuls. With the bucket, Dale scooped up as much snow as she could, feeling a bout of coughing build in her chest. With a grunt, she slid the snow-filled bucket across the floor away from her and let out a long series of ragged hacks. From the floor, Dale closed the back door and sat gasping, the rawness of her throat now worse than ever. She ate some of the snow from the bucket and that helped, if only a little. Shivering, she inspected her clothes, which were cold but dry.

Dressing took time, which passed fluidly for her.

What little energy she had was flagging, but once she'd gotten her clothes back on, she felt warmer. The shaking in her bones seemed to lessen.

In the dim light, she spotted the hatch lid in the floor, below the table.

The kitchen's cold box.

Her stomach growled.

Dale pushed the table aside, an effort that left her coughing again. After another mouthful of snow, she opened the cold box door but couldn't make out the contents without lighting a candle. Inside were jars, crocks and wax-clothed preserves, kept cool and dry in the ground. Dale's appetite flared up and she pulled several of the preserved foods out of the box. Sitting cross-legged on the floor next to the armchair, Dale found salted pork in one of the jars, a wheel of homemade cheese sealed in wax cloth and discovered strawberry jam in another jar. Hungry as she was, she fought through the pain of swallowing, which tore at her throat. She stopped herself from eating too much, both to save her food supply and to keep from overdoing it with her stomach. After her candlelight meal, she packed everything back into the cold box and returned to her armchair. She'd just wrapped the heavy quilt around her and sank into the chair, her head swimming on the edge of dizziness, when fevered sleep took her again.

* * *

The nightmare that followed made even less sense to her than the last one.

The ghost Laura O'Malley stood over her, pointing, her face expressionless.

Someone else was there in the room with her, a dark figure.

The shadow man, Dale thought, and she tried to get up.

"You can't be here," said the voice of Rose.

Dale looked around for the schoolteacher, rising from her chair. Hands grabbed her and Dale fought to push them away, but the effort was feeble as she was forced back down in the chair. Her mind reeled and spun through the terrible ache pounding in her skull.

Laura's ghost approached her and Dale wanted to flee, but couldn't.

"I stopped Henry, what more do you want?" Dale asked.

Hands took her under her arms and lifted her, but Dale only comprehended in a distant haze. She didn't struggle, but tried to make out what the stern voice was telling her.

It's finished, Dale thought, *I've been found, but I'm too sick to do anything about it. I'll wake up in a jail cell again... if I wake up at all.*

Then she felt cold. When she opened her eyes she saw the sun peeking out from behind thick clouds in the blue sky overhead. The world around her spun, but she wasn't sure if it was her own dizziness. The black silhouette of a person towered over her, blotting out the sun and the sky. The person spoke, but Dale was already falling back into unconsciousness and could make none of it out.

* * *

Emery Dale's blurred vision tried to focus in the dark as she floated back to lucidity through the haze of sickness. The surface underneath her was firm, but not the hard wood of a kitchen floor.

I'm on a cot, back in my cell, Dale thought, the gloom taking shape around her.

Candlelight and shadows flickered across the ceiling. No bars encaged her. She was covered in blankets, with a damp cloth on her head. Dale tried to move, but didn't have the energy. She let loose a violent burst of sneezes, followed by a wretched cough that made her roll on her side, causing the cloth to drop from her forehead. When the sneezing let up and Dale opened her eyes again, a slender hand held out a handkerchief for her.

91

Dale took it, falling back on the bed, blowing her nose and whipping her face. She felt the damp cloth placed back to her forehead.

"Where am I?" Dale whispered, not wanting to aggravate her throat any more than she had already.

No one answered, but Dale sensed the other person moving just out of sight in the shadows. It hurt to keep her eyes open, so she closed them. A moment later, she felt the edge of a cup against her lips. Water trickled over them. Dale took the cup and drank, letting the water work to calm her throat. Once empty, the cup disappeared and Dale slid back into unconsciousness.

* * *

Pale light cut through the haze of Dale's fever when she opened her eyes again. More of the room came into view, lit from the soft daylight streaming through the window above her bed. The low ceiling and thick log walls told her she was not at the O'Malleys' farmhouse, nor was she in jail. The light hurt her eyes, so she closed them, listening to the sound of birds outside. It mixed with the crackle of a fire in a cast iron wood stove. It reminded her of Rose's cottage. The two of them would sit next to each other some nights and simply enjoy the calming pantomime of sounds, the fire, the rain, the wind. The sounds of spring had an intoxicating effect those evenings in particular, accented by the fresh air. Dale let the memory take her back to sleep.

* * *

Another nightmare...

The bloody face of the woman from the photograph leaned over her, emerging from the shadows and into the candlelight.

"Fight, Sheriff," the woman said, *"You're stronger than this illness, I reckon."*

"Who are you?" Dale asked.

"Your Angel of Mercy, it would seem," the woman said, sitting on the edge of Dale's bed. Her face changed then, the bloody wound faded away, replaced by hard features of a kind face. Dale struggled to recognize her.

Something white and like vapour moved behind the woman and Dale watched as Laura O'Malley's ghost drifted into view, staring at her.

"Laura!" Dale gasped.

"No," the woman replied, "Her mother."

Dale tried to focus on the woman sitting at her bed and saw it was Mrs O'Malley. She smiled down at Dale, a sweet expression so unlike the wretched, grief-fuelled madness Dale had witnessed from her after Laura had been murdered.

"Laura came to me the other night," Mrs O'Malley said, "and motioned for me to come outside. I was reluctant, but when I saw the storm had broken, I followed her. It did not take me long before I heard you traipsing through the woods. You passed about a dozen yards from me and this cabin, but I'm not at all surprised you didn't see me; so much snow and so much darkness that night covering everything. I saw your lantern, though, and heard you. I didn't know it was you, Sheriff, until a few days ago, but that night I watched from a distance as you went to my house and let yourself in. I almost went to investigate, but stayed back and watched, day after day. When I saw you open the door, all sick and naked, gathering snow, I knew something was wrong. If the sheriff's posse hadn't come down the road a few minutes later, I'd have come to retrieve you earlier. But come they did, and they stopped at the edge of my land. They gave it a good long look and I thought for sure they'd decide to ride up and knock on my door looking for you. They didn't, maybe because the sun had set and the light was failing. My house looks a haunted fright that time of day, all shuttered and dark. They rode on and I returned to my little hunting cabin in the woods. I prepared everything I'd need to tend to your sickness. It's a dreadful flu, with pneumonia chasing hot at its hindquarters. I went to the farmhouse to bring you back here, but you were asleep and a sick person needs their rest, so I sat in my kitchen, something I hadn't done since the new year came, and I watched over you. You slept the sleep of the damned, sometimes tormented, sometimes at rest, but at sun-up I knew we had to go. The new sheriff and his posse could return at any time, less afraid of this place by the light of the day. You put up such a fuss, but I got you here. Now whether you live or die is up to you. I'll do my best to tend to you because I owe you that for finding Laura's killer and putting an end to his evil ways."

Mrs O'Malley leaned forward and whispered, "Thank you for that."

Her face changed again and Dale gazed once more upon the woman with the bloody slash from eye to chin. The blood dripped onto Dale's face, cold when it ought to have been warm.

"Thank you for that," the woman said, more blood dripping from her face as she spoke. Some landed on Dale's lips and it didn't have that bitter, coppery taste, but instead was like water. Dale's dry lips welcomed the liquid, no matter what it was. She was too sick and too thirsty to care as she drank the—

water

—blood.

"You're welcome," Dale mouthed, unsure if any sound came out when she tried to speak. She succumbed to the blackness again, and she didn't fight it.

* * *

The smell of cooking food brought Dale back to the world of the living. She coughed and sneezed and shivered, still sick and weak, but damn if that delicious odour didn't wake up her appetite again.

Mrs O'Malley sat once more at the edge of Dale's bed, black-clad, the only clear thing the former sheriff could make out. The bright sunlight bounced off the silver cross around Frances O'Malley's neck. Dale blinked, squinting against it. Mrs O'Malley had a bowl of the wonderful-smelling food and offered Dale a spoonful, the way a mother does with a sick child. Dale accepted, pondering again the stark contrast between this woman and the one who had raved and cursed people in the streets of Orchard Bend only months before. The stew was as tasty as it smelled and not so hot as to aggravate her throat.

She wolfed down several bites before Mrs O'Malley said, "That's enough for now, Sheriff, your stomach may reject any more. It's been days since you ate properly. I tried to feed you yesterday, but you would only take a few bites."

"I don't remember that," Dale said, her voice still raspy.

"I'm not surprised, sick as you are," Mrs O'Malley said. "Your fever is still hot and I expect you've lost weight. You labour to breathe, especially at night. I fear I'll awaken to find you taken by Our Lord. If it's pneumonia, that's a devil who's taken many a-soul. We thought Laura had contracted it, the winter before you came to Orchard Bend, if I recall. Doc Shaw said it was a nasty flu. Laura pulled through, strong, healthy girl as she was."

"Did they find Shaw?" Dale asked. "Do you know?"

"They did, the morning after the storm," Mrs O'Malley said. Dale wondered how she knew, but another, more pressing thought came to her.

"You said Laura told you about me, that I was in the woods?" Dale asked.

"She came to me that night," Mrs O'Malley said, stirring the bowl of stew in her lap. She scooped up a spoonful and started feeding Dale again as she went on. "She gestured for me to follow her outside and I did. She pointed to you as you charged through the woods just as quick as you please."

"Do you see her often?" Dale asked between spoonfuls.

"Time and again, she comes to visit," Mrs O'Malley said. "It started on the first of the year. I didn't then know why exactly, but when I found out what you had done, ending Henry McCabe, I knew that must have been why. Somehow I think it set her soul free."

Mrs O'Malley patted Dale on the hand, fed her the last of the stew and stood up.

"You should sleep now, Sheriff," she said, tucking the blanket and quilt up to Dale's neck.

"I'm not the sheriff anymore," Dale said as she closed her eyes, but not before Frances O'Malley smiled. It was a kind smile, one that masked pain, but also one borne of deep affection.

"I don't think you will ever *not* be sheriff here," Mrs O'Malley said.

And Dale fell back asleep.

* * *

No nightmares. Just dreams.

* * *

Emery Dale opened her eyes in a blackness broken only by the dim light from the wood stove on the other side of the room. She coughed, but very little phlegm came out. The air tickled her throat and she called out for water as she rested on her elbow at the edge of the bed, her chest muscles tightening, threatening to unleash another bout of dry hacking.

With her gaze directed at the floor, Dale saw the hem of a dress as a woman approached. Another series of coughs gripped her and Dale felt a hand on her shoulder. Through squinted eyes, she saw the woman hand her a cup of water and Dale took it. She swallowed the drink in gulps and dropped back down on the bed, eyes closed. She let out a long sigh. She put her hand on her chest, took another deep breath and coughed again as she exhaled, a short cough, almost out of reflex, not nearly as bad as the others. Her head felt clearer, too. It still throbbed, but the thick, heavy feeling had let up. She put her hand on her forehead, trying to gauge her temperature. She didn't feel feverish or sweaty. Despite being hungry, weak, tired and still unwell, Dale knew she felt a whole lot better.

"Sheriff Dale?" said a voice that belonged to a young woman.

Not Mrs O'Malley, Dale noted, her heart rate rising. *So, who?*

Dale sat up as the young woman knelt by the bed with a fresh cup of water, half her face lit by the glow from the stove.

"Rebecca Clarke?" Dale whispered.

"Yes, Sheriff," Rebecca answered, handing the cup to Dale. The former sheriff saw the girl's hands tremble just a little.

Dale took the cup and Rebecca sat down on the chair by the stove.

"Where is Mrs O'Malley?" Dale asked between sips.

"Mrs O'Malley?" Rebecca asked, her brow furrowed in confusion. "Mrs O'Malley was here?"

The girl looked around the small cabin and Dale focused in on her expression, one of surprise.

Dale sipped the water.

Rebecca stood up and reached across the bed to the inside shutter of the window above Dale. When she opened it, pale light filled the room and Dale closed her eyes against it.

"Mrs O'Malley is not here, Sheriff," Rebecca sighed. "No one has seen her since the night of the big storm. The night you escaped."

"She brought me here," Dale said.

Rebecca nodded and opened the wood stove door. Dale tasted the ash in the air more than she smelled it, as Rebecca put a piece of wood in the fire.

"Your fever broke last night," Rebecca said. "It looked like pneumonia. I arrived yesterday and found you here, practically knocking on death's door, what with that rattle in your chest. Feeling better, are you?"

"Much better," Dale said, handing Rebecca the empty cup. The girl went to the basin that sat on the small table against the far wall.

"Good, because I can't stay long right now," Rebecca said, filling the cup.

"Wait," Dale said, sitting up. "How did you come to be here?"

Rebecca looked out the window, her eyes glassy with the hint of tears.

"Laura," Rebecca said. "Laura brought me here."

Dale waited for more, but Rebecca only wiped at her eyes and started for the door.

"I have to get to school," Rebecca said, putting on her coat and scarf. "Miss Adelaide doesn't like it when we're late."

"Are you coming back?" Dale asked.

Rebecca paused for a moment.

"I guess I have to," Rebecca said.

Dale forced herself out of bed and held her balance with the help of the headboard.

"You don't have to," Dale said. "It's dangerous for you to be here. I expect they're still looking for me."

Rebecca slipped on her boots and answered without looking at Dale.

"I do have to," Rebecca said, opening the door. "It's what Laura wants."

Dale shivered and sat down on the bed as the cold air filled the room. Then she called out, "Wait!"

Rebecca stopped.

"Can I borrow a piece of paper and a pencil?" Dale asked.

Rebecca hesitated, then reached into her pail full of schoolbooks, took out her well-whittled pencil and handed it to Dale. She then took out her tablet, flipped to the very back page and tore it out. Dale took it without a word. Rebecca dashed out of the cabin, pail in hand, closing the door behind her. Dale grabbed a blanket, threw it over her shoulders and went to the door. She disregarded the freezing air that made her chest tighten. It threatened her with another coughing attack as she opened it and looked outside. The snow-covered steps led up from the door and Dale realized the cabin was set halfway in the ground. Rebecca's tracks had broken the snow, leading both to and from the cabin, and bent away around the side, off into the woods.

Birds chirped and whistled in the trees, and light came down in pale shafts. Beyond, Dale could see blue sky and clouds. Her breath floated away from her mouth in the cold and her bare legs shivered. She looked around the inside of the doorway and found her boots sitting neatly by an almost empty bookshelf. Her clothes, apart from the under-things she was wearing, were folded on one of the shelves. Dale took her time getting dressed, but was relieved when no dizziness tried to force her off her feet, even when her chest seized with a coughing fit. Once clothed and with the blanket back over her jacketed shoulders—the very same blanket she'd taken from the jailhouse, she noted—Dale ventured outside.

She followed Rebecca's tracks for a few feet, until they arced away into the woods. There, Dale turned and looked at the cabin. The snow provided a natural camouflage, made more effective with the building half buried in the ground. One of the only give-aways to its existence was the grey smoke wafting from the chimney, which dissipated in the air soon after, failing to escape the cover of the trees. Dale felt confident that unless someone came looking for it, or knew it was here, few people would just happen upon this cabin.

"More like a bunker than a cabin," Dale said.

Dale took in the surrounding woods and picked out the tracks of some small animals criss-crossing the snow. Rabbits, she guessed. She walked toward them, thinking about maybe snaring one if it came to that.

That's when the bolt of pain in her head almost knocked her to the ground.

The world around her became grey and smoke-like, transparent and distorted. Dale had experienced this before, on New Year's Eve, when the shadow man had guided her to the McCabe barn.

This was *his* world.

As the headache eased, Dale turned this way and that, looking for the dark apparition. The blanket slid from her shoulders, but the cold she expected did not fall upon her. She saw a rabbit approach and, despite the bizarre circumstance, Dale stood still and watched it. As it got closer, she saw its hide was smoky and translucent like the trees around her. The rabbit stopped and watched her as well, allowing Dale a moment to see its tense muscles and even the outline of its internal organs before it sprang off across the snow. As it disappeared into the undergrowth, Dale bent to pick up the blanket. She had an unnerving moment when she realized that, like with the rabbit, she could also see through her own hand, to the bones and tendons and veins. Nausea welled up inside her. She looked to the cabin and could see through the thick log walls, picking out the shapes of the stove, the bed, the chair—

Something white moved to her left and Dale spun about, her hand dropping to her hip out of instinct, grasping for a revolver that wasn't there. A pale form moved between the trees several yards away, spectral and quite unlike the dark shape of the shadow man she'd seen several times before. Dale could make out the shape of a body, slight and shorter than herself. The spectre weaved through the woods, examining each tree as she passed, raising her hand as if to touch the bark, but the misty digits only passed through the trunk. As she got closer, Dale backed away. The former sheriff's movements got the attention of the spectre and she looked right at Emery. Dale stopped, not out of fear, but from recognition.

"Laura?" Dale said.

The expression on the face of the spectre of Laura O'Malley remained impassive, but her silky, translucent form moved toward Dale, who took another step back. The migraine returned. Dale's foot caught on something buried in the snow and she stumbled, falling back. Once more, she felt the cold of the snow and air. The world returned to normal, the grey, smoky appearance fading back to the sun-dappled woods. The breeze caught the snow Dale kicked up when she fell and the lighter crystals wafted about her as she looked back in the direction of Laura O'Malley's ghost. In a fleeting few seconds, Dale thought she saw the young woman's form standing over her, but she couldn't be sure it wasn't a play of sunlight and glittering snow on the air. Just as fast, the figure disappeared from view.

But are you really gone, Miss O'Malley? Dale thought. *Or are you watching me, just out of view?*

It took Dale some effort to get to her feet as the adrenalin rush gave way to fatigue borne of her illness. She made slow progress back to the cabin, fighting through another bout of coughing along the way.

Inside, her stomach gave a fierce growl. Dale looked around the room, hoping Mrs O'Malley had left her something to eat. Seeing nothing in plain sight, she sat on the bed. She thought about the stores of preserves in the O'Malley farmhouse, in the cold box under the floor. Dale cast her gaze about the floorboards of the cabin. After a minute's search, she found the trapdoor below her bed, smaller than the one in the house. On her hands and knees, Dale opened it and reached inside, retrieving two jars, one of dried meat and one of a dark red jam. The small jars meant there wasn't much of each, even though they were full. As Dale took out a piece of dried jerk meat and ate it, she knew she'd be wise to ration the food, at least until Mrs. O'Malley or Rebecca Clarke returned.

Dale then dragged the solitary chair next to the bed and set on it Rebecca's pencil and paper. Taking a second piece of meat from the jar and tearing the tough, sinewy flesh with her teeth, Dale put the pencil to the paper. Before she could write even a word, her tired thoughts turned to the woman who brought her here. Dale had not known Frances O'Malley before her daughter had been murdered by Henry McCabe. By all accounts, the woman had been a kind, decent, God-fearing person, a strict mother, but not unreasonable. After Laura O'Malley's murder, Mr O'Malley had left her and she declined into a grief-filled madness, raving in the streets and railing against the lack of progress in her daughter's case.

Has she come back to herself now? Dale wondered. The Mrs O'Malley who carried Dale here and tended to her illness seemed a far cry from the person Dale had seen spewing words of fire and brimstone at the onlookers in town months before.

Months, Dale thought. *That was November, but what month was it now? Still January, or are we in February? Have I been out of it that long?*

She had no way to know, not out here. When Rebecca returned, Dale planned to ask her. She pushed away the chair with the blank paper on it and laid down on the bed. She closed her eyes and the image of the woman with the scar came to her. Dale sat up and patted the pockets of her jacket, feeling for the newspaper. She found it in her breast pocket and let out a long breath. Had she put it there in her delirium or had Mrs O'Malley retrieved it for her? Dale couldn't remember and it didn't matter much anyway. She unfolded the paper and looked at the picture of Doc Reed and the scarred woman again.

Dale had done the math.

Assuming the woman in the image to be thirty years old at the time and knowing the photo was taken twenty-five years earlier, she'd only be about fifty-five today.

If she's still alive, Dale mused.

"I have a feeling you're out there somewhere," Dale whispered, replacing the newspaper back into her jacket pocket. She took off the jacket and lay back down on the bed under the blanket.

I'm going to try to find you, whoever you are, Dale promised, staring up at the cabin ceiling. A bout of coughing seized her and Dale clutched her chest. It didn't last long. Afterwards, Dale closed her eyes to go to sleep.

Just as soon as I'm better, I'm going to try, Dale thought, and she let sleep take her.

18

June 15, 1862
Orchard Bend

With the sky clear and the summer sun hazy and warm overhead, old Doc Reed sat on a rickety chair, watching from the grassy lawn as Freddy Wood helped Earl McManus hang the hand-stitched banner over the door of the church. Twice Freddy shifted on his tall ladder and both times came within seconds of putting it too far off-balance. Wood's wife Nell directed the two men not far from where Reed sat. Not wanting to become a widow if Freddy fell and broke his neck, she then decided to foot the ladder herself as her husband tacked the nails in to hold the cloth banner aloft.

When the two men finished securing the banner, Earl called out, "Ready?!"

The townsfolk gathered on the church lawn answered him with cheers and claps, but Daisy Sullivan, holding her two-year-old daughter Irene in one arm and gesturing with the other, shouted, "Wait, wait! The photographer isn't ready!"

Earl called out, "Well, tell him to hurry! My arms are getting tired up here."

"Ditto," added Freddy.

The photographer stood at his camera, adjusting his tripod. Doc smiled at the man's fumbling, which lasted half a minute more before he proclaimed, "Ready!"

"On three," Earl shouted to Freddy. "One... Two..."

"Three!" cried out the town, drowning out McManus's voice. The men let the banner unfurl to the sound of cheering and applause. *Welcome to Orchard Bend!* read the sign, marking the town's official incorporation.

Freddy and Earl climbed down and admired their handiwork as Sean McCabe, looking ever the gentleman in his slim suit and silk top hat, ascended the steps of the church with a paper in his hand. The jubilation died down at once.

"It's a shame my father did not live to see this historic day," Sean began, looking back at the hand stitched banner, the work of many of the ladies in town.

"Here, here!" cried a man from the crowd.

"Liam was a great man," said another.

"Yes," Sean said, pointing to the crowd. The paper in his hand fluttered in the afternoon breeze. "But I may be a little biased making that determination."

The crowd laughed.

"But one man who is still with us," Sean went on, "the last of Orchard Bend's founding fathers you might say, *is* bearing witness today."

Doc felt the eyes of the townsfolk upon him even before Sean said, "Mr Doc Reed!"

More warm applause and Doc raised his cane in a strong, knobby fist. He smiled and it was genuine. He thought of his old friend Liam and the first time they met, when a party of twenty-five settled on the then-empty plain not far from this very spot.

As if reading his mind, the ever perceptive Sean continued, "Fifty-one years ago I hadn't even learned to walk when my father and mother arrived to make their home here. They thought they were the first to put down roots in this place, but Doc Reed had beat them to it, didn't you, Doc?"

"I had this place all to myself till you lot came along!" Doc joked. Everyone laughed. Doc gave a hearty smile that made the many lines on his face stand out.

"And now here we are," Sean said, beaming. He held the paper up, saying, "I hold in my hand the notice from the State's House of Representatives *approving* our Charter and By-laws, thus incorporating the Town of Orchard Bend!"

As the townspeople cheered, even louder than before, Sean's son Maxwell, also looking smart in his suit jacket, stepped up next to his father and placed the document carefully in a leather folder. The Council of Aldermen no doubt planned to have it framed. It would hang in the McCabe home, on the hill overlooking the town. Doc snickered to himself, knowing Liam wouldn't have had it any other way, and his son Seam was no different.

"But enough of my endless prattle, we're here to celebrate! And celebrate we shall!" Sean said with a sweeping wave of his arms. On cue, the small but enthusiastic group of local musicians burst into melody. Everyone partook of the food spread out on the mismatched collection of tables. Sounds of laughter and merriment filled the air and Doc Reed watched it all, marvelling in the way only a man in his position, of his experience, could. And it was not because he had only a month earlier celebrated his ninetieth birthday in a similar fashion at his nephew Sully's tavern. Nor that the many years under his belt gave him a distinct perspective. No, it was a good deal more than that.

Take the war, for example.

Doc's grandson Edmond had talked seriously about joining the Union Army. Men and boys from all over had signed up, including friends of Edmond's, and the young man had talked about doing the same. Doc's own son, Gabe, had been aghast. The arguments between Edmond and he were fierce for weeks. Doc saw that Gabe would lose in the face of Edmond's determination in this time of deep emotion and rigid points of view. So at his own ninetieth birthday party, as the guests around them danced and made merry, Doc pulled Edmond to him with his hard, boney grip and sat the young man down.

"Edmond, I'm going to tell you something," Doc said. And when his grandfather spoke, Edmond knew to listen.

Doc ringed his hands around the handle of his cane and considered his words carefully.

"The war will be won by the Union without your help," Doc said.

"Grandpa, you can't forbid me to fight. The Union has to be preserved—!" Edmond started, but Doc cut him off with a wave of his hand.

"I'm not forbidding anyone anything," Doc said. "I'm telling you what I *know*: this war will end and it will be a Union victory. It will bring about a better country than the one we had before. Not a perfect one, but better in so many ways. And I want you to be a part of that better world, at least the start of it. You don't have to fight. The war *will* be won without your going."

"So others fight defending our country?" Edmond protested.

Doc shook his head.

"It will be a bloody, horrific thing, this war," Doc said. "It will tear apart so many lives and so many families, but the Union will prevail. You don't have to die, but you can help make the world after the war better. You're a good person and when I'm gone—"

"Grandpa, enough of that talk, you're not going to die," Edmond said, but Doc waved him off.

"We all die," Doc said, "but my point is that you'll be needed here with your family after the war is won."

Edmond looked as though he was about to cry. His cheeks quivered and twitched with emotion and his eyes glistened. Doc knew the young man had all but made up his mind to go, but now he was not so sure. Doc watched Edmond compose himself, wiping his eyes on his sleeve and sitting up.

Doc spoke again.

"I could use some of that famous McCabe cider," Doc said. "All this talking leaves a man parched."

Edmond chuckled and Doc heard a measure of relief in it. After that conversation, Edmond no longer talked of joining the fight.

At the picnic, Doc spotted Edmond with Miss Sarah Cavanaugh, standing in the shade of some Atlas Cedars, talking close the way two people do when they're smitten.

Good, Doc thought, *if he's focused on her, he won't be thinking about joining the army.*

Some yelling children tore past Doc and one boy almost knocked him off his chair, bumping his arm so hard Reed dropped his cane.

"Clement Arnold Wilson!" scolded Dorothy Sullivan. Doc watched his sister-in-law, a woman in her sixties still blessed with the momentous fortitude she'd had all her life—enough even that she still taught school—take the young Wilson boy by the arm as she leaned over him.

"Now you apologize to Mr Reed this instant," Dorothy ordered her pupil.

"I'm sorry," the boy muttered, looking at his feet.

"And pick up his cane," the schoolteacher said, "You're lucky he doesn't whip you with it."

"Now, now, Dorothy," Doc said. He gave the child a forgiving smile as the boy picked up his cane and handed it to him. "Apology accepted, young man."

"Go play over by the trees, away from the grown-ups," Dorothy said. The Wilson boy bolted off to join his friends, who teased him for getting caught.

"You can't escape Miss Sullivan, Arnie," one of them laughed.

"Don't call me that, I told you! My name is Clem!" Wilson barked as they headed off. Dorothy knelt next to Doc and put her hand on his shoulder.

"Don't you want to sit in the shade, Doc?" she asked.

Reed looked around at the townsfolk socializing. Many were talking in groups of threes and fours, some sitting on the green grass in front of the church, some standing about with a cup of cider or water in their hand. Still others gave into the festive mood and danced with a friend or loved one or just by themselves on the hard, dry dirt of the street where the band played. They kicked up their heels and Doc smiled at the sight of it all.

"I'm quite content where I am, Dorothy," Doc said, "but I appreciate you thinking about me."

"Well let me get you some water, then," Dorothy said. "We can't have you drying out and blowing away like a leaf in autumn, can we?"

Dorothy dashed off to fetch him a cup of water and was intercepted by Matilda Bentley. Doc knew their conversation would not be a quick one; both ladies were well known to chat

107

up a storm about the town's goings-on, sometimes for hours on end.

Doc turned his attention to the photographer, who had moved his tripod across the lawn for a wider shot and who at that moment fussed and argued with the great wood and metal contraption as he set it up. After several minutes watching the man, Doc felt a cough rise in his drying throat. He gave a short hack, covering his mouth with his fist.

"You could use some water, Doc," said a voice beside him.

He turned and saw a woman in her late twenties holding out a cup of water. She wore a white blouse and a plain brown skirt, and had her pulled back tight in a ponytail.

Doc didn't really see the deep scar on her face at first. In fact, once their eyes met, Doc saw with such clarity memories of a life long gone, moments strung together in his mind's eye from years of working in that underground facility. He saw a shiny, shadowy place of metal, computers monitors and hazard signs, where men and women in lab coats milled about, diligent in their work.

And this woman was both here before him at the picnic and there in that other place and time.

"Hello, Doctor," the woman said, in her dark uniform, complete with tactical harness, greeting him as the glass doors slid open at his approach, its sensors activated by the signal from his watch.

"Hello, Doctor," the woman said, there at the picnic, still holding the cup of water out to him.

Looking past her and into the lab, Doc gave the woman a familiar nod, "Hello,..."

"...Sergeant Decker," Doc whispered as she took his hand and put the cup of water in it. The name fit with such ease on his tongue as he spoke it, yet it had not been there just seconds before, having been lost in the recesses of his memory.

She smiled at him and that's when he first noticed the scar.

"That's right, Doctor," Decker said, "And you better drink up. We have a lot to talk about, I think."

* * *

108

June 13, 1862
Orchard Bend

The sensation of being pulled along by some invisible tether seemed to only become more intense as Kenna Decker walked down the road heading west. Whatever its source, she intended to find it out here. The fedora she wore didn't quite fit right, being a little too large for her, but it kept her face out of the sun well enough. She couldn't take off the bulky jacket in this heat, as it hid her tactical harness and service weapon from any passers-by who might happen upon her. Lots of farms spread out over the land in these parts, west of the little town of Orchard Bend, and the few farmers who passed had not troubled her. A man calling himself Staid had offered her a lift to wherever she was going, but Decker had declined with a forced grin, so the man had ridden on. Still, she might appear an easy target for anyone with more nefarious intentions, so Decker felt it best to keep her sidearm on her and out of sight.

Lush foliage and tall trees rose up on either side of the road as it began to slope downward in a gentle curve toward a ravine. Wild flowers bloomed in an array of colours all around her and the air became thick with the mingling aromas. Decker walked on, not allowing herself to be distracted. Finding the reason why she felt drawn in this direction meant staying focused. Reaching a bridge of stone and timber that spanned a not insignificant river, Decker paused. The feeling in her gut, the *pulling* which brought her here, only intensified. Decker stood in the middle of the bridge and looked around for anything unusual.

You're exposed out here, she told herself, yet saw nothing out of the ordinary. She continued on across the bridge and would have ventured up the hill, but that persistent urge seemed to point her off the road and into the woods, still onward due west. Decker saw a well-worn path along the river's edge and left the road to follow it.

After some long minutes making her way along the bank next to the rushing water, Decker spotted what looked like a building farther on ahead through the trees. She resisted the urge to draw her weapon, but still flexed her hands and readied herself as she approached. The path gave way to a clearing and there stood a low, stout, wood-framed cabin made of solid, sturdy timber on a foundation of stone.

Sitting on the step by the cabin door was a girl of twelve or thirteen years. Her eggshell blue dress and matching bonnet stood out against the green foliage. With a stick she drew lines in the loose dirt at her feet. She didn't look up at Decker, who couldn't see her face under the girl's bonnet. Decker checked her surroundings with practiced glances, taking in a wealth of detail in a matter of seconds. Besides the girl, she saw few signs of human activity.

Decker stepped into the clearing and toward the girl, who she now heard humming a tune Decker couldn't make out.

"Excuse me," Decker said.

The girl started and jumped up from the step, holding the stick out between her and Decker, even though the woman was more than a dozen feet away.

"I, um..." the girl stammered, "Who are you?"

"I'm a traveller," Decker said. "Do you live here?"

The girl looked at the cabin, then back to Decker.

"I..." the girl said, "no, I don't."

"Who does?"

"Nobody," the girl said. "I mean, not anymore. My best friend Isla used to live here. Her family had to move away."

"So why are you here now?" Decker asked.

"I come out here sometimes, even though Isla's gone," the girl said. "It's peaceful and I like to just sit and remember."

"Nobody else lives out here?" Decker asked.

"My family's ranch is just up the road a ways," the girl said. Decker noted the defensiveness in her voice. "No one lives in the ravine, if that's what you're asking."

Decker nodded, her attention now on the cabin.

"And my family knows I'm here," the girl added, using the stick in her hand to point toward the road.

"Good," Decker said, walking away from the girl.

She looked around the property, verifying what the girl said with a visual inspection of the premises. The empty stall behind the cabin, the closed shutters on the windows, the lack of any signs of work being done on or about the cabin told Decker she could believe the girl's assertion. No one lived there.

As she walked around the vacant property, Decker found herself moving in the same direction as before, drawn west. She didn't have to check the compass app on her watch, tucked safe in a pocket of her jacket, to know that. The literal gut feeling told her she was getting close.

But close to what? Decker wondered.

On the far side of the clearing lay a grove of aspens, their white bark stunning in the late spring sun. A breeze picked up and rose in pitch through the trees. That lonely sound spread out for miles in every direction. Kenna Decker stood motionless at the edge of the grove, her senses heightened. She could see no reason not to go forward, yet she didn't move.

"Are you looking for the carving?" the girl said behind her.

Decker turned around.

"What carving?" she asked.

"There's a strange carving on one of the trees," the girl said, pointing with her stick. "Isla's father said Indians put it there, but I don't think that's true."

"You've seen this carving?" Decker asked.

"Yes," the girl said. "Isla and I used to play in there. We pretended the trees were a great white palace and we were queens of all the lands."

Decker gave her a genuine smile and said, "How about you show me where it is, this carving."

The girl looked back toward the path by the river, unsure of Decker or her intentions.

"How did you get that scar on your cheek?" the girl asked.

A frown replaced Decker's smile.

"It's pretty bad, isn't it?" Decker replied.

The girl shrugged.

"It's an interesting story," Decker said. "I fought off some bandits who were trying to take something valuable from me."

111

The girl's eyes narrowed and she cocked her head to one side. "Did that really happen?" she asked.

"Yes," Decker said. "In the struggle, I was left with quite a cut on my face."

"What happened to the people who attacked you?"

"I honestly don't know," Decker said. "Now how about you show me this carving, alright?"

"I supposed I can do that for you," the girl said. "What's your name, may I ask?"

"Kenna," Decker said.

"That's your first name?" the girl asked.

"Yes, Kenna Decker."

"I'm Gertrude," the girl said. "Gertrude Kiley."

"Nice to meet you," Decker said. She gestured to the grove, "Lead the way."

Gertrude passed her and stepped into the grove. The heavy undergrowth made for a slow march between the trees, but never did the girl pause or appear unsure where they were going as she wended her way between the aspens. A few yards in, Decker felt the soft pulse of her watch in her jacket pocket. The vibration was not audible over the sounds of nature all around them, but Decker wondered what would set it off. She reached into her pocket and switched the watch off. Ahead of her, Gertrude gave no indication she had noticed at all. She twirled her stick between her fingers and ran her other hand over the occasional tree they passed.

Then all at once, Gertrude stopped and picked out an aspen that, to Decker, looked no different than the many others all around them. Catching up to the girl, however, Decker saw why this tree was different. She didn't know what she had expected to see, but the symbol carved into the tree had not been it. She recognized the rough-hewn carving and her breath caught in her chest.

"How...?" she asked, amazed and confused at the symbol that resembled an "L" growing out of a "P." Yet the confusion did not last long.

Of course, Decker thought, *someone put this here. Someone from the facility arrived before I did. That's how it works, isn't it, when the Breach spits us out? It scatters us all over time. So somebody came here first and carved this. But who?*

Decker had an idea who.

"Is that what you're looking for?" Gertrude asked.

"I don't know," Decker answered. The sensation in her stomach that had drawn her to the ravine eased and Decker suspected that she had reached her destination. She looked at Gertrude, "You've been a tremendous help, Gertrude. You have my thanks. You should get on home, I think, though."

Gertrude frowned, then smiled as she remembered something.

"The town is having a picnic on Sunday to celebrate Incorporation, if you plan to be here until then," Gertrude said. She nodded to the carving, "I don't know if anyone else knows more about this, but you might ask Mr Reed. He's the oldest man in town. Ninety years, they say. He might know more. I've really never talked to him myself."

"That might not be a bad idea," Decker said, looking at the carving again.

Gertrude started back to the clearing.

"It was a pleasure to meet you, Miss Decker," Gertrude said.

"You can call me Kenna," Decker said. "I'm not that much older than you."

"I hope to see you at the picnic," Gertrude said.

"I expect you will," Decker replied.

Gertrude waved and walked back out of the grove. Decker watched her go until at last the sergeant stood alone before the carving.

Before she could ponder the "L-P" shape more, she remembered that her watch had given her a notification. She pulled it out of her jacket pocket and pressed the power button. On the small screen, the following appeared:

Signal Acquired
Connecting...

"What the hell?" Decker said. "Connecting with what?"

The watch pulsed again.

113

Signal Connected
Syncing…

Decker could only stand speechless and unmoving, not wanting to interrupt the process. Whatever it meant that her watch from the future could now sync up with something in the 19th Century, Decker hoped that once it finished, she'd have some answers.

Sync Complete
1 New Message
Device Clearance Recognized
Sgt. K. R. Decker
Enter GvSci Passcode

_ _ _ _ _ _ _

Decker tapped in her passcode.

W h i s k e y
[Select?]

A green circle swirled around the screen, then the new message appeared. Decker leaned back against the tree with the carving on it and read every word, slowly sliding down the trunk as all feeling left her legs.

* * *

From the road, Decker saw the thin column of smoke rising from the bank of the river northeast of Orchard Bend. The rays of the setting sun turned it a faded yellow and orange. The same golden sunlight cast her shadow long across the wild grass. She tipped the ill-fitting hat back from her brow and the sun warmed the smooth skin of her left cheek. She reached up and her fingers traced the marred surface of the healed wound, the uneven flesh cold in the shade.

Her camp lay a few dozen yards ahead, the covered wagon a solitary mound rising above the grass, the plume of smoke reaching to the sky, but Decker stopped on the worn dirt road and faced the sun, closing her eyes and letting it cast its heat on her entire face. A gust of wind moved across the flat land and she heard it coming, a soft white noise passing over the grass. When it reached her, Decker's long skirt flitted and rippled against her legs. The wind pulled at her hat, forcing her to hold it in place. Behind her, the sound of the shifting grass carried away along the empty plain mile after mile.

Decker let go of her hat and pulled it back down to shield her eyes, then she started on again toward her camp. The fragrant aroma of cooking meat made her stomach growl and Decker picked up her pace.

"I just put on those cuts of steak we picked up in Ashleyville," Winstone said, standing up from his crouch by the low fire and stretching his legs and back. "Your timing is impeccable."

The golden light gave way to a crystalline blue all around them as the sun dropped below the horizon. Kenna offered him a smile. With a tin cup, she scooped some water from the black scorched pot and sat on an upended crate by the fire without a word.

Charles watched her sip the water as she stared into the crackling fire. She could feel his eyes on her. When she spoke, she didn't take her eyes off the flames that licked the grill and pan he had balanced over them.

"I see you got the spokes of the wheel fixed," Kenna said, closing her fingers around the metal cup.

"I did," Charles said, looking away and poking at the steaks cooking on the grill. "A farmer named Picton lives nearby. He came down the road and saw we needed help. You'd been gone an hour by then. Agreeable fellow. He went to his farm, got what he needed to replace the spokes and rode back out here. I offered to pay him for his time and materials, but he wouldn't have it. I wasn't going to argue with the man. So the wheel is just about good as new."

Charles put a pair of potatoes on the grill next to the pan as the steaks sizzled. He flipped the steaks over and pulled his own crate close to the cooking, making himself comfortable.

"You've been gone a while, so I'm going to ask: did you find anything?" Charles tried to sound casual, but Kenna knew the curiosity was getting too much for him, what with her muted demeanour upon returning.

"I did," she said, dropping her head down, but not in frustration at the question. She wished she had a better answer for him. She brought her head back and eased her hair back from her face to look at him. "There's a lot to it and I don't have all the answers yet. We'll talk about it, just maybe not tonight."

Charles turned the potatoes over.

"I understand," he said.

A short time later, Charles served up dinner. Darkness descended around them and Kenna spotted the W-shaped constellation she guessed to be Cassiopeia not far above the horizon to the north. Draco sat higher up in its frozen writhe. The near-full moon would wash out many of the stars when it rose behind her to the southeast before too long, but everything in the night sky spread out in the peaceful deepening blue as she ate in silence and took it in.

After she washed the plates, pan and the grill, and set them out to dry, Kenna pulled her crate close to Charles, who had thrown another scrap of driftwood on the fire. She took his hand in hers. They watched the moonrise and Kenna at last spoke again.

"We have to stay here a few more days," she said, "Until Sunday. A pleasant young lady told me the town is having a picnic that day. And there will be someone there I want to talk to."

"Alright," Charles said.

They spoke very little after that and let the fire burn low. When it died, Charles poured water on the embers and they climbed into the back of the covered wagon. Kenna tried to burn off some of the frustrating, conflicting emotions as aggressively as she and Charles could on their makeshift bed,

116

but in the afterglow, little had been resolved. Charles slept, but Kenna stared out at the moonlit sky for a long time.

19

June 15, 1862
Orchard Bend

Doc Reed looked up into Decker's face, oblivious to the din of the town's jubilance but no longer overwhelmed by the wave of memories he thought lost forever.

"Your face, Sergeant..." Reed said, but Decker took his hand in hers and knelt next to him.

"I survived," Decker said. "And so did you."

"You were compelled to travel here, weren't you?" Reed asked. "That's how you came to be here, isn't it?"

"I ran into a girl named Gertrude who told me to talk to the oldest man in town," Decker smiled.

"Gertrude Kiley," Reed said, "Her family has a ranch not far from the ravine. So you've been there then? You went there before coming here, didn't you?"

"Yes," Decker said. "I found your message."

Doc looked away from her for the first time since she had appeared next to him. His eyes stung with tears and he dabbed them with a handkerchief.

"And I saw the carving in the aspen tree," Decker said.

"Rateliff. That was his name," Reed said, his voice low. Leaning forward on his cane, Doc stood up. Decker slid her own arm around his and helped him up. "He wanted to get home so badly, but he wouldn't listen. I tried to stop him opening a Portal to the Breach..."

Doc stopped himself and forced back the rush of memories, the ones that had never really gone away; his first memories of his new life here.

Decker gave his hand a comforting squeeze. Doc looked around at the picnic's revellers, all smiling and carrying on.

"After that, I made this my life," Reed said, pointing at the town with his cane. "I stopped thinking too much about the Breach, but even after so many long years without seeing anyone else, I never gave up hope that others would arrive. And here you are, Kenna Decker."

Half a dozen yards away, Doc saw the photographer tucked under his hood and taking aim in their direction. Doc straightened up and Decker looked at him, then saw the camera. The photographer exposed the plate with a flick of his hand and closed it just as fast.

"So that's it, then," Decker said. They walked on across the grass toward the shade of the cedars on the far side of the church, where few had gathered. The gravity of her situation weighed heavy in Decker's voice, "There's no way home."

It wasn't a question, so Reed said nothing, letting reality take hold.

On the other side of the trees next to the church lay the town's small public cemetery. Beneath the cedars and out of the sun, Reed took off his hat and settled himself on the weathered stone bench, placed there for mourners to sit when visiting passed loved ones. Moss grew around the thick legs at their base where they sunk into the ground. Decker paced in a tight circle before him, with her arms crossed and a hand on her chin, her head down, deep in thought.

Doc marvelled again that this woman had come here. He had so many questions for her, but some he could deduce on his own. She must have exited the Breach not long ago, as she hadn't aged at all and still looked uncomfortable here.

Weeks, Reed thought, *maybe months. This is all still new to her.*

As Decker turned to pace back in the other direction, Reed looked at her scar.

She got that at the facility, trying to stop the take-over, Reed now remembered. There had been so much blood as the blade sliced her face.

She's lucky to still have her eye, Doc mused.

Decker stopped pacing and faced him.

"Your control computer," she said. "You brought it with you through the Breach. I have my watch. They can sync up. The extra processing and two points of reference could be enough—"

Doc shook his head and interrupted her train of thought.

"No, no," Reed said, "It wouldn't be enough, nowhere *near* enough. There were too many variables we knew about back then and so many more we *didn't* know about. Remember the volunteer?"

"The volunteer?" Decker repeated back, not understanding.

Reed stamped his cane into the dirt in frustration.

"What was his name?!" Reed asked, looking around, trying to remember. "We sent him out to try to open a second Portal off-site."

"You mean Sergeant Liszt?" Decker asked.

"Liszt! Yes," Reed said. "We thought we knew everything we needed to know. We checked and rechecked our data, had dozens of reference points, atmospheric intelligence, hi-rez GPS monitoring, satellite imaging that could read the name tag on his uniform from orbit, the works. The Breach swallowed him up. We didn't expect that, but we hoped he'd reappear in the facility at our Portal. It made sense, right? Go in one end, come out another. I can guess now that if it didn't kill him going in, it deposited him in some other time. Or it will if it hasn't yet. Or it did and he's out there somewhere, lost like you and I were."

"Or he's long dead," Decker said under her breath, hands on her hips and her head down.

"Or worse," Reed said, "and that doesn't need to happen to anyone else."

Head still down, Decker looked at him.

"You made a life for yourself here," she said.

"That's all there is left to do," Reed said.

"What if I can't?" Decker said, looking back at the happy picnickers on the lawn of the church.

"Sergeant, there's so much about my life I don't remember before I arrived here," Reed said, "but I remember you. I know who you are and I know you will make the best of things. This time is home now. You *will* adjust."

120

Decker gave her head a little shake, still not looking at him, but her expression changed, her eyes narrow and her mouth drawn tight.

"You said you don't remember much about your life before the Breach brought you here?" she asked, her tone interrogative.

"That's right," Reed answered.

"Maybe I can help you fill in the gaps," Decker said, "starting with your real name."

Reed did not respond at once. Over the last sixty years, he would not have expected to feel fear at such an offer, but here it was. By now he had gone more than half his life as Doc Reed. He had wed Mary Sullivan and now had a son, daughter-in-law and grandson.

"No," Doc said. Decker shifted her gaze back to him, her expression alone telling him she did not understand. He went on, "But I thank you, Sergeant. There was a time I wanted to know. I thought it would drive me insane not knowing. Things have come back to me over time, small jigsaw pieces of memory, like your name when I first saw you again. Maybe my own name will return in such a fashion on its own, but believe me when I tell you that even if I knew, it's not who I am anymore."

Decker appeared to get it.

"It comforts me, though, to know that *you* will remember it," Reed said, "That *someone* out there will remember."

* * *

The middle-aged woman in the pink bonnet behind the table gave Charles Winstone a bright smile as she filled his tin cup with apple cider.

"You're new to Orchard Bend, aren't you?" she asked.

"We're just passing through," Winstone replied.

"You picked a good day to be here," the woman said. "As you see, we've just been incorporated. Isn't that exciting?"

"Very much so," Winstone said, raising his cup to her in thanks. "Congratulations."

"Aunt Laura!" called a girl in her early teens as she came running up to the table.

The woman in the pink bonnet turned around to face the girl.

"What is it, Frances?" Aunt Laura asked.

"Matilda, Janey and Gertrude and I were going to go down to the river and put our feet in the shallows," Frances said.

"That's fine, Frances, you don't need my permission for that," Aunt Laura said, looking to Winstone and rolling her eyes.

"I know, but can you hold onto my cross?" Frances asked, reaching behind her neck to undo the chain. "I don't want to lose it in the river."

"Of course, of course," Aunt Laura said, the exasperation leaving her face, returning it to its pleasant demeanour.

Frances pulled the shining silver cross out from under her dress, re-latched it and handed it to her aunt, who tucked it into her apron pocket.

"Thank you," Frances said as she turned and dashed away, joining her friends. Together they hurried away from the picnic.

Charles cast about for Kenna and saw her walking with the old man Reed. The pair reached the shade of trees near the small cemetery and disappeared around the corner.

"So where do you hail from?" Aunt Laura asked as Charles sipped his cider.

"Black Barrel," Charles said, trying not to let the tension show in his voice.

"That's pretty far south of here, isn't it?" Aunt Laura asked.

"Southeast, yes," Charles said, his pleasantness now somewhat feigned, "and it has been quite a ride, I must say. This cider, though, pretty well makes the journey worth it."

"Made locally from the McCabe Orchard," Aunt Laura said, beaming at the chance to impart some local knowledge upon this newcomer. "You probably saw it as you drove into town. The family's home sits on the top of the hill overlooking the orchard."

"Yes," Charles said, "quite the sight, both that big house and the orchard. And thank you for the cider. I think I'll try some of the baked goods, they look delicious."

He stepped away from Aunt Laura's table with a wave and she waved back, happy to dispense cider to another picnicker who approached.

He moved about the lawn, keeping to himself and admiring the scene. Amid the lively music and gaiety of the whole affair, Charles felt more relaxed than he had in a long time. Yet, Kenna had brought them here for a reason.

"I can't shake this feeling," she'd told him one early April afternoon as spring set in. "West. There are answers out there and I have to travel west."

Charles didn't protest or even ask how she could know that. Kenna Decker knew a great many inexplicable things. The woman from another time and place spoke little of her world, but the morning after her arrival, after he himself stumbled into what she called the Portal to the Breach, not once did he doubt her story. Kenna had showed him her watch, a thing far removed from his own pocket watch and its workings of springs and cogs. The small glass-like contraption, only a little larger than a postage stamp, had a flexible band to keep it attached to one's wrist, but the face was what held the real wonders. Kenna could tap the flat, blank surface and bring the whole thing to life. She entered the date and the time and the watch communicated back, asking her questions in text and providing information in the same fashion. Charles did not understand its workings, but seeing a map of the area on the tiny machine and hearing its little bells and whistles, for example, left little room for disbelief.

"I could show you more, but there are no satellites in this time," Kenna told him. "And no internet. No GovNet. It's using the basic built-in mapping system as best it can."

The watch wasn't all. Kenna's clothing, the ingenious rig of straps she'd worn around her body, which collected her bevy of equipment. Its funny locking mechanisms, which you squeezed to released, and the materials used to make all of it, fibres of a substance she called 'plastic.' And her gun. A small, blocky, yet sleek and lightweight weapon that could hold more bullets hidden in the grip than any pistol he'd ever heard of. Charles

123

had witnessed her disassemble and clean it, marvelling at the design.

No, Charles Winstone did not doubt Kenna Decker. And he would help this extraordinary woman get home if he could.

* * *

The girl's cries for help carried up the street as Frances came running from the direction of the river.

Leaning against the back of his covered wagon as he waited for Kenna to return from her talk with the old man, Charles heard the commotion and went to investigate. He walked from the cluster of parked wagons and buggies to the church lawn just as the girl Frances came running up the road, soaked and distraught. The nearby townsfolk went to her aid as the music stopped amid the commotion.

"AUNT LAURA! ANYONE! HELP!" Frances cried. "JANEY FELL IN THE WATER!"

"Where?!" asked a man in a wide-brimmed hat wearing his Sunday best, as his wife tried to calm the girl.

"The bridge! They're at the bridge!" Frances gasped, unable to catch her breath.

A crowd began to form on the road and the man took off on foot in the direction of the east bridge, with several other men following.

"Where's your doctor?" Winstone asked the woman tending to Frances.

"He went back to his office," another man said from the lawn, pointing in the opposite direction of the river.

"She fell and hit her head on a rock and floated away," Frances said, pale and sobbing. "We pulled her out of the water, but she wasn't breathing!"

Charles had heard enough and ran to the bridge himself at a full sprint. Up ahead, he could see the men gathered around the girl. The man in his best Sunday suit pulled off his jacket and was warming the unconscious girl with it. Off to the side, her two friends stood still, holding hands, watching. A man stood with them, whom Charles thought to be one of their fathers. Another man, distraught and calling out the unconscious girl's name, knelt at her side on the ground holding her hand.

Charles reached the scene and hunkered next to Janey, who was soaked and pale, her lips an ashen blue. Her father started sobbing.

"Give me room, I'm a doctor," Charles said.

A bystander pulled Janey's father away to let Winstone work. Charles pulled the jacket off the girl and started pressing on her breast bone in slow, regular compressions.

"Lift her legs up, bent at the knees, hold them there," he said to the owner of the jacket. The man did as told and Charles stopped his chest compressions, worried that no water had come forth from her lungs. He examined the head wound through her thick, wet hair. The rock had split the girl's scalp, but had not done any greater damage that he could see.

Charles put his mouth to Janey's and gave a strong breath of air.

"What's he doing? Stop!" shouted Janey's father behind him.

Charles heard the man restraining him say, "He's helping her, Terence, just let him. He's breathing for her."

Still no result, so Charles started again pushing on her chest. More townsfolk came running.

"Sheriff!" cried one of Janey's friends.

"He says he's a doctor," said the man holding up the girl's legs.

A man with stubble on his hard features, a six-shooter on his hip and a badge on his vest knelt across from Charles, looking down at Janey.

"How is she?" the sheriff asked.

"If we can get the water out of her lungs..." Charles said, glancing up. The sheriff locked eyes with him. Charles broke the gaze and looked to the man standing with the girls. A woman had joined him, her arms around both of Janey's friends. Charles nodded to the man, "You there, I need you to take over for me."

The man hesitated, but his wife said, "Go, Bradley, for Janey's sake!"

Bradley knelt next to Charles.

"Just do what I'm doing," Charles said. Then he took his hands away and Bradley took over.

"Your name's Winstone, isn't it?" the sheriff said, his voice so low only Charles heard it. "I know you."

The sheriff kept his gaze fixed on Charles, who moved to Janey's head. Before he could tell Bradley to stop so that he could try breathing into the girl's mouth again, a voice called out, "No, you're doing it wrong!"

Kenna Decker rushed to Charles' side and put her hand on his shoulder.

"Let me," she told him, her expression serious. He nodded. She looked at Bradley, "You have to go faster. And harder. Press right down. 1, 2, 3, 4!"

"I can't, I'll break her ribs, or—!" Bradley said, but Decker pushed him off.

"I'll do it," she said, ignoring the collective gasps and mutterings of the bystanders. As she positioned herself over Janey and began the most rapid, hard compressions Charles had ever seen, he rose to his feet.

The sheriff drew his gun and levelled it at Charles, who for a moment didn't even comprehend what was happening.

"You stay right there, *Doctor*," the sheriff said, his eyes narrow and unflinching.

"What...?" Charles said, his voice weak with disbelief.

"The name's Anderson," the sheriff said, "You killed my wife, *Doctor* Winstone."

When Janey gagged and coughed and expelled more water than most would think could fill a pair of lungs, Sheriff Anderson didn't move. Charles moved toward the girl and Anderson all but growled, "Don't you touch that girl."

Decker rolled Janey onto her side as the girl coughed and flailed. The man holding her feet let go and Janey's father and mother rushed forward.

"O'Toole, Barrow, place this man into custody on my authority," Anderson said, not taking his stern eyes off of Charles. The two men each grabbed Charles by an arm, but he put up no resistance.

126

"What is this all about?" Decker protested as Janey's parents held their soaked and crying daughter.

"Miss, your *doctor* friend here is guilty of killing a whole lot of innocent people," Anderson said. "I'd be doing the world a favour if I put him down right here and now."

"He was convicted of this crime?" Decker asked, looking from the sheriff to Charles. Next to them, Janey's father carried his daughter to a nearby wagon.

"No, he wasn't," Anderson said, "but they took his license. He's no doctor anymore and I can arrest him for claiming he was."

"He did say that," Bradley muttered and the other men who heard it all agreed.

"I was trying to help, there wasn't any time—" Charles said.

"Shut it," Anderson said, his gun still aimed at Charles.

Decker, her expression calm and even, stepped between Anderson and Charles, right in the path of his gun.

"Sheriff, he and I just saved that girl's life," Decker said, unflinching, "So you're not going to shoot him and you're not going to arrest him. He's going to leave this town and you'll never see him back here again."

"That isn't going to happen," Anderson said.

"James Anderson!" said the aged but powerful voice of Doc Reed. "Holster your weapon, *right now.*"

Anderson hesitated as Reed shambled forward with the help of his cane, standing quite tall in spite of it. Flanked by his son and his niece, the town elder carried himself with such dignity and strength that Anderson lowered his weapon and slid it back in his holster. Decker held her ground.

The sheriff's jaw clenched as he spoke.

"Mr Reed, you knew my Emiline," he said, "this man killed her."

"An epidemic killed her," Reed said, his tone firm, but edged with compassion.

"Because this man is a drunkard," Anderson said, pointing at Charles. "He was supposed to be treating those people but he went off to find a bottle somewhere. He was stone drunk when

I claimed her body. Afterwards, I read what happened. He was held accountable. That's why he's not a doctor anymore."

Charles dropped his head to his chest, his eyes stinging with tears. O'Toole and Barrow still held his arms.

"Let him go," Reed said to the men. They did as they were told.

Free, Charles covered his face with his hands and wiped the tears away.

Anderson approached him, making no effort to hide his anger and contempt. He stood a foot taller than Decker, but still she held her ground between him and Winstone.

"You're going to walk back to your wagon, mister," the sheriff said to Charles, "and then you're going to get on it and you're going to ride far, *far* away. If I ever set eyes on you again—"

"James," Reed said, reining the sheriff in.

Anderson held his hard stare on Charles for a moment longer and then turned away with a grunt of disgust. The sheriff walked down the short hill to the riverbank and knelt by the rushing water.

The townsfolk splintered into smaller groups, some hurrying away from the site of the afternoon's drama, while others stood around talking amongst themselves, casting furtive glances in Charles' direction. He noticed that Bradley and his wife had taken Janey's friends away at some point.

Decker saw him looking at the spot where the girls had stood and she took his hand in hers.

"Hey," Kenna said, her voice soft now, gentle, "take a deep breath."

Charles did, letting it fill his lungs, then letting it out in a long exhale.

Doc Reed came over to them.

"Kenna, you two had better get on your way," Reed said. He put a boney hand on her shoulder and leaned close to her, speaking with a wise sort of sadness, "I wish things were different, but they aren't."

"I know," Kenna said. Charles saw her eyes tearing up now, too.

"Seeing you again, though," Reed smiled, his weathered features becoming more pronounced. Yet he somehow looked much younger than his ninety years as he said, "It was a gift."

"I'll come back," Kenna said, "when things have settled down."

Doc just smiled and said, "At ease, Decker. Dismissed."

"You aren't my commanding officer, doctor," Decker said, shaking her head.

Reed's smile faltered.

"No," he said, "no, I wasn't."

"Kenna," Charles said, his throat tight with emotion, "it's time we got a move on."

"Yes, you're right," Decker said, looking down to the river, where Anderson still knelt hunkered, head down.

They turned to go, but Reed snagged Charles' arm with his firm grip.

"We all have a past, young man," Reed said. The old man's eyes flicked about Winstone's face, looking for something. Then, satisfied, Reed relaxed, saying, "You did a good thing today."

Charles wanted to say thank you, but couldn't. He just wanted to get far away from Sheriff Anderson and the gawking stares of the people of Orchard Bend.

Charles and Kenna left the river's shore by the bridge and walked up the road to the church lawn in silence, where more of the townsfolk watched them, speaking in hushed tones amongst themselves. Charles went to the front of his wagon to untie his horses from their post.

"Mister?" said a girl's voice behind him. He turned around with a start. A girl in a pale blue bonnet approached, holding something in her hands. Charles recognized her as one of Janey's two friends from the river.

"Yes," Charles said, his voice cracking.

"You dropped this," she said, holding up his tin cup. Charles didn't remember dropping it at all. All he could do was look at it in the girl's hands, the sunlight bouncing off the weathered metal. When the girl realized he wasn't about to take it from her, she stepped forward, saying, "I cleaned it off for you."

Charles blinked, then took the cup from her. Kenna came around the post where the horses were tied and saw the young woman.

"Gertrude," Kenna said.

"You saved Janey's life," Gertrude said. "Both of you. She's with Doctor Moore right now."

"Gertrude, best let these folks be on there way," called out a man who looked to be her father. He kept his distance, tipping his hat to Kenna, but keeping his eyes fixed on Charles.

Gertrude turned to go, but after a few steps spun around and ran up to Kenna and Charles.

"I don't care what Sheriff Anderson or anyone says," Gertrude exclaimed, her eyes wet and her face blushing. "Thank you for saving her—"

"Gertrude!" her father barked.

"—God bless you both," Gertrude said, smiling through her tears as she clasped each of their hands before running back to her father. Charles thought the man might scold her, but when she ran to him, he just put his arm around her and she him. They walked away across the lawn and Charles watched, feeling somewhat dazed and light-headed.

That's when he saw the shadow.

He blinked and rubbed his eyes, thinking the sun and clouds and stress might be playing with his vision, but there was no mistaking the faint shape standing on the lawn. Gertrude and her father walked past it and the shadow turned.

Charles took several steps forward, horrified, but he knew he'd seen something like this before, that morning on the plain after Kenna had arrived, when he'd seen the shadowy shapes that looked like people. And the grey world in which they lived. The Breach, Kenna has called it, the passage through which she'd travelled to get here.

Decker appeared at his side. He watched the shadow on the church lawn turn as Gertrude and her father passed by it.

It's watching them, Winstone thought. *But they can't see it.*

"Charles, it really is time we left," Kenna said. "That sheriff wasn't fooling around."

130

The shadow turned the direction of Kenna's voice and despite the warm spring air, Charles felt a chill.

Can it see us? Charles wondered.

"What is it, Charles?" Kenna asked, now following his gaze. "What's wrong?"

To his relief, the shadow turned away from Charles and Kenna and moved away. As it did, its already translucent form became less distinct. Then it disappeared altogether, trailing after Gertrude and her father as they left the picnic. Charles guessed that they were going to check on Janey.

"You're right," Charles said to Kenna, "it's time to go."

The two crossed the bridge, driving east and out of town. They rode past the McCabe Orchard and saw the McCabes' large house on the hill with the afternoon sun behind them. Kenna sat next to him and wrapped her arm around his as he drove. Later, as they made camp far past the town's limits, they would talk by the fire about Janey's near-drowning and Kenna's effective technique which saved her. They would not talk about Kenna's visit with Doc Reed, nor about the events that led to Charles losing his medical license. Those subjects would still feel too close, too fraught with emotion to discuss. However, sitting on the wagon under a blue sky dotted with white clouds, the newly incorporated Town of Orchard Bend growing more distant behind them, Charles found himself not thinking about any of those things.

The shadow man occupied his thoughts as the landscape of farms changed to wilder backcountry around them. Charles felt no lack of relief in putting ground between themselves and such a spectre, but he wondered with some dread what business it had with Gertrude and her family.

20

The Ledger of Owen McCabe

The Orchard Herald, March 15, 1887
ORCHARD BEND IN MOURNING
by Thomas Buchanan, Editor

On Saturday past, the 12th of the month, Mrs. Gertrude McCabe, wife of Maxwell McCabe, mother of Master Owen McCabe and predeceased by son Henry, lost her short battle with a cancer of the lungs and died peacefully in Sutter Grove. Born Gertrude Eavan Kiley A.D. 1849 in Orchard Bend, she was the only child of late ranchers Aidan and Anna Kiley.

A benefactor of the town for many years alongside her husband, Gertrude McCabe was much-loved for her philanthropy and dedication to the well-being of Orchard Bend.

The McCabe family is expected to return to Orchard Bend this week for a private service.

* * *

"I'm so sorry," said Rebecca Clarke.

She stood before Emery Dale silhouetted in the cabin's doorway, the bottom of her dress fluttering in the cold breeze below her winter coat.

Dale stared at the short obituary on the front page of the *Herald*, no longer reading the words, but unable to look away.

"I should go," Rebecca said, fidgeting with the pail that held her books. "My mother asks a lot of questions when I come home later than she expects. I let her think I'm slow to walk home with Billy..."

She trailed off, looking at the freshly snared rabbits hanging by the door next to Dale's walking stick.

"Thank you for delivering this news," Dale said, still holding the paper, but letting it drop to her side. "How did Miss Adelaide take it?"

"Quite hard, I reckon," Rebecca said, shuffling on her heels and looking at the floor. "She didn't want to show it, but most of us could see it there, just underneath."

Rebecca looked behind her out the door and then back at Dale.

"I best be off, Sheriff Dale," she said, not hiding the urgency in her voice.

"Of course," Dale said.

Rebecca left without closing the door. Dale stood in the cold air, her breath turning to crystals as she looked out across the snow-covered woods around the isolated cabin. She went to the doorway and leaned against it, taking in the yellow streaks of clouds against the darkening blue of the late afternoon sky. Wrapping her arms around her, still holding the newspaper, Dale slid down the doorframe and curled her knees to her chest, tears flowing unchecked down her cheeks.

21

March 17, 1887
Orchard Bend

"Miss Adelaide?" echoed Ruby Sumner's hesitant voice in the vast space of the grand hall.

Rose Adelaide looked up from the lesson plans on her desk to find her students all regarding her with quizzical, amused expressions. Several of her pupils loosed quiet chuckles and Rose gave a sharp "Ahem!" to restore order.

"Yes, Ruby?" Rose asked.

"I think it's after the bell," Ruby said, looking from her teacher to her classmates around her, who nodded in agreement. She sat in the second row of plain tables and chairs, all clustered between the tall columns in the middle of the Town Hall's makeshift schoolhouse.

Rose consulted her watch.

"My, yes, you're quite right, Ruby," Rose said, standing up. The children shuffled in their seats and started packing away their readers. Rose spoke over the growing din, "A few things before you leave: Senior scholars, remember to study for tomorrow's history test. Chapters five, six and seven. Junior scholars, your themes are due next Monday. If you haven't started already, it's wise to not leave it all to the last minute. Class dismissed."

The sound of chairs scraping on the floor and the excited chatter of the students filled the Town Hall's grand space. After the snowstorm left the old church in ruins, Rose and the school board asked the Council of Aldermen to relocate classes there. The Town Hall had a number of unassigned rooms and offices, but an inspection by Rose showed them to be too small to accommodate a school, leaving the grand hall as the only option until a new structure could be erected. The council did not anticipate any such work being done until the summer.

Rose crossed the grand hall to the lobby entrance ahead of her pupils. As was part of her routine, Rose helped the younger students with their winter boots and scarves.

After she bid a cheery good afternoon to the last student that day, Rose let her smile drop away. She crossed her arms against the frosty air that had bled in from outside and walked back to her desk. The hard soles of her boots clicked on the wooden floor. The sound moved around the room in a way that haunted the space, climbing high into the ceiling above her and staying there longer than welcome.

Rose stopped in the middle of the room, letting the echo drift away. From the south-facing windows high in the walls, she saw the blue late afternoon sky. A thick, grey cloud rolled into view, darkening the room around her. Rose straightened the tables and chairs, went to her desk, packed her books, papers and supplies, then donned her winter attire and crossed the long, empty hall to the lobby. The lock to the double doors of the grand hall gave a hollow rattle as she turned her key. Slipping it back into her pocket, she felt the engraved initials "R.A. Schoolteacher" along the length of the key, put there by Mr McManus, the smithy. He had made the key for her at the behest of the Town Hall's caretaker, Mr Field, who had grown somewhat weary of locking and unlocking the hall five days a week.

"Make one for Reverend Thomas while you're at it," Mr Field was reported to have said, "He'll need it for Sunday services."

The cold bit at her nose and cheeks the moment she stepped outside. Rose pulled her scarf over her face and descended the steps to the path etched across the snow in the Town Hall lawn. Despite the cold, Rose stopped to feel the sun on her face as it reappeared from behind the clouds. It provided little in the way of warmth, but Rose moved her scarf down nonetheless and closed her eyes against it.

The breeze picked up and Rose felt flecks of icy snow dab her cheeks. The wind shifted about her and she opened her eyes, blinking against the crystals swirling across her vision, wetting her eyes.

And then she caught her breath.

For the briefest instant, Rose saw the form of Laura O'Malley in the glittering snowflakes before her. Rose couldn't mistake Laura's kind, open face and slight frame looking back at her.

The vision lasted but a second or two, and when it vanished as the snow dispersed, Rose rubbed her eyes with a mittened hand.

"Miss Adelaide," a voice called out to her.

Waving from the street, Eloise Langford stood arm in arm with her mother, Kate Picton.

"Hello, Ellie, Mrs Picton," Rose said, greeting them where the path ended at the edge of the lawn and giving her eyes another rub with her mitten.

"Is anything the matter?" Mrs Picton asked.

"Oh, well," Rose said, blinking, "I'm afraid some snow got in my eye and now my eyes won't stop watering."

Before Rose had finished her explanation, Mrs Picton snapped a handkerchief from her coat pocket and was handing it to the schoolteacher. Rose thanked her and wiped her eyes.

"Doesn't it just seem like this winter won't ever let up?" Ellie asked, tightening her dark blue scarf to her chin as the wind shifted again. Rose recognized it as the same scarf her former student had worn to school.

"Seems most of the continent has been buried, from what I hear," Mrs Picton said, shaking her head, "Dreadful for the ranchers and cattlemen. Just dreadful."

"What brings you both into town," Rose asked, giving the handkerchief back to Mrs Picton.

"My father arranged to pick up Dr Shaw's horse from the Statlers today," Ellie said, frowning.

"Dr Shaw's horse?" Rose asked, not understanding.

"Yes," Ellie said, "You see, the Statlers actually *owned* the horse, but they agreed to loan it to Dr Shaw in exchange for him not charging them for his doctoring services."

"I see," Rose said, giving a slow nod, "and now your father is buying the horse from them?"

"The horse is getting on in years and they're asking a fair price," Ellie said, taking Rose's arm as they walked north. The three women locked arms to keep their balance on the uneven snow-covered ground. Ellie went on, "Pa says it's a real bargain. After hearing that the horse made its own way back to the Statler livery—and my word, that was an awful snowstorm that took Dr Shaw. Tragic—Well, Pa says any animal that does that still has a good many years left in her."

As they left the Town Hall behind them, Rose glanced back at the spot where she imagined she'd seen Laura O'Malley. She resisted the urge to cross herself, lest she draw questions from Ellie and her mother that she didn't want to answer.

They reached Church Street and found a ragged line of townsfolk gathered there. People dotted the street in both directions.

"What in heaven's name is going on?" Mrs Picton asked, but neither Ellie nor Rose had an answer for her.

When Rose saw the McCabes' shiny black coach clatter down the street toward them, all at once she knew what was going on. Her stomach knotted and she wanted to be ill, but didn't let herself look away. She felt Ellie's hand take her own and squeeze it.

Mr Burke held the reins. Inside the coach, Rose saw a gaunt Maxwell McCabe with his surviving son Owen on his lap. In the scant seconds she witnessed him pass by, Rose thought McCabe had lost weight. Too much weight, in fact, but perhaps that was simply fatigue. The man sat looking straight ahead, oblivious to the onlookers watching him pass by.

Owen looked from one side of the coach to the other and back. His red cheeks shined from tears, but he didn't appear to be crying in the moment he looked at Rose. He made eye contact, but Rose wasn't certain he even registered her or any of the people on the street. Going on only eight years old, the burden of death would be too much for a boy his age to carry, Rose mused.

The McCabes' coach trundled past and Rose watched it go, then turned to see the hearse following behind it. The driver Edgar Allman held the horse's reins in one gloved hand while the other kept the wind from taking his black hat from his head. With his ears and face red against the elements, Rose thought the undertaker must be freezing during this slow journey from the railway station, but the man's expression betrayed no discomfort while performing his solemn duty. Around her, the men on the street removed their hats and many onlookers crossed themselves. The splatters of dirt and snow on the windows of the hearse did little to obscure the sight of Gertrude McCabe's coffin inside.

"Miss Adelaide?" Ellie said, but Rose did not turn her gaze away from the funeral procession. Ellie then pulled at Rose's grip, "Miss Adelaide, you're squeezing my hand."

Startled, Rose let go.

"Oh, Ellie, I'm so sorry," Rose said.

"It's quite alright," Ellie said, massaging her hand. "A sobering thing as this affects a person."

The hearse made its slow progress down the road and the townsfolk remained still, doing nothing more than watch it drive away.

"Curious thing," Kate Picton said. "No wake and only a private service. It's quite unlike Maxwell McCabe."

Ellie nodded.

"The suddenness of her passing and it being so soon after their son," Ellie said. "I expect such a wealth of tragedy could drive a man to reclusion. Worse, he has to wait until the spring thaw to bury both of them."

"For whatever comfort it's worth, mother and son will rest side by side now," Kate said, as the gathered townsfolk went back about their business. "May it be in peace. Come now, Ellie, we best hurry to meet your father. He ought be finished inspecting that horse. Always a pleasure, Miss Adelaide."

"Likewise," Rose said.

They said their goodbyes and Ellie and her mother continued north, rounding the corner at Reed's General Store and out of sight. Rose turned and walked east down Church Street, not questioning why, but following the route of the funeral procession. She had intended to stop in at Reed's herself before returning to her cottage, but now something compelled her otherwise.

Ahead, Rose could see the McCabes' coach and Mr Allman's hearse. They reached their destination and came to a stop. Rose stepped up her pace on the slick boardwalk, careful not to lose her footing.

She caught up to them with little trouble and stopped a short distance away. Nothing remained of the church that had also doubled as her schoolhouse except the stone receiving vault. Snow now blanketed the property. The vault reminded Rose of a solitary gravestone in the empty lot and any other day she would have avoided going there.

Mr Allman climbed down from the hearse and walked to the McCabes' coach. Next to it stood Mr Burke, the two Statler brothers, Mr McManus and Mr Griesbach, who stamped his feet in the snow and clutched his coat tight around him. The men exchanged words, then Mr Allman went to the receiving vault and out of view behind it. When he returned, Rose saw him put his large key ring in his pocket. He passed by the men gathered near the coach and said something to them. They made their way to the hearse while Mr Allman knocked on the coach door.

"It's time, Mr McCabe," he said.

Rose didn't hear a response, by the door opened and Maxwell stepped out. He reached back in and lifted Owen out. The boy looked around and saw Rose. His gaze made her think he might draw attention to her, but Owen did nothing, looking away a moment later. Maxwell fixed the boy's winter hat and then nodded to Mr Allman. As Maxwell led his son to the receiving vault, the other six men went to the hearse. Mr Allman directed them in a hushed voice, too low for Rose to quite make out, but his gestures showed his instructions to the pallbearers. He glanced over at Mr McCabe and then turned and opened the back of the hearse.

It wasn't until Rose saw Gertrude's coffin lifted by the six men that she understood what drove her to witness this.

"I hope you can forgive her now, my friend," Rose said. Her throat tightened and her eyes grew wet, but she made no move to wipe them, only blinking the tears loose so that they rolled down her cheeks.

Carrying Gertrude's coffin, the pallbearers reached the vault, passed Maxwell and Owen, and moved to the rear of the building out of view. The McCabes followed and Rose crossed herself. She did not want to be there when the funeral party re-emerged, so decided to take to her leave. The horses gave her a disinterested glance as she walked past the coach and the empty hearse.

With no boardwalk that far down the street and no shovelled path, Rose tramped through the snow, wondering if she might have been wiser to take the longer way around back to her cottage, a route more well-travelled.

Rose had made it a dozen yards when she heard the panicked whinny of the horses behind her. Surprised, the schoolteacher spun around to see Mr Allman's horse rear up and pull hard on the reins tied to the post. The McCabes' horse backed way, also spooked, its eyes wide with fright.

"Miss Adelaide!"

Sheriff Turnbull rode up next to her, a hand on the brow of his thick wool hat to shield his eyes from the sun. His own horse also seemed restless when he brought the animal to a stop.

Mr Allman's horse whinnied again, whipping his head from side to side, straining the leather reins.

"Sheriff—" Rose started to say, but the Allman stag reared up again, pulling the post's rail loose.

"Damn thing's going to tear that post apart and bolt!" Turnbull said. "Get off the road, Rose!"

Mr Allman and the pallbearers reappeared just then, running hard through the snow toward the horses. The McCabes' mare continued her efforts to back away, but had nowhere to go with the coach boxing her in. She kicked up plumes of snow and dirt in her struggle. Before the men could reach them, the Allman stag broke free.

Just as predicted, the horse bolted, hearse and all.

And it ran straight towards Rose and Sheriff Turnbull.

The sheriff kicked his mount forward. Rose dropped her bag and hiked up her skirt in one motion, though her mittens did not provide much of a grip. She lost no time charging out of the path of the horse, kicking up snow herself, until her footing gave way and she dropped to the ground. She scrambled forward, but heard the horse and hearse clatter behind her. Rose rolled onto her back in time to see the two roar past her, right over the spot where she'd been standing mere seconds before.

Sheriff Turnbull raced after the horse, pursuing it down the street. Rose got to her feet and took a few shaky steps back to the road, her heart pounding. She glanced back to see that the men had gained control of the McCabe mare and Wayne Statler had started running in her direction, pointing past her and yelling, "He's headed for the river!"

Rose turned just in time to see the hearse reach the end of the road, hit the river's embankment and topple out of view.

The sheriff's horse stood rider-less a few yards from where the hearse crashed.

Rose started running down the street toward the river, unsure what she'd find when she got there. When she got closer, Rose made out the unmoving form of the sheriff lying in the snow. Wayne Statler sprinted past her and Rose staggered to a walk, out of breath and holding her side.

"Dear Lord, let him be alright," Rose prayed between heavy breaths.

Wayne reached the sheriff and knelt by his side. Rose started running again, a sick feeling in her stomach as Turnbull, lying on his back, still had not moved. She ran harder than she thought she could have and somehow didn't lose her footing. Wayne reached down and took the sheriff's hand and, to Rose's astonishment, Turnbull sat up. She slowed to a stop and knelt on the other side of him.

"I saw you go off your horse, Sheriff," Wayne said. "That was some fall. Is anything broken?"

"You need to see the doctor," Rose said.

Turnbull clutched at his ribs, grimacing.

"My ribs," the sheriff. "It's still hard to breath."

Wayne looked to Rose.

"Stay with him, Miss Adelaide," he said. "Sheriff, I'll ride your horse to fetch the doctor."

Turnbull only nodded, wincing, a tear of pain running down the old ragged scar tissue that covered his cheek.

Wayne went to the sheriff's horse, climbed onto the saddle and looked back at Rose.

"Go," she said, and Wayne Statler rode off. Rose watched him go until Turnbull took her hand.

"Idiot thing to do," he groaned. "Thought I could stop it before—"

He winced again, his breathing shallow. Rose suspected he was right, that he'd broken some of his ribs.

"Don't try to talk now, Sheriff," Rose said.

"Call me Reggie," Turnbull said. "All the pretty ladies do."

"*Sheriff*, it's best you spare yourself the effort of talking," Rose said.

"It'll be easier to breathe if I stand up," Turnbull said, bending forward with great difficulty and bringing a knee up.

"Nonsense, you're in no such condition," Rose protested.

"I'll freeze to death," Turnbull said, grunting with each movement as he forced himself up, holding Rose's hand for balance, "if I have to sit... in the snow... any longer."

He turned to look back to where the street ended at the river. The straight lines made by the hearse's wheels framed the tracks of the stag, and both pointed to the stone foundation of the old wooden bridge that had years before spanned the rushing water.

Turnbull took an uncertain step, clutching Rose's hand, and she had a mind to tell him to not try to walk, but something in his pained expression said in no uncertain terms that he meant to do this with or without her assistance. So she said nothing and helped him make his way to the river's edge. They stood on the stone foundation of the old bridge and took in the carnage below, the hearse's broken wheels were twisted on their axles, its windows cracked and shattered. And the dying horse lay bloody and struggling beneath the hearse's wrecked carriage, half submerged in the river.

Turnbull drew his revolver and took aim at the animal. His gloved hand trembled, but he pulled the trigger.

The round sent up a puff of smoke near the horse's head, missing it by more than half a foot.

"Damn," Turnbull said, dropping his arm to his side, against the broken ribs, "The pain makes it hard to get a clean shot."

"I'll do it," Rose said.

"No, we'll wait for someone else," Turnbull said. "Statler will be back soon."

The horse let out a pained whinny.

"We have to do it now," Rose said. "I'll steady your hand. You pull the trigger."

Turnbull raised the gun again and aimed with both hands. Rose took off her mitten and put her bare hand under his, feeling the soft leather of his gloves and the cold bottom of the grip in her palm. The tremble in his hands from the pain eased and his aim stilled.

Turnbull pulled the trigger and the shot hit its mark, putting the horse out of its misery.

* * *

When she reached her cottage, Rose wanted nothing more than to draw a bath, pour herself some hot cocoa and relax. Opening the front door, the light of the pale dusky sky drew a narrow band across the floor of the dark interior. That's when she saw the folded paper on the floor. She did not pick it up right away, instead regarding it for several seconds as she stood in the doorway. When the air caught the paper and sent it sliding away, Rose followed it, closing the door behind her. She dropped her snow-covered bag and lit the lantern on the table by the kitchen. She retrieved the paper and sat at the table, not even taking off her shoes. Turning the paper over in her hand, Rose discovered the dried, flat wax that sealed the letter shut.

Rose broke the seal, unfolded the paper and began reading.

I am alright.

I heard about our friend and wept. There's nothing to be done for her now, so we must mourn and make our peace with everything that happened.

You are in my thoughts every day, please know that. And please understand that I did what I did for a reason. There's somewhere I need to go, but first I need something from you: the wooden box I entrusted to your care.

You'll find a loose stone in the side of the bench beneath the cedars by the cemetery and you can leave the box safely inside. Don't wait there for me to retrieve it, but trust that it will be collected in due course. If you are unable to place it there tonight or tomorrow morning, please continue to keep it safe with you.

We will see one another again soon.

Yours Always.

Even absent a signature, Rose knew Emery had penned the letter.

"Clever, darling," Rose smiled in the warm lantern light. "Always so clever."

She brought the letter close to her face, closed her eyes and breathed in, hoping to detect some residual scent of Emery. Whether she picked up on a real odour of burnt wood or not, Rose couldn't be sure, but she allowed herself to imagine Emery putting pencil to paper somewhere safe and warm, writing something more than just a letter by firelight, reaching out to Rose from her dark exile, hoping the message would be received and understood.

Rose knew Emery would not want the letter to incriminate the schoolteacher if found by anyone else, so had not signed it, nor left any detail identifying herself as the author. Rose recognized the tablet paper as the kind used by her students.

Of course Emery knew I would spot that, Rose thought.

The errand with the wooden box gave her pause, however, not because she was unable or unwilling to follow Emery's instruction, but because the idea of Emery risking capture to retrieve it was foolhardy. And Emery Dale was anything but foolhardy.

Rose re-read the letter and one sentence stood out:

> *Don't wait there for me to retrieve it, but trust that it will be collected in due course.*

Rose put the letter down and leaned back, looking at the lantern's flame through tired eyes.

You have an accomplice, Emery, Rose thought. *Clever woman, indeed.*

22

March 18, 1887
Orchard Bend

A red dawn bathed the town.

It seeped through a crack in the window's shutter, casting a thin line on the floor of the room, lighting the glass of the whiskey bottle beside the bed and drew a line across the face of the sleeping Deputy Allen Green. As the light grew brighter, he brought a hand to his face. The pounding in his head made falling back to sleep impossible. To make the situation even more unpleasant, he had to relieve himself something fierce. Rolling out of bed onto unsteady legs, he crossed the cold wood floor to his bedpan and did his business, leaning against the wall, head down and eyes closed. Once finished, he didn't move, didn't open his eyes, not even when his bare feet began to tingle from the draft coming in under the door.

"Today will be different," Green told himself, his mouth dry. He repeated the words two more times, hoping God or someone would hear him.

Hell, there's a Father, Son and Holy Ghost, so each can have one, he thought.

That little ritual done, Green went to his dresser and looked in the mirror. The dark bags under his eyes had faded, so maybe bedding down early last night had been worth it. Not that it had been his choice, come to that. After Turnbull's accident the day before, the new doctor, Faraday, had ordered the sheriff off duty, which left Green as the only active lawman in town.

It had been on him to clean up the mess of the McCabe funeral. No one there had any clue what set the horses off. The one that bolted damn near ran over the schoolteacher and damn near killed the sheriff. It had taken a team of men an hour and a pair of wagons to get the hearse out of the riverbed. It had taken another hour to haul the body of the horse away. Most of the work had to be done after dark by lantern light.

Green had wanted to help, to get right in and get his hands dirty, but the way men looked at him, snickering under their breath, he felt it best to hang back and hold one of the lanterns. When at last the gruesome task was done, the men had made their way to Sully's for a drink. Green bought the first round, but didn't stay to drink with them, instead disappearing up to his room above the tavern where his own bottle of whiskey awaited. There hadn't been much left, however, and when he emptied it he couldn't bring himself to go downstairs to Sully's to buy another one. Other nights he had done just that, but each time he felt the accusing eyes of the patrons watching him. Even Sully, or his wife Daisy, would give him a look, something like disappointment. Their daughter Irene, would give him a smile, but Green knew she wasn't working that night, so no, he had not gone down to restock on alcohol, instead opting for bed and an early night.

His stomach growling, Green retrieved the basin of fresh water from the hall and washed himself, looking out the window to watch the sunrise. The low, thick clouds turned crimson and orange as the sun climbed behind them and vanished. It began to rain a light drizzle. He dressed, donned his gun belt and then straightened the badge on his winter coat. Hat in hand, he left his room and made his way downstairs to the tavern.

"Good morning, Deputy Green," Irene smiled as she swept around the tables.

"Good morning, Miss Sullivan," Green said, parking himself at the bar.

"We have fresh eggs from the Reeds this morning," Irene said, joining him at the bar. "And hot biscuits in the oven. We can throw on some bacon and gravy."

"I'll take some coffee with that, too," Green said. "Many thanks, Miss Sullivan."

She took his order to the kitchen and returned with two cups of hot coffee, handing him one.

"Is it true that Sheriff Turnbull's ribs will take six weeks to heal?" Irene asked, holding her own cup with both hands.

Green took a sip and nodded.

"Dr Faraday bandaged him up tight and that's about all he could do," Green said. "You can't rightly use plaster just for some ribs, so he ordered Turnbull to a spell of bed rest so he can heal up. Until he's well enough to come back to work, I suppose it's on me to keep the peace."

"I'm sure you'll manage," Irene said.

Green sipped his coffee again rather than reply. Irene left him in silence and moved to the end of the bar to polish glasses. When the kitchen bell rang, she dashed away to get Green's food for him.

Green closed his eyes, enjoying the quiet, the only sound coming from the rain that pattered the snow into muddy puddles outside.

When Irene returned, Green's stomach all but jumped at the smell of the breakfast she set down in front of him.

"I had the cook add an extra piece of bacon for you, Deputy," Irene said. "I reckon you have a long day ahead of you, being the sole lawman in town."

"Heaven help us, if that's the truth of it," said Martin Griesbach, who stood at the tavern door shaking the rain from his overcoat.

Green slammed his cup down and coffee splattered the bar, but didn't turn around to face the lawyer. Irene gave him a stern but sympathetic look that told him not to answer back.

"What can I get you, Mr Griesbach?" Irene said, moving away from the deputy and no doubt hoping to pull the lawyer's attention away.

"What he's having looks mighty fine," Griesbach said, taking a seat at a table behind Green.

"You're up awfully early this morning," Irene said with a chipper air. Green could tell she was forcing it. He took a bite of his bacon and tried to ignore the man.

"A long day awaits me," Griesbach said, his chair scraping the floor as he made himself comfortable. "Meeting a client and I expect the business will take much of the day. But that's to be expected of a man who does his job *thoroughly.*"

Irene looked at Green as she went to the kitchen, her expression telling him what he already knew, that Griesbach was sneering behind him.

I'm not turning around, Green told himself, stabbing at his eggs and taking a big mouthful. *I'm not going to do it.*

He relaxed a little at the sound of paper rustling at Griesbach's table.

Good, Green thought, *let him read his newspaper and I can eat in peace.*

Irene returned and refilled Green's cup.

"Why I'd love a cup of coffee, Miss Sullivan," Griesbach said from behind his paper. Irene rolled her eyes and poured him a cup. "Thank you, Miss Sullivan. Isn't it a pleasure to see someone who takes pride in their work, Deputy Green?"

Green swallowed his food hard, biting back the urge to answer.

"I will say that I am relieved that Sheriff Turnbull's injuries were not more serious," Griesbach went on, "Not only is he a fine, *competent* man of the law, he's the fourth sheriff to hold the post in Orchard Bend in less than a year. Two met tragic fates, God rest their souls. And the third...? Why, what did happen to the third? Deputy Green, do you recall?"

Green downed the last bite of food and chased it with coffee.

"Oh, I remember!" Griesbach said. "She *escaped* custody!"

Green stood up from the bar and slammed his empty cup down. Irene's expression again told him not to do something he'd regret.

"Thank you for a wonderful breakfast, Miss Sullivan," Green said, his back rigid and his jaw tense. "Good day to you."

She put her hands on her hips and glared at Griesbach, who sat oblivious and reading his newspaper. Green donned his hat, adjusted his badge and crossed to the tavern door.

He expected Griesbach to fire a parting shot, but the man said nothing and Green left, careful not to hurry, his pace measured.

Outside, the light rain continued. Brown patches formed on the street as the snow and ice melted away. Green stayed dry under the covered boardwalk, putting up the collar of his coat against the gusts of wind until he reached the jailhouse.

He lit the potbelly stove and sat in the chair at the desk, not bothering to take off his hat or coat. The jail cells were empty, but Green stared at the one Sheriff Dale had escaped from and gave a slight shake of his head.

"How?" he asked.

It didn't matter at this point, what was done was done and everyone knew the fault lay with him. People like Martin Griesbach would remind him every chance they got.

Green stood up and walked to the cell. He leaned against the bars, as he often had since that stormy night, and wondered how Dale had gotten out. He and Turnbull had searched her upon her arrest, even deputizing the midwife Ester Wright for the duration of the search to make quite certain that Dale had not brought any weapons or other contraband into the cell with her, contraband like lock picks or other small tools. Dale had entered the cell with nothing but the clothes on her back.

She had not used the jail's own key, which had remained untouched on its ring in Green's own pocket. Her visitors, Miss Adelaide and Dr Shaw had been supervised and not allowed to venture close to the bars. And after she'd vanished, he and Turnbull inspected the inside of the cell, looking for weaknesses, looking for any clue, but the secret did not reveal itself.

Emery Dale was simply gone.

Green slammed a fist on the crossbar of the cell and the clatter filled the jailhouse. Turnbull had at one point tried to make light of the unbelievable situation by joking that maybe Dale had been helped by spirits, like some magicians in the cities back east had claimed. Ridiculous as it sounded, it was the best answer either lawman could come up with.

How pathetic is that? Green thought.

With even the empty cell now seeming to mock him, Green had to get out of the jailhouse. Back on the boardwalk, he considered returning to Sully's, but Griesbach would in all likelihood still be there. And if he wasn't, someone else would be, ready to offer an accusing eye or a snide comment.

A wagon rolled past and Green thought about the hearse running wild the day before. With the rain thinning out, Green decided he'd ride over to the scene of the crash and check it out by the light of morning, overcast as it may be.

Taking a horse from the Statler Livery, Deputy Green trotted down Anderson Street, turned south at Reed's General Store, then east again onto Church Street. He passed the site of the old church and stopped, regarding the broken hitching post. The horizontal beam, a four-inch thick, round piece of timber, had been torn from one of its vertical supports by Allman's horse, leaving it twisted and cockeyed, pointing upwards. The nails that once held it to its post sticking out from the end.

Green made a note to find Mr Field at the Town Hall and ask him to come take care of this.

When the breeze picked up and Green put his hand on his hat to keep it from blowing away, he realized the light rain had stopped and that the sky had grown brighter. The warmer air on the cold ground created low misty swirls of vapour. Some tendrils moved across the lot and around the receiving vault, while others weaved between the cedars and the gravestones at the cemetery. Turnbull's comment came back to him, the one about spirits helping Dale escape, and Green decided then it might be best to ride on to the river.

As he approached the intersection, he spotted Miss Adelaide rounding the corner. Leather bag in hand, she moved at a brisk pace, her focus on avoiding the puddles and patches of ice and slush. Mud already speckled the hem of her dress and bottom of her coat.

Looking up, she stopped at the sight of the deputy.

"'Morning, Miss Adelaide," Green said, tipping his hat.

"Hello, Deputy," she replied with a quick smile, not slowing on her way to the Town Hall.

"Feeling alright, Miss Adelaide?" Green asked.

"Yes, I'm quite well," she answered, not looking at him.

Green looked ahead of him, in the direction of yesterday's crash at the river.

"After what happened, I thought maybe you'd be wary of walking this way to school, that's all," Green said.

Rose stopped, her gaze fixed on the ground. Green couldn't see her face beneath her bonnet.

"Thank you for your concern, Allen, but I'm fine," Miss Adelaide said. Then she added, looking up at him, "I came this way out of old habit and did not want to turn back around when I've come this far."

"Well, avoid the hitching post," Green said, tipping his hat as he started away, "It's still ripped apart and I don't want anyone getting themselves cut on those nails. Good day, Miss Adelaide."

"Good day, Deputy," she replied, continuing her trek through the melting snow.

Green rode on to the river and there sat looking at the spot where they'd cleared out the hearse and stag the night before. Some broken pieces of glass and wood littered the ground, but the rain had done a good job of melting away the bloodstained snow. If anyone came out here curious to see the aftermath, they would find little evidence, and that suited Green just fine.

The deputy turned back toward town and trotted up Church Street, watching the thin plumes of mist as they crept along the ground. Passing the old church lawn, Green slowed when he noticed Miss Adelaide sitting on the stone bench beneath the cedars. She saw him and sat up straight, wiping her eyes with a handkerchief.

Uncomfortable at interrupting his former teacher in a personal moment, Green rode on.

Gertrude McCabe, he thought, *that's why she came this way. It might even explain why she had been nearby when the horse bolted. She'd come to see her friend placed in the vault.*

So Green left the schoolteacher to grieve in peace and headed to the Town Hall to find the caretaker, Mr Field. Children would be heading to school soon and any one of them could stick themselves on those nails.

Rose Adelaide folded the damp handkerchief in her hands and watched Deputy Green trot away. She hoped her red eyes would return to normal before school began. She picked up the stone hidden behind her bag and, casting a quick look up the road, saw Green continuing on his way. She counted to sixty before replacing it in the hole in the bench, concealing Emery's wooden box inside.

Rose took one last look at the receiving vault and resisted another bout of real tears for Gertrude. She put the handkerchief away, picked up her bag and headed on to the Town Hall.

Whoever Emery had enlisted to retrieve the wooden box, they would find it in the precise spot as planned.

* * *

Word of the hearse crashing into the river did not take long to spread throughout the town. Those students who had not heard prior to coming to school were well informed by their classmates as they gathered on the lawn before Miss Adelaide rang her morning bell. The students spoke of little else, with the children of the men who had helped pull the wreckage from the riverbank enjoying the attention of their peers as they repeated all that they had heard from their fathers.

Billy Howard's father had been among that group of men, so Billy wasted little time telling Rebecca Clarke what he knew as they walked to school in the light rain.

"That's terrible, all of it," Rebecca said as they passed by the McCabe Mill on their way into town.

"Maybe Miss Adelaide will cancel school today," Billy said. "I could use the weekend to study more, you know?"

Rebecca started to reply, to scold Billy for such a selfish thought, but she herself now wondered if the crash would affect Sheriff Dale's plan. Neither she nor Rebecca had anticipated such a thing happening. Rebecca tried to sort through all the

153

possible complications, such as whether Miss Adelaide had not been able to place the wooden box in the stone bench. Or if she did, what if people gathered at site of the old church to see where the excitement had all started, preventing Rebecca from retrieving the box? What if someone decided to rest on the bench and found the box instead?

Rebecca's head swam with possibilities, few of them reassuring.

"I was only joking, you know?" Billy said after a minute's silence between them, breaking Rebecca's train of thought.

"Pardon? Oh, I'm sorry," she said. "I was thinking about Miss Adelaide. I hope she's alright."

"My dad said she had to put the horse down with the sheriff's own gun," Billy said, "but I don't believe it."

"Surely not," Rebecca said, horrified at the thought.

"She's strict and all, but I'm not even sure *I* could do that," Billy said.

On Anderson Street they passed Mr Griesbach's office and watched him lock his door and climb onto his buggy. The rain had stopped, but the dirty, melting snow would make the lawyer's journey a slow one, wherever he was going this early in the morning.

Farther on, Rebecca and Billy stopped at the Statler Livery, whose wide doors sat open. In a heap inside, past the stalls, lay the disturbing remains of Mr Allman's hearse. The sight made Rebecca nauseous.

"It's like some kind of dead animal," Billy said without a trace of humour.

Sam O'Toole, their friend and former classmate, joined them at the door of the livery.

"My dad says they can put the hearse itself on a new carriage," Sam said. "I think that's what Mr Allman plans to do."

"He'll need new windows, too," Billy said.

Rebecca didn't want to look at the ugly, broken vehicle any longer, so she started on her way again. Sam and Billy followed behind her.

"Do you miss school?" Billy asked his friend.

"A little bit," Sam said.

"We have a history test today. You can write mine for me if you want," Billy said, slapping Sam on the shoulder.

"I'm actually going to the jailhouse to see about becoming a deputy," Sam said.

Rebecca stopped and spun around.

"A deputy?!" she said. "Are you serious?"

"Yes, I am," Sam said, looking from Rebecca to Billy and back. "You don't think I should?"

"It's just..." Rebecca trailed off, throwing her hands up and letting them drop to her side in frustration. "I don't want you to get hurt. Or worse. Remember Sheriff Anderson's funeral? That wasn't even a year ago. Or Sheriff Wilson's for that matter."

"What did your parents say?" Billy asked. "You told them, haven't you?"

"My mother reacted the same way you did," Sam said to Rebecca.

"Smart woman," Rebecca said.

"But she supports it and said she'd be proud to see me wearing a badge," Sam added. "And my father, well, he just smiled as wide as he could. I think he knew I wanted to do this for a while."

Rebecca put her hands on his shoulders and fixed him her most serious look.

"If you do this, Sam O'Toole, you promise me you'll be careful," she said.

"I promise," Sam said.

Rebecca gave him the tightest hug she could, hoping it would help keep him safe.

"We should get a move on," Billy said.

Rebecca let Sam go and Billy shook his hand.

"I think you'll make a great deputy, Sammy," he said.

"Thanks, Billy," Sam said. "I told Ellie Picton—"

"Ellie *Langford* now, you mean," Rebecca corrected him.

"Yes, Ellie Langford. That still sounds strange, though," Sam said. "Anyway, I saw her and her mother yesterday and told them, too. Ellie said 'who knows, you might make sheriff someday.' And I'd actually planned to see Sheriff Turnbull yesterday, but then all that business with the horse happened and now he's laid up, so I guess I'll talk to Deputy Green."

"Good luck," Billy said.

"Remember, you promised," Rebecca said with a wag of her finger, offering a strained smile nonetheless.

"I know. And I'll be careful," Sam said.

Rebecca and Billy hurried on down the boardwalk as Sam watched them go. They rounded the corner past Reed's General Store and Rebecca looked ahead to the intersection of Church Street, wondering what they'd find when they got there. Apart from people stopping to look at the hearse in the Statler Livery, the town seemed to be going on about its usual morning activities as shops opened for business and wagons rumbled along the muddy streets.

When they reached the corner and looked east, the sight of a group of their classmates hurrying in the direction of the cemetery made Rebecca stop and shake her head. One of their friends, Quinton Reed, waved from across the street and called out, "Hey, Billy, Rebecca, are you coming?"

Billy waved back, then turned to her.

"We've got time to take a look, if you want," Billy said.

Rebecca shrugged, feeling downright sick from the knot in her stomach. She and Billy followed their friends up the street, past the millinery and the Harvest Moon hotel. They found Herman Statler by the broken hitching post at the edge of the old church lawn, recounting the tale of what had happened.

"...The stag whinnied again, heaving against the post!" he said, gesturing and pointing. It reminded Rebecca of Reverend Thomas when he would work himself up during one of his sermons. Statler's audience gasped and muttered, enthralled by his story. Rebecca saw Mr Buchanan, the owner and editor of the Orchard Herald, scribbling notes next to Herman.

She looked to the bench under the Atlas Cedars by the cemetery and let out a relieved sigh that no one was sitting on it, nor even standing near it. Rebecca wrestled with the urge to go there and retrieve Sheriff Dale's wooden box right then, just to get it over with.

The sound of Miss Adelaide's bell, still quite loud more than a block away, forced her hand. By way of a shortcut down the alley next to the millinery, Rebecca raced off to school with Billy and her friends, leaving the task for later and hoping she had made the right choice.

* * *

The Ledger Of Owen McCabe

The Orchard Herald Special Edition, March 20, 1887
STAMPEDING HEARSE CRASHES INTO RIVER
by Thomas Buchanan, Editor

Thursday last the earthly remains of Mrs. Gertrude McCabe were interred within the receiving vault on the lot where once stood the town's venerable church. Intended to be a quiet affair for the grieving widower, Mr. Maxwell McCabe, and his son, Master Owen McCabe, the solemn occasion was marred by a most sudden and unexpected turn of events.

For reasons known only to the Lord above, the horses belonging to both the McCabe family and to the undertaker, Mr. Edgar Allman, became so riled as to attempt escape from the post to which they'd been hitched, all while the mourners were attending to the deceased Mrs. McCabe in the receiving vault. The disturbance caused by the horses drew the attendees' attention, and while the McCabe's horse was brought under control, Mr. Allman's broke free. The great animal charged wildly down Church Street, still secured to Mr. Allman's hearse, which it pulled behind it as it ran. The beast nearly trampled our schoolteacher Miss Rose Adelaide, who jumped out of harm's way with nary a moment to spare. She was miraculously unhurt.

Sheriff Turnbull, who witnessed the horse break free of its reins, tried to stop the stampeding creature but was injured in the attempt, being pulled from his saddle at high speeds and suffering several broken ribs.

157

The horse proceeded down Church Street, but failed to stop at the east river and met its fate when it and the hearse upended down the riverbank. Sheriff Turnbull used his gun to spare the badly injured animal further suffering.

As there were no direct witnesses to what spooked the horses, thereby setting off the unfortunate chain of events, no fault or liability has been laid on any parties.

"He was a good stag, well-tempered," said Mr. Wayne Statler, at whose livery Mr. Allman kept his horse, and who was a pallbearer at the interment service when the horse bolted, "There ain't no reason I can see for the animal going off the way it did. It must have been scared by something, but I can't reckon what."

Mr. McCabe has requested privacy for his family in this time of sadness and was unavailable for comment.

* * *

The Ledger of Owen McCabe

May 13, 1895
Orchard Bend

Of course it was the Prisoner who spooked those horses during my mother's interment all those years ago. The infernal things sensed him and reacted the way only big, stupid animals do, by losing their fucking minds and running away.

I remember it all, though not in acute detail like the night Henry died. Mr. Burke was there, and as the article notes, so were the Statlers and Mr. Allman. I forget who else. Not many showed up. I remember the teacher, Miss Adelaide. She was on the street when we drove past. She was my mother's friend, so came to the interment and watched from a distance. My father wouldn't have wanted her there, so it's a good thing she stayed away. Then the horse bolted, dragging Allman's hearse behind it, and it damn near killed her for her trouble. When we ran out of the vault to see what the hell all the commotion was

158

about, my father stayed with me while the men ran to the horse.

They couldn't see the Prisoner, but I could. His dark shape was faint, but unmistakable, leaving no trace in the snow as he walked across the lawn in our direction. I thought at the time he was coming to see me, but I found out later that wasn't the case at all.

We returned home once Mr. Burke and one of the Statlers got our horse back under control. My father wanted us away from that madness as fast as possible. We crossed the bridge on Anderson Street and I looked out to see the schoolteacher and the sheriff shoot Allman's horse as it lay dying on the bank downriver. I remember the sound of the gunshot, a quick pop. I didn't see the bullet actually hit the horse, but I could picture it and maybe that was worse.

We drove on for a while until we reached the house. One thing I remember quite well is thinking how different it looked on the outside. Nothing had changed since we'd left, but it still looked different.

My father held my hand as we went inside, while Mr. Burke unloaded our bags from the coach. We'd come straight from the train to the vault and then home. There were a lot of bags, including our big trunk. As we left the vault one of the Statlers had remarked that the weight of all of it might have been what kept our horse from tearing loose and following the hearse.

I don't remember much from the rest of the night, except playing in my room at one point and hearing someone coming upstairs. For a brief moment, so absorbed was I with my toys, I thought it was my mother. When I remembered it wasn't and that I'd never see her again, I cried on the floor. Later my father came in, read me a story and put me to bed.

Then the Prisoner emerged from the shadows.

"I'm sorry about your mother, Owen," he said.

I asked him why he had been at the vault and the answer he gave bombarded my mind with images and his thoughts, starting with a girl named Isla Cormack.

Her family moved into the cabin by the west river in the ravine when she was quite young. The Prisoner had been

159

trapped for many years, unable to enter the Breach and unable to open a Portal to escape. Decades had passed and the Prisoner had watched Orchard Bend grow, unseen at first, until with great effort he strained against the barrier between our world and his, and he learned to manifest as a shadow, but only for brief moments.

Still it was progress and the Prisoner knew he had time, lifetimes worth of it, because that's what it would take.

He also knew he'd need help from the outside if he was ever to escape.

When the Cormacks move ·in to the cabin in the ravine, the Prisoner watched them, hoping their little girl Isla would be the one. She was a bright, outgoing and happy girl, who played make-believe among the aspens or by the river, often with her friend Gertrude, my mother.

—And seeing my mother in the Prisoner's memories, as a child, so youthful and healthy, so soon after watching her eaten away by that son of a bitch cancer, well, it was almost too much to bear—

The Prisoner struggled to reach out to Isla, to make contact, to speak to her in his unusual way. Years passed where for all his efforts, the only result was his dark, spectral form appearing in and around the cabin. He learned that nighttime worked best if he wanted to be seen, and after the sun had set or before it rose, because in those hours his shadowy form didn't have to fight against the sun. More than once, he knew Isla could see him. As dusk settled and she fed the family's horse, he'd struggle to appear, a wrath in the gloom, and Isla would glimpse him and be startled at the sight. Just as fast, the Prisoner would vanish and leave Isla to no doubt think it was just her overactive imagination.

One summer evening, however, he discovered something else very much by accident. The Prisoner followed Isla and Mrs. Cormack to my mother's home, the Kiley ranch. My mother's family, consisting of my grandparents and my great grandmother, had all fallen ill, feverish and delirious. Somehow my mother had been spared, but could not take care of her family alone.

160

"We've come to help, Gertrude," Mrs. Cormack told my exhausted mother. "You get some sleep before you get sick yourself, understand?"

My mother did as she was told. She and Isla went to her room, leaving Mrs. Cormack to tend to the stricken adults. The Prisoner stayed with her, following Mrs Cormack from room to room as she saw first to my mother's parents and then to my great grandmother, Trudy (after whom, incidentally, my mother Gertrude was named). Trudy was in much worse condition than her son and daughter-in-law. The Prisoner knew what it was that had befallen the ranch: malaria, likely contracted from mosquito bites.

Mrs. Cormack tried to get my great grandmother to drink, but when she put a cup of water to her mouth, most of it ended up streaming down her chin and neck. Mrs. Cormack kept at it, telling her patient that some of the water was bound to make it down her throat. Then Trudy surprised Mrs. Cormack with a burst of strength, pushing the younger woman away and raving for someone named Hans, before falling back on the bed and gasping for air.

(There are no Hanses in our family history, so who this man was to my great grandmother remains a mystery. We all have our secrets.)

Mrs. Cormack was at her side in a flash, but the Prisoner, who stood beside her, wasn't sure there was much the woman could do. Trudy was just too far gone.

And then it happened, old Trudy Kiley looked at him.

She saw *him*.

Somehow, she saw the Prisoner.

He moved around her bed and her eyes stayed fixed on him.

You can see me! *the Prisoner said.*

Yes, *Trudy answered, but not with her voice. She was thinking it and the Prisoner could hear her in his own thoughts. She never took her eyes off him, asking,* Are you the Angel of Death?

Others would later ask him the same question, but old Mrs. Trudy Kiley was the first. And when she spoke, he saw into her

161

thoughts and memories, fragments connected to what she was saying.

No, I'm not, *the Prisoner told her.* You're sick and I think you *are* going to die, but it is not my doing.

I would like to see my Hans again, *Trudy told him.*

That's not up to me, *the Prisoner said.*

The old woman's eyes narrowed on him.

You look odd, *she said, and the Prisoner caught a glimpse of his reflection in her mind, that of an almost solid, grey-black human form. And she was correct, his face was not right. The eyes and mouth were missing, only deep, black voids where those features ought to be.*

I've been trapped a long time, *the Prisoner said.*

Then the old woman's eyes went glassy and vacant as she rattled her last breath. Mrs. Cormack shook her, felt for a heartbeat, and even leaned over her mouth to try to find any sign of life, but there was none to be found. She covered the body with a sheet and left the room, but the Prisoner remained, looking down at the late Trudy Kiley, the first person he had spoken to in decades, if you could call their exchange of thoughts and images speaking. She would not be the last one, either. Something about a person's dying moments, he learned, thinned the barrier between the living world and his prison.

As time passed, the Prisoner continued his efforts to make himself seen in our world, enduring the discomfort as he struggled against the barrier. In time, he could hold his shadowy presence longer. And after the encounter with Trudy, he set about trying to communicate with Isla.

But then she left.

An opportunity presented itself back east by way of a cousin of Isla's father, and the Cormack family packed up on a windy, damp spring afternoon and rode off. The Prisoner watched them go, then returned to the ravine and waited, much as he had for all those decades of his imprisonment in that place between worlds.

And one day, she *arrived.*

My mother Gertrude Kiley, the now-lonely friend of Isla Cormack, came down the path from the road and walked around the abandoned Cormack property. The Prisoner watched her as he had once watched her play in the grove with Isla, but dared not show himself so as to not frighten the teen girl. She sat in front of the cabin door and cried for her absent friend. After a time, Gertrude left, returning to the ranch.

The Prisoner was not surprised when she returned again.

And again.

And continued returning, sometimes staying for only a few minutes, while other times she stayed and played by herself amongst the aspens, recreating the make-believe worlds she and Isla had shared. When my mother left the ravine one clear evening, the Prisoner followed, still resisting the urge to reveal his shadowy form. Until he knew how to speak with her the way he'd spoken with her grandmother Trudy, the Prisoner dared not approach her.

More years passed and the Prisoner observed Gertrude Kiley and the town of Orchard Bend, moving unseen among the townsfolk. By the time my mother married my father, the Prisoner had not been back to the ravine in quite some time, ignoring the pull that had drawn him there in the first place. After she gave birth to my brother Henry, the Prisoner remained close to her in our house on the hill, overlooking the town.

He did return to the ravine when a Portal to the Breach opened there. That was the night before I was born, the night that woman emerged from the Breach—Emery Dale.

The less said about her right now, the better. I bring her up only because the Prisoner was there when she killed the Underwood Gang at the bridge in the ravine.

And she was there when Marshal Saunders tried to murder my family. So much death and killing that night and the Prisoner saw it all. And the dying men saw him. In the barn that night, Henry truly believed his life was about to end. The barrier grew thinner and at last the Prisoner could reach out to him, to talk to him with his noisy voice.

Henry didn't die that night, however, and the barrier returned to normal, but this was something altogether new and the Prisoner wasn't about to lose the ability to communicate with someone on the other side. He struggled against the barrier. With a willing person in Henry, someone who didn't fear him, the Prisoner fought and railed and clawed with his mind to hold on to that connection.

And it worked.

Now that he had broken through, so to speak, with Henry, his plan shifted from my mother, Gertrude, to her son. But he did not ignore her. She had been his focus too long for that to happen. He remained aware of her. When the Prisoner lost influence with Henry, he considered shifting his intentions back to her, but after Dale gunned my brother down, he chose me instead.

When my mother grew sick and we travelled to Sutter Grove, the Prisoner did not follow us. I wonder if he was even capable of leaving Orchard Bend.

That's why I came to the vault when you interred your mother, *the Prisoner said as the images of the past faded, leaving a curious stretched sensation in my mind, something close to a headache.* To see her off now that she is gone, to stand at her side as I did for your grandmother, Trudy, those years before.

His parting words before fading back into the shadows that night were, Remember that I am your friend, Owen. I'll always be here.

To this day, the Prisoner has kept his word.

* * *

"Senior scholars, you have one minute to finish your essay answers," Miss Adelaide announced, looking up from her pocket watch and rising from the seat at her desk. Those students still writing doubled their efforts to get their final thoughts down. Rebecca reread her short essay, saw a missing word near the end and scratched it in with her pencil. Miss Adelaide put her watch away and said, "Very well, time to put down your pencils. Quinton Reed, don't make me repeat myself."

164

"I was just on the last sentence, Miss Adelaide," Quinton said, setting his pencil down and putting his hands up the way a boy does when he's caught.

"In that case, I expect I'll find it to be quite a fine example of prose," Miss Adelaide said with a wry smile. "Scholars, remember to put your name, the date and each page number at the top of each sheet. Do so now if you haven't already. Mr Reed, no adding to your masterpiece."

"I wasn't!" Quinton protested, but his friends only laughed.

"When you've completed that, please bring your pages to the front and place them neatly in a stack on my desk," Miss Adelaide said, crossing to the side of her desk to wipe the test questions off the blackboard as the students got up. Without turning around, she added, "And Mr Howard, if you place your test in the stack upside down for a fourth time, I'll deduct five marks."

Rebecca smiled and gave Billy a playful punch in the arm as he tried to look as innocent as possible. When they reached Miss Adelaide's desk, Rebecca saw on his face that Billy was considering putting his test answers on the pile upside down anyway and she gave a whispered hiss, "Don't you dare, Billy. She'll do it, just you watch."

Billy thought better of it and put his papers down the correct side up. Rebecca put hers on the stack and they looped back around to their seats.

Miss Adelaide finished with the blackboard, turned to face the class and took out her pocket watch again.

"Seeing as it's Friday and the rain has cleared up, I'm inclined to let school out a little early today," she smiled, then put her hand up to silence the excited chatter at the announcement. "Remember, junior scholars, your themes are due on Monday. Class dismissed."

Rebecca gathered up her things and hurried to put on her boots and coat, wanting to waste no time getting out of the Town Hall and over to the cemetery. With Billy trailing behind, she rushed through the lobby and out onto the steps. Thick clouds rolled low overhead and the sun cast shafts of light across the lawn.

"Rebecca, slow down," Billy called after her. She stopped and waited. He came up beside her and put a hand on her arm.

"Is something the matter?" he asked with genuine concern. "Was it the test?"

"No, it wasn't the test," Rebecca said. She actually thought she did quite well on it, even near the end when she started thinking more about the task that lay ahead, trying not to get distracted by it.

"Was it Sam?" Billy asked. "We can go talk to him now, we have a bit of time. I don't need to be at the mill until four o'clock."

"Billy, I'd like to go sit somewhere," Rebecca said. She glanced about, pretending to decide on a location, "How about by the cemetery? There's a bench there where we can sit."

"Alright," Billy said.

Hand in hand, they walked up to Church Street and headed for the cemetery. They passed the broken hitching post and walked under the cedars to the stone bench. They sat with their backs to the gravestones, looking out at the lawn.

"It's really strange without the church here," Billy said. "I can't get used to it. It's as though I can still see it in my mind."

"I know what you mean," Rebecca said.

"But there's still the vault," Billy said. "And *he* is in there."

Rebecca hadn't thought of that and said nothing. The body of Henry McCabe, who Sheriff Dale believed to be Laura's killer, was still in the receiving vault, where it would stay until the spring thaw.

Billy stood up and walked toward the vault.

"You killed her, didn't you, Henry?" Billy asked, facing the cold, grey structure.

"Billy, please sit down," Rebecca said.

"Dale thought *I* did it, Henry, but it was you!" Billy said, clenching his gloved fists. "She was smitten with you and you *killed* her!"

"Billy, sit down before someone hears you!" Rebecca pleaded. She leapt up and took Billy by the arm, her touch gentle as she pulled him away and back to the bench.

Yet, she couldn't deny she felt much the same way, and watching Billy seethe with rage made her want to tear the vault down stone by stone to get to Henry McCabe herself.

"I'm sorry," Billy said. "The newspaper and everyone has made such a fuss over Henry's mother's death, but no one talks about Laura anymore, you know?"

"I know," Rebecca agreed, holding his hand in both of hers.

"And she, Laura I mean... her *you know*... it's still missing," Billy said. Rebecca did indeed know what he meant. It pained her to think about Laura's head still out there somewhere. Rebecca had wondered more than once whether that was why she couldn't find peace and why her spirit still walked the earth.

"Someone will find it one day," Rebecca said, her voice shaky. Tears of rage would flow if she let them, but she held firm as best she could. She gave Billy's hand a loving squeeze, "And when that happens she'll be able to rest at last. We all will.

Billy nodded, his head down. Then he looked into her eyes and leaned forward. Rebecca didn't hesitate to kiss him.

"I should get going," Billy said.

"Be careful at work," Rebecca said, letting go of his hand. He stood up and gathered his school supplies. He glanced at the vault, but turned from it at once to give Rebecca a smile. She smiled back, her eyes wet. Billy walked back along the line of cedars to the street and there gave her a wave, which she returned.

Rebecca watched Billy avoid the puddles and muddier parts of the streets on his way to the McCabe Mill.

Once he was out of sight, Rebecca took in a deep breath to collect herself. She then looked around to make sure no one was watching.

* * *

Billy Howard didn't look up as Deputy Green rode past him, heading in the opposite direction. Green wondered what he was smiling about, but didn't ask, seeing as he himself was in something of a foul mood. No one had seen the caretaker, Mr

167

Field, all day, so Green suspected he'd shirked off the job again. Any other day and Green would not have cared a wink what the man did, Green wasn't his boss after all, but that post at the old church lawn still needed fixing.

After wasting the better part of the day looking for the fellow, Green thought he should just knock on the man's door, but in all honesty, Green didn't feel up to a confrontation. He'd decided to just ask one of the Statler brothers to take care of it. He could pay them out of the sheriff's petty cash and Turnbull would bill the town later. Or they could bill the town themselves, whichever they preferred, Green just wanted the job done before someone complained or got hurt.

When he'd arrived at the Statler Livery, both men were hard at work on the undertaker's hearse.

"Sorry, Deputy, Mr Allman has promised us a bonus if we can have this fixed and refitted by Sunday," Wayne Statler explained. "It's a big job; new spokes for some of the wheels, a pair of axels. And we lost part of the day when David Langford busted an axel on his own wagon out on the tracks, so we've got to make up some time on this."

"Wouldn't it be faster to just fit the wagon onto a new carriage?" Green asked.

"It sure would be, but who has a wagon carriage to spare? Do you know anyone?" Wayne shrugged. "No, we can salvage a good lot of the old one and rebuild the rest. You're welcome to borrow some tools and fix that post yourself."

He pointed to the array of tools on the worktable in one of the unused stalls. Green fetched what he needed, along with some lumber and nails. He thanked Wayne and mounted his horse. He carried the lot to Church Street, where he passed Billy Howard.

Miss Adelaide's let school out early, it seems, Green noted. He picked up his pace, wanting to get started before any children passed by the broken post.

Riding past the cemetery and up to the old church lawn, Green noticed someone at the bench under the cedars. The girl wore a dark red dress and a heavy grey winter coat. A bonnet obscured her face and she stood bent over the bench as though she'd dropped something next to it.

Green's horse let out a grunt as he brought it to a halt at the end of the line of cedars. The girl spun around, startled. Still on his horse, Green tipped his hat.

"Sorry to scare you, Miss Clarke," Green said.

The girl put her hand on her chest and let out a relieved sigh.

"Oh, it's fine, Deputy," Rebecca said with a pleasant wave.

"What brings you here?" Green said.

"Well, I was just... You see, Miss Adelaide let school out early, it being Friday and all, and the rain has blown on and the sun is out," Rebecca explained. "Billy Howard and I were just talking, but he had to go to work, so I was just getting ready to head home myself. My mother will be expecting me."

"I just passed Billy on the road," Green said, dropping the lumber on a patch of wet snow and swinging his leg over the saddle to climb down. As he did, Rebecca fumbled with the pail in which she carried her school supplies. She stood back upright as he stepped off the saddle and stretch his back. He asked, "Is everything alright?"

"Of course," Rebecca said, smiling, "but I really should be going."

"Don't let me slow you down, Miss Clarke," Green said, tipping his hat again as he tied his horse to the nearest cedar. "You have a good day now."

"You too, Deputy," Rebecca said, collecting her pail and walking toward the street along the other side of cedars next to the cemetery fence, not looking at Green at all as she left.

The deputy scratched his head and picked up the piece of lumber from the ground. He brushed the snow off it and leaned it against the tree. Then he took the nails and tools from his saddle bag and brought them to the broken hitching post. A group of boys ran up the street, stopped at the edge of the lawn and one of them pointed in the deputy's direction.

"That's where it happened!" the boy said. Green recognized him as one of the Powell boys.

"That's enough, fellas," Green said, thinking he'd gotten to work on the post just in time. "You've had your look, now get on home."

"Let's go see the riverbank where the hearse crashed!" said another boy in the group, Roger Cane. The others agreed and started up the street. Almost out of earshot, the boy added, "My pa says Deputy Green let Sheriff Dale escape..."

Green didn't catch the rest of what the boy said, but the other laughed and looked back in his direction, sneering before they broke into a run, splashing in the puddles and kicking muddy slush everywhere.

Green shook his head, fighting off hot anger and embarrassment. He set about tearing off the broken rail of the hitching post, prying it the rest of the way off with the claw of the hammer.

He brought the broken rail, with its bent nails still jutting out, back to the cedar where he'd tied his horse. His gaze fell upon the stone bench where Rebecca Clarke had just been.

Popular place today, Green thought.

He leaned the broken piece of wood against the tree and picked up the new one. A cloud moved across the sun and dulled the light around him, but it was still nicer that afternoon than it had been earlier in the day. He thought about Miss Adelaide weeping, sitting at the bench in the mist, sheltered from the rain, come there to mourn her friend, Gertrude McCabe.

With some effort, Green straightened up the post that the horse had twisted as it had struggled against the rail, then he put the new piece of lumber down across it, lining it up with its partner several feet away, squaring up the edges so there was no overhang. Taking care not to mash his thumbs, he drove first one nail through the wood to the post, then a second and a third, making a triangle of the three. He did the same to the other side, fixing it to the post. At one end, the excess lumber extended more than two feet out from the post. As he walked back to his horse to trade the hammer and nails for a handsaw, Green looked at the bench again. He thought about Rebecca

Clarke's reaction to his arrival, the genuine surprise at his being there.

Green put the hammer and nails in the saddle bag and took out the handsaw. The sun came back out and the town lit up. The deputy stopped and admired the spectacle. Even with the trees still bare and the ground mostly mud and snow, he welcomed the coming change in season. Just about anything was better than the winter they'd had, with its blizzards and death.

Returning to the hitching post, Green began sawing the excess lumber from the rail, so that it lined up with the post. He thought about the blizzard when Emery Dale made her escape on his watch. Anger swelled and he forced that memory away, sawing even harder, directing his frustration there. He tried not to think about anything but getting this task done.

With a few short breaks to rest his arm, Green sawed through the lumber. The excess length first bowed then dropped to the ground as the last fibres of wood cracked and separated. It hit the ground with a wet splat. The sound brought with it another awful, vivid detail memory.

It was the previous summer and he was standing in the west field where Laura O'Malley's decapitated body had been found. He'd still been new to the job (himself not much older than the boy Sam O'Toole, who had come by today to ask about becoming a deputy). That day in the field, Sheriff Wilson had left Green and Doctor Shaw with the headless body to go tell Laura's parents.

Green looked up at the receiving vault where the late Doctor Shaw now rested. Also in the vault was Henry McCabe, whom Dale insisted was Laura's killer.

An excitement welled up in the deputy, but he couldn't quite place what in these connections was causing it.

Another memory arose, of being back in the same field on a cold, overcast autumn day, now accompanying the new sheriff, Emery Dale. She had asked Green to take her to where Laura's body had been found. Once there, she'd walked him through deductions he would never have made himself. Later that day over coffee, he even said as much.

"All you needed," Sheriff Dale told him, "was to be pointed in the right direction. You're a smart man, you just never thought in those terms before."

High praise and Green took it as such. After all, it had led him to the murder weapon. He'd felt the same rush of excitement in that moment, too, pulling the hatchet from the river.

Now he felt it again, standing on the lawn of the old church lot.

But what is the connection here? Green wondered, wishing for clarity.

Green turned his attention to the stone bench beneath the cedars.

Miss Rose Adelaide.

Rebecca Clarke.

Emery Dale's friend.

Laura O'Malley's friend.

A popular spot today, he'd thought earlier.

Green dropped the handsaw in the snow without noticing it and walked to the bench, his heart racing and blood rushing in his ears.

It's probably nothing, his doubt told him, but Green had to see for himself.

Something about this bench was important.

* * *

With the sun setting later each day as spring drew closer, darkness no longer engulfed the land quite as early as it had in the preceding weeks and months. For Rebecca, it would have made navigating the woods from the road to the sunken cabin so much easier if not for the soggy ground and treacherous patches of ice everywhere.

Well, I'm not freezing, so that's good, Rebecca mused.

Up ahead, she spotted the cabin low in the ground and resolved to get there without stopping. In the trees, the birds sang and squawked and called out everywhere, as was their custom late in the day. The noise would get so loud, it reminded Rebecca of some mornings at school in the old church. In that small space, crammed with children laughing and talking, Miss Adelaide would rap her yardstick on her desk to bring about quiet. Now in the Town Hall, the voices carried to fill the vast openness of the space and were not as deafening. A touch of sadness wrenched at Rebecca's heart as she thought about all the years she'd attended classes at the little church schoolhouse. The town would rebuild the church, of course, but it would never be the same.

And by the time the new church went up, she herself might no longer be a student. Rebecca smiled at the prospect, thinking of the hints Billy had dropped of late, things like how he had been saving his money and how he wanted the two of them to travel and see something of the world before they put down roots. Rebecca had never been to the city, nor been much beyond the county. The thought of going farther away and setting foot in distant quarters of the country, perhaps even abroad, it all seemed like something out of a storybook.

The sheer excitement of it, my word, Rebecca thought. Any other day, the thought would have had her giddy, but the stress of the day tempered that excitement.

Sheriff Dale's wooden box rattled in the tin pail, next to her books and school supplies, swinging from the crook of her elbow. Rebecca touched it as she approached the cabin, curious as to its contents and relieved that Dale's plan had worked.

At the cabin door, she knocked twice, paused, and knocked once more.

"Come in, Miss Clarke," Sheriff Dale called from inside.

Rebecca entered.

"Sheriff, it all went exactly as you said it would!" Rebecca said, her words just about running into each other as she hurried to make her delivery. "Miss Adelaide followed your note and put the box inside the secret spot in the bench. It was there after school, like it was waiting for me..."

Rebecca's pace slowed to a stop as she realized Dale had not gotten up from where she sat on the bed, her back against the wall, her knees up and her arms crossed, with her face almost hidden from view. The sheriff wasn't even looking at her.

"What is it?" Rebecca asked. "What's the matter?"

Dale continued to stare at some far away point, her face bearing an expression Rebecca's mother would have called the long away gaze, seen when Rebecca and Laura were girls, lying on their backs, staring at the clouds. Unlike the wistful long away gazes of Rebecca's youth, Dale's held something darker and a little disquieting.

"So you have the box?" Dale asked, after letting Rebecca's questions hang in the air unanswered.

"Yes, I have it here!" Rebecca pulled the box out of the pail and held it out to Dale. The sheriff didn't look at it, but her eyes darted about. Rebecca turned to see what she might be looking at, but saw nothing but bare log walls. She put the box on the bed next to Dale and took a step back.

Rebecca had intended to ask what was in the box. She had even harboured the idea that Dale might show her what was so valuable that she'd go through all this scheming to get it back, but everything about the woman sitting on the bed spoke of a melancholy Rebecca could not fathom.

"I'm going to leave now, Sheriff," Rebecca said.

"Thank you for everything you've done, Miss Clarke," Dale said, still unmoving. Her gaze shifted to Rebecca and she made eye contact. "I mean it."

"You need my help," Rebecca said. "And... I owe it to Laura."

"You best get home," Dale said, turning away and casting her long away gaze back at the wall. "Your mother will be waiting for you."

Rebecca looked from Dale to the wooden box on the bed beside her and then back to Dale.

"Goodbye, Sheriff Dale," Rebecca said, turning to the door to let herself out.

"Goodbye, Rebecca," Dale said.

Rebecca opened the door, thankful for the fresh air and clear sky above the woods. She closed the door and put on her mittens, thinking she could still make it home before her mother started wondering why she was late.

* * *

174

Rebecca Clarke kept her eyes on the ground as she followed her route back to the road. With her bonnet on, she didn't see Deputy Green hunkered down and using some brush as cover.

The deputy again weighed the option of confronting the girl. Now would be his chance to escort her to the road and question her about what she was doing out here. Green would have done just that, but he already knew what she was doing. Maybe not the specifics, but he knew enough.

No, he thought, *let her go, for now. The person I'm actually after is inside that cabin.*

He watched Rebecca make her way through the woods in the direction of the road until he could no longer see her, then he waited an additional two minutes.

Best to let them settle back into their routine, he told himself. *The Clarke girl can go on home thinking all is well. And the person in the cabin can think the delivery was made without a hitch.*

The person in the cabin.

Green knew who it was.

The time had come for him to fix his mistake, to bring her to justice, and to silence the snide comments from people like Griesbach.

What little remained of the sun cut through the trees, casting long shadows across the forest floor. Green rose from his hiding place and, taking great care with each step, made his way to the cabin, an unusual structure built half in and half out of the ground. Like before, at the stone bench, his heart was racing.

Steady, boy, he told himself. *She's fast and she's clever, but you have the element of surprise.*

The rush of adrenalin eased as Green drew his six-shooter. He didn't want to use it and hoped the woman inside would choose to surrender without a fight.

If not, well...

Steady and tense, Green came around to the front of the cabin, where the door sat in a recess in the ground. It looked like a strong kick would take it down with ease. He paused and listened, hoping to hear her moving about, to get a sense of where she was inside. The cabin was not that large and probably had only the one room. Since Green first spotted the place and saw smoke drifting from the chimneystack, he knew someone was in there, that *she* was in there.

Green considered again whether he should go back to town and tell Sheriff Turnbull. In his condition, Turnbull wouldn't ride out himself, but Green could gather up a posse. They could come back here and surround the place. It was not a bad plan, but all that would take time and she might be gone when they returned.

Wouldn't that be a right goddamn daisy? Green thought.

If she did slip away, people might not even believe that she'd been there in the first place. And if they did, how would it look that Green let her escape? *Again.*

No, Green resolved, *it ends here and now, one way or the other.*

He reared back and fired his boot into the door, which put up no resistance. By some miracle it stayed in one piece as the hinges split from the frame and it hit the cabin floor with a crash.

The instant he saw her, Green ducked against the doorframe, gun levelled.

"Emery Dale!" he shouted. "You're under arrest!"

Dale stood in the middle of the room, facing the door, her hands already up to show she was unarmed.

"Hello, Deputy Green," Dale said.

* * *

When the knock at her front door jolted her from her idleness, Rose Adelaide didn't know just how long she had been staring out the kitchen window. Outside, the sun had gone down and the sky had turned a deep blue. The tranquility of the scene settled her wayward thoughts.

As per Emery's instructions, Rose had not returned to the stone bench at all after she had dropped the wooden box off that morning, but after school, while she had graded the seniors' tests and while she had prepared and then ate her dinner, Rose's thoughts returned to the wooden box.

Had it been retrieved?

Had it been delivered to Emery?

What did it contain that Emery needed?

As she pondered these questions, she made every effort to avoid the deeper ones, such as where Emery was going and when she might return—

—if ever.

As winter's end drew closer, Rose let herself take in the simple beauty of the evening's dusk. The questions ceased and that was peace enough.

The knock at the door brought her back. She picked up her lantern and crossed from the kitchen through the dining area to answer it.

Upon opening the door, dread gripped Rose at the sight of Deputy Green there, his hands behind his back.

"Deputy," Rose said, "what brings you by this evening?"

She found Green's expression difficult to read, being one of seriousness, almost brooding. He brought his hands out and held one of them up, presenting Rose with Emery Dale's small wooden box, the very one she had left in the stone bench that morning.

"Miss Adelaide," Deputy Green said. "We need to talk."

177

23

Orchard Bend Historical Society Museum Archives

Eloise Langford Memories 3 of 3
Recorded 06-06-35
Transcript [Excerpt]

...Oh, and that reminds me of the winter of '87. Such a blasted winter that was, never wanting to end, even when March arrived to send Old Man Winter packing, the stubborn coot just refused to leave. Ever hear of a false thaw? Well, that's what happens when the Old Man decides to trick everyone into thinking he's resting his aching, frosty bones for a spell. Days that were once so frigid your breath froze to your face feel downright balmy by comparison. You wake up one morning and could swear spring is on the way. The temperature climbs and the snow starts to melt, and you can't help but go outside.

March of old '87 one such false thaw came to Orchard Bend (there are always a few each winter, they try to fool you like that). For days at a time we hardly left our house, and those days that we did go out were just so nasty cold. But when this thaw arrived, David suggested we enjoy the outdoors.

"Ellie," David said, sipping his coffee and looking out the kitchen window, "I think this rain is clearing up. How about I take you for a wagon ride?"

I didn't take much convincing. And David was right, the clouds had thinned and the patches of blue sky were unmistakable.

"A capital idea, David!" I answered. But I'd bring an umbrella for us just in case.

So out we went that day for a ride on the wagon and mind you the air was still quite cool, but not the kind of cold that wants to claw off your face. After the light rain, the snow was melting and puddles had formed. This was before we had a sleigh carriage, which if you don't know, well, see, you could take the bed of the wagon off the wheel carriage and put it on the sleigh carriage. We didn't have one in '87, but David thought our wheels were sturdy enough, and we didn't plan to go far, just out to get a taste of fresh air while it lasted, you see?

The muck on the road from the thaw wasn't too bad when we set out, and the ground still held firm. It made travelling easy. By the time we reached the railroad tracks by the trestle bridge—you know the one over the East River?—by the time we made it that far, the snow and the mud and the puddles were getting too treacherous for comfort. I told David we should go back. He agreed. He made the turn 'round at the tracks because it was harder-packed soil, with the rail bed and all. He got the wagon halfway around when we heard a crack of wood and felt a shudder from underneath. The wagon jostled and dipped, and David held the horses up fast. He looked at me and I looked at him and we both knew something was broken. We were half on and half off the tracks, which is never the place you want to find yourself stuck, so David eased the wagon forward and it gave a mighty jerk. I turned and saw the back wheel on my side was all wrong, pointing outward and at a lazy angle. Before I could tell David, we bucked and bounced again and he called "Whoa! Whoa!" to the team. He turned and saw what I saw and shook his head.

"Reckoned as much," he said with a shake of his head. He climbed down, inspected the carriage and declared the axle was broken on that side, the wheel barely clinging to the frame. He sighed, "Damn fool thing to do after all, coming out here. But least we're off the tracks, my dear!"

"Is it broken all the way?" I asked.

"Most of the way," David said. "I could maybe rig some braces, enough to keep the wheel squared up and we could get it home."

I looked around, hoping to see someone else out on the road who might help us, but there was no one. I suppose we were the only damn fools witless enough that day to go for a ride.

David crossed the tracks and looked toward town, which was a long ways on, easily three quarters of an hour walk or more. The walk home would be longer still. As he came back to the wagon, though, David paused, looking east along the rails. His gaze was fixed there long enough for me to know what he was thinking.

"David Langford, don't add another damn fool deed to the day," I told him. He smiled as he looked back at me.

"My parent's farm is just a short skip that a-ways, Ellie," he said. "Half the time it would take to get to town. Maybe even less. My father could bring me back here with everything I need to fix the axle."

"That bridge is covered with snow and slick and Lord knows what else," I told him. "You'll make a widow out of me!"

"I can make it," David said. "Remember when you and I ran across it when we were kids?"

"Clear as this blue sky," I told him. "But that was summer and we didn't know any better. We were lucky we didn't fall to our deaths."

"I'll be careful, Ellie," he said and started toward the trestle bridge. I climbed down from the wagon and watched him approach the river, a glistening dark current cutting through the blanket of snow forty or fifty feet below. David's boots crunched on the timber as he walked between the rails. He stopped where the bridge extended over the deep scar in the earth and looked back at me. He didn't say anything, but he was smiling and gave me a wink.

"Go on, then!" I said and David turned back to the bridge. He took a deep breath and started across. I almost called out for him to stop and come back, to forget this silly notion. But I didn't. I wonder how different things might have been if I had.

David took each step carefully, his arms out at his sides. He neither hurried nor tarried. He took his time, and kept a steady pace. A gust of wind made him stop and crouch down. When it settled, he stood up and continued on. By then, he'd crossed

180

maybe a third of the bridge, with the rushing water full of
melted snow far below him.

He made it halfway before I heard the train.

I spun around and saw the dark shape in the distance. I
didn't want to believe it, but a blast from the whistle left no
doubt. I looked back to my husband and saw him turned back
to me, not moving. I guessed he was trying to figure if he could
make it to my side of the span or not. He gave a wave and
darted off in the other direction, less cautious now and moving
faster. The train was catching up. I whipped my head left to
right and back again, my heart racing, helpless but to watch. I
didn't even think to pray, the train was gaining so fast.

When I looked back to David I saw him lose his balance and
flail his arms. I stopped breathing. The train must have seen
him then, for it gave a mighty, deafening blast of the whistle.

David regained his footing and charged on, now three
quarters of the way across. The train's whistle screamed over
and over. Without thinking, I slowly backed away from the
tracks, all the while keeping my dear husband in view. I didn't
turn away to look at the train, my only focus was David, racing
for his life.

He can make it, *I thought, but I wasn't at all sure.*

When the train blew past me, the air twisted around and
pushed me away. I held onto the back of the wagon for support.
When I looked back in the direction of the bridge, I could see
nothing. The freight carried by the old CUC company seemed
to take forever as it clattered past. When at last the caboose
sailed by I raced to the tracks as if chasing the behemoth. I
stopped where the bridge met the steep hill and on both sides
of the opposite bank I saw no sign of David. He had not jumped
to escape the train.

The freight carried on and I watched it go. The caboose
reached the far side and shrank smaller and smaller away.

"David!" I yelled. The cry carried and bounced off the opposite
bank. I waited for a reply, anything, a sign that he was alright.
I looked back down at the snowy slope again, then up at the
bridge. I called out again, "Daaaa·viiid!"

181

A dark shape appeared from the tree line on the opposite side and raised a hand. An echo-y voice came on the air, "Ellieee!"

My oh my, the relief that swept over me, I tell ya! David waved his arms back and forth and I waved to him in return. He turned away and I did the same, walking back to the wagon where I sat and laughed. Maybe I should've been upset or cussing him for a fool, but only laughter came, wetting my eyes and somehow making me appreciate the day even more.

When the laughter eased, I sat thinking about how long it would take David to return. He'd reach his parent's farm soon. I pictured him knocking on the door, explaining to his father what happened and what tools and supplies he'd need to fix the wagon's carriage. They'd gather what they need, hitch up the team and make for where he'd left me. I expect his mother would give him a fresh cup of coffee and he'd protest, saying he left his love by the side of the road, but would take a few sips because coffee on a winter's day is hard to resist.

What I didn't expect was to hear footsteps behind me. I turned to see David coming back along the tracks.

"David! What in the world...?" I gasped, climbing down and hurrying to him. "Why are you here? Why did you come back?"

I'd known David Langford all my life and never before had I seen the expression he carried on his face in that moment. It was troubled and scared and confused. I thought it was the train, that he was somehow in shock from nearly meeting his end, but he said it wasn't that.

"I saw something," he said. "On the other side."

"What?" I asked. "What did you see?"

"I think I should go to the sheriff," David said. "It's..."

"It's what, David?" I asked, taking his hand.

"Laura," David said. "She's over there."

"Laura who?" I asked.

"O'Malley," David said.

Laura O'Malley, the girl murdered that past summer. That's who he meant.

"You saw her?" I asked, becoming afraid myself, I admit. "You saw a ghost?"

"I don't know," David said, looking back across the bridge, speaking slowly. "The snow and sun play tricks and I was winded from outrunning the train. After I heard you calling, I sat on a rock to catch my breath. I closed my eyes and when I opened them I could see her standing before me, like fine silk in the wind. Her face, I swear, it was looking at me. Her mouth was moving. I got up at once, I didn't believe it, but she approached me. She was reaching out. I ran. To the tracks. I had to get away. When I reached the bridge, I stopped, remembering why I crossed. I turned around and she was still there, standing on the tracks, looking at me. Still trying to speak. Her mouth was moving, but there was no sound."

I followed his gaze to the opposite side of the river, but saw nothing.

"Do you see her now?" I asked.

"No," David said. "I ran. I ran back here, Heaven help me. It was probably not very smart, but I ran just as fast as when the train was coming."

He looked at me, shock mixed with panic now.

"You believe me, don't you, Ellie?" he asked.

"I do," I said. And I did. David was not the sort of person to spin yarns or make believe like this. I didn't doubt him then and I don't doubt him now, all these years agone. I can't right tell you what he saw, but he saw something out there that looked like Laura O'Malley.

David walked into town and arranged with Herman Statler to give him a ride back to the wagon. They were able to fix it up nice and good, and we rode back through the muck not saying another word about the trestle bridge or what he saw on the other side.

It weighed on him the rest of the day. He would stop what he was doing and look out in the direction of the bridge. I hoped a good night's sleep would rest his heart on the matter, but even the next day the encounter occupied his thoughts. I asked him what he wanted to do about it and he said he thought he ought to tell the sheriff. Poor Laura O'Malley had been murdered after all. Even if the sheriff laughed him out of the jailhouse,

David felt he had to tell someone so as to have a clear conscience.

So, that afternoon David went back into town and told the sheriff what he saw. David said the sheriff listened and didn't poke fun or anything like that. David said his piece and came home.

It stayed with him, though, I can tell you that for certain. Every time we crossed those tracks by the trestle bridge, David would let his gaze linger in that direction a little longer.

Every time.

24

The Ledger of Owen McCabe

Sheriff's Report, March 19, 1887
Acting Sheriff Reginald Turnbull

After a day of boredom and discomfort, recovering on Dr. Faraday's orders, I had had my fill. I felt my ribs could tolerate checking in with Deputy Allen Green in the jailhouse. I did not find him there and guessed he was somewhere about the town on duty.

At half-past eleven in the morning, Mr. David Langford approached me as I was heading to Sully's for some lunch. He was of a serious disposition, but eager to share what was on his mind. I asked him to accompany me to the jailhouse. He did so and told me the most bizarre of tales.

He said that yester-day, March 18th, his wagon had broken down near the tracks north of town. He related how he'd attempted to cross the trestle bridge on foot. After avoiding a train, his story became fantastic and I harboured doubts as to its veracity. Simply put, Mr. Langford claimed to have seen the ghost of Laura O'Malley.

At the mention of the deceased girl, I paid closer attention to Mr. Langford's story. It was a simple one. Her apparition tried to speak to him, but was devoid of sound. So frightened was Mr. Langford that he fled back across the trestle bridge and told his wife what happened.

As he related this story, his manner was calm and edging toward sheepish embarrassment, aware that such a claim might be met with skepticism, but he remained firm in his conviction that this unusual event took place. Upon questioning him, he neither evaded nor came up inconsistent.

Whatever had happened, he believed his senses and seemed trustworthy in the telling.

Satisfied, I sent him on his way.

After Langford left, I pulled documents originally written by Sheriff Wilson, who had conducted the initial investigation into Laura O'Malley's murder. The Langfords' had been hosting a dinner with their in-laws the evening of the girl's death. None of them left the farm until dusk and then only the in-laws, who travelled home. No one had seen anything unusual that day. David was not then a suspect and I held to that conclusion. Nothing in his telling of the encounter with this "ghost" left me to question his character.

What then to make of his extraordinary story; a fugue of the mind or a genuine visit by a spirit? Being neither a man of medicine nor spiritualism, I am not qualified to say. As a lawman, my attention must be to the facts and David Langford left me with one I could not ignore.

The trestle bridge where Mr. Langford allegedly encountered the ghost of Laura O'Malley is north of town over the east river. Of greater importance, however, is that it is the site of Deputy Green's discovery of the hatchet believed to be the murder weapon used on the girl.

I dwelled on the issue for some time, but decided to visit the trestle bridge. The journey there on horseback was not a pleasant one, to be sure, with my ribs still in a very sensitive state. So much did they ache and jab me with pain that I did not dismount my horse once at the bridge. Cautious for any oncoming train, I looked across the span to the opposite side and saw nothing out of the ordinary. I made to ride back to town when something on the far side move. I waited and watched, thinking perhaps it was a shadow in the bright sunlight. What emerged from the underbrush was a stray dog, followed by a pup. They looked around, then ducked back into the undergrowth within the trees. I considered leaving, but decided that since I was out there I'd best be thorough.

I dismounted—with no small amount of aggravation to my ribs—tied up my horse to a tree and walked across the bridge.

It unnerved me to recall Mr. Langford's harrowing account of outrunning a train on that very trestle the day before.

I glimpsed the dogs as I approached, moving about their business amongst the trees. As I drew closer, I saw three of them, the two adults digging at the soil under a large rock and their pup, who approached me. One of the parents was none too keen on that. He stopped digging at once and began to growl at me. I drew my gun and fired a warning shot into the air. The dogs fled.

Curious what they were digging after, I went to the rock, reckoning it to be the one Mr. Langford said he sat upon after fleeing the train. The dogs had made good work of the soil around it.

It was there that I found the severed head. The distinctive jaw and teeth of a person, bare of skin in places and exposed to the elements. Heaven help me, I was both ecstatic and disgusted.

I moved the rock, which took extra effort in my condition, and with my knife dug out the grave. I will spare the details as to the state of the head, but suffice to say insects and worms had set upon it, though the cold of winter had stopped the rot sufficiently from making me sick.

Repulsed as I was, I could not leave it out there, particularly with the dogs already aware of its presence. I pried the head lose, cutting the strands of long dark hair still sunk into the deeply frosted earth. I took care as best I could to preserve what remained of the head. It was quite unpleasant an experience and not one I care to ever repeat. I welcomed the distraction of the train that passed as I worked, loud and close as it was.

I wrapped the head in my scarf and crossed the bridge back to my horse. I rode into town with great haste to the doctor's office.

My sudden arrival bearing human remains took Dr. Faraday aback. I braced him before revealing the contents of the scarf, but it came as no less a shock to him, even as a medical doctor. He asked me to leave the head with him so he could examine it, as well as study Dr. Shaw's notes from Laura O'Malley's original autopsy.

He also admonished me thoroughly for not following his orders by venturing out.

Several hours later, Dr. Faraday came to the jailhouse and asked me to take him to the place where I found the head. We rode out on his buggy, which put less stress on my ribs, I'm happy to report, and crossed the trestle bridge on foot. The day had grown long, but the rock and the hole were as I had left them. Dr. Faraday found the hair I had cut to free the head still protruding from the frozen earth. He examined the site in silence, but our visit there did not take long.

He said: "After examining the remains and seeing this for myself, I can conclude that what you found here and brought to me is without a doubt the head of Laura O'Malley."

I asked: "On the record, that's your official conclusion?"

Dr. Faraday answered: "Yes. I'll write up an autopsy report for you. It's her."

Acting Sheriff Reginald Turnbull

25

The Ledger of Owen McCabe

The Orchard Herald Special Edition, March 20th, 1887
MURDER OF LAURA O'MALLEY SOLVED!
by Thomas Buchanan, Editor

On this first day of spring, Orchard Bend reels after an unexpected and dramatic turn of events in the case of Laura O'Malley's murder. During the course of his investigation, Sheriff Reginald Turnbull made a ghastly but important discovery. When Laura O'Malley's life ended prematurely last August, her killer did the unthinkable and mutilated the body by decapitation. Her headless corpse was found in the days that followed, but her head remained missing.

Yester-day, Saturday the 19th, Sheriff Turnbull unearthed that vestige of poor Laura's remains and Doctor William Faraday confirmed her identity.

"The remains were found on the edge of the McCabe estate," Turnbull told the Herald. "There is no doubt now that Henry McCabe was responsible for Miss O'Malley's death. The evidence is overwhelming."

This discovery comes after former Sheriff Emery Dale's arrest and incarceration on the charge of negligence leading to manslaughter in executing her duties while investigating the murder. While awaiting trial, Ms. Dale escaped custody and fled, not having been heard from since. The Council of Aldermen met in an emergency session yester-eve and Mr. Griesbach now confirms they are withdrawing the charges against Ms. Dale.

The would-be prosecutor told the Orchard Herald, "After consultation with the Council, our charge of negligence is no longer supported by the facts of the case. It has been decided, in light of new evidence pointing to Henry McCabe as the murderer of Laura O'Malley, that Ms. Dale acted within her duties to defend herself against a deadly threat by ending Henry McCabe's life when he left her no other recourse. I have telegraphed Judge Grenville and hope he will withdraw the standing warrant for Ms. Dale's arrest."

Thus, both the Sheriff and the Council consider the case of the murder of Laura O'Malley solved.

Mr. Maxwell McCabe did not make himself available to comment on the matter, having only recently returned to Orchard Bend following the death of his wife Gertrude.

When asked how he came to make his discovery of Miss O'Malley's remains, Sheriff Turnbull would only cite anonymous sources he interviewed this past week, whose information led him to the burial location near the train bridge spanning the East River.

Of the O'Malley family itself, Sheriff Turnbull could provide few details.

"I visited the O'Malley homestead in the hope of delivering the news," says the sheriff, "but found no one there. Laura's father travelled south last year following her death, so I've been told, while her mother has not been seen in these parts in some months and may also have moved on."

May Laura O'Malley at long last truly rest in peace.

* * *

Rebecca Clarke clutched the newspaper tight in her hand, not wanting to risk dropping it on the wet ground as she hurried through the woods towards the cabin.

Elation, relief and intense sadness boiled under the surface, making her want to cry out with excitement one moment and stop to weep the next. The murder case was closed, with Sheriff Dale vindicated, and like the paper said, Laura could now rest in peace. All the many weeks of sneaking to this remote place, bringing Dale news and the occasional supplies, watching her recover from the sickness in her lungs, the stress of keeping the secret from everyone, even Billy, all of it was over and Emery Dale could return to Orchard Bend.

Would she get her job back, be made proper sheriff again? Rebecca wondered. *After all, she'd done nothing wrong, except maybe break out of jail. But she never should have been there in the first place.*

Anger replaced the relief, anger that any of this ever needed to happen in the first place, that the council hadn't believed Sheriff Dale about Henry McCabe.

"I hope the taste of crow was tough and bitter for Mr Griesbach," Rebecca said under her breath.

The cabin came into view and Rebecca doubled her pace, her boots sinking into the mud with each step.

In the past, Rebecca would have knocked on the door to let Dale know it was her, but with the veil of secrecy no longer needed, the girl called before she got there, "Sheriff Dale, it's Rebecca! You won't believe it! Sheriff Dale!"

Rebecca rounded the front of the cabin and saw the door ajar.

"Sheriff Dale!" she said, eager to break the news.

Still, no one answered.

Rebecca approached, uncertain, and then saw that the door was not in fact ajar. It had been ripped from its frame and lay on the cabin floor.

Rebecca took in the scene inside the cabin and let out a choked whisper.

"No..."

26

March 18, 1887
Orchard Bend

"Hello, Deputy Green," Dale said.

"Come peacefully, Miss Dale," Green said, his voice steady. More to the point, his hand was steady, the gun aimed at her from the cover of the doorframe not wavering. Dale kept her hands up.

"Allen, I'm not armed," Dale said.

"On the floor, Miss Dale," Green said.

Dale knelt, not taking her eyes off the deputy.

"You'll have to tell me how you tracked me down," Dale said.

"After you tell me how you broke out of jail," Green answered, and this time his voice betrayed biting anger. Dale resisted smiling as she remembered that night, fleeing the jailhouse in the blizzard.

"I will," Dale said. "I owe you that."

"On the floor, all the way," Green said, "on your stomach."

Dale did as ordered, lowering herself to the floor.

"No one's let me forget that you got loose on my watch," Green said as she put her cheek against the cool, rough wood. "I'm a laughing stock around here, but that's all going to change when I bring you in. Mr Buchanan's headline will read *Deputy Green Re-Captures Dale.* Then they'll stop with their comments and their opinions. "

He stepped into the room, the soles of his boots scraping on the wood floor as he stood in the doorway looking around.

"I'm sorry, Allen, you don't deserve that," Dale said.

"You're right, I don't deserve it," Green said.

Out of the corner of her eye, Dale could see him at the door, his hands on his hips, standing over her.

"I've always respected you, Allen," Dale said.

"Is that so?" Green said.

"Yes," Dale replied. "You're smart and you learn quickly. You found the hatchet that day we went out to the field, remember?"

"You said I had never thought in those terms before, thinking like the criminal," Green said. Dale could almost hear that he was smiling as he said it.

His boots shifted and he walked around her, giving her arms a wide berth.

Good technique, Dale thought, *stay out of reach of the suspect as you move to restrain them. You are good, Deputy Green, you've done everything right.*

"I'm willing to bet that's how you found me here, with good old-fashioned detective work," Dale said, turning her head to follow him.

"What was in the bench?" Green asked. Dale heard him uncock his gun and drop it into its holster. He knelt behind her, putting his knee on her lower back to keep her from moving. He took her left wrist and brought it to her back. She heard the rattle of his handcuffs and then felt them close around her wrist. "I found the hiding place there. What did Miss Clarke take from there to bring to you? Was it that little box on the bed?"

Green brought her other arm back and cuffed it. Dale felt her blood rising and the sick feeling of panic clawing at her chest. Green stood up and when he did, Dale took in a deep breath, steadying her nerves against the claustrophobic feeling of being handcuffed. The deputy took her by the arm and helped her to her feet. He then pulled up the chair and sat her on it.

He parked himself on the bed across from her, which creaked under his weight. He picked up the wooden box, and held it in his hands, looking at her. The box's key rested in the lock.

"You can open it, Allen," Dale said.

Green did, unlocking it and examining the contents, then looking at her. He reached in and pulled out a stack of dollar bills of various denominations.

193

"What you have there is most of the original five hundred dollar reward I got for ending the Underwood Gang," Dale said, dropping her head and looking at the floor. "I didn't spend a lot of it because almost immediately I was employed by Maxwell McCabe. And he paid me very well."

"I'll bet he did," Green said, standing up.

Dale remained seated.

"Do you know why I became sheriff of Orchard Bend?" Dale asked. "Because I couldn't work for him anymore. I couldn't live that life. I wanted to do good, to protect this town and the people I care about here. It's why we all wear a badge, isn't it?"

Green said nothing, but shifted on his heels, his boots again scraping on the wood floor.

"Henry McCabe murdered Laura O'Malley," Dale said, looking up at Green. "He followed me to the barn and attacked me. I was forced to shoot him. He left me no other choice."

Green said nothing, but his jaw clenched and his lip twitched. His eyes grew narrow.

"I killed my good friend's son," Dale said. "And that's something I have to live with. I'll never be free of that, I'll never escape that fact. Not ever. And now *she's* dead, too, along with any hope of forgiveness from her.

"I've thought about it every day since it happened, what I did to protect myself and to protect the town. It cost me everything," Dale said, "but I know I'd do it again to keep Orchard Bend safe."

"Stop!" Green said, throwing the money down on the bed. He rubbed the back of his neck and shook his head, letting out a long breath through his teeth.

Dale watched him.

"I have to take you in, Sheriff," Green said. "You can go before the judge and tell him what you told me. Show him the evidence that Henry McCabe was guilty..."

Dale shook her head, looking back down at the wood floor.

"Now that his wife is dead, do you think Maxwell McCabe will let the judge release me after you bring me in?" Dale asked. "Remember, I worked for McCabe, I know how he operates. I killed his son and now he has me over a barrel. He and Griesbach have probably already paid the judge to lock me up for a good long time."

Green straightened up at the mention of Martin Griesbach.

"So you're going to run?" Green asked. "You needed this money to get away, start a new life."

"I can't stay here," Dale said.

Green reached into his pocket and pulled out the small key for the handcuffs. He held it up and looked at it.

"I woke up this morning and told myself that today was going to be different," Green said, turning the key this way and that in the candlelight. Without another word he walked over to Dale and unlocked her handcuffs. Dale rubbed her wrists and stretched her arms.

"Thank you, Allen," she said.

He nodded, still not saying anything. He didn't look at her as he tucked the handcuffs into his gun belt and slipped the key back into his pocket. He stared off out the open cabin door, where the late afternoon light had begun to fail toward dusk.

Dale rose from her chair.

"Orchard Bend should be grateful they have you as a deputy, Allen," Dale said.

Green turned and looked at her.

"Thank you, Sheriff," he said.

"May I ask a small favour of you, Allen?" Dale asked. She picked up the now the empty wooden box and held it out to him. "Return this to Rose. I have what I need from it and I want her to have it. She's the only friend I have left in Orchard Bend."

Green took the box, turned the key and locked it.

"Is there a message to go with it, Sheriff?" Green asked.

Dale shook her head.

"Nothing that need be put into words," Dale said. "The box is enough."

Green nodded and walked to the door, then stopped.

"You're wrong about one thing," he said, not turning around. "She's not the only friend you have in Orchard Bend. Godspeed, Sheriff Dale."

He stepped out of the cabin and out of the shallow recess, his boots making wet sounds on the thawing dirt. He disappeared around the corner and she listened as his footfalls grew distant. Dale sat on the bed next to the scattered bills, put her face in her hands and let herself weep for several minutes.

Drying her eyes and letting out a long, weary groan, she rose to her feet and walked to the cold wood stove. She opened the door, pulled out the fresh, unburned log and put it back on the small pile from which she'd taken it mere minutes earlier. Then she reached inside the stove and pulled out her watch, the small black rectangle with the smooth, flat face. The watch, like Dale herself, which was not of this time or place.

Dale had seen Green approaching, just as she'd seen Rebecca coming to bring the wooden box to her. Dale had seen it all from inside the cabin, through what she called the grey sight, the smoky, translucent view of the world she had discovered the morning she awoke there.

With little else to do all alone expect trap small game and recover from the sickness that almost killed her, Dale focused on practising using this grey sight. With all but the barest pieces of her old life lost to her, Dale hoped the grey sight would offer some clarity or a way to learn more about who she had been. After a month, the nature of the grey sight still eluded her, but she knew it was tied to her headaches and her amnesia, and that drove her on, kept her level against the tide of loneliness and isolation and sorrow.

When Rebecca brought news of Gertrude's death, Emery Dale knew the time had come to depart Orchard Bend. She had escaped jail, but to what end, the thin hope that another person from her time had visited Orchard Bend decades ago and might still be alive?

Dale had to know, she had to try to find this woman with the scar on her cheek.

With Rebecca's help, she formed the plan to get the wooden box, but Rebecca had been followed by Deputy Green. Even as she sat on the bed talking to the girl, seeming distant and shut off, Dale was watching Green outside, seeing him through the walls of the cabin with the help of the grey sight. When

Rebecca had left, Dale knew she had only seconds to act. She'd jumped from the bed, opened the wooden box and took out the small, black watch. With a glance over her shoulder to confirm Green was still approaching around the cabin, Dale hid the watch in the stove, setting it in the thick ash, placing the piece of wood on top of it. She closed the stove door and waited, watching Green approach until he kicked his way into the cabin.

Now she wiped the ash from the screen and the wristband, cleaning the surfaces with a little spit and the corner of her shirt. She tapped the screen and the green circle there spun around before the display filled with options. Content that the watch had suffered no damage in the stove, Dale tapped it off and sat back down on the bed.

She closed her eyes and concentrated, focusing on memories, those from her life before Orchard Bend, few and fragmented as they were.

Dale recalled the woman from the newspaper photo, her face bloody from the gash on her cheek. It lasted only a few moments, but it was the clearest of the old memories, from the pain and anger on the woman's face to the residue of urgency and fear, almost panic, rising up inside her.

Next, she saw soldiers firing on a family in a desert, soldiers under her command. Hard as it was to face, she needed to play that memory out. She felt no shame, no remorse, only horror at the deaths brought about by her order to fire. Then she recalled her superior officer pinning a medal to her dress uniform and congratulating her on her actions.

Did I deserve recognition and support? Dale wondered, but she could not say for certain.

Then came the memory of the blonde woman with the pale green eyes sparring with her, the two crashing wooden practice blades together, swinging, dodging and blocking with uncanny precision. Her opponent's face, lined with determination, very much in the moment, was so familiar. It brought up so many emotions now—hurt and envy, but there was also comforting warmth. Each time Dale brought that memory forward, those feelings—and many others tangle together—grew stronger and it became difficult to separate them.

Each memory made her headache grow. It swelled to an almost unbearable pounding, until at last, with a fierce suddenness, the pain ebbed.

Dale opened her eyes and beheld the world once more through the grey sight. She rose from the bed and walked to the cabin door as everything around her shimmered translucent grey. Through the thick logs, Dale could glimpse the shape of the trees beyond. If she leaned up close to the cabin walls, which she'd done before, she knew she could make out details in the nearest tree's bark.

Outside, she stood before the cabin and looked around.

"Laura?" Dale said. "Are you there?"

Dale expected the apparition of Laura O'Malley might slip into view, moving through the trees in her direction. Dale waited, looking all about her, but Laura was nowhere to be seen.

Dale thought she might be out there anyway, so continued, "I wanted to tell you and your mother 'thank you.' You both saved my life. I hope one day you both find peace."

Silence and stillness answered her from the woods. Dale guessed that would be the only response she'd receive. It would have to be enough.

* * *

"Miss Adelaide," Deputy Green said. "We need to talk."

Rose drew in a breath, then caught herself. Her hand tightened on the handle of the door as she eyed the wooden box in the deputy's hand.

Is this it? Am I caught? she wondered. *Is he going to arrest me?*

In her hesitation, Green stepped forward, not quite crossing the threshold of her door, enough to make her back away. He looked around, up and down the street, then gave the wooden box a shake in her direction, his expression urgent.

"Take it," Green said, his voice still low.

Wide-eyed and not quite comprehending what was going on, Rose reached for the box. Green shoved it into her hand and stepped back from the open door, looking around again. Rose peered past him, but could see no one.

"Allen..." she started, wanting to ask what in the world this visit was about, but she stopped herself.

"Sheriff Dale asked me to return the box to you," Green said. "Best keep it out of sight."

"Sheriff Dale?!" Rose said, setting the box down on the table next to the door. Her thoughts began as she pieced the situation together. "I don't understand entirely what you mean, Deputy."

The sound of conversing voices down the street caused Green to straighten up and look around. In the pale dusk, a man and woman approached.

Mr and Mrs McManus.

Green snapped his attention to Rose. When he spoke, his voice was loud and full of authority.

"And you don't recall seeing anything that could have spooked the horses yesterday?" Green said, giving her a wink.

"Why no, Deputy," Rose said, almost as loud. Green's horse was tied to the post by the cottage's white picket fence and Rose watched the McManuses pass by the animal. She asked Green, "How is the sheriff? Was he hurt quite badly?"

"Some broken ribs, mainly," Green said, as Rose saw the couple slow at the fence gate, both trying to be discreet as they watched the schoolteacher and the deputy and both failing. "Doctor Faraday says he'll be up and about in no time."

"Well then, you have a good evening, Deputy," Rose said. She fixed him with a serious stare but kept her voice light. "And thank you for your news about the sheriff. It's most comforting."

The McManuses picked up their pace and continued on, no doubt heading into town for dinner at the hotel. Rose started to close the door and for a moment Green seemed uncertain. She'd seen the same torn expression on many students' faces over the years and guessed he had more he wanted to say.

"We shall speak more another time," Rose whispered. Green nodded and turned away. As Rose closed the door, she saw him cast his gaze up at the deepening blue sky and the stars above before heading back down the path to the fence gate.

Inside, Rose leaned back against the door frame, her heart racing.

"Emery," she said, and picked up the wooden box from the table by the door, noticing for the first time the key in the lock. She sat at her dining table, set down the lantern and put her hand on the lid. Rose had really not expected to see the box again after leaving it inside the stone bench, but it had made its way to Emery, who had held it and then delivered it back. Rose grinned, her eyes watery; first had come the letter the day before, and now the box. Again, Rose tried to picture Emery, this time holding the box, thinking about Rose, before handing it to Allen Green.

Was he the courier? Rose wondered. It made sense, since he'd been out by the old church lawn that morning.

Rose turned the key and the lock released the wooden lid. Whatever had been inside was gone now, but Rose didn't give the absent contents much thought as she closed the box and locked it, leaned back in her chair and ran her fingers over the varnished wood grain.

* * *

As Miss Adelaide closed the door, Deputy Green stood on the path leading to her gate and beheld the stars far overhead. The cool air held the faint smell of the spring thaw and he breathed it in before walking down the path to his horse. As he rode away from the schoolteacher's cottage, his stomach growled. He couldn't remember when he'd eaten last. It must have been hours.

Green made his way to Anderson Street, left his horse at the Statler Livery and walked to Sully's, where the jangling sound of the tavern's piano carried outside. Green stepped up onto the boardwalk and through the door, crossing straight to the bar. He passed tables where patrons paused in their conversations to watch him go by, but Green took little notice of it. Sully himself glanced up from the piano, saw who it was, looked away with a slight shake of his head and kept right on playing.

At the bar, Irene Sullivan poured the young Doctor Faraday a whiskey as Green approached. At the doctor's feet, Green noticed an apple crate full of odds and ends sitting on the floor. Faraday took the shot, downed it and straightened the pointed ends of his black moustache.

"A fine potation, Miss Sullivan. Truly splendid, indeed," Faraday said, putting a coin down on the bar and tipping his hat to her, "A capitol evening to you."

Stepping away from the bar, he spotted Green and greeted him with a polite, "Deputy," and proceeded on his way out.

Irene watched the doctor leave, shaking her head with a smirk.

"Easterners," she said, then turned her attention to Green.

"Did I just witness the new doctor's first visit to this fine establishment?" Green asked.

"*The Harvest Moon's* dining room was full, what with three stages passing through," Irene said. "Two heading to California and one heading east. So the good doctor at last graced us with his presence."

"Did the man forget this?" Green asked, walking over to the apple crate on the floor.

"No," Irene said as she came around the bar, "Doctor Faraday figured that since he was coming here anyway, he would bring these over."

From the crate, she pulled out a stack of what looked like several framed pictures and laid them on the bar. Two were documents and one was indeed a photograph.

"These belonged to Doctor Shaw," Green said.

"Doctor Faraday has settled into his office and was wondering what to do with all of these things," Irene explained, "Pictures, his old army papers, his degree, not to mention everything else in there."

"What are you going to do with it all?" Green asked.

"I don't rightly know yet," Irene said, picking up the framed photograph. Green had only ever known Shaw in his later years, so the young man in the image seemed like a stranger. Green guessed it had been taken around the time of the doctor's graduation from medical school.

Irene to the wall overlooking the bar, where several other photographs hung, and added, "But I think I can give this a home right here."

She walked back around the bar and knelt down, disappearing for a moment and re-emerging with a fountain pen. With some care, Irene slipped the photograph out of its frame and set it flat on the bar. She took the pen, dabbed the tip on her finger to make sure it had ink and began writing on the lower quarter of the picture. It took only a moment, but when she finished, she held the photograph up. In her neat cursive, Irene had penned *Dr. Alfred Shaw.*

Green nodded his approval and Irene replaced the photograph in its frame.

"I'll hang this up tomorrow," Irene said, setting the picture on the shelf next to the liquor bottles. "Now, what can I get you this evening, Deputy?"

Before Green could answer, a voice called out behind him.

"Why if it isn't Deputy Green!"

Green turned to find Martin Griesbach sauntering across the floor toward him. The lawyer stopped halfway there, smiling, his hands holding his lapels.

Green looked around the room and saw just about every pair of eyes on him. Even Sully was watching, his fingers slowing on the piano keys and then stopping altogether.

"Now, Deputy, I swear I saw you riding out of town earlier, in something of a hurry," Griesbach proclaimed, his smile turning acidic. "I thought to myself, 'There goes a man on a mission! What could be so urgent?' And then it dawned on me: you had a break in the case! You were going after the former sheriff Ms Dale."

Green felt his cheeks flush, and not just at how uncanny Griesbach's taunting was.

"And now I see you tracked her all the way to this watering hole," Griesbach went on. He turned and pointed around the room at the onlookers. "Quick, everyone! Check under your tables. Dale's got to be around here somewhere!"

Laughter erupted.

Griesbach revelled in it and then made his way to a table across the room. Sully resumed his playing.

Green turned back to Irene, who was not laughing. The dark expression she shot at Martin Griesbach would have been enough to wither most anyone else, but Green knew the lawyer would pay no attention to the barmaid.

"I'll take your dinner special tonight, Miss Sullivan," Green said.

Irene left to take the order to the kitchen and Green took up a stool, leaning back with his elbows on the bar. Across the room, Griesbach made himself comfortable at his table and pulled out his pipe.

Green watched him, then looked down at the mud still on his boots, mud from the woods outside the cabin where Sheriff Dale was holed up.

Mud from where I tracked her, he thought, and a ghost of a smile crossed his face.

Irene returned and from behind the bar she leaned forward, talking low.

"Don't let him get to you, Deputy," she said.

"No, Miss Sullivan, you're dead right," Green said, looking back at Griesbach, who caught his eye, sneered again and gave a puff of his pipe. "That man has nothing over me."

27

The Ledger of Owen McCabe

Ashleyville Republic, March 29, 1879
*UNDERWOOD GANG ROBS STAGECOACH, THREE
DEAD!*
by Percival Wright

The murderous Underwood Gang has resurfaced and after a
harrowing attack on a Western Star stagecoach, many surely
wonder whether anyone is safe. Having robbed banks in Spring
Pass, Gravestone and Pine River, where a deputy was shot and
killed, the group of Ernest Underwood, Arthur Underwood and
Andrew MacReady are wanted men. Their associate James
Olsen was shot dead during the Pine River robbery.

In the early evening on the 27th, the Underwood Gang set
upon the Western Star stage, which at the time was
transporting passengers from Ashleyville to destinations south.
Employing a ruse of blocking the road with debris, the
stagecoach's driver, armed escort and passengers were
ambushed. Charles Warren (driver), Branch Beckham (escort)
and two yet-to-be identified passengers were fatally shot. The
third passenger, an eyewitness who the Railroad Police would
not identify (citing the integrity of an active investigation), was
travelling with the others on business when the robbery
occurred. The gang also put down the pair of horses pulling the
stage, thereby stranding it in the far outskirts of Ashleyville's
town limits. The victim was forced to wait overnight in the
wilderness before being discovered by a travelling minister and
his wife, who brought the sole survivor to Ashleyville, where
they immediately informed Lieutenant Douglas Harper—the
new head of the Railroad Police—of what had transpired. Lt.

Harper and his officers located the stage and from there began their investigation and the pursuit of the wanted men.

A reward of $500 now stands for anyone able to bring them to justice, dead or alive, including for information provided which directly leads to their apprehension.

* * *

March 27, 1879
Ashleyville

Holding the Smith & Wesson revolver they found at the side of the road, Lieutenant Harper surveyed the scene of the attack.

Even before the posse of officers and recruited men reached the stagecoach, Harper had put together a detailed picture of what had happened. Miss Eagan, the dishevelled, tired and hungry survivor, had given her dramatic account, but as Harper spotted the stage on the road ahead, and more to the point now saw the scene for himself, the picture of the events became quite clear.

The Underwoods could not have planned it better.

The stretch road made a gradual descent into a dell lined with trees and undergrowth. A smart driver would pick up his pace to clear it all as fast as he could, but Ernest Underwood and his brother had thought of that, too, with a little help from Mother Nature. A storm had blown through to the north, but wind had torn through the entire region, taking down signs from storefronts in town and even knocking some people off their feet. Harper had even heard reports of whole trees being damaged and their limbs being torn off. Sitting in his office at the CUC Railroad Police station, he had heard the wind howl and carry on for hours as it slammed the windows. On the road approaching the scene of the crime, branches and debris lay all about.

Perfect subterfuge, Harper thought. *Most of this is probably genuine. And there's enough of it to sell the illusion up ahead.*

The driver sees all this mess and isn't surprised to see a whole tree limb blocking his path.

When the posse was a dozen yards from the stage, Harper stopped them.

"Sergeant Barnes, you first," Harper said to his second-in-command, who saddled up beside him. "Take Crenshaw and start tracking. Miss Eagan said they lit off west. Find their trail."

Barnes rubbed his chin through his thick beard, an affectation the CUC had often insisted he trim. Barnes just as often resisted the request.

"You know, Doug, the trail is gonna be close to cold by now, if it's not already," Barnes said. "Crenshaw's good, but this is going to be a doozy of a job."

Harper turned around, leaning over on his saddle.

"Crenshaw!" he called out.

The tall, clean-shaven man rode up to join them.

"Today you work for your supper," Harper told him. "Get on up there and figure out where these sons of bitches skedaddled off to."

"Right, Lieutenant," Crenshaw said, but he didn't move.

Harper waited, then looked to Barnes, who gave an amused shrug. Crenshaw's face went slack and he didn't blink, even when one of his long, stray blond hairs whipped across his face in the breeze. Harper made to say something, but Barnes saw this and put his hand up to stop him, giving a curt shake of his head and a look that said, *Leave him be.*

Then Crenshaw blinked, but his expression remained passive, almost bored, and he said in a soft voice, "Now."

Without another word, Crenshaw trotted on toward the stagecoach. Harper looked at Barnes again, who shrugged and followed the tracker. Harper watched as Crenshaw went to work and Barnes stayed out of his way. They reached the stage and Crenshaw gave it a cursory look before dismounting and turning his attention to the dirt road. He moved this way and that, sometimes kneeling to get a closer look at some key mark on the road that would go unnoticed by most anyone else. All the time he did this he didn't say a word. As he placed each

206

puzzle piece, he drew away from the stagecoach step by step. Soon he stood at the road's edge looking west.

"Good man, that fits the woman's story," Harper murmured.

Crenshaw continued on, not stopping to consult Barnes or anyone else. He peered into the knee-high grass and undergrowth at the side of the road, then without looking back, gave a wave for Barnes to follow. Not waiting to see if they would, he stepped into the grass and kept right on tracking. Barnes trotted over to Crenshaw's horse and took the reigns, then turned back to the rest of the posse and waved for them to come forward.

Harper shifted in his saddle to address them.

"Alright, tracking team, you know your assignment," Harper said. "Go with Sergeant Barnes and get those murdering bastards. Watch your backs and do as he says. Everyone come home safe. Now go."

Most of the dozen men charged forward, some letting loose determined shouts. Up ahead, Crenshaw had remounted and was guiding his horse through the grass past the tree line, his gaze fixed on the ground. He remained out front, with Barnes following right behind him and the others bringing up the rear single file. Harper watched them for several minutes, then rode to the stage. Following behind him was the remaining officer, the undertaker with his hearse, and the two men who had volunteered to help clean up the mess—not out of any sense of duty, but because it paid well.

Even though he knew what he was going to find, Harper still braced himself for the carnage. The two dead horses lay crumpled on the road in a kneeling position that almost looked like they could stand up and continue their journey. The stagecoach wasn't too worse for wear, except for the dozen bullet holes splintering the wood in the doors and the frame. None of the glass had been shot out, which for some reason surprised Harper. All those bullets flying around and not one hit any of the windows. Nor had any hit Miss Eagan. The others hadn't been so lucky, like the driver, whose body lay by the thick tree limb blocking the road.

The Underwoods either dragged the limb there to stop their next prey or it had fallen there during the windstorm and they took full advantage of it, Harper mused. *Either way, it came to the same result: a perfect ambush.*

The Eagan woman hadn't seen the initial attack, having been inside the coach. Harper knew he would have to exercise considerable discretion later when he wrote his report. Eagan surviving and a CUC executive dead made a messy situation worse. Not for the first time did Harper wish it had gone the other way for the victim and the survivor. And they had not been alone. Harper had assigned Officer Mills as an undercover agent to prevent just this sort of outcome.

I'll be lucky to keep my job, Harper thought.

When they stopped, the grey-haired driver, Warren, climbed down to move the heavy tree limb. He called for the fellow riding shotgun, a man named Wallace, to help him, but before Wallace could answer, the Underwoods had opened fire. Wallace was killed, his shotgun dropped mere feet from the driver.

Warren, were you stupid enough to try to grab the gun? Harper wondered. Warren's body now lay face down next to it, a bullet in his back and one in his head. *Or were you running for cover and they only thought you were going for the gun?*

Either way, the man had taken a bullet to the back, dropping to the ground next to the horses, who by now had met their own ends.

The Underwood Gang broke cover then and advanced. Mills, the armed officer inside the carriage, had pushed both the CUC executive and Miss Eagan to the floor and maybe thought he could surprise his attackers, because his next move was to fling the coach door open and start firing on Ernest Underwood as he came galloping out of the tree line. It had not been a wise plan. Mills got off a single shot before Ernest returned fire and killed him. His body lay outside the coach door, two rounds in his chest. That's when the executive threw up his hands and surrendered. Ernest ordered him out of the stagecoach and the man did as he was told, surrendering his money and his valuables. Then Underwood shot him and ordered Miss Eagan out of the coach. She did so, praying the entire time.

While all that was going on, Andrew MacReady was rooting through the luggage and Arthur Underwood stood watch a ways up the road. When he finished with the luggage, MacReady moved on to the driver's body, but it turns out the man wasn't dead. The Eagan woman said that when MacReady started rifling through his pockets, the man jerked and coughed up blood, then tried to talk. It startled MacReady, who jumped back, but Ernest just aimed his Colt .45 Peacemaker and shot the driver in the back of the head.

"Hurry up, would you!?" Ernest told MacReady.

MacReady took the driver's watch and the money from his wallet, which he dropped next to his body. And there it still lay, untouched. Then MacReady picked up the shotgun and mounted his horse. He joined Ernest and gave the gun to him. Ernest levelled the weapon at Miss Eagan, who later admitted she thought her own time was up right then.

Instead of shooting Eagan, Underwood swung the butt of the shotgun and knocked her cold. When she came to, it was full-on night. The Underwoods had fled and she was alone with a splitting headache, her head covered in drying blood. Eagan spent the night curled up on the floor of the coach, clutching one of the dead officer's pistols and praying for dawn, jumping at every suspicious sound and hoping the gang wouldn't decided to return to finish her off. Dawn arrived and a few hours later along came the minister and his wife. They too were heading out of Ashleyville. When they saw the bodies and the shot-up stagecoach, they turned right around to hightail it back the way they came. Eagan heard their wagon clattering to make the turn on the narrow road. She jumped out of the stage, causing the pair quite a fright. With her blood-soaked face, ragged appearance and still holding the gun, they thought her somehow responsible for the whole ugly scene. In a moment of clarity, Eagan realized how she must have looked and dropped the gun on the side of the road, where it lay until Harper and his posse of officers came upon it. Crying for help, Eagan had climbed into the back of the wagon against their protestations and just about got herself shot when the minister's wife pulled their rifle on him. She kept it trained on Miss Eagan all during the long trip back to Ashleyville that day.

Harper finished his survey of the scene around the stagecoach and rode over to the corpse of the CUC executive. He dismounted and hunkered down next to him.

"Your little getaway with Miss Eagan didn't go quite the way your planned, huh, Mr Cobbler?" Harper whispered as he straightened the man's coat over his bloody shirt. He stood up, waved to the two volunteers and they dismounted. They walked over and picked up Cobbler's body, carried it to the hearse and laid it on the heavy canvas sheet inside.

Harper then looked down at the body of Mills, the officer who had been riding with Cobbler and Miss Eagan. Harper hunkered down beside him next.

"Mills," Harper said, wiping the blood from the man's badge. Harper held up the Smith & Wesson. "I return this to you, officer."

Taking care not to jostle the body, Harper slipped the gun back into Mills' holster, where it would stay until they returned to Ashleyville. When that ritual was finished, the two volunteers carried Mills' body to the hearse.

Harper then walked over to the body of the guard, Beckham, gunned down from the seat of the stage. The way he landed sickened the lieutenant. The man's left arm was bent back at an unnatural angle with his face in the dirt and one knee bent under him, leaving his hindquarters pointing in the air. Harper rolled Beckham onto his back, a much more dignified position, and dusted off the man's face. No blood had splattered it. Ernest Underwood had rode off with Beckham's shotgun, so Harper couldn't return it, but at least the man still had his sidearm.

The two volunteers picked up Beckham's body to carry it to the hearse as the young officer, Rogers, walked up to Harper.

"We're sure the Underwood Gang did this, Lieutenant?" Rogers asked.

Harper gave the fresh recruit in his new uniform a hard look.

"We are indeed sure," Harper said. "Our eye witness description fits and she picked them out from their pictures."

Harper could see that Rogers wanted to ask who the eyewitness was, but the kid had sense enough not to. *The identity of the eye witness is not something you need to concern yourself with, officer,* Harper had told him back at the police station. *That should be enough for you if you want to keep this job.*

"First banks, now stage coaches," Rogers said, staring wide-eyed at the dead horses. The two volunteers were unhitching the team from the coach, a job made harder by the fact that the steeds were crumpled on the ground.

"Crime of opportunity, perhaps," Harper said, leaning over the driver's body. "Or they might have decided banks were too high risk now. Every one of them has been increasing security, so I hear."

Harper knelt and rolled the driver so that he was lying face up, not that there was much of his face left after the bullet had made its exit, his right cheek blown outward. Rogers stood behind him and Harper wondered if now was when the kid would upchuck, but apart from disgusted sigh, the new recruit kept his stomach.

There's hope, Harper thought, and wiped the dirt from the intact side of the driver's face. He picked up the man's wallet and opened it, finding no money, but spotting a folded piece of paper. Harper took it out. He read the contents several times, then handed it to Rogers.

"Tell me what you make of that," Harper said to the recruit.

Rogers took the paper and read it aloud, "'Preston Medical College. Admit One. Josiah Hampstead, M.D., for Charles Winstone. Lecture on Physiology. Session of 18... something, I can't make out the year, but the next number is a 2, so February. Lieutenant, is this ticket to see a lecture?"

"It is," Harper said, turning the wallet over in his hands and regarding the body of Charles Warren with great interest. "You see, medical students attend lectures at their school. They get the ticket and the doctor giving the lecture signs it, as does the student. The student keeps them as a record of what lectures they've attended, I guess."

"So the student this belonged to was Charles Winstone," Rogers said. "Then how did the driver get this ticket?"

Harper didn't reply. He motioned to the volunteers, who were still undoing the harnesses and bridles from the dead horses.

"When you two finish with that business, take care of this man," Harper said, pointing to the driver. "Then you can drag those horses off the road."

Rogers handed him the lecture ticket and Harper folded it up. He tucked it back into the driver's wallet, secured the wallet to the dead man's belt and rose to his feet.

Harper looked west, where Crenshaw had led to the posse in pursuit of the Underwoods.

"Do you think they'll find them, Lieutenant?" Rogers asked.

"Best not to engage in speculation," Harper said.

Rogers started to say something, but stopped himself, opting instead to stare thoughtfully past the trees that lined the road.

The kid has potential, Harper thought. *He knows when to hold his tongue.*

28

April 30, 1879
Ashleyville

"Sergeant Barnes, the station is yours for the remainder of the evening," Lieutenant Harper said. He walked past Barnes' desk, adjusting his coat and hat as he made his way from his office.

Barnes scratched his beard and leaned back in his chair.

"Going to dine at that new hotel?" the sergeant asked.

"The Clementine, yes," Harper said, doing up the buttons on his coat. Outside, the wind had picked up and the heavy clouds threatened rain. Harper knew he better hurry if he planned to beat the weather.

Barnes shook his head.

"Their menu is too expensive for a family man on sergeant's pay," he said. "If I start saving now, I might get in the door with the missus sometime in the next ten years, I reckon."

Harper laughed.

"Good night, Sergeant," he said, and left the station's office area to cross the lobby to the front door. Pulling it open, he fought against the gust of wind that pushed him back. Stepping outside, his coattails whipped about his legs. He lowered his head, pulling his hat down on his brow to keep it from blowing away.

"Excuse me," called a woman's voice.

Harper looked up and saw a woman approach in a plain dark skirt, the colour of which Harper couldn't make out in the gloom of the overcast evening. Her coat, which appeared a light grey but could well have been a pale brown, seemed ill-fitting and baggy. Most of her hair was tucked up under her dark, wide-brimmed hat, but some stray dark locks flitted about in the wind. Her hands she kept tucked in her coat pockets.

Harper didn't make out the long, vertical scar on her cheek until she was a few feet from him.

"Yes, ma'am?" he said.

"I've come to speak to Lieutenant Harper," the woman said. "Do you know whether or not he's still in the station?"

"I'm Lieutenant Harper," he replied, feeling his stomach sinking. He hoped this conversation would be a quick one.

"My name is Kenna Warren," the woman said as she took her hand from her pocket.

Harper tensed up.

Warren, he thought, *I know that name.*

For a split second he thought she was pulling a gun, but instead she produced a folded leather wallet.

Harper relaxed, but stared at the wallet for several seconds before it fit together.

"Mrs Warren, your husband...?" he started.

"...Was the driver of the stagecoach," she finished. "The one attacked by the Underwood Gang."

"I'm so very sorry for your loss," Harper said. He looked up at the sky, which had only grown darker and more ominous. The wind had picked up and he thought he could smell rain in the air.

"Thank you, Lieutenant," Mrs Warren said. "How is your hunt for the Underwoods going? The newspapers have written little about it since the initial report of the robbery."

"Unfortunately, there's very little to tell," Harper said, taking a step away from the woman and hoping she'd get the suggestion that he needed to be elsewhere right then. "The investigation is ongoing."

She moved to block his path and he stopped.

"But there *is* an investigation going on, right?" Mrs Warren snapped at him.

Harper didn't care much for her tone, but seeing as she was a grieving widow, he set that aside.

"We're doing all we can, Mrs Warren," he said, trying to sound patient.

"Which is what, exactly?" she asked, her eyes piercing below the brim of her hat.

"Police work, Mrs Warren," Harper said, his impatience simmering just below the surface. "It takes time."

"So you're following leads, questioning suspects?" she asked.

"Yes, yes, all of that," Harper said.

"It's been over a month, Lieutenant," Mrs Warren said. "I need to know if you're making any progress. I came all this way. The least you can do is spare me a few minutes to tell me what steps you've taken."

"Mrs Warren, I had my men out hunting for the Underwood Gang for over a week," Harper said, letting out a long, resigned sigh. "Before the trail ran cold, all they found was the shotgun belonging to the armed escort. They either dropped it or got rid of it as they made their escape. I had the best tracker in the region leading the hunt, but the Underwoods know that terrain and they know how to disappear. But they're wanted men, and wanted men often make mistakes. I can't say any more than that without compromising the investigation. I'm sorry."

Mrs Warren held his gaze with her uncomfortable stare. He felt she was sizing him up. He held fast and didn't flinch.

"Fine," she said, looking away and taking a step back. "Thank you for your time, Lieutenant."

Mrs Warren turned and walked away as Harper remembered something.

"Mrs Warren?" he called out.

She stopped and turned around.

Harper waited for her to approach, but she didn't, so he went to her.

"May I ask a question, one not entirely related to the case?" he asked.

"Go on," she said.

"I found a ticket in your husband's wallet," Harper said, "for a medical lecture. I am curious why he would have such a thing on his person."

Mrs Warren looked down at the wallet still in her hand. A pained smiled crossed her mouth.

"Before he became a driver for Western Star, my husband was a doctor," Mrs Warren said.

"So he was Doctor Warren, then?" Harper asked.

"No," Mrs Warren said, "he changed his name. When we met he was still Charles Winstone, but he had not been licensed for several years."

"I see," Harper said, though in all honesty he did not. Nor did he really care to.

"Is that all, Lieutenant?" Mrs Warren asked.

"Yes, it is," Harper said, tipping his hat to her. "Have a good night."

Without another word, Mrs Warren turned and walked away down the street. Harper watched her go, then crossed the street and continued on in the direction of the Clementine hotel.

Harper cursed under his breath and quickened his pace as the sky opened up and the first heavy drops of rain hit.

29

March 19, 1886
Sutter Grove

Under a searing, unforgiving sun, as dust swept about and cast the village into a shifting haze, Major Emery Dale drew her service weapon and pointed it at the toothless, grey-haired old woman standing with her family a half dozen paces away. The crone pleaded, tears in her eyes, but contempt and rage filled Dale. The old woman's broken English became indistinct, just more noise in the windy desert. With her scarves and cloths draped about her aging frame, the woman positioned herself between Dale and the man Dale guessed to be the old woman's son, trying to protect him from the automatic weapons levelled at him by Dale's squad of soldiers.

Dale refused to listen to anything more the old woman had to say. She could go to hell for all Dale cared, her and her son and her entire family. Dale lowered her pistol as the wind gusted and sand scratched at her face and hands.

"Fire," Dale ordered.

The soldiers let loose a deafening barrage of rounds, cutting the family down.

Dale jerked out of her slumber as the sound of the train wheels grating against the tracks blended with the gunfire in her dream.

She had not intended to fall asleep in the boxcar, but between the steady rhythm of the jostling train, the growing darkness and the ache of fatigue in her legs and lower back, her body had decided otherwise. Nestled in a corner, Dale had dozed off still upright atop a shipping crate, the blanket she'd taken from the Orchard Bend jail wrapped around her. How long she'd been asleep she did not know, but a kink in her neck brought her back around.

As she opened her eyes, the dream of hazy sunlight faded, its uncomfortable heat replaced with the dry, musty cold of dust and wooden crates. Blackness surrounded her, except for the faint line of blue where the boxcar's door had jammed partway open.

The sight of the family in the desert being gunned down flashed through her mind. She pushed it away, but couldn't shake the feeling of anger and disgust toward those unnamed people.

This is something new, she thought, *where are these feelings coming from?*

The horror she felt was nothing new. The memory had always filled her with horror because it had no context. Dale remembered doing it in her long-ago life, but not why.

The anger, though, the loathing she'd felt in the dream when she looked at the old woman and her family, that was new.

I hated those people, Dale thought. *Whatever my tactical reasons for having them shot, I hated them.*

But why?

Dale didn't know.

She climbed off the crate, massaging her sore neck. She pulled her watch from her coat pocket. She tapped the face and saw it was a little after ten PM. She'd been asleep for just over an hour. Dale turned on the flashlight app and by its soft, white light she folded the blanket she'd been sitting on and packed it in the pillowcase she'd brought from the cabin. She tied the pillowcase closed, with a loop at the top just large enough to thread her walking stick through.

Dale tapped off the light and leaned against the large open door of the boxcar, her hair loose and dancing about her head. Through the blur of passing treetops, she stared up at the constellations glittering in the clear night sky. With no moon visible, the speckle of clouds appeared as dark smudges, but they did little to hide the canopy of stars. When the train passed into an open stretch and the trees flanking the railroad tracks gave way to a view of open fields and farms broken up

218

by hills, rivers and lakes, Dale took it in. Pinpoints of light identified the farmhouses, but much of the land remained bathed in the deep shades of blue and black as the Milky Way stretched overhead.

Dale picked out Hydra and Cancer the crab. In the distance, the three stars of Orion's belt announced his presence behind a large cloud spreading along the horizon.

Dale yawned, but it felt damn good to be outdoors and on the move. Not for the first time since departing Orchard Bend did she admit that to herself. Even the act of abandoning the cabin in the woods had brought an unexpected sense of freedom. Of course she'd fled as a fugitive, leaving so much behind. It tempered the exhilaration a good deal, but it did not outright erase it.

She watched as the train began a gradual turn, banking around the curve of the hillside. Far up ahead, she could see the steam engine and the grey trail of smoke billowing out from the chimney. The engine turned again, curving in the other direction. In the distance, a cluster of lights on a vast riverbank rolled into view. Dale stood up, keeping her eyes on the town up ahead. The train passed a large sign of black text on white.

Sutter Grove.

Dale retrieved her pillowcase and her walking stick and knelt by the open door. The train weaved to and fro as the lights of Sutter Grove grew larger. When the hills dropped away and the train rattled across a trestle bridge, Dale looked down into the black rushing water far below, gripping the door of the boxcar. On the far side, halfway up the hill, a campfire glowed orange and yellow against the blue night. A bearded man sat next to the fire watching the train pass overhead. Soon after her boxcar reached the far side, the train began to slow as it approached the town.

Dale slid the walking stick through the loop halfway up the shaft, then took her watch from her jacket and hooked it around the knot in the pillowcase. She tapped the flashlight app and pointed the light out at the rail bed.

It didn't offer a lot of light at that distance, but it was something.

The ground and rail ties glowed a little brighter and Dale could better gauge her jump. She watched for a flat stretch, knowing it would be only a little less dangerous. She would only have a second to decide. Even slowing down, the train still sped along at a fierce clip. A clearing shot by, and then another. Dale timed her eventual jump. When she saw the next decent spot, she held her breath and went for it, throwing the walking stick and pillowcase out and away from her. The rush of air hit her as the boxcar flew off down the tracks without her. Dale tucked her legs together, bent at the knee, and tried to relax. She wanted to twist her body to the side to cushion her ankles from the full brunt of her landing, but the distance proved too short. Her landing ended up far from graceful.

Coming to a stop on the ground, Dale lay still and listened as the last train cars sail on. The sound grew quieter and quieter until it became lost in the wind and rustling trees. She thought she'd heard the last of it when a distant blast of its whistle carried through the night.

Dale remained on the ground and assessed her condition, flexing her muscles and going easy on moving her legs and arms. Sore, but otherwise unhurt, she sat up and spotted the white glow of the watch's light nearer to the tracks. Dale got up and rubbed her lower back and hip, walking off the throbbing as she retrieved her luggage.

* * *

March 20, 1887
Sutter Grove

Dale reached Sutter Grove just before midnight. Ten minutes after that, she realized that she was being followed.

After jumping from the train, Dale had followed the tracks until she was within sight of the great artificial canal that linked to the river. A line of barges sat docked against the break wall, waiting until morning to either set off on their deliveries or to load their cargo from arriving trains like the one Dale had rode in on. The canal sat adjacent to the gated

220

train yard, with its signs reading 'No Trespassing'. Even at this late hour, people moved between the trains, inspecting the boxcars and keeping the shipments secure. Dale left the rail line and made her way toward the canal and the area of Sutter Grove everyone called Barge Town.

The wet smell of fish and damp in this quarter, even on the driest days, had always taken Dale some time to get used to. When she'd come to Sutter Grove on business for Maxwell McCabe, she always tried to keep her visits to Barge Town as brief as she could. Her first time there, a pair of gentlemen had come to explore the festive atmosphere of nightlife at the water's edge, with its music and booming laughter pouring onto the street from the public houses. The men soon learned that the laughter could be harsh when it reached the shadowed alleys and the music would mask their cries for help. Dale didn't see the men beset upon, but one of them staggered into the *Black Water* pub, where Dale was meeting a contact, crying that he and his companion had been mugged. To their credit, a few of the less drunk patrons followed the man back outside to offer some assistance, but most ignored him and went on drinking. After Dale had concluded her business with her contact, she found the man outside the *Black Water* trying to negotiate with a wagon driver to take him and his unconscious, beaten friend to the doctor across town.

"I can't pay you right now, friend, they took everything of value," the gentleman sobbed as his friend lay unconscious in the wagon. "After we get Stanley to the doctor, I promise to pay you handsomely!"

"Then I ain't movin'," the driver said, getting comfortable, "...*friend.*"

Dale had seen enough.

"I'll pay you a dollar to get these men out of here and back uptown where they belong," she said to the driver. "His mewling is getting on my nerves."

The gentleman stared at her, speechless for several seconds.

"Done," said the driver, reaching down from his wagon to take her money.

221

"Thank you!" the gentleman said. "I won't forget your generosity this night!"

"Not generosity," Dale said. "A debt I'll collect on."

"Of course! Of course!" the gentleman said, climbing into the back of the wagon next to his friend, who let out a moan of pain. "My name is Price, of Stand Hill."

Dale reached up and handed him a ten-dollar bill.

"For the doctor's trouble," she said.

"Thank you!" Price said, tears in his eyes.

Dale nodded and they sped off. She watched them go, then returned to the *Black Water* to arrange accommodations for the night.

Not a lot had changed in the Barge Town quarter in the intervening years, Dale noted.

Balancing her walking stick on her shoulder, the pillowcase hanging from the notch in the middle, Dale stepped up her pace on the unnamed narrow street, letting out a series of coughs to clear her chest.

Still not a hundred percent, she thought. *This wet air isn't helping.*

Behind her, not more than two-dozen yards away, the unmistakable shuffle of cautious feet and low, dangerous voices moved between the buildings. Dale half-turned and saw the shape of two men in the shadows, one of them never breaking his leer in her direction.

Dale continued on toward the *Black Water* pub. Without warning, her chest seized and she bent over, coughing again and spitting up phlegm on the dirt. When the fit eased, she wiped her mouth with her sleeve, still leaning on her knees.

"Barge Town's not fit for a girl to be out alone."

Doubled over, Dale saw the pair of dirty work boots that belonged to the man blocking her path. The broad shoulders, thick neck and calloused hands suggested he was a bargeman. Dale backed away and angled herself sideways at the sight of the long, straight knife in his belt, a common tool in the trade. She pivoted to see the two men she'd spied before approaching from the other direction.

"For a fee, my pals and I would be happy to escort you about," the bargeman continued.

"I'm fine on my own, thanks," Dale said, her eyes casting about to see if any more men might be lurking in the shadows.

"I'm afraid I have to disagree with you," the bargeman sighed, straightening his belt, his fingers sliding along the hilt of his knife. "There's a decidedly unpleasant element in these parts. Just yesterday a shopkeeper's daughter had an unfortunate run in with some criminal sorts. We'd hate to see the same fate come to a pretty thing such as yourself."

One of the men behind Dale spoke up, the smaller of the two men who looked no less dangerous as he rolled up his dirty sleeves

"It won't cost you much," he said, not hiding the sneer that edged his tone. "Money is good. Whatever you have in the sack there. And if you don't have anything of sufficient value, I'm sure we can come to some *alternate* arrangement."

Dale looked from him to the larger bargeman, whose finger gave a casual tap on the hilt of his knife. She cocked her head, then tilted the walking stick backward on her shoulder so that the pillowcase slid out of the notch. It landed on the ground with a soft thud and Dale took the stick from her shoulder and planted one end in the ground.

"Big girl carrying a big stick," said the larger bargeman, drawing his knife. "Look, little lady, we asked nice and polite. No need to make a fuss. Put the stick down before I have my friend take it from you."

Dale heard the other two snicker behind her and turned to face them. Her eyes narrowed to slits as she fixed the small man a hard stare.

"I guess we do it the hard way," he said. He gave a nod past her, "Milt?"

Dale heard the one called Milt move behind her and she pivoted again, planting both hands on the stick. She gave it a flick upward, sending dirt at the large bargeman's face. She swung the stick around, her motion almost a pirouette, and the wood connected with Milt's head, sending him reeling.

The third man, who had not spoken at all, lunged at her exposed flank with his own knife and Dale had only a second to react. She twisted and dropped to a knee, balancing with one hand and parrying the knife's blade with the stick in the other. The move didn't offer much force to the block, so Dale scooped up a handful of dirt and threw it in the man's face. In his moment of blindness, she swept his feet out from under him and swung around to face the bargeman, dropping into a ready stance with her stick in both hands.

Still wiping dirt from his face, the quiet bargeman lumbered forward, knife in hand. Dale waited for her moment to strike, then with three rapid blows, she struck the man's forearm as he lashed out with his knife. The weapon fell from his hand and dropped blade-first into the ground. The bargeman lurched at her, swinging his numb, broken arm, not understanding why his hand wouldn't function the way it should. Dale drove the tip of the stick into his gut, knocking the wind from his lungs. He crumpled to the ground, gasping.

"Bitch!" cried the smaller man.

Dale saw the flash of the blade in the darkness and out of sheer reflex got her face out of the way of the knife as it flew past her head. Dale didn't know if the man had another weapon on him and didn't wait to find out. A white-hot anger drove a succession of blows from her stick. As each thrash made contact with the man, it felt good. He hit the ground a beaten mess, writhing in pain. Dale stood over him, a dark smile of her own crossing her lips.

"You're fortunate I'm leaving you alive," she said, a deep well of anger burning in the pit of her stomach.

The quiet bargeman found his breath again and wheezed as he reached for his knife with his good hand. Dale drove her walking stick into the dirt, blocking his grasp and shaking her head as he looked up at her. She saw the fear and pain in his eyes and said nothing. The bargeman staggered up, clutching his broken forearm, and shuffled to Milt, who sat up holding his head.

"Grab him," the bargeman muttered to Milt, nodding at the smaller man on the ground. Milt swayed on his feet, but pulled his comrade up from the dirt. Without looking back at Dale, Milt helped the man stumble away down the street. The bargeman followed behind, looking back at Dale several times. She wondered if he thought she'd follow them to finish the job or if he was thankful to be walking away at all.

Overhead, a pair of curtains drew shut in one of the rooms above a closed shop. Dale became aware of the eyes of people in the shadows watching her and decided it would be best to leave. She pulled the bargeman's long knife out of the ground and tucked it into her belt. She found the smaller man's knife embedded in the wood doorframe of a shuttered pawnshop and put it in her belt. Scooping up her pillowcase, Dale continued on her way to the *Black Water*.

* * *

"I need a room," Dale said, dropping her pillowcase on the dusty floor next to the bar, "and a meal, if your kitchen is still open."

The barkeep was a stick of a man whose short-cropped beard and white hair stood out against the dim murk of the pub. He didn't look up from wiping a rag across the top of the bar.

"A room I can do," he said, "but the cook's gone home. I've got a bag of potatoes open in the back and there might be some bread and cheese around. That's the best I can offer."

"It'll do," Dale said, taking out some money. "I may be here for several days. This should cover it."

"Your room's up in the back, number six," the barkeep said, putting a key on the bar and gesturing to the crooked stairs against the far wall.

Dale put some bills on the bar and the barkeep snatched them up. His eyes flicked over her as he counted the money, but he said nothing. Dale picked up her pillowcase and took it to one of the empty tables across the room. She passed a group of bargemen playing cards and a man propositioning a young prostitute Dale guessed had not been in the trade very long. The girl, nineteen if she was a day, had not yet lost the sparkle in her eyes, nor did she carry the lines of that hard life on her face. Unlike women in some houses-of-ill-repute of which Dale had a passing knowledge—from her days working for Maxwell McCabe—this girl's attire was suggestive but still modest. Her open blouse showed just enough skin, and her skirt rode a little too high, exposing the fringe of her petticoat. The girl glanced at Dale, but Dale kept walking.

A log burned low in the fireplace. Dale dropped the pillowcase on the tabletop and dragged the table closer to the flame. She leaned her walking stick against the stonework and picked up the bent iron poker. She stirred the fire and put another log on, relishing the warmth after a day in the boxcar.

Pulling up a chair, Dale sat at the table facing the fire. She leaned forward with her elbows on her knees and put her head down. Her fingers twitched and she squeezed them into fists until her knuckles turned white. Her back tensed up. Her knee bounced up and down as the adrenalin ebbed. She replayed the fight with the men in her mind. Speed and surprise had been on her side, but she knew full well that her technique with the walking stick had been sloppy, even after the practice she'd put in while recuperating at the cabin. But she had walked away and they had all but scurried back to whatever hole they'd crawled out of.

Dale sat up, flexing her hands. She pulled out the two knives she'd taken from her attackers. She placed them on the table and noticed the nearby patrons look away. The prostitute rose from her table and led her customer away by the hand to slink off up the rickety staircase. They disappeared into the shadows. Dale held the bargeman's knife up and let the firelight glint off the blade.

The migraine came on at once.

So did the memory.

The glare from the overhead work lights hit the knife's blade as Dale held it before her. Consoles and computers glowed and indicator lights flickered.

There were other people in the room, soldiers, and a tall man in a suit and tie, but her attention was fixed on the blonde-haired woman next to him with the pale green eyes.

Frustration burned in Dale's gut and she slammed the knife flat on the table, causing the gambling bargemen to glance in her direction. Dale paid them no heed and turned to look at the fireplace.

All these faces, she thought, *all these people from a life I can't remember, in a time that hasn't happened yet.*

She pulled out the folded piece of newspaper with the picture of the scarred woman. Dale stared at it by the firelight. The woman's eyes stared back.

In Dale's memory, the woman was holding her bloody face.

I was there when you suffered that injury, Dale thought, *but that was before either of us came to Orchard Bend. If I find you will you even remember me? Or, like me, will there be only shadows of memories of your life before?*

Dale put those thoughts to rest when the barkeep brought her dinner; a bottle of wine, a plate with a thick chunk of bread, some crumbing cheese, jerky and two raw potatoes. Dale held one of the potatoes up and shot the barkeep a confused look.

"I told you, the cook's gone home," he said, and pointed to the fireplace. "Perfectly good fire burning right there, though."

He didn't wait to receive the icy glare she cast him as he darted back to the bar. Dale picked up the bargeman's knife and held it over the fire to sterilize it, turning it over, this way and that, watching the firelight reflect off it. Then she impaled it into the first potato and cooked the vegetable over the fire as she gnawed on some of the jerky. The cheese and bread were still fresh enough. When each potato was cooked through, Dale split them open and let some chunks of the cheese melt inside for flavour.

The gamblers ended their game and two of them departed. The others nursed their mugs and started singing a version of "Oh Shenandoah." The prostitute and her john re-emerged down the stairs, the man fixing his clothes and saying something to the girl. She laughed, a clear, happy sound that brightened the gloomy pub. The man left. The prostitute went to the bar and took a drink from a bottle of sparkling water. She put some money on the bar and the barkeep wasted no

227

time stuffing it in his pocket. The two started talking. With the bargemen singing, Dale couldn't hear what they said, but she didn't really care to. She took a long pull from her wine bottle and let her eyes move down the girl's body, taking in the curve of her breasts and the roundness of her behind. Dale wondered if the skin of the girl's legs were as soft, porcelain white and perfect as her face. The barkeep said something that made the prostitute laugh again and the sound made Dale close her eyes, her fingers caressing her thigh under the table.

The bargemen rolled into "I'm Bound For The Rio Grande" and Dale drank from her bottle again. She opened her eyes and saw the prostitute swaying to the rhythm of the song and smiling, watching the men. Dale smiled as the girl moved a long lock of hair and tucked it behind her ear. The girl's eyes flicked in Dale's direction and Dale did not look away. The girl did, returning to watching the men. Dale took another swallow of wine and the girl glanced back at her, looking away just as fast, biting her lip.

Dale knew she wanted this girl.

The girl must have known it, too, for she looked back at Dale once more and held her gaze. The bargemen finished their singing and pounded on the table, laughing as they rose and made their way out of the *Black Water*. The girl looked away from Dale to watch them go, then bottle in hand, slinked her way to Dale's table by the fireplace as Dale put her knives back in her belt.

"I see you over here, darling," the girl said, her voice soft, but with just enough sulte to make Dale catch her breath for just a moment.

Dale put a bill on the table and said nothing, her fingers circling the lip of her wine bottle. The prostitute took the money and slipped it into her blouse.

"I have a room," she said, "and I don't often entertain ladies."

Dale took her finger off the lip of the wine bottle and put it on the lips of the girl. She felt the prostitute's tongue on her finger, licking the drop of wine from it.

"I have my own room," Dale said.

The girl smiled. Dale looked around the room and saw the barkeep failing to be discreet watching them. Dale didn't care what he thought. The girl picked up both her bottle of water and Dale's wine as Dale collected her pillowcase and walking stick.

"Room six," Dale said, and the girl nodded, leading the way across the pub. The stairs groaned and shifted as they made their way to the second floor. Lit only by a single lantern at the end of the hall, the cramped passage didn't look to Dale to have a square angle anywhere, age having bent the structure so much out of shape. They reached room six and Dale unlocked the door as the girl caressed her arm. Inside the unlit room, Dale dropped the pillowcase and her walking stick on the floor and took the bottles from the prostitute. She set them on the dresser. Then she picked the girl up by the waist, kicked the door closed and carried her to the bed. The girl laughed and Dale undid her blouse all the way, pressing her face against the prostitute's chest.

"What's your name, honey?" the girl asked.

Dale hesitated, her hand cupping one of the young woman's breasts over her corset.

"Caroline," Dale lied.

"Well, Caroline, it's a pleasure to make your acquaintance," the girl said. "My name is Amelia-Rose."

Dale stopped.

She put her hand over her mouth and stumbled back against the wall. Amelia-Rose propped herself up on her elbows, confused as she watched Dale slide down the wall to sit on the floor.

"What's the matter? First time?" she asked.

Dale shook her head, her hand still over her mouth. Whether because of the alcohol or the shock, Dale couldn't say, but the dizziness she felt was real.

"I can't do this," Dale said. "I can't do this to her."

Amelia-Rose's expression became dark very quick.

"Well, sweetie, it's clear you've got something on your conscience," she said. "I don't have all night, so if you—"

"Get out," Dale said, not looking at her. "Keep the money."

"Oh, I *always* intended to keep the money, darling," Amelia-Rose said, doing her blouse back up as she crossed the room. She stormed out and left the door ajar. Dale gave it a kick and it slammed shut. Dim light and dull sounds from the street poured in through the murky glass.

Dale remained sitting on the floor, tense and trembling for a long time.

30

March 20, 1887
Sutter Grove

Emery Dale stopped in her tracks in the foyer of the *Sutter Grove Gazette*. In the room to her left, a man cranked the wheel around and around as fresh newspapers came off a cylinder one by one to be folded. A group of men at one end gathered the folded papers and stacked them into bundles, tying them with twine. At a row of tables sat women labelling the bundles for delivery. These bundles made their way out the loading door at the other end of the room to waiting wagons. A large man with a thick brown beard, broad shoulders and a good deal of weight around his middle barked directions at each team. He spotted Dale and crossed the printing room to her.

"You lost, Miss?" he asked, his scowl not at all hidden under his dark, sweaty facial hair.

"I need to talk to someone about the photograph used for this engraving," Emery Dale said, unfolding the scrap of newspaper and handing it to him.

"This ain't from the Gazette, I can tell you that by the stock," the man said, examining the paper. "Too light weight, we'd never use this. Never seen this picture before, either."

"No, it was printed in the *Orchard Herald*," Dale said, "but the photograph came from your offices here. It says so in the article."

"*Orchard Herald*, huh?" the man said with disgust. He looked at the paper again, then handed it back to Dale. "You want to talk to Whitaker, the Editor-in-Chief."

He pointed to the other side of the foyer, to the closed door of the *Gazette* offices. Through the glass, Dale saw a room of

231

empty work desks. The clock on the wall read 8:17 in the morning. Being a Sunday, Dale wondered if any other staff would be working today.

"His office is through there," the man said. "Little bald fella, you can't miss him."

"He'd be in at this hour?" Dale asked.

"Usually gets here around seven," the man said as he returned to the printing room and continued shouting orders, chastising the speed at which the men were loading the wagon.

Dale let herself into the newspaper's office and waited for someone to come out and greet her, but no one did. She looked around at the empty room and the vacant desks, some tidy, some a mess of papers, notes and books. Dale began to think that maybe the man from the printing room had been mistaken, but then she heard a voice from behind an unmarked closed door next to her mutter, "Shit."

A chair scraped along the floor, followed by the stamping of hurried feet. A shadow moved behind the door's frosted glass window and when the door flew open, out stomped a little bald man in a suit. He passed Dale without seeming to see her, crossed the foyer to the printing room and yelled, "Typographical error on Page 2, line 22, column 4! Typesetters, what are you paid for? Proofreaders, my blind granny could spot that mistake! Do better, people, our readers expect no less."

The little bald man returned to the office and only then appeared to see Dale, giving her an unimpressed once over.

"And you are...?" he asked.

"Someone with a very important question," Dale said, straightening her jacket and pulling out the newspaper clipping again. "Are you Mr Whitaker? I need some information on this image."

Whitaker took the paper and held it up into the light, then looked at Dale again, once more sizing her up.

"Come into my office," he said.

Dale followed him through the unmarked door.

"Your office isn't labelled, Mr Whitaker, otherwise I would have knocked," Dale said.

"New office," Whitaker said. Dale waited for more, but the man offered nothing else by way of explanation. The office itself was cluttered, but not untidy. Dale sensed Whitaker had a system at work that few but himself would comprehend. A map covered a good part of the wall and Dale's gaze followed the rail line along from Sutter Grove past the intervening towns to Orchard Bend. She shifted on her feet and pulled her eyes away at once.

Whitaker, meanwhile, sat at his desk and read the article, nodding as he did.

"Thomas Buchanan," he said with a shake of his head. Again, Dale waited for more, only to be left hanging.

"So, you recognize the picture?" she asked.

"Of course," Whitaker said. "I sent it to Buchanan just after the new year. We were emptying out this very room, as a matter of fact. It used to be the paper's archive, but we moved that to the basement. The owner told me if I wanted this as my office, I had to clear it out myself. Not all the boxes were labelled, though, so I went through them one at a time. I found a box of photographic plates, including that one. I feared they might deteriorate, so I had them developed and printed to preserve Sutter Grove history. Sometimes I lament that too few in this town care about its past. When I realized that photograph was actually of Orchard Bend, I sent a copy to Tom Buchanan. Glad to see he made good use of it. I've got a copy here, too, somewhere."

Whitaker rummaged through a cabinet next to his desk and pulled out an original print of the photograph, one not much larger than his hand.

"Here you go," Whitaker said, handing Dale the picture. "You'll see right away that it's a lot clearer than this engraving from the newspaper."

Dale sat in the chair opposite Whitaker's desk and poured over the image.

There she is, Dale thought, *clear as day.*

The higher quality of the picture highlighted subtle details Dale had not seen in the newspaper clipping. The excitement of familiarity intensified. Once again, the memory of the woman clutching her bloody face flashed through Dale's mind.

"Do you know anything more about this photograph?" Dale asked, "Anything not in the article, like who this woman is?"

Whitaker sat up in his chair, again giving her a curious look, assessing her.

"She was right," he said to himself.

"I'm not following," Dale said, confused.

Whitaker stood up and went back to the cabinet. He rifled through a drawer and took out an envelope.

"Six weeks ago, a woman came here with the same newspaper you took that article from," Whitaker said, sitting back at his desk. "She sat right where you're sitting now."

"What woman?" Dale asked, growing impatient. She pointed to the woman with the scar in the photograph. "Was it *this* woman?"

Whitaker shook his head.

"No, but she was looking for information on that woman, same as you are now," Whitaker explained. "I didn't have much to tell her. I told her who took the picture, Sherman Pitt. He puts his name on the back of the plates, you see. She didn't stay long and I didn't think I was much help."

Dale waited for more, dumbfounded and wondering who this other woman was.

Whitaker saw the expectant look on Dale's face and smiled.

"You'll be happy to know that the woman came back here," he said. "She sat there and did not look well at all. She said she needed my help. She said another woman, with blonde hair, might come asking the same kinds of questions, 'Who is this woman with the scar in the picture?', that sort of thing. She didn't give me your name, but you fit the description, just as she said."

"She didn't tell you *her* name either?" Dale asked, frustration mixing with excitement.

"No, ma'am," Whitaker said, "but I deduced she was a woman of means. She came here escorted by a gentleman who waited outside my office and drove her in a fine rented coach both times."

Dale looked out the office door, past the desks and out to the street, trying to picture the scene.

Whitaker leaned forward, elbows on his desk.

"Our woman of mystery said that when you showed up, I was to give you this," he said, holding out the envelope.

Dale looked at it, hesitant. The envelope contained answers, but also proved forces were at work around her that she had not known about. Someone knew she would be here, that this moment would arrive. It unsettled Dale as she took the envelope from Whitaker.

She ran her fingers over the paper. Nothing marked either side of the envelope, no name, no indication of whom it was from or to whom it was addressed. Yet Dale knew Whitaker was right, it was meant for her.

Delaying no more, she cut the paper open, taking out the folded sheet inside. It read:

Emery,
Her name is Kenna Warren.
Gertrude.

The weight of the moment crashed down and left Dale lightheaded as she sat back in her chair. She looked at Whitaker, who said nothing, but raised an eyebrow.

"I...," Dale said, looking out the window again to the street, "I was not expecting this."

Dale could see it now. Gertrude, sick and dying, coming here to try to track this woman down, a woman named Kenna Warren. In the flood of deductions and possibilities, Dale turned the name over in her head, but could not match it. The name meant nothing to her. Yet Gertrude had uncovered it. How?

Why?

You knew I'd come here, Gertrude, Dale thought. *You knew I would be looking for her. Just as you pointed me to the ravine all those years ago at the start of our friendship, now you point me to this woman I seek even as our friendship has ended. Was this a last act to try to save a piece of what we had? I know you could never forgive me for killing Henry, but maybe something of our friendship survived.*

A tear ran down Emery Dale's cheek and she drew a deep breath to collect herself.

Whitaker tapped the photograph on the desk.

"You can keep that," he said. "I can make more."

"Thank you," Dale whispered, not wanting him to hear her hoarse voice as her throat tightened.

"The woman who came here before you," Whitaker said, "her name was Gertrude McCabe, wasn't it?"

Dale wiped the tear from her face.

"Yes, it was," Dale said.

"I put it together after her last visit," Whitaker said. "We ran a notification in our society column about the death of 'Mrs McCabe of Orchard Bend,' but I wasn't entirely certain it was the same woman."

"How was she?" Dale asked. "In her final days, how did she seem, how did she look?"

"Every bit a lady," Whitaker said. "She coughed some during her first visit, but I had no idea just how ill she was until she returned. It was difficult to bear seeing someone in such discomfort."

Dale nodded.

"Does the name Kenna Warren mean anything to you?" Dale asked.

"I don't know the name, no," Whitaker replied. He nodded to the photograph. "Is that her?"

"Gertrude believed it was," Dale said.

"I see," Whitaker said, picking up the photograph. "Why is she important to you both? This photograph is twenty-five years old."

"I knew her," Dale said, "in another life."

Whitaker stared at her and she could see him weighing the answer, picking it apart, assessing her once more.

Dale stood up, taking the photograph and putting it with the letter in the envelope.

"Thank you, Mr Whitaker," Dale said. "You have been a tremendous help."

"It's been quite an enlightening conversation," he said, also getting to his feet to see her to the office door.

Dale made her way outside.

From the top of the stairs she watched the bustle of traffic on the street, wondering what to do next.

She'd left Orchard Bend with the thin hope of learning something about the woman in the photograph. She hadn't before grasped how much of a long shot it was that she would discover anything. The image had been all there was to go on and hitching a ride on a train to Sutter Grove to track down its source had been a gamble. Yet here she stood, with a name and the knowledge that her dying friend had been on the same course. Her mind reeled and she wished she could speak to Gertrude—about this and so much more—but all that remained between them was a seven-word letter.

What's the next step, Gertrude? Dale wondered. *You found her name somehow, but what comes next?*

Dale put the envelope in her jacket pocket and through the passing wagons, buggies and pedestrians, saw a tall, lean, grim-faced man in a black suit and badge watching her from across the street.

Time to go, she told herself.

Far from Orchard Bend, Dale thought less about her status as a fugitive, but seeing the lawman reminded her that her wanted poster would probably be up in stations all over by now. When she had been sheriff, she had made a point to study the posters, to know their names and faces should any arrive in Orchard Bend. Dale had to assume this man did the same.

Not wanting to look out of place, Dale walked down the steps and strolled along the wooden planks of the boardwalk. She did not look back, nor did she hurry. Both might tip the lawman off. When she reached the intersection, she stopped and waited for a chance to cross, rather than changing direction and disappearing from view. On the other side of the street, she paused to look in a shop window, using its reflection to try to spot the man. She saw him, still standing where she'd first spotted him, but he didn't seem to be watching her. His attention appeared to be elsewhere, his gaze toward some point out of her view. Still, she felt she'd been at the window long enough and continued on her way, turning down the next street and heading to Barge Town and the *Black Water.* Dale thought about the short letter and wondered why Gertrude had left only a name and nothing more.

Halfway down the block, Dale stopped cold in the middle of the boardwalk. She pulled the envelope out of her jacket pocket and looked at it.

"Of course," she said, smiling, "a letter. Clever girl."

31

March 21, 1887
Sutter Grove

Emery Dale couldn't remember the last time she'd worn a skirt. Even loose fitting, the weight of the wool fabric and petticoat moving around her legs as she walked left her feeling restricted and slow.

If Rose could see me now, Dale thought as she fussed and fidgeted with her new hat and pulled at the collar of her new blouse beneath her drab coat. She forced herself to stop, since such behaviour would attract attention. The entire point of her altered attire was to remain inconspicuous.

After spotting the lawman on the street the day before, Dale realized that her fashion sense, such as wearing trousers, made her stand out against the well-dressed ladies in their Sunday best more than she would have liked. Her first stop that morning had been a shop on the edge of Barge Town. Their selection of women's clothes was neither colourful nor flashy, thus perfect for Dale's needs. With the brim of her smart, straw country hat set low to shield her eyes, Dale hoped she'd disappear amongst the townsfolk of Sutter Grove.

The *Gazette* had not been a far walk from the Barge Town quarter, but this day her destination would take her to the center of town.

Her past visits to Sutter Grove in the employ of Maxwell McCabe had kept her either in Barge Town or the neighbouring industrial quarter, where the rail yard and warehouses lay. Uptown Sutter Grove lay on the other side of the downtown shops and businesses. Dale would not be going quite that far, but even as she drew closer to the municipal buildings between uptown and downtown, she could see the impressive wealth on display in the form of houses dotting the hills beyond. They belonged to CUC and mining executives, and the rich owners of the shipping trades that continued down the river and back. A few wealthy families from the city also had summer retreats in the hills. All of them overlooked the town. It reminded Dale of the McCabe home, which sat atop a hill overlooking Orchard Bend.

All of them want a view, she thought, *and all of them want to be seen.*

The red brick and white trim of the Municipal Building shined in the midday sun and Dale could imagine how pleasant the scene would be in the coming spring bloom. The brisk air told her that spring weather would have to wait a bit this year. More snow would descend upon the region before the month was out. Men tipped their hats to her as she ascended the steps and entered the front door. She followed the signs marked 'Post Office' and there joined the short line of townsfolk at the counter. At the front of the line, a scruffy man dropped off a package, paid his postage and the clerk stamped the top of it before taking it away. The man frowned as he exited the line, looking sad and uncertain. The clerk waved the next costumer forward, and older woman, and the scruffy man shuffled past Dale—who wondered what his story was—and left the post office.

With several people ahead of her, Dale looked around the room. A young man came out from behind the counter and went to the notice board on the wall. He gave it a quick inspection and then started removing outdated items. With space limited, some had been pinned overtop of even older notices. When the young man pulled one of the sheets away, it revealed a Wanted poster Dale recognized.

Anson Tull, she remembered, having had the same notice up in the jailhouse in Orchard Bend. She knew what it said without needing to read it. Beneath the ugly drawing of the man it read: *Brown hair, blue eyes, 35 years old; Wanted for assault, attempted robbery, horse theft; $50 Reward.*

The clerk began rearranging the notices to make more space and he spotted another item to take down. As he did, Dale found herself looking at her own Wanted poster, the simple drawing of her own face staring back at her.

The line moved again and Dale looked away as she stepped forward.

Don't panic! Dale told herself. *The truth is that few people pay attention to those Wanted posters. No one ever thinks the person will show up in their town, let alone be standing beside them in a line at the post office. It's not even that good a drawing of me, certainly not Gertrude's pencil work. Hers were uncannily good.*

Dale tried her best to appear relaxed and casual, just another person going about their business. Behind her, she heard a young child talking to her mother as they took their place in the line. Dale half-turned and the little girl of about six or seven years old waved at her. Dale waved back and faced forward again.

"Mother, can I look at the pictures over there? Please?" the girl asked.

"Very well," her mother said.

Dale watched in silent horror as the girl walked over to the notice board and stared at the Wanted posters.

"He's ugly," she said of the picture of Anson Tull. Dale felt cold sweat on her skin as the girl moved to the next poster. She pointed at the drawing of Dale and said, "She's pretty, though."

"Clara, hush," her mother said.

Dale knew her cheeks were going red.

Stay calm, she told herself. *Take care of your business and get out.*

The line moved again and Dale found herself one person away from being served, after the gentleman approaching the counter.

"'Emery Ann Dale' is a funny name," the girl said, twirling a finger in one of the long curls of her hair.

"Clara, know your place," her mother hissed. "Come here at once. If you can't keep your thoughts to yourself, you'll stand quietly here with me."

Clara returned to her mother's side behind Dale and the two said nothing. Dale could hear Clara shifting and sighing from the boredom. Dale wanted to let out a long sigh of her own to tell the gentleman at the counter to hurry up. His protracted discussion with Elizabeth the clerk about the delivery time and postage had dragged on long enough.

"I like your hat," said Clara.

Dale clenched her jaw and forced a smile, half-turning toward the girl.

"Thank you," Dale said. "Your curls are very pretty."

"You look like the lady in the picture," Clara said.

Dale went cold as Clara's mother let out a gasp.

"Clarabelle, apologize this instant!" her mother said.

Clara dropped her face down and said nothing.

Her mother leaned in to Dale.

"I'm so sorry," she said. "Clara forgets her manners sometimes."

"It's alright," Dale said. "No harm done."

Clara's mother turned to her daughter.

"I've never been so embarrassed," she whispered at Clara. "We're going home right now, young lady!"

And with that, she dragged her daughter out of the post office. Dale let out a quiet sigh of relief.

Elizabeth waved Dale to the counter, as the gentleman ahead of her concluded his business.

"How may I help you?" Elizabeth asked.

Dale collected herself.

"I need your help," Dale said, smiling, but not too much. "I'm trying to locate a dear friend of mine and last I heard she lived in or around Sutter Grove. I thought if anyone could help me find her it would be fine staff of the Post Office."

"I see," Elizabeth said, "Well, I certainly hope we can assist you."

"All I have to go on is her name," Dale said. "Kenna Warren."

Elizabeth gave Dale a look of complete surprise.

"I'm sorry, 'Kenna *Warren?*" she said.

"Yes," Dale answered. "Why?"

"Um, one moment, please," Elizabeth said and stepped away from the counter. Without looking back, she went through a swinging door to a back room.

Dale looked around the now empty post office.

Something's wrong, she thought. *I should get out now.*

She didn't, though. She was too close to finding Kenna Warren and answers about her own past. She clasped her hands behind her back, trying to look casual as she waited, comforted by the feeling of the knives tucked under her coat in the waistline at the back of her skirt.

Elizabeth came out and stood at the door, looking awkward. Dale started to ask what was the matter, but the clerk stopped her, raising her finger in a 'just a moment' gesture.

Dale waited.

Out stepped another person.

Dale stood in shock at the sudden appearance of Kenna Warren.

* * *

"It's you," Kenna Warren said, looking just as wide-eyed as Dale herself. "You're... *here.*"

Dale blinked and gave a shake of her head, taking in every detail, her thoughts overwhelming her; Warren's eyes, the very same as had stared back at her from the photograph, real before her now; the straight, clean scar line on her cheek—

The memory of Warren clutching her face, blood seeping through her fingers from the wound, her eyes—

Those same eyes—

—piercing and focused through her pain.

—but this Kenna Warren had lived these past twenty-five years and it showed in the crow's feet around her eyes and the lines around her mouth. Her once dark hair now streaked grey by half.

"I've come a long way," Dale said, her voice cracking with emotion. "We... we both have."

Warren nodded. Her eyes darted to Elizabeth, who took in the scene with great interest.

"We can't talk here," Warren said, reaching over the counter and taking Dale's hand. "Now isn't the time. Where are you staying? I'll come see you when my shift is over at 5 o'clock."

"The *Black Water* in Barge Town," Dale said, fighting off impatience. After everything that had happened, after eight years of not knowing who she really was, Dale couldn't help but hold onto Warren a moment longer, looking her straight in the eye to ask, "You remember, do you? You remember... back then?"

Warren smiled, put her other hand over Dale's and gave it a pat.

"I have so much to tell you," Warren said.

* * *

Dale pushed open the door of the Municipal Building and squinted against the glare of the sun. Her heart racing and her thoughts excited and scared at the promise of learning what had long been forgotten to her. As her eyes adjusted to the brightness, she flew down the steps and only then did she see the six armed men pointing guns at her, a mix of six-shooters, rifles and shotguns.

"Emery Dale!" said the lawman in black she recognized from the day before. "Come quietly. This doesn't have to be difficult."

Dale cursed herself for walking into the trap, blinded by finally tracking down Kenna Warren and not paying attention to her surroundings until it was too late. Beyond the parameter townsfolk watched the confrontation with great interest, including Clara and her mother as they retreated up the boardwalk. Closer to the action, however, was Whitaker, the *Gazette's* editor-in-chief, pencil and notebook out, documenting everything.

You did this, didn't you? Dale wondered, anger welling up. *You figured out Gertrude's identity and you figured out mine. Did you go straight to the sheriff after I walked out of your office?*

Dale couldn't dwell on that.

What's done is done, she told herself.

Dale knew she had a chance, though. With her two knives and her speed, she could try to take out the men nearest to her, the ones brandishing shotguns. Each also had a revolver on his hip, so once Dale reached one of those, her odds would improve.

It won't work, she realized.

Her fingers twitched as she struggled against the urge to fight.

Dale knew she might take them out, but she also knew she might die. And if she lived through the shootout, she'd have murder charges on her, complete with witnesses.

I swore I'd never be taken like this again, her anger burned.

"Dale!" said the lawman. "It's over."

Her eyes narrowed and darted back and forth, fixed on the barrels of the guns.

I guess I was wrong, Dale sighed.

She raised her hands and knelt on the ground.

* * *

The larger cell meant Dale had more room to pace back and forth, but not by much, and it did little to ease the strain of her captivity.

Two armed deputies stood watching her, never taking their eyes off their prisoner. Dale didn't have to guess that the sheriff knew about her escape from the jailhouse in Orchard Bend.

Smart precaution, Dale thought, *I would have done something similar.*

The cells were located at the back of the jailhouse, at the end of a corridor and away from the front hall and the sheriff's office. If Dale had to guess, she figured that since the office of Sheriff was an elected one in Sutter Grove and required the support of the wealthier residents, everyone would feel it best to keep the prisoners and drunks well out of public view.

The sheriff had not spoken to her since she'd been brought to the Sutter Grove jail and Dale had a good idea why. He and Maxwell McCabe had moved in some of the same circles. While not a corrupt man of office, at least not from McCabe's pocketbook, the white-haired sheriff had proved to be a valued ally in many business dealings. No doubt he'd feel it in everyone's best interest to let his senior deputy, Connelly, the lawman in the black suit, handle the arrest and incarceration of Emery Dale.

When she wasn't pacing, Dale sat on the cot and closed her eyes, trying not to think about everything in her life now coming apart. She'd hoped Kenna Warren would come to see her.

Surely she saw the arrest outside the Municipal Building, Dale told herself. *Connelly might even have questioned her and the clerk, Elizabeth, about my business there.*

Dale knew that if that were the case, Connelly would know she had a room at the *Black Water.* He might even be there now with a deputy or two, questioning the barkeep, searching her room.

They won't find my watch, at least, Dale thought. A lockbox at the local Wells Fargo would see to that.

Dale could only hope she might be able to retrieve it sooner rather than later. She also considered if she might have been better off leaving it in the stove in the cabin back in Orchard Bend, buried in ash and forgotten. With luck, someone might have lit a fire in the stove and destroyed it. Better that than a piece of future technology falling into the hands of someone from the 19th Century. Keeping it hidden as a fugitive herself had proven a complication Emery Dale could have done without.

She figured she'd be on the next train to Orchard Bend to face the outstanding charges there. It might be a while before she was able to return and get her watch back.

For the time being, though, the watch was safe. And in the cell, Dale could do nothing about it.

"Dinner," announced a deputy as he approached the cell. One of the guards motioned for her to back up and face the far wall. Dale did so and her plate of food clattered as the deputy put it on the floor. He slid it under the bars and said, "You can turn around now."

Dale looked at the plate and her stomach turned at the sight of the mouldy bread and rancid meat. The three deputies snickered, then laughed as Dale slid the plate back under the bars and out of the cell.

"Don't complain to us in the morning if you're still hungry," said the deputy as he picked up the plate and took it away.

"Tell me, *former Sheriff Dale*, were you expecting anything better here?" asked one of the two guards, running his fingers over his moustache. "The last lawman to go bad sat in that cell for three days before we served him the 'special of the day.' He wasn't so quick to turn his nose up as our hospitality as you were. Good thing you're leaving in the morning. You can go back to being Orchard Bend's problem."

"Are you finished?" Dale asked.

"Oh, she's got a mouth on her, doesn't she?" the other deputy laughed, scratching at his stubble.

"Better watch it, *Sheriff,* I might be inclined to do something about that lip," the moustachioed deputy taunted, leaning close to the bars. So close Dale could have belted him in the face right then. Or grabbed him and slammed him into the bars. It would have only taken a second to draw his weapon after that. Instead, Dale only smiled.

"Try it, kid," she said.

The deputy's smirk vanished and he kicked the bars of the cell. Dale didn't flinch.

"Alright, that's enough, Chambers," the other deputy said. "She ain't worth it."

Dale parked herself on the cot and stretched, then leaned against the wall and closed her eyes again, her arms folded across her chest. She thought of Rose, knowing full well that the schoolteacher would attend her trial.

At least I'll be able to see you again, Dale thought, picturing Rose in her mind. *Though it may well be for the last time.*

The sound of a pair of footsteps coming down the corridor interrupted that depressing train of thought. She cracked an eyelid open and saw Connelly enter the wing of cells.

"Dale, wake up! You have a visitor," he said.

Warren?! she hoped.

Before she could open both eyes, Whitaker strode in, a newspaper tucked under his arm and his pencil and notebook out. He stopped when he saw her and looked at Connelly.

"Well, what are you waiting for?" he said, gesturing towards her.

Connelly rolled his eyes and took out his ring of cell keys.

"That's it, fellas," he said to the deputies. "Guard duty's over. The sheriff wants you out front."

The deputies looked as confused as Dale.

"What's going on, Connelly?" the moustachioed deputy asked, shooting Dale a cold look.

"The sheriff will explain out front, Dobbs," Connelly snapped.

Something's happened, Dale realized. *And Connelly is not happy about it.*

Whitaker jotted something in his notebook as the two deputies left. Connelly then looked at her.

"Emery Dale, you're free to go," Connelly said.

"I am?" Dale asked, wary as she stood up.

"The charges in Orchard Bend have been dropped," Connelly said in a matter-of-fact tone, looking at his ring of keys and avoiding eye contact with her.

"And Judge Grenville dismissed your arrest warrant," Whitaker added, scribbling a note. He glanced up from his writing and added, "Effective *yesterday,* it seems."

"The sheriff only just found out," Connelly added. "He had to verify the information, of course, which takes time by wire."

Dale took a cautious step out of the cell.

"Clearly I'm missing something here," Dale said. "I mean, the charges were outrageous to begin with, but why were they suddenly dropped?"

Whitaker took the newspaper from under his arm and passed it to her. Dale read the front page:

The Orchard Herald Special Edition, March 20, 1887
MURDER OF LAURA O'MALLEY SOLVED!
by Thomas Buchanan, Editor

248

*On this first day of spring, Orchard Bend reels
after an unexpected and dramatic turn of events
in the case of Laura O'Malley's murder...*

Dale read the entire article as she walked away from the cell, ignoring Connelly as he slammed the bars shut behind her. She re-read portions, letting the details sink in. Turnbull had found Laura's head. And on the McCabes' land, no less. The Council dropped the charges.

"I'm free," Dale said as she reached the end.

Next to her, Whitaker took notes.

"How does it feel, Ms Dale, to be vindicated after everything that's happened?" Whitaker asked.

Dale looked at him, unsure what to say. She didn't quite know how she felt. She looked down at the article, which was accompanied by an engraved image, that of Laura O'Malley and her parents, from a photograph taken at the Jackson Picture Studio the year before—the engraver had left Jackson's mark on the picture. Below the portrait was the same drawing of Dale used in her Wanted poster.

"Laura O'Malley and her loved ones deserved justice and I hope this will be enough to bring them peace," Dale said, still regarding the picture of the O'Malleys. Her gaze shifted from Laura to her mother, Frances. It stayed there a moment longer, then she started down the corridor, leaving the cell behind. As she did, she asked Connelly, "What time is it?"

* * *

Dale rushed through the door of the jailhouse and onto the street, her straw hat in her hand and the *Orchard Herald* newspaper under her arm. She stopped at the edge of the ditch, looking in either direction. At half past six and with the sun setting below the hills, Dale knew the post office would be closed. Despite the relief of her freedom, Dale kicked the dirt in frustration. She could only hope Kenna Warren would be at work the next day.

Dale put her hat on and started down the street in the direction of Barge Town. Her stomach growled, but she took little notice. She took the paper from under her arm and read the headline again: *MURDER OF LAURA O'MALLEY SOLVED!*

Just like that, the entire affair was done with.

She had so many questions that her head ached as the lack of answers drove her thoughts in circles. She tucked the paper back under her arm and walked on, passing other townsfolk. Beneath the brim of her straw hat, she watched their faces, half expecting one of these men or women to recognize her from her old Wanted poster, to stop and point at her and exclaim, "It's her! Call the sheriff. Arrest this woman!"

None did. They just went about their lives with little notice of her. Some men tipped their hats, while others even smiled. But the smiles lacked warmth. They were perfunctory gestures, the thing you do in polite society.

I'm not a fugitive anymore, Dale thought, *but I'm still on the outside.*

At the next street corner, Dale stopped as two wagons passed.

"One of the first things I truly noticed when I arrived was fresh air," said Warren behind her.

Dale spun around to see Kenna Warren emerge from the shadows behind her to stand beneath the gaslight, her bonnet casting her face in darkness. She continued, "Where we come from, even on the clearest day, it was never as clean as this."

Relief swept over Dale as she realized Warren must have followed her from the jailhouse.

"I have so many questions, Kenna," Dale said as she went to her.

Warren straightened, tilting her head and taking in a deep breath. The light caught her cheek and the deep line of her scar.

"I know," she said. "I did, too. But we can't talk here. You said you had a room at the *Black Water.* We best talk there."

32

The Ledger of Owen McCabe

May 9, 1895
Orchard Bend

In my mother's last days, she had many visitors in the form of her wealthy friends. And no shortage of doctors. As she grew worse, the wealthy friends visited less often and soon only the doctors—and a tall man in black I now think was an undertaker—called on us at the hotel in Sutter Grove. I remember wondering why the wealthy friends had stopped coming around. Mr. & Mrs. Wilson had always brought me a paper bag of candy when they came to see my mother. Mr. Wilson would talk at length with my father while Mrs. Wilson sat and talked to my mother. When she was well enough, my mother would be out of bed and entertaining in the sunshine at the table in the small parlour. I'd sit and eat the candy until she told me I'd get a tummy ache if I tried to eat the entire bag.

I missed the Wilsons and their candy when they stopped visiting.

One of my mother's guests who was not a wealthy friend was the woman with the scar on her cheek. I remember wondering how she received such a wound, but children back then were to be seen and not heard, so I didn't ask. The pink line of scar tissue went from her jaw line, past her cheekbone, nearly to her eye.

She called at our hotel two times. The first was no more than a week after we settled in. I know this because I was playing in the hallway outside our rooms when she arrived, led to our suite by the uptight prick of a concierge. Every time he passed by, he would scowl at me with his ugly, moustachioed face and say I shouldn't be out of my room. Finally he had me banned from playing in the hallway for the duration of our stay. I'd get so mad when I saw him and sad that Henry wasn't around to stick up for me.

The woman with the scar first met with my mother while she was still well enough to receive guests at the sunlit table. She didn't bring me candy, but unlike the nasty concierge, she did smile at me that first visit.

The second time she came to the hotel was the morning my mother passed away, before we returned to Orchard Bend. It's my last real memory of being at the hotel, sitting in the chair next to my mother, with my father beside me. My mother lay in her bed, asleep, her breathing shallow and raspy. My father told me to talk to her even though she was asleep. He said she could still hear me. So I told her about how pretty the sunrise had been, that her table by the window was glowing, and when she woke up we could have tea there if she felt up to it.

My mother never did wake up.

Instead, she stopped her raspy breathing and lay still. I cried for her to come back. When my father said she was not coming back, that she was with Henry now, I was so upset I ran out of the room and into the hallway.

That's when I saw the woman with the scar.

She was at the top of the stairs with the concierge, both of them walking to our suite. The concierge told me to get back inside that instant or we'd be kicked out of the hotel and it would be all my fault. Through my tears and sadness I felt a rage unlike anything I had ever known before, even after losing Henry.

"SHUT YOUR MOUTH!" I screamed at him, "MY MOTHER IS DEAD!"

Both of them stopped in their tracks, the woman in shock and the concierge in anger. His face went completely red and he stormed at me. Part of me was scared and wanted to run, but another part made me stand my ground, my fists at my side and my chin out. I didn't know what he thought he was going to do when he reached me—pick me up and carry me inside, maybe even hit me?—but I knew I'd put up a hell of a fight. I *wanted to gouge out his beady eyes and rip his moustache from his face.*

Before he could reach me, though, the woman with the scar caught up to him, grabbed him by the arm and in one quick move had him pinned face first against the wall.

"What were you planning to do to that young man, huh?" she said, not raising her voice much above a whisper. The concierge squirmed and tried to wrestle free, but the woman twisted his arm so hard he cried out in pain. I remember thinking that this is what Henry would have done, too, standing up for his little brother. I wanted to run over and kick the asshole in the shin.

"I was..." the concierge started to say, "...I mean, the boy needs to be taught a lesson! You can't—!"

"Quiet!" the woman said, her voice still low, but sharp and clearly in control. "I think I can make my way to the McCabes' suite unescorted, sir. You can return to the lobby and send for the undertaker, then stay there until called upon by the McCabes. If you return to exact any sort of punishment on young Mr. McCabe here, I will hear about it and I will pay you a visit. You do not want to fuck with me to-day. Understood?"

All the concierge could do was sputter and nod his head. The woman pulled him from the wall and shoved him back toward the stairs. He scurried off, rubbing his arm and looking at us with stunned and icy glares.

The woman came to me and put her hand on my shoulder.

"Owen, I'm sorry about your mother," she said. "Wherever she is now, it's a better place. And she's smiling at you for standing up to that man."

At the mention of my mother, it all came crashing in on me again and I started to cry. The woman gave me a hug and said, "You're not alone, alright?"

I thought about the Prisoner, who had not come to Sutter Grove with us. I wondered if I'd see him again when we returned.

After I got my crying over with, the woman let me go and said, "I'm going to pay my respects to your mother now."

She went inside and I sat on the floor of the hallway, leaning against the wall and not really feeling much of anything. Mr.

Burke came out of the suite and we talked, but I don't really recall what we said except that he tried to cheer me up. Then he left to arrange our train tickets back to Orchard Bend.

The woman with the scar came back out of the suite and sat on the floor next to me. From her coat pocket she took out a candy stick wrapped in paper and handed it to me.

"I found this by your mother's bed," she said. "I think she would like you to have it."

I unwrapped the stick and licked it.

"If you want to talk," the woman said, "I'll listen."

I didn't say anything. I didn't know how to tell her what I was feeling. I was sad, but I was also angry. I licked my candy until all I could come up with was, "It's all Sheriff Dale's fault."

The woman looked at me sharply.

"If she hadn't murdered Henry, he would still be here," I said. "My mother got sick after he died and now they're both gone. She was my mother's friend even."

The woman nodded and patted me on the back. I think she was going to say something, but my father came out of the suite and beckoned me inside. The woman and I got up off the floor and I said goodbye to her. She smiled and walked away as my father closed the door.

33

March 21, 1887
Sutter Grove

"I don't know where to begin," Dale said, sitting on her bed by her window in the *Black Water* as the sky sank deeper into a dark blue. "For eight years I've been struggling to remember."

"What *do* you remember?" Warren said, taking a seat on the room's solitary, creaky chair.

"Not much," Dale said, looking out the window. A star flickered above the horizon. "I woke up in Orchard Bend and I didn't even know my own name. And before that, there are only pieces."

Dale turned from the window to see Warren nod to herself.

Dale asked, "Was it like that for you?"

Warren shook her head.

"No," she said. "I mean, I don't think so. If anything is missing I haven't noticed."

"You remember *everything?*" Dale asked, unable to hide the excitement in her voice. "You have to tell me what happened. How did we get here?"

"Do you remember something called the Breach?" Warren asked. "Or the Portal?"

Dale winced and closed her eyes against the thin pain that cut through her head.

Warren clutching her face, eyes wide through the blood from her wound. But now Dale saw more. In the vast room of harsh light and black shadows around them, where monitors glowed and LED indicators flickered, the injured Warren backed away from her. Dale's attention shifted to a shimmering, watery break in reality to her left.

"Yes," Dale said, not opening her eyes. "You were there, in that place. And you were hurt."

"My face was cut just before it happened," Warren said with a slight tremble in her voice.

"*What* happened?" Dale asked, her head in her hands. She opened her wet eyes and tried to fight off the migraine.

"The captain," Warren said, her voice catching in her throat. "I bought her enough time to grab her watch and set off the lab's destruct sequence."

The chair creaked again as Warren got up.

"I still don't understand," Dale said, shaking her head, massaging her temples. It didn't help. The headache still threatened to overwhelm her. "Why destroy the lab?"

When she spoke again, Warren's voice didn't tremble, nor did it offer any comfort or warmth. Her words seemed to create a vacuum devoid of all other sound around them.

* * *

"Because of *you*," Warren said.

34

April 16, 1886
Blue Creek

"They're going to close the other two mines, mark my words," Jerry Abernathy whispered.

"Shush!" Bart Edwards said in a voice just as quiet.

He glanced toward the bar, where Phelps, the bartender, had been wiping the same glass for several minutes, staring across the room and out the window at the inviting girls of the *Golden Sunset*.

Abernathy took a sip of his lager and shook his head.

"The man's not paying no mind to us," he said with disgust. "Not with Birdy across the way looking as fresh as summer sunshine."

"What do we do if that happens?" Daniel Underwood asked. "All I got on my pocket is scrip. The company will exchange it for us, won't they?"

"If it suits them," Edwards said, sipping the last of his beer.

"They have to!" Underwood said, horror growing on his nineteen-year-old face. "What am I supposed to do with it otherwise?"

"First, you quit your pissing. Listen to your elders," Edwards said, pointing to himself and Abernathy.

"Hey, who are you calling an 'elder?'" Abernathy said with a swipe at Edward's hand.

"Second, if they don't, Miss Holly at the *Golden Sunset* will exchange your scrip for real money if you ask her nice," Edwards said, looking down at his empty glass.

"She will?" Underwood said.

"Only at half the dollar value," Abernathy said.

"That's crazy!" Underwood said, look from one man to the other.

Edwards put his finger to his lips in a 'shhh' gesture, nodding back towards Phelps at the bar, who now took his time polishing a different glass while admiring the view.

"She has a *special* arrangement with Mr Peachtree," Edwards said.

"And third..." Abernathy said with a wag of his finger. He then paused to finish his beer in a single gulp, "...it's time for you to stop asking questions, lad, and fetch us another round."

The two men dropped a scrip paper each on the table and Underwood collected them and their empty glasses, hoping his own half-finished beer would still be there when he got back.

Keeping his eye on the girls across the street, Phelps made his way down the bar. With some reluctance he broke eye contact to take Underwood's order.

As Phelps refilled the men's glasses, Underwood looked at the mining photographs on the wall. Even in the place where the men often came to forget about the drudgery of working the mines, the company made sure to remind them where they were. Underwood looked at the photograph of a group of miners gathered around Shaft 3. Edwards once told Underwood that he had known every last man in the photograph and that they were all dead now, most still buried when the mine collapsed in the explosion the previous November. Underwood himself had only been working for the company a week when the explosion happened. He guessed that maybe he had met a few of those men in that time, but to be frank he recalled none of them. What he did remember was the blast hitting the company store, where he'd gone to buy a warmer shirt that snowy November day. He remembered running outside to see what had happened. People on the street were already speculating that one of the mineshafts had blown up and then the strangest thing happened. Burning shards of wood and rock rained down all around them, with some of the lumber as big as a man. One such piece came down from the sky and into the company post office, injuring the postmaster inside. To Underwood, the scene looked like Armageddon, but he soon

258

realized that the people had been right, one of the mines had indeed gone up. Even before they knew it was safe, folks began rushing around to put out the fires. Someone put a bucket in Daniel's hand and soon he was in a ragged line passing water from a pump to the fire in the post office.

Phelps started filling the second glass of beer as the tavern door opened and in walked a woman in a plain brown skirt and a dark jacket. Her bonnet shielded her face as she stopped inside the door and scanned the room. She saw Daniel watching her, tilted her head and walked straight to him.

"I've been looking for you," the woman said. Closer now, Underwood got a better look at her. Locks of dark hair framed her face beneath her bonnet, and a few strays came down over her eye and cheek.

"Looking for *me?*" Underwood said, scoffing. He wondered if she was from the *Golden Sunset*, a new, older girl dressed up proper so as not to get the boot from Phelps for peddling in a company establishment.

"You're Daniel Underwood," the woman said.

"That's right," Underwood said, knowing it wouldn't be too hard for the woman to get the name of a particular man in town if she really wanted to.

Phelps brought the glasses of beer over and returned to the important business of getting an eyeful of the girls on the porch across the street.

"It's about your father," the woman said low as Underwood reached for the beers.

He stopped.

"You best tread lightly now, you hear?" Daniel said without looking at her.

"Meet me at that table over there," the woman said.

Not waiting for an answer or an acknowledgement, she walked away, crossing the tavern to an empty table in the corner. She sat with her back to the window, through which poured shafts of bright afternoon light.

Daniel dropped the glasses of beer off at his table for Edwards and Abernathy, collected his beer—untouched by either of the other two—and joined the woman at her table. He squinted against the light behind her.

"So what about my father?" Daniel asked, wanting to get this conversation over with as fast as he could.

"His name was Ernest Underwood," she said.

"I know," Daniel said, raising his glass to take a sip.

"The woman who killed him lives in Orchard Bend," she went on, "and I'm prepared to pay you handsomely to kill *her*."

Underwood sputtered in his beer and wiped his mouth with his sleeve.

"And don't pretend you're as pure as the driven snow," the woman said. "I made the acquaintance of Mrs MacReady, the widow of Andrew, your father's 'business associate.'"

Underwood fixed the woman a hard stare, his jaw clenched. He peered into the shadow of her bonnet as she spoke and picked up more than a few details. Her hair had begun to go grey and she was older than his mother would have been, God rest her soul.

And beneath the stray locks of hair covering her cheek was a nasty scar, straight as a ruler.

"Believe me when I say that she has it coming," the woman continued. "Even before she killed your father, she did a lot of bad things, ruined a lot of lives. She deserves this."

Daniel Underwood took a slow, deliberate sip of his beer, never taking his eyes off the woman with the scar. She held his gaze without so much as a blink.

Daniel knew she was serious.

And he knew she was right.

Setting his glass down, Underwood nodded and gave a little snicker. He had a gun and belt back in the locker under his cot and he was going to need it.

"How much?" Underwood asked.

"Five hundred dollars," she said. "Same as she got for killing your father and his friends. I'll give you a hundred dollars now to recruit some men of your own. You'll get the rest when she's dead."

She slid an envelope across the table. Inside, Underwood could see the money. He could have counted it, but he didn't want to draw attention. Instead he nodded again, looking out the window at the whores across the street as he tucked the envelope into his shirt. He wouldn't need a hundred dollars to convince the Mercer brothers to join him. Last he heard they were in Ashleyville. That left more than enough to pay a visit to the *Golden Sunset* before he rode out.

"Deal," he said.

"Her name is Emery Dale," the woman said.

"I know that, too," Daniel said, "kind of hard to forget."

This time she nodded.

"My wagon will be parked ten miles up Whisper Pass for the next seven days," the woman said. "You have that long and no longer."

Underwood smiled, downed his beer and stood up.

"One more thing," the woman said.

"What?" Daniel asked. "You want to shake on it?"

"Watch out for the sheriff," she said. "He's a real son of a bitch."

Underwood snickered again, turned and left, giving Edwards and Abernathy a nod goodbye as he passed their table.

35

March 21, 1887
Sutter Grove

"Because of *you*," Warren said.

Dale sat stunned on the bed, her migraine burrowing deeper, tears rolling down her face. She looked up at Kenna Warren and saw no sympathy, no compassion. The woman's lip twitched as she watched Emery Dale struggle.

"You and your team attacked the lab," Warren said, "You killed my friends. You slashed my face!"

The pain exploded in Dale's skull as Warren said those words, sending her to the floor where she writhed in pain, her hands gripping her head.

Through tear-blurred eyes, Dale saw Warren lean over her, the woman's expression one of bemusement at Dale's agony.

"And my name," Warren hissed, "was *Decker.*"

The memory flashed clear in her mind.

Decker attacking, moving fast and taking full advantage of the element of surprise to engage her target: Dale.

A fraction of a second later, a voice called to her, 'Major! Behind you!'

Dale already saw the movement to her right and was spinning around as Decker leapt from cover. Dale saw the gun in her hand and ducked, moving to her right and dropping the sword in its sheath. As Decker advanced, closing the distance, firing and missing the moving target, Dale drew one of her knives from her harness and engaged her opponent.

Anger took hold of Dale as Decker anticipated the attack, moving just as fast as Dale. They were so close to each other that Dale could read Decker's name on her dark uniform. Decker holstered her weapon to free up both hands, dodging to avoid the blade, but the move gave Dale the opening she needed. Letting out a cry of rage and satisfaction, Dale slashed upwards, her blade tearing Decker's face. She staggered back and Dale dropped into the ready position.

"Stand down!" Dale ordered Decker as the woman clutched her face, blood gushing from between her fingers, her eyes wide with shock and pain.

And hatred.

When the grey vision replaced Dale's normal sight, the pain broke. Warren, with the same cold hate in her eyes, reached beneath her coat and withdrew a knife of her own, one Dale recognized as US Army issue. Still curled on the floor, Dale drove her boot out at Warren's knee, but her the long skirt got in the way, so only part of her heel connected. Warren's knee twisted and she grunted, but she slashed at Dale's leg as it recoiled, slicing the cloth and the meat of her calf. Dale grabbed the thick leg of the dresser and pulled, dragging herself across the floor to put some small amount of distance between her and Warren, who limped as she tried to put pressure on her knee.

Through the grey sight, Dale saw the gun in the shoulder holster beneath Warren's jacket as she reached for it. On her side, Dale drew one of her knives from the waist of her skirt and launched it, but Warren saw the move and got out of the way with less than an inch to spare. As the blade sunk into the cheap wood door, Dale got her legs under her. Warren charged again. Dale tried to get behind the blade, but Warren caught her and slammed both of them into the dresser and then into the wall, knocking the empty porcelain washbasin to the floor, where it shattered. Dale felt her head crash into the plaster wall. With one hand locked onto the wrist of Warren's knife hand, she went for the gun under Warren's coat. Warren twisted around to prevent Dale from reaching it, crying out with angry pain as the move pulled her too far around. She let go of the knife and Dale caught it before it hit the floor, letting go of Warren's wrist. Warren pulled away and drew her service weapon, pivoting to put her back in the corner of the room. Dale saw this and knew her angle was bad to throw the knife.

Warren had her.

Dale froze in a crouch as Warren drew down on her. She dropped the knife and Warren hesitated.

"I'm sorry," Dale said between gasps, her voice shaking from adrenaline. "Whoever I was, I'm not that person anymore."

"How convenient," Warren spat.

"Eight years," Dale said. "That's how long these fragments of memory have haunted me. That's why I wanted to find you, why I tracked you down."

"Except you didn't track me down," Warren said. "*Gertrude* led you to me. Or hadn't you figured that out yet?"

The statement stopped Dale cold and she dropped to a knee. She looked away from Warren, who could shoot her at any moment, and tried to make sense of what she'd just been told.

"Gertrude... How...?" Dale trailed off, "She found you?"

"No," Warren said. "See, I've known for some time that you were in Orchard Bend. But when I read that you had killed her son, I reached out to her. She remembered me."

"Remembered you?" Dale asked, her head still hung low.

Warren only nodded.

"So I visited her here in Sutter Grove," Warren said. "I told her who you really were. She believed me. She was a perceptive one. And apart from *when* exactly you came from, she had already put some things together about your past just by watching and listening to you. And she knew what bread crumbs to use to lead you to me."

"If you knew where I was and you wanted me dead, why not come for me before?" Dale asked.

"Who said I didn't?" Warren said.

Dale tried to sort out what she meant, but decided it didn't matter anyway, not now, and she closed her eyes. She felt the grey sight ease and then slip away, leaving only stinging blackness in her swollen, damp eyes. Somehow the dark made it easier to fathom the magnitude of what Gertrude McCabe had done. Her friend had not been trying to mend one last bridge between them in her final days. Instead, she'd been torching it, along with eight years of love and friendship.

Dale reached into her pocket and waited for Warren to shoot her. When she didn't, Dale took out the envelope Gertrude had left at the *Gazette*. She unfolded the letter and put it on the floor, then set the photograph of Warren down next to it.

My mistakes led me to this, Dale thought. *Even ones I can't well remember.*

Out of the corner of her eye, Dale saw Warren move.

Dale waited, but no killing shot came.

She looked up at Warren and saw the woman had lowered her gun, her expression still intense, her eyes troubled. Warren said nothing to Dale as she holstered her weapon. She took her bonnet off the hook on the back of the door and tied it around her chin. When her gaze went to the knife on the floor near Dale, she exhaled.

"I'm taking my knife," she said. "I don't intend to kill you anymore. This all ends here, for me anyway."

Dale got up from the floor and took a step away from the knife. Warren reached out with her boot and dragged the weapon across the floor to her. In a swift motion, she picked it up and twirled it around in her hand as she sheathed the blade. Her gaze went to the photograph on the floor—her at the picnic in 1862.

"May I have that?" she asked. Dale heard many years of fatigue in her request.

"So long as I can keep the letter," Dale answered, her voice rough and her throat tight.

Warren didn't reach for the photograph, so Dale picked it and the letter up from the floor. She held the photograph out to Warren, who took it. Their eyes locked and both held the picture in the darkening room, lit only by the failing light outside the window. Dale let it go with a nod. Warren turned and opened the door. Loud conversations and laughter drifted in from the pub below. The bargemen sang and drank and Warren walked out of the room, not shutting the door behind her. Dale put Gertrude's letter on the bed next to the *Orchard Herald* newspaper and closed the door. She picked the candle up off the floor and struck a match to light it. Dale brought it to the window. Below, she saw Warren in her bonnet walking up the street away from the *Black Water*. Dale followed her progress past the dark shops and storefronts, passing beneath the lampposts until she turned a corner and was gone.

* * *

Dale sat on her bed in her underclothes and shredded her petticoat for bandages.

I won't need to wear this ever again, she thought as she tore the fabric into strips.

She began to clean and dress the gash on her calf as well as she could. The long slice was clean and straight, but not too deep. It both throbbed and stung and caused Dale to swear more than once as she worked. It also reminded her of the scar on Warren's cheek. Dale forced the thought away.

She tied the bandages tight, dressed in a more comfortable shirt and trousers, and sat on the bed with her back against the wall and her arms on her knees. Through the open window, a fresh breeze cut through the dank smell that characterized Barge Town. Dale breathed it in. She thought about getting something hot to eat before the kitchen closed, but whatever appetite she'd had earlier was now long gone.

So she sat staring out the window and listening to the noise of the street below. Men shouted both in anger and jocularity, women laughed and scolded. A fight broke out, but it ended just as fast when a peacemaker stepped in. An old man came parading down the street singing "What Shall We Do With a Drunken Sailor?" and as he got closer to the *Black Water* several men and a few ladies joined in. He continued on down the street and out of earshot. All the while, Dale sat on her bed and tried not to think about anything from the past two days. She wondered if she'd even be able to sleep.

Footsteps came and went down the hallway and Dale paid them no mind until one set stopped outside her door. Dale flew from her bed, grabbing one of her knives, and crouched low.

A soft knock came, followed by a voice.

"Dale," the man said, "it's Turnbull."

* * *

Dale unlocked the door and left it open a crack before returning to sit on her bed as she had before. When Turnbull pushed it open, the door gave a long creak. Still in the hallway, he scanned the room, lingering on the shards of porcelain on the floor. Dale's gaze returned to the window and Turnbull let himself in. He carried her weathered satchel, which gave a heavy, dull thud on the wood floor when he set it down. Turnbull righted the chair and sat on it, favouring his ribs and wincing. The chair groaned under the weight and Dale gave a slight wince at the sound.

Turnbull leaned back, a move that caused even more discomfort. He adjusted his position until he found an angle that suited him. He grimaced, but said nothing. That was fine with Dale. Minutes passed in silence between them, with the only sounds drifting in through the window and from the pub below.

Turnbull at last broke the stalemate by reaching into the pocket of his vest. He tossed the object on the bed next to her and the flash of metal in the candlelight told her what it was without her needing to look at it.

A badge.

Her badge.

"It's time to come home, Sheriff Dale," he said.

Dale continued looking out the window, listening to the sounds of the street's nightlife, but then picked up the badge and held it up. As she turned away from the window, she ran her thumb over the words.

ORCHARD BEND
SHERIFF

DALE

"I suppose it is," Dale said, "but it won't be the same. It will never be the same."

"No, I don't reckon it will be," Turnbull said.

She looked at him for the first time since he had knocked on the door. She could tell he'd hurt his abdomen, maybe even broken some ribs, but the dark rings around his eyes told her he'd not had much sleep in days.

There's something else, though, Dale thought, *something in his expression. Not quite a thousand-yard stare, but in the neighbourhood. He's seen something that weighs on him.*

Dale thought it might be his discovery of Laura O'Malley's head, but perhaps it was something more.

Dale closed her hand around the badge and got up from the bed.

Wincing again, Turnbull picked her satchel up from the floor and put it on the bed next to her.

"The next train heading to Orchard Bend leaves at ten in the morning," Turnbull said, making his way to the door. "But you don't have to stay here tonight. I've arranged other, less pungent accommodations. Meet me downstairs when you're ready."

He closed the door behind him and Dale stared at the satchel on the bed for a long time, suspecting she knew what lay inside.

* * *

As Emery Dale came down the stairs and into the pub, she relished the barkeep's double-take at her appearance. He wasn't the only one who took notice. Men paused a moment to look in her direction, some playing cards, glancing over at her before returning to the game. Like the bartender, some noticed the sheriff's badge on her jacket and took a second look.

She adjusted the satchel by the strap and tucked the back of her cloak under it to keep it off her shoulders. She thought she might pull the hood up outside in the chilled air, but for now she kept it down.

Her gun belts criss-crossed her waist, shifting on her hips as she walked. Dale had forgotten how good the weight of the guns felt.

But it's more than that, she thought. *I have my life back.*

Turnbull stood at the bar with a shot glass of whiskey. As Dale approached, he raised it in salute.

"Looking alright, boss," he said and downed the shot.

"I accidentally broke the basin in my room," Dale said to the barkeep, putting some money on the bar, along with her room key. "Sorry. This should more than cover it. And I'll be checking out."

The barkeep said nothing, but snatched the money and the key, stuffing both into his pocket.

"Time to go, Sheriff," Turnbull said, leaving the bar and gesturing to the door.

"And where *are* we going, Deputy?" Dale asked as they stepped outside. The cold air seeped under her cloak and she flipped the hood up to cover her head.

"Oh-ho," Turnbull said in mock offence, "I'm still an Acting Sheriff until we're back in Orchard Bend I'll have you know."

"My mistake, Acting Sheriff Turnbull," Dale said.

"As to where we bunk down tonight, only the finest establishment in town," Turnbull said, "the Sutter Grove jailhouse. They have a bunk room for me and a spare office for you."

"I think I might go back to the *Black Water*," Dale said. "Unless you tell me Deputies Connelly and Dobbs are still on duty."

"Which one is Dobbs?" Turnbull asked.

"Deputy Moustache," Dale answered.

Turnbull snorted out a laugh.

"I believe he is," Turnbull said, "as was Connelly. I don't think either of them like you very much."

"I wonder if they'll like me more now that I'm wearing a badge," Dale mused.

269

36

March 23, 1887
Orchard Bend

Snow dusted the ravine as Emery Dale guided her horse down the road. The sun broke through the clouds, casting the falling snow in shafts of light where they glittered and shined. Dale breathed in the air and held out her hand. The flakes landed on her glove and melted, leaving only drops of water. She pulled her hood back and looked up at the sky, letting the sun light her face. She smiled as the snow touched her cheeks and her forehead.

At the bridge, she slowed and looked down at the rushing water that always ran high and fast this time of year. On the other side, she turned off the road and onto the trail by the riverside. When she reached the clearing, she stopped and regarded her cabin. The hollow, distant sound of wind in the trees filled the ravine and she soaked it in.

"It's good to be home," she said.

Dale dismounted and led her horse to the stable. She didn't remove the saddle because she'd be riding out again later, but she watered the horse and fed it.

Carrying her satchel over her shoulder, Dale walked back to her cabin and rounded the corner.

She stopped when she saw the mark on her door.

Scratched in pencil, it depicted a flower.

A rose.

Dale smiled and wondered when the schoolteacher had put it there. She planned to ask her later that night.

She unlocked the door and opened it, standing in the doorway and looking inside; everything was as she left it, nothing had changed.

Everything's changed, she thought.

Dale stepped inside, closed the door and took off her satchel. From her cloak, she took out her watch and set it on the windowsill above the sink, allowing the solar cells to bathe in the light. She sighed, wanting nothing more than to take a long, hot bath and a nap before riding back out.

That's when she saw the cross on her bed.

Silver and polished, glinting in the light from the window, Dale recognized it immediately. It belonged to Laura's mother, Frances O'Malley.

Dale went to the bed and picked the cross up by the chain, letting it tangle there in the light. She looked around the one-room cabin again, found everything as it should be, so turned her attention back to the cross.

Why leave this here? Dale wondered. *And how did you get in, Mrs O'Malley?*

Dale thought she might have to change the lock on the door very soon. She put the cross back down on the bed, picked up her water bucket from beside the door and went outside.

Standing at the end of the trail from the road was Maxwell McCabe. In his black hat and coat, he was a stark contrast to the green and white surroundings.

Dale dropped the bucket and her hand went to the gun on her hip.

McCabe threw his hands up and Dale saw he had a white handkerchief in one of them.

"Sheriff, I've come to talk," he said.

Dale's eyes scanned the woods beyond the clearing.

"Where is Burke," Dale asked.

"Back at the coach on the road," McCabe said.

Dale scanned the area again and could see no sign of an ambush. Still, she remained on guard.

"I understand your trepidation," McCabe said. "The events of the past few months would leave anyone suspicious."

"Why are you here, Mr McCabe?" Dale asked.

"I wanted to tell you that I harbour you no ill will for what has transpired," McCabe said, lowering his hand. Dale watched his every move, waiting for some sign of betrayal.

271

"I didn't want to kill Henry," Dale said. "He left me no choice."

"I understand that," McCabe said. "I don't like it, but I understand it. I know now that my son was... that he kept hidden a monster inside him. I didn't see it. I can't tell you if my wife saw it because I don't know."

Dale's jaw clenched at the mention of Gertrude.

"What she did at the end," McCabe continued, "what she wanted to do to you, I had no knowledge of it until the other day."

He raised a hand again, slow and careful. Dale did not relax her grip on her gun.

"I received a letter from her, mailed to our house here in Orchard Bend, sent before she died," McCabe said. He moved to reach inside his coat, but paused and gave Dale a nod that asked for her permission. She nodded back and McCabe took out an identical envelope to the one Whitaker had given her in Sutter Grove. He took out the letter and unfolded it. He read aloud...

* * *

My Beloved Husband,

Just as our son was a victim of brutal disregard, so too am I a victim of all-consuming grief. It eats at me and casts a pall on all I see and hear, save for you and our blessed angel, Owen. I will be gone by the time you read these words. We will have said our farewells as husband and wife. I don't know what lies before me, as my faith has withered, but perhaps we shall meet again if it is of Divine will. If not, if we never cross paths in that eternal place, know that I loved you and our children more than anything else. I hope to find our Henry after I am gone from this world and I will tell him how much you and his brother miss him.

All of that I'm sure you already knew, so now I must inform you of something which you do not yet know.

I made arrangements with an old acquaintance to kill Emery Dale. It is vengeance, right and simple. I kept you out of those plans to protect you. The business was mine alone and I will accept any punishment God sees fit to exact for my deeds in that matter. It can't be any worse than the pain and torment I feel at losing my son the way I did.

I trust that when you read this the act will have been committed successfully. Now you know the truth of it should any questions linger in your mind.

You and Owen can live your lives in peace now, knowing revenge was exacted. It is my last gift to both of you.

> *With all the love in my heart,*
> *Gertrude*

* * *

McCabe finished reading and waited for Dale's reaction.

Dale took her hand from the gun and looked around the clearing.

"I knew she wanted me dead," Dale said, "but to hear her tell it so plainly…"

"My wife failed," McCabe said. "Her assassin let you live."

"Murder is not in everyone's heart," Dale said, not looking at him. "Sometimes we think it is. Sometimes we believe it is, so completely, but when the moment comes we find it's not what we're after."

McCabe waved the letter as he spoke.

"If I had known about this," he said, "I would have done everything in my power to stop it."

"But not my arrest," Dale said.

"I wanted you held accountable," McCabe said. "And you would have been. And it turns out you were right. It's not easy for me to admit what my son did to Laura O'Malley, but he did it and you acted in self-defence. It's why I recommended to the council that you be re-instated as sheriff."

"*You* made that recommendation," Dale said. "You opposed my getting the job in the first place."

"People change, Ms Dale," McCabe said, turning back to the trail that led to the road. "And Turnbull, I'm told, didn't want the job anymore."

He stopped at the edge of the clearing and turned to face her.

"I'm going to take my son and travel for a time," McCabe said. "You were always effective while in my employ, Ms Dale, so I trust Orchard Bend will still be here when we return."

He continued up the trail and left her standing in the clearing.

37

April 19, 1887
Orchard Bend

"I'm sorry to lose you, Allen," Sheriff Dale said as she got up from her desk. "But our loss is the Pinkertons' gain, I suppose. I have no doubt you'll do good work for them."

She put out her hand.

"Thank you, Sheriff," Green said, shaking it. "Like I said, I don't leave for a couple of weeks, so I'll work the rest of the month if that's alright, then spend time with my family before I go."

"If you get tired of the big city, know that you'll always have a job here," Dale said. She put her other hand on his shoulder. "And if I don't get the opportunity to tell you this later, thank you, Allen, for *everything.*"

"You're welcome, Sheriff," Green said.

"Which reminds me," Dale said. "I made you a promise once."

She walked to the jail cell and opened the door, gesturing Green to follow her. Dale stood at the door and looked inside, saying nothing. Her breathing became shallow.

"Sheriff, are you alright?" Green asked.

Dale gave a nod and took a deep breath.

"When I first came to Orchard Bend," Dale said, "Sheriff Anderson detained me while he investigated what happened with the Underwood Gang at the ravine. I was held here for an uncomfortable amount of time."

"Your clauster-phobia," Green said.

"Claustrophobia, yes," Dale said. "Doc Shaw explained it to you. While I was in this cell I told myself 'never again.' I would not let myself be put in a cage I could not get out of, so when I became sheriff, I decided to ensure I could always get out of this jail."

She took another deep breath and stepped inside, fighting down the gnawing panic at the memory of that long week in January spent behind bars. Dale sat on the cot and looked at Green, who waited for her to explain further.

Dale smiled.

"Turnbull and I searched the cell after you were gone," Green said. "We didn't find anything to tell us how you might have escaped."

"Come inside, Deputy," Dale said, standing up.

Green did so.

Dale climbed onto the outer frame of the bed in the corner of the cell, balancing against the wall. At that height, her head reached almost to the ceiling. She put her hand on the end of one of the slats of wood overhead and pushed it up. The end of the slat raised up two inches. Dale put her hand in the crevice, felt around, then produced a key.

"You're kidding with me," Green said, shaking his head.

"This board is on a hinge at the other end," Dale said, holding the key out to Green. "I added a cross piece to hold the board in place, to keep it dropping down."

Green took the key and looked at it, then walked to the lock of the open door. He put it in and turned. Sure enough, the lock closed. He turned the key the other way and unlocked it, shaking his head again.

"Just like that," Green said with a snort. "You hid a key in the cell."

He handed it back to her and she replaced it in its hiding spot overhead.

"It never occurred to either of us to check there," Green said. "We thought we'd checked every possible inch. Tell me, who thinks to check the ceiling?"

"*You* will, from now on," Dale said, climbing down from the bed. She left the cell and Green closed it behind her. She checked the time on her brass pocketwatch.

"So how did your parents take the news?" Dale asked.

"About my leaving for the city? Well, my mother wasn't happy about me being so far away," Green said with a guilty smile, "but I told her the train can get me home to visit in no time. I said she won't even notice I'm gone. She made me promise to come home at least one weekend a month for some home-cooked dinner until she gets used to me being away."

"Well, when you're in town you be sure to visit us," Dale said, taking her cloak off the peg on the wall. "And speaking of a home-cooked dinner, *I* am dining with Miss Adelaide this evening."

"Give her my best, Sheriff," Green said, settling into the chair at Dale's desk.

"I will," Dale said, throwing her cloak over her shoulders. She kept it draped over one arm, leaving the other free. It also displayed her badge and that was not an accident. "Have a good night, Allen. Stay safe."

Dale left the jailhouse and walked along the boardwalk, taking in the spring evening, happy to be leaving work while the sun still lit the sky.

At the intersection, she saw Herman Statler atop a ladder working on the wall of the new bakery. As she got closer, she saw he had a sign in his hands that couldn't have been longer than two feet.

"Evening, Mr Statler," she said when she reached the corner, "that's a pretty small sign for a bakery, wouldn't you say?"

Still clutching his hammer, Herman tipped his hat and took the nails out from between his lips.

"Evenin', Sheriff," he smiled, "Um, no, this isn't the sign for the bakery. This is the street sign. You know, for the street."

He held it up. In clean, neat font it read 'ANDERSON STREET.'

"Did you make that?" Dale asked. "It's lovely."

"I did, in my free time,' Herman said. "It's the anniversary, you know? Of Sheriff Anderson's passing."

Dale's heart sank. She hadn't known. Even with so much on her mind, she felt she ought to have remembered. She was one of his successors after all.

"You honour him, Mr Statler," Dale said, "and you do the town proud."

Herman smiled and got back to work, driving the nails into the sign, securing it to the wall. Dale crossed the street and walked in the direction of Rose's cottage.

"Sheriff Dale! Sheriff!" a voice called out behind her.

Dale turned to see the widow Mrs Bentley rushing up the street towards her, waving a letter. Dale walked back and met her at the corner.

"I'm sorry I'm delivering this so late!" Mrs Bentley said. "We had quite a day for mail today and Mrs Green and I talked at length about her son's new career in the big city and—"

She caught herself and stopped, covering her mouth.

"I hope I'm not telling stories out of school, Sheriff," she gasped. "I assume you know already."

"About Deputy Green's new job with the Pinkertons, yes, I do," Dale assured her. "Is that letter for me?"

Mrs Bentley looked at the letter in her hand, then thrust it at Dale.

"Why, yes," Mrs Bentley exclaimed, "I nearly forgot. I'd forget my head if it wasn't attached."

Dale looked at the envelope. It was addressed to her, *Emery Dale, Orchard Bend*, but she didn't recognize the address on the postmark.

"Where is Black Barrel?" Dale asked.

"I couldn't say," Mrs Bentley answered. "Clearly someone there knows *you*."

* * *

Dale ran her hand along the white picket fence in front of Rose's cottage as she approached the gate. Warm light glowed from the windows and Dale smiled. She walked along the path to the front door and knocked.

Rose answered and frowned.

"Emery Ann Dale, how often must I remind you?" the schoolteacher scolded. "*You* never need to knock before entering my home. Now come inside at once."

Rose's frown broke into a smile and Dale beamed as she entered the cottage.

"I simply enjoy reminding you just how delighted you were to see me at your door," Emery said, taking off her cloak.

"Always and forever," Rose said, putting Emery's cloak on the coat hook. "And your timing is impeccable. Dinner is prepared."

* * *

Emery sank down onto the sofa and put her hands over her face. The heat from the wood stove in the corner washed over her and Emery soaked in it. She dropped her hands onto the sofa and that's when she saw the sword on the mantle. She stared at it as she listened to Rose humming and making hot cocoa in the kitchen.

Emery stood up and went to the weapon, which sat behind the photo in the silver frame, of Dale herself, taken by accident a year ago to the day in the Jackson Picture Studio, when she had been pursuing Daniel Underwood.

I'm sorry I couldn't have reached you sooner, Sheriff Anderson, she thought.

The grey sight came on without warning or headache. Emery swayed, her hand steadying herself on the mantle. It took a moment to regain her balance and she found herself looking at her sword. Through the smoky-glass of the world, Emery could make out the blade beneath the sheath. She could also see the lines of thread in the stitching of the sheath. Emery followed the edge of the blade to the guard, finding a kind of beauty in the straight edge and seeing the layers all together. The metal of the blade continued past the shoulder, where the edge stopped, and right into the hilt, the part known as the tang. She could make the tang out underneath the bands of leather wrapped around the hilt.

And that's when she saw the writing.

Startled, she stepped away. With some focus, she pushed the grey sight from her eyes and stared at the sword. Rose came in and set the tray with the rich-smelling cocoa on the dining table behind Emery.

279

"It's been one year since that picture was taken," Rose said. She started to pour cocoa into the mugs as Dale picked up the sword from the mantle. Rose stopped and watched her as she held the sheathed weapon out on its side, resting it on both hands. Dale carried it to the dining table.

"Emery, what are you doing?" Rose asked.

"I'm not sure," Dale said.

She put the sword down and looked at it, bending over the hilt and the damaged pummel, where the metal had become misshapen from the bullet hit.

Emery looked up at Rose, who watched in fascination and confusion.

Dale took the deformed round pummel in her palm and gripped it. She took the hilt in her other hand and twisted them in opposite directions, straining as the pummel refused to turn. Rose sat and sipped her cocoa, eyes wide. Dale let go and flexed her hand, wiggling her fingers. She gripped the sword again the same way and twisted, this time doing so in short, steady motions.

"Come on!" she growled.

The pummel gave and started to turn. Rose picked up the lantern from the center of the table and brought it close to Emery.

Her heart racing, Dale unthreaded the pummel from the end of the tang. Once free, she slid the hilt off, leaving the guard loose at the shoulder.

"Is that writing?" Rose asked, leaning in close.

The fine, etched text read:

MARA

"'Mara,'" Rose read aloud.

Emery turned the sword over to see whether anything more had been etched on the other side of the tang and found only the same name there.

Mara.

"Who is 'Mara?'" Rose asked.

—The blonde woman with the pale green eyes, sparring with a wooden sword—

Emery Dale sat down and set the sword on the table.

"Someone from my old life," she said.

But there was more to it, only she couldn't pin it down.

"I understand," Rose said. Emery could hear the frustration in her voice, along with something else, something close to fear.

"Rose," Emery said, "it's time I told you some things about who I am and who I was."

* * *

Deep in thought, Rose stared at the glowing orange fire behind the glass of the wood stove. She held Emery's watch in her hand, turning it over and over, this way and that. She ran her thumb over its smooth, black surface and let the band slide between her fingers.

Emery watched Rose, trying to read her expression.

To her surprise, telling Rose about her amnesia had not been as difficult as Emery had often imagined it would be. Telling Rose about her past had proved more difficult. If not for the watch, Emery might not have even considered trying. She showed Rose the message app, which identified her as having held the rank of major in her old life.

Rose had listened to everything, taking it all in, and asking very few questions.

Emery told Rose all she knew about this Mara person, which not very much, that she had been there when the facility exploded and that she remembered sparring with her at some point before that.

"I may never find out who she is," Dale had explained. "Warren might know, but she's gone."

Emery finished her story, and Rose had said nothing, instead turning to look at the stove.

Emery sat in the chair holding her lukewarm cocoa, waiting for a reply. The minutes ticked away. Rose looked at the watch, then back at the glow of the stove.

"Emery?" she said at last, turning to look at her, "Do you love me?"

"Yes," Emery said without hesitation.

"I love you, too," Rose said.

She stood up and kissed Emery, taking her hand and leading her to the sofa. As they sat together, Rose held up the watch.

"Turn it on for me again," she said.

Relieved, Dale tapped the screen for her and watched as Rose took great care examining the tiny icons. Rose opened the message app, bringing up the display:

1 New Message
Device Clearance Recognized
Maj. E. A. Dale
Enter GvSci Passcode

_ _ _ _

Rose bit her lower lip and gave the screen a tentative poke. Letters appeared and Rose gasped.

"You can use those to enter the passcode," Emery said.

"Yes, of course," Rose said, not taking her eyes off the screen. "That's why I sought this out."

Emery's brow furrowed and then her eyes went wide as Rose taps the letters with her finger.

"I told you I don't know what it is," Dale said.

Rose finished typing and showed her the screen, a mischievous smile on her face.

1 New Message
Device Clearance Recognized
Maj. E. A. Dale
Enter GvSci Passcode
M A R A
[SELECT?]

Emery took the watch in disbelief. She looked at the sword, still disassembled on the dining table.

Could it be that simple?

Emery looked to Rose, who nodded.

Emery hesitated.

Opening this message could change her life more than she knew, more even than the events of the last few months. Dale wasn't sure she was ready for more upheaval. She looked at Rose, who patted her leg and smiled. The trepidation in the schoolteacher's expression told Emery that she felt the same, but also that whatever revelations were contained with the message, they would face them together.

Dale tapped "[SELECT]."

She held her breath as the green circle spun around in the middle of the screen.

It winked out and the screen filled with text.

38

Passcode ACCEPTED
Maj. E. A. Dale
New Message

Date Sent: 14-08-11
Date Received: 15-05-79

If you're reading this, I expect you found your way to the grove of aspens. I don't know how many of us survived the journey through the Breach, but I know I wasn't alone. Another man, Rateliff, arrived here years before and has since been lost trying to get back to our own time. I tried to stop him, but it was no use. The Portal he opened failed and trapped him in the Breach.

Let me be clear on this point: There is NO going back.

Do not try or you will suffer the same fate he did.

Another thing about the Breach is that it affects the mind. When I arrived in the past, my memories were incomplete. So were Rateliff's. I suspect his sanity was affected, too, and I often wondered about my own in the years that followed. I don't remember my name, the one I had before the explosion in the lab. I do know who I was, though, the lead scientist studying the Breach. I remember the attempted takeover, all the shooting, and the captain detonating the explosives to stop the Breach falling into the wrong hands. We were pulled in and scattered throughout time, so I theorize. If Rateliff was the first to exit into the past—chronologically speaking, that is—and the first to venture here, and I was the second, the rest of you must also have felt drawn to this place, a pull deep inside your stomach, feeling like a hook tugging at your gut. I think that's the pull of the Breach, but I don't really understand what it means.

I also remember another person, whose name also eludes me. I know her only as the captain and I know I love her. If you're reading this, if you remember me and what we had, know that I never stopped loving you, no matter where or when you ended up. You are the bravest person I ever met and I know you will survive.

I've tried to make a life for myself here and I encourage you all to do the same. I've wondered about the paradoxes we could create, how we might affect history, but there's no way to know. We are trapped whenever we ended up, so live your life in the here and now, keep future knowledge and technology to yourself and don't go out of your way to change history. I don't know if that's the right answer, but it feels like it is, like the tugging sensation that brought us here against our will.

This will be my parting message in the control computer I've hidden in the ravine. It will stay powered by the solar cells and will transmit as long as the hardware withstands the elements. I may come to check on it from time to time, I don't know.

As I said, I don't remember my real name, but I have chosen one that I think has a nice ring to it. Some settler families have arrived in the area and plan to start a town. They've welcomed me into their group and after years alone out here, I am glad to be with people again.

That's all.

Heed what I said about not trying to re-enter the Breach.

Live. That's all you can do now.

Doc Reed

39

April 20, 1887
Orchard Bend

With no moon in the sky, the canopy of stars glittered overhead as Emery and Rose moved through the dark and empty streets of Orchard Bend. At the river's edge near the McCabe Mill, they stepped onto the landing of mortar and stone, and took care laying out the supplies.

One by one, they set each of the small candles in its bed of wax paper and lit the wick.

"Doc Reed," Emery whispered as she placed the makeshift boat on the moving water. It floated on down the river, a tiny point of yellow-white light, only a little brighter than the reflection of the stars overhead.

Rose knelt with her candle, its light glinting off her damp eyes.

"Laura O'Malley," she whispered and sent the candle bobbing down the river.

Emery knelt next.

"Sergeant Rateliff," she whispered, and let the candle join the line forming along the water.

Rose touched the water with one hand and set the candle atop it with the other, whispering, "Doctor Alfred Shaw."

Emery held the next lit candle close to her face, feeling its warmth against the tears rolling down her cheeks. Rose took her trembling hand and guided it to the river.

"Gertrude McCabe," Emery stuttered. "I forgive you."

"As do I," Rose whispered.

Together they let it go.

Emery took the last two candles, handed one to Rose, and lit them, saying, "For the souls still lost or traveling. You are not forgotten."

"Frances O'Malley," Rose whispered.

"Kenna Warren," Emery whispered, "and for Mara. I hope this light helps guide you home."

They launched the candles together and stood on the landing to watch them pierce the blackness as they floated away.

* * *

Just before dawn, Emery Dale climbed out of bed and walked nude across the cottage's bedroom. Halfway to the door, she picked up her shirt and put it on. The brisk morning had a refreshing bite as it touched her sweat-dampened skin and ahe shook the last few sleepy cobwebs from her brain. She found her jacket hanging on the peg over her cloak by the cottage's front door. Dale searched first one pocket, then the next before she found the envelope. She sat at the dining table and lit the cord wick of the lantern, mindful to keep it low so as to not wake Rose in the next room.

Dale read the postmark again, Black Barrel, and then slit the envelope open with the butter knife on the table.

She unfolded the single piece of paper, trying not to dwell on the memory of doing the same with Gertrude's last letter to her.

> *Dale,*
> *I'm not entirely sure why I'm writing this letter to you, except maybe because I want one of us* <u>*travellers*</u> *to have an idea of where I went and what I'm doing. By the time you read this I'll be venturing east. I know the Breach tries to draw us in the direction of the ravine in Orchard Bend, but that pull* <u>*can*</u> *be resisted, so that's where I'm headed. I have no specific destination as of yet, but maybe I'll know where I'm going once I get there. I may or may not tell you when that is. For*

287

*now, someone knows I'm out there and that's
enough.*

*The last thing I'll say is that there were others
of us pulled into the Breach. Any who survive
will travel to Orchard Bend just as we did. It
may even happen in your lifetime, so expect
them. Doc Reed knew this, too. It's in his
message.*

That's all I have to say.

Don't expect to see me again.

Warren

* * *

April 5, 1887
Black Barrel

Kenna Warren set the pen down next to the letter and waited
for the ink to dry. Rays of morning sunlight came in through
the trees around the old Winstone farmhouse, flooding in
through the kitchen window. She sipped her coffee and thought
of Charles, letting her heart ache as long as it needed to. She
guessed this would be the last sunrise she'd see from this
kitchen, so she soaked it in. By the afternoon, she planned to be
on her way down the road. All that was left was to pack up the
blankets in the bedroom and clear the kitchen out. She'd leave
the door unlocked for the next people who might take up living
here, whoever they may be. She and Charles had done the
same things years ago when they travelled west on their great
adventure. Now it seemed right to do it again as she planned to
go east.

All of that would come later, though. For right now, the
morning light shone pretty in the kitchen and Kenna Warren
would enjoy it while it lasted.

She sipped her coffee and smiled.

40

The Ledger of Owen McCabe

The Ghost that Guards the Mad Mountain of Siberry
Brochure, printed circa 1919

For more than thirty years, residents and visitors of Siberry, New Jersey, have borne witness to the spectral form of Robert Ludlow. In the mountains overlooking the town, his ghost serves as a reminder of the dark winter that began 1887.

The story begins with a prospector, Robert Ludlow's own grandfather, Fred, who early in the early 19th Century struck gold while working a pan in the mountain. As it turns out, he was one of the last in the state to make a successful claim. Fred sold the rights and made a moderate profit, but within a decade, the mine spawned from his discovery dried up. All across the state, backers determined that the amount of gold to be found in the ranges did not support the expense needed to mine it.

Fred Ludlow invested wisely, so they say, but his son did not, and by the time young Robert came of age, his family lived in a one-room shamble at the base of the very mountain where his grandfather had once struck gold.

Frustrated with his soured investments, Robert's father William attempted to repeat the discovery made by Fred. At every opportunity, William would prospect for gold on the mountain and every time would return a failure. His friends told him over and over that the odds were against him. On his death bed, old Fred had told his son to take his family and move west, to build a new life, but William was stubborn and returned again and again to the mountain.

He wasn't alone.

While the mining companies had given up on the mountain, men like-minded as William dreamed of finding personal wealth amid the crags and rocks and streams. And some did, despite the odds. Seeing others succeed, even rarely, drove men like William to keep at it. And William felt he had more at stake than all those others did. If he could make back even some of the money his own father had made from those mountains, he could once again provide for his family.

Then something strange happened.

William heard about another prospector who, with no warning, lost control of his mind and ran gibbering from the mountain. William didn't think much about it. After all, some men's minds break, either from despair or the thin altitude or any number of reasons. William told young Robert that such a thing would never happen to him because Robert, and Robert's mother and Robert's sister, too, all gave him something to live for, even when his hopes of ever finding gold were dashed day after day.

When word spread of another man being consumed by mental fits, William began to wonder. The second man had been working an area not far from where the earlier prospector had been when *he* succumbed to madness. And both those men had been working near William's own stretch of water and rock.

William wondered about it, but did not stop. Wondering would not feed his family or restore their lost savings. So as the people of the town began to refer to it as the Mad Mountain, William went on panning for gold, all the time hoping.

One day, young Robert was just coming home when he saw his father racing down the path from the mountain, grinning ear to ear. Robert froze, believing that at last his father had done it, at last he had struck gold.

Alas, that was not the case. In fact, it was far worse.

William did not stop at the family's ramble-down shack, but kept running towards town, his grin never wavering. He passed Robert with nary a look and Robert knew what had happened.

The Madness had taken his father.

Robert had to grow up fast after that, to help take care of his mother and sister. They moved into town, where they lived in a single boarding house room, where his mother took a job cleaning. It paid poorly, but included meals, so no one complained. Robert worked, first helping his mother clean, then taking a job at the mill. After a few years, his sister married and moved west with her husband, taking their aging mother with them.

An accident at the mill left Robert lame, his left arm partially paralyzed. He couldn't work as he'd used to, nor pay for his room at the boarding house, so he moved back to the small shamble of a cabin at the base of the mountains and considered following his sister and mother west. But he'd be a burden, he told friends, a lame man with only one good arm. He couldn't do that to them.

The night was December 31st, 1886, and, both near and far, people toasted the end of the old year and the arrival of the new. Siberry was no exception in this regard, with the streets bustling and revellers having a grand ol' time. Robert's friends convinced him to join the merriment, to look at the coming new year as a chance to see his life afresh.

It worked, for a time.

As midnight passed and his friends one by one left for home, Robert sat alone in the saloon, negotiating with the owner for another drink in exchange for helping clean up.

"What, with *your* arm?" the barkeep asked, though not without pity. He was about to agree to Robert's offer when a stranger walked in. He had a beard and a wild air about him, and spoke in a peculiar way.

"I'll buy you a drink, friend," the stranger said to Robert, "If you tell me everything you know about the Mad Mountain."

Of course, Robert agreed. He told the stranger about his grandfather's claim and his father's failed attempts to find gold himself. He told him about the madness that had struck down his father and others, before and since.

"No one goes up there anymore," Robert said. "No one dares."

The stranger nodded and put his hand on the bar, palm down.

"I'm going up there," the stranger said, "and I need a guide."

He lifted his hand from the bar and underneath was a small pebble of gold. Both Robert and the barkeep gasped.

"Where did you get that?" Robert asked.

The stranger nodded in the direction of the mountain.

"But if you've found gold up there," Robert said, "why do you need me?"

"I found gold," the stranger said, "but I'm looking for something else."

Robert looked at the nugget on the bar and then to the stranger.

"You can take that right now if you agree," the stranger said. "And there's more to follow. You show me what I need and I'll show you where that came from, where you can find more. The claim will be all yours. You even have the barkeeper here as a witness."

Robert's jaw hung open, hardly able to believe the offer. When he looked to the bartender for advice, all the man could do was shrug in return. No doubt visions of gold wrestled with Robert's memories of his father returning from the mountain in a state of insanity. Robert looked at his lame arm, which still possessed a small amount of life in its muscles, and tried to make a fist. The result was feeble and Robert looked at the stranger.

"I agree to be your guide," Robert said, "In exchange for this piece of gold and the right to your claim on the mountain. Coleman here is our witness."

"Wait," the barkeep Coleman said, picking up the gold nugget, "We test it first."

He produced a touchstone, having been called upon in the past to test such claims. The nugget was indeed gold and of high purity.

The deal struck with a handshake, Robert led the stranger up the mountain the next morning. For two days no one saw or heard from them. On the third day, Robert returned.

A grin spread across his face from ear to ear.

The Madness had taken him.

In his good hand he held the gold nugget and when asked what happened, Robert was silent for a long time as he stared back the way he came, back toward the mountain. The grin faded. As he spoke he was almost sane.

"We walked high up the mountain," Robert said. "I showed him where dad panned at the stream. He said we were close to where he wanted to go and asked me to take him to where the other men had gone mad. I took him as far as I knew. It was a long time ago that it all happened, but I had a pretty good memory. When we reached the spot where the first man had broken, I told him that was all I knew. The stranger stopped and closed his eyes. 'You hear it, don't you?' he asked, and God help me, after a moment I could hear it, a single terrible, beautiful note. We pressed on. Higher and deeper into the mountain range we went. It started getting dark and that's when we saw it: Something there and not there, like moving glass."

Robert stopped and jerked his head this way and that.

"No, that's not right," Robert said. "It was like a broken mirror, because we could see ourselves, but not just ourselves, not just our reflection, but inside. I saw inside myself, inside my mind. I couldn't look away. The note was in my head and I loved it. I asked the stranger if he heard it to and he said he used to be able to hear it, in another life, but not anymore. 'If I could hear it, I wouldn't have needed you,' the stranger said, 'but I remember the sound. I couldn't remember before, but I do now. It's all coming back.'"

Robert dropped to his knees in the snow and mud, still staring miles away at the mountain.

"He had a contraption with him," Robert said, "a box of magic he called it. 'I heard the stories about this place,' the stranger said, 'of both the gold and madness to be found up here. I sought you out, Robert Ludlow, I knew I could get you to agree to help me and I spent weeks in the cold doing my own panning and looking for this place. I was holed up further south. Boy, was I off, but no matter. Here we are.'

"The stranger held up his little box of lights and tapped it the way one does when wiring a telegram or sending Morse code,"

Robert continued, "The great broken mirror that was both there and not there changed, the reflections disappeared, but it wasn't what the stranger wanted and he got very upset, claiming his contraption was broken. He stopped working his little machine and the mirror returned to normal, the sound of that note filling my head. It's so beautiful."

And just like that, with no warning, Robert Ludlow died right there in the street.

His friends, shocked and dismayed, talked of gathering a search party to seek out the stranger in the mountain, but Robert's story scared them all to their core and they did not go out that day or any other day to search for the stranger, instead leaving him to his fate.

Spring came and a hunter tracking a deer followed it from the base of the mountain along the stream where they used to pan for gold. Whether he knew of the men stricken by madness on that mountain or not isn't known, but he came back just as fast as they did and claimed a ghost gestured to him to turn back, a ghost with a lame arm. Everyone knew it was Robert Ludlow. The hunter wasn't the last to see Robert's ghost. A young couple looking to build their home near where, years before, the Ludlow shack once stood, they claimed a one-armed ghost pointed them away.

The most compelling evidence came when Robert's sister, Margaret, came to Siberry to visit the grave of her brother at the site of their old home. After paying her respects, Margaret turned to see the ghost of Robert. She made it clear to everyone it was him.

Few are brave enough to visit the Mad Mountain now and those who do likewise report being warned away by the ghost of Robert Ludlow.

As for the stranger he once guided into the mountains, no one ever saw him return to Siberry and for all anyone can tell, he disappeared atop that mountain.

What *is* known for sure is that Robert Ludlow's ghost still haunts the Mad Mountain.

Heed his warning, lest you fall to madness.

About The Author

Patrick Lemieux is a Canadian artist and writer based in Toronto. He has exhibited his work internationally and it has featured in magazines and album sleeves.

He is currently working on the fourth *Orchard Bend* book, expected for release in 2021. A collection of his photography will very likely be his next project to come out, hopefully in early 2020.

You can find him on Facebook and Instagram at *Patrick Lemieux Artist* and on Twitter @MadTheDJ

www.ingramcontent.com/pod-product-compliance
Lightning Source LLC
Chambersburg PA
CBHW031205020726
47499CB00002B/498